P9-DDS-059

**Praise for *New York Times* bestselling author
Linda Howard**

"Linda Howard writes with power, stunning sensuality
and a storytelling ability unmatched in the
romance drama. Every book is a treasure
for the reader to savor again and again."
—*New York Times* bestselling author Iris Johansen

"Ms. Howard can wring so much emotion and tension
out of her characters that no matter how satisfied you
are when you finish a book, you still want more."
—*Rendezvous*

"Linda Howard knows what readers want."
—*Affaire de Coeur*

"This master storyteller takes our breath away."
—*RT Book Reviews*

"Already a legend in her own time, Linda Howard
exemplifies the very best of the romance genre.
Her strong characterizations and powerful insight
into the human heart have made her an author
cherished by readers everywhere."
—*RT Book Reviews*

LINDA HOWARD

SHATTERED

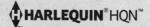

If you purchased this book without a cover you should be aware that this book is stolen property. It was reported as "unsold and destroyed" to the publisher, and neither the author nor the publisher has received any payment for this "stripped book."

ISBN-13: 978-0-373-77913-0

Shattered

Copyright © 2014 by Harlequin Books S.A.

The publisher acknowledges the copyright holder of the individual works as follows:

All that Glitters
Copyright © 1982 by Linda S. Howington

An Independent Wife
Copyright © 1982 by Linda S. Howington

Recycling programs for this product may not exist in your area.

All rights reserved. Except for use in any review, the reproduction or utilization of this work in whole or in part in any form by any electronic, mechanical or other means, now known or hereafter invented, including xerography, photocopying and recording, or in any information storage or retrieval system, is forbidden without the written permission of the publisher, HQN Books, 225 Duncan Mill Road, Don Mills, Ontario M3B 3K9, Canada.

This is a work of fiction. Names, characters, places and incidents are either the product of the author's imagination or are used fictitiously, and any resemblance to actual persons, living or dead, business establishments, events or locales is entirely coincidental.

This edition published by arrangement with Harlequin Books S.A.

For questions and comments about the quality of this book, please contact us at CustomerService@Harlequin.com.

® and TM are trademarks of Harlequin Enterprises Limited or its corporate affiliates. Trademarks indicated with ® are registered in the United States Patent and Trademark Office, the Canadian Intellectual Property Office and in other countries.

Printed in U.S.A.

www.Harlequin.com

CONTENTS

ALL THAT GLITTERS

CHAPTER ONE

CHARLES SAID BLUNTLY, without warning, "Constantinos arrived in London this morning."

Jessica looked up, her mind blank for a moment, then she realized what he had said and she smiled ruefully. "Well, you did warn me, Charles. It seems you were right." Not that she had ever doubted him, for Charles's instincts in business were uncanny. He had told her that if she voted her stock in ConTech against the Constantinos vote, she would bring down on her head the wrath of the single largest stockholder and chairman of the board, Nikolas Constantinos, and it appeared that once again Charles had been exactly right. The vote on the Dryden issue had been yesterday. Despite Charles's warnings, she had voted against the takeover and her vote had carried the majority. Less than twenty-four hours later, Constantinos had arrived in London.

Jessica had never met him, but she had heard enough horror tales about him to count herself lucky in that respect. According to gossip, he was utterly ruthless in his business dealings; of course, it stood to reason that he would not have achieved his present position of power by being meek and mild. He was a billionaire, powerful even by Greek standards; she was only a stockholder, and she thought humorously that it was a case of overkill for him to bring out his heavy artillery on her, but it looked as though no problem was too small for his personal attention.

Charles had pointed out that she could have voted for the takeover and saved herself a lot of trouble, but one of the things that Robert had taught her in the three years of their marriage was to stand up for herself, to trust her instincts and never to sell herself short. Jessica had felt that the move against Dryden was underhanded and she voted against it. If Constantinos was unable to accept that she had the right to vote her stock as she wanted, then he would just have to learn to deal with it. Regardless of how much power he wielded, she was determined not to back down from her stand, and Charles had found that she could be very stubborn when she set her mind to something.

"You must be very careful around him," Charles instructed her now, breaking into her thoughts. "Jessica, my dear, I don't believe you realize just how much pressure the man can bring to bear on you. He can hurt you in ways you've never imagined. Your friends can lose their jobs; mortgages can be called in on their homes; banks will cease doing business with you. It can even extend to such small things as repairs to your auto being delayed or seats on flights suddenly becoming unavailable. Do you begin to see, my dear?"

Disbelievingly, Jessica stared at him. "My word, Charles, are you serious? It seems so ludicrous!"

"I regret that I am very serious. Constantinos wants things done his way, and he has the money and the power to ensure that they are. Don't underestimate him, Jessica."

"But that's barbaric!"

"And so is Constantinos, to a degree," said Charles

flatly. "If he gives you the option of selling your stock to him, Jessica, then I strongly urge you to do so. It will be much safer for you."

"But Robert—"

"Yes, I know," he interrupted, though his voice took on a softer tone. "You feel that Robert entrusted that stock to you, and that he would have voted against the Dryden takeover, too. Robert was a very dear and special man, but he's dead now and he can't protect you. You have to think of yourself, and you haven't the weapons to fight Constantinos. He can demolish you."

"But I don't want to fight him," she protested. "I only want to carry on as I always have. It seems so silly for him to be upset over my vote—why should he take it so personally?"

"He doesn't take it personally," explained Charles. "He doesn't have to. But you've gone against him and you'll be brought into line, regardless of what he has to do to accomplish it. And don't think that you can appeal to his better nature—"

"I know," she broke in, her soft mouth curving into a smile. "He doesn't have one!"

"Exactly," said Charles. "Nor can he be feeling very charitable toward you; your record in voting against him, my dear, is very nearly perfect."

"Oh, dear," she said wryly. "I hadn't realized. But at least I'm consistent!"

Charles laughed unwillingly, but his cool eyes gleamed with admiration. Jessica always seemed in control of herself, capable of putting things into their proper perspective and reducing crises to mere annoyances, though he feared that this time she was in over her head. He didn't want her hurt; he never again wanted to see the look in her eyes that had been there after Robert's death, the despair, the pain that was too deep for comforting. She had recovered, she was a strong woman and a fighter, but he always tried to protect her from any further hurt. She had borne enough in her young life.

The phone rang and Jessica got up to answer it, her movements, as always, lithe and as graceful as a cat's. She tucked the receiver against her shoulder. "Stanton residence."

"Mrs. Stanton, please," said a cool, impersonal male voice, and her sharp ear caught the hint of an accent. Constantinos already?

"This is Mrs. Stanton," she replied.

"Mrs. Stanton, this is Mr. Constantinos's secretary. He would like to see you this afternoon—shall we say three-thirty?"

"Three-thirty?" she echoed, glancing at her wristwatch. It was almost two o'clock now.

"Thank you, Mrs. Stanton," said the voice in satisfaction. "I will tell Mr. Constantinos to expect you. Good day."

The click of the receiver made her take the phone from her ear and stare at it in disbelief. "Well, that was cheeky," she mused, hanging up the instrument. It was possible that he had taken her echo of the time as an affirmation, but her instincts told her otherwise. No, it was simply that she was not expected to make any protest, and it wouldn't have mattered if she had.

"Who was that, my dear?" asked Charles absently, gathering up the papers he had brought for her signature.

"Mr. Constantinos's secretary. I've been summoned into the royal presence—at three-thirty this afternoon."

Charles's elegant eyebrows rose. "Then I suggest you hurry."

"I've a dental appointment at four-fifteen," she fretted.

"Cancel it."

She gave him a cool look and he laughed. "I apologize, my dear, and withdraw the suggestion. But be careful, and try to remember that it would be better to sell the stock than to try to fight Constantinos. I have to go now, but I'll ring you later."

"Yes, 'bye," she said, seeing him out. After he had gone, she dashed upstairs and took a shower, then found herself dawdling as she selected her dress. She was unsure what to wear and stood examining the contents of her wardrobe for long moments; then, in swift impatience with herself, she took down a cool beige jersey dress and stepped into it. It was classically simple and she wore it with four-inch heels to give her enough height to make her look more than a child.

She wasn't very tall, and because she was so fragile in build she tended to look about sixteen years old if she didn't use a host of little tricks to add maturity to her appearance. She wore simple clothing, pure in cut, and high heels whenever possible. Her long, thick, tawny hair she wore twisted into a knot at the back of her neck, a very severe hairstyle that revealed every proud, perfect line of her classically boned face and made her youth less obvious. Too much makeup would have made her look like a child playing grown-up, so she wore only subtle shades of eye shadow, naturally tinted lipsticks and a touch of peach blusher. When she looked into the mirror, it was to check that her hair was subdued and her expression cool and reserved; she never saw the allure of long, heavily lashed green eyes or the provocative curve of her soft mouth. The world of flirtations and sexual affairs was so far removed from her consciousness that she had no concept of herself as a desirable woman. She had been a child when Robert had taken her under his protective wing—a sullen, self-conscious, suspicious child—and he had changed her into a responsible adult, but he had never attempted to teach her anything about the physical side of marriage and she was as untouched today at the age of twenty-three as she had been when she was born.

When she was ready she checked the clock again and found that she had three-quarters of an hour to reach the ConTech building, but in the London traffic she would need every minute of that time. She snatched up her bag and ran downstairs to check on her dog, Samantha, who was very pregnant. Samantha lay in her bed, contentedly asleep even though her sides were grotesquely swollen by the puppies she carried. Jessica made certain there was water in her dish, then let herself out and crossed to her car, a sleek dark green sports model. She loved its smooth power and now she needed every ounce of it as she put it through its paces.

The traffic signals were with her and she stepped out of the lift on the appropriate floor of the ConTech building at precisely three-twenty-nine. A receptionist directed her to the royal chambers and she opened the heavy oak door at the appointed time.

A large room stretched before her, quietly furnished with chocolate-brown carpeting and chairs upholstered in brown and gold. Set to one side of massive double doors was a large desk, and seated at that desk was a slim, dark man who rose to his feet as she entered.

Cool dark eyes looked her up and down as she crossed the room to him, and she began to feel as if she had violated some law. "Good afternoon," she said, keeping all hint of temper out of her voice. "I am Mrs. Stanton."

The dark eyes swept over her again in a manner that was almost contemptuous. "Ah, yes. Please be seated, Mrs. Stanton. I regret that Mr. Constantinos has been delayed, but he will be free to see you shortly."

Jessica inclined her head and selected one of the comfortable chairs, sitting down and crossing her graceful legs. She made certain that her face remained expressionless, but inside she was contemplating scratching the young man's eyes out. His manner set her teeth on edge; he had a condescending air about him, a certain nastiness that made her long to shake the smug look off his face.

Ten minutes later she wondered if she was expected to cool her heels here indefinitely until Constantinos deigned to see her. Glancing at her watch, she decided to give it another five minutes, then she would have to leave if she was to be on time for her dental appointment.

The buzzer on the desk sounded loudly in the silence and she looked up as the secretary snatched up one of the three telephones on his desk. "Yes, sir," he said crisply, and replaced the receiver. He removed a file from one of the metal cabinets beside him and carried it into the inner sanctum, returning almost immediately and closing the double doors behind him. From all indications, it would be some time yet before Constantinos was free, and the five minutes she had allowed were gone. She uncrossed her legs and rose to her feet.

Coolly uplifted eyebrows asked her intentions.

"I have another appointment to keep," she said smoothly, refusing to apologize for her departure. "Perhaps Mr. Constantinos will call me when he has more time."

Outraged astonishment was plain on the man's face as she took up her bag and prepared to leave. "But you can't go—" he began.

"On the contrary," she interrupted him, opening the door. "Good day."

Anger made her click her heels sharply as she walked to her car, but she took several deep breaths before she started the engine. No sense in letting the man's attitude upset her, perhaps enough to cause an accident, she told herself. She would shrug it off, as she had learned to do when she had been battered with criticism following her marriage to Robert. She had learned how to endure, to survive, and she was not going to let Robert down now.

After her dental appointment, which was only her annual checkup and took very little time, Jessica drove to the small dress shop just off Piccadilly that her neighbor Sallie Reese owned and operated, and helped Sallie close up. She also looked through the racks of clothing and chose two of the new line of evening gowns that Sallie had just stocked; perhaps because she had never had anything pretty when she was growing up, Jessica loved pretty clothes and had no resistance to buying them, though she was frugal with herself in other matters. She didn't wear jewelry and she didn't pamper herself in any way, but clothing—well, that was another story. Robert had always been amused by her little-girl glee in a new dress, a pair of jeans, shoes; it really didn't matter what it was so long as it was new and she liked it.

Remembering that made her smile a little sadly as she paid Sallie for the gowns; though she would never stop missing Robert, she was glad that she had brought some laughter and sunshine into the last years of his life.

"Whew, it has been a busy day," sighed Sallie as she totaled up the day's revenue. "But sales were good; it wasn't just a case of a lot of people window-shopping. Joel will be ecstatic; I promised him that he could buy that fancy stereo he's had his heart set on if we had a good week."

Jessica chuckled. Joel was a stereo addict, and he had been moaning for two months now about a marvelous set that he had seen and just had to have or his life would be blighted forever. Sallie took all of his dire predictions in stride, but it had been only a matter of time before she agreed to buy the new stereo. Jessica was glad that now her friends could afford a few luxuries without totally wrecking their budget. The dress shop had turned their fortunes around, because Joel's income as an accountant was just not enough nowadays to support a young family.

When Robert had died, Jessica had found herself unable to live in the luxurious penthouse without him and she had left it, instead buying an old Victorian house that had been converted into a duplex and moving into the empty side herself. Joel and Sallie and their twin five-year-old hellions, who went by the names of Patricia and Penelope, lived in the other side of the old house and the two young women had gradually become good friends. Jessica learned how Sallie had to scrimp and budget and make all of their clothing herself, and it was Sallie's needlework that had given Jessica the idea.

The Reeses had not had the capital to open a shop, but Jessica had, and when she found the small, cozy shop off Piccadilly, she leaped on it. Within a month it was remodeled, stocked, and in business with the name of SALLIE'S RAGS on the sign outside. Patty and Penny were in kindergarten and Sallie was happily installed in her shop, making some of the clothing herself and gradually expanding until now the shop employed two salesgirls full time, besides Sallie herself, and another woman who helped Sallie with the sewing. Before the first year was out, Sallie had repaid Jessica and was flushed with pride at how well it had turned out.

Sallie was now rounding quite nicely with a third little Reese, but she and Joel no longer worried about expenses and she was ecstatic about her pregnancy. She was fairly blooming with good health and high spirits, and even now, when she was tired, her cheeks had a pink color to them and her eyes sparkled.

After they had closed up, Jessica drove Sallie by to pick up Patty and Penny, who stayed late on Friday nights with their baby-sitter, as that was the night Sallie closed out the week. The twins were in school for the best part of the day, and when summer holidays came, Sallie intended to stay home from the shop with them, as her pregnancy would be advanced by then. When Jessica pulled up outside the baby-sitter's home, both of the little girls ran to the car shrieking "Hello, Auntie Jessie! Have you any candy for us?" That was a standard Friday-night treat and Jessica had not forgotten. As the girls mobbed her, Sallie went laughing to pay the sitter and thank her, and by the time she came back with her hands full of the girls' books and sweaters, Jessica had them both settled down in the car.

Sallie invited Jessica to eat dinner with them, but she declined because she did not like to intrude too much on the family. Not only was she rather reserved herself, but she sensed that Sallie wanted to be with Joel to celebrate the good news of the week's business in the shop. It was still new enough to them that it was a thrill, and she didn't want to restrain them with her presence.

The phone started ringing just as she opened the door, but Jessica paused for a moment to check on Samantha before she answered it. The dog was still in her basket, looking particularly peaceful, and she wagged her tail in greeting but did not get up. "No pups yet?" asked Jessica as she reached for the phone. "At this rate, old girl, they'll be grown before they get here." Then she lifted the phone on the kitchen extension. "Mrs. Stanton speaking."

"Mrs. Stanton, this is Nikolas Constantinos," said a deep voice, so deep that the bass notes almost growled at her, and to her surprise the accent was more American than Greek. She clutched the receiver as a spurt of warmth went through her. How silly, she chided herself, to melt at the sound of a faint American accent just because she was American herself! She loved England, she was content with her life here, but nevertheless, that brisk sound made her smile.

"Yes, Mr. Constantinos?" she made herself say, then wondered if she sounded rude. But she would be lying if she said something trite like "How nice it is to hear from you" when it wasn't nice at all; in fact, it would probably be very nasty indeed.

"I would like to arrange a meeting with you tomorrow, Mrs. Stanton," he said. "What time would be convenient for you?"

Surprised, she reflected that Constantinos himself did not seem to be as arrogant as his secretary; at least he had *asked* what time would be convenient, rather than *telling* her what time to present herself. Aloud she said, "On Saturday, Mr. Constantinos?"

"I realize it is the weekend, Mrs. Stanton," the deep voice replied, a hint of irritation evident in his tone. "However, I have work to do regardless of the day of the week."

Now that sounded more like what she had expected. Smiling slightly, she said, "Then any time is convenient for me, Mr. Constantinos; I haven't any commitments for tomorrow."

"Very well, let's say tomorrow afternoon, two o'clock." He paused, then said, "And, Mrs. Stanton, I don't like playing games. Why did you make an appointment with me this afternoon if you did not intend to keep it?"

Stung, she retorted coldly, "I didn't make the appointment. Your secretary phoned me and told me what time to be there, then hung up before I could agree or disagree. It rushed me, but I made the effort and waited for as long as I could, but I had another appointment to keep. I apologize if my effort was not good enough!" Her tone of voice stated plainly that she didn't care what his opinion was, and she didn't stop to think if that was wise or not. She was incensed that that cockroach of a secretary had *dared* to imply that she was at fault.

"I see," he said after a moment. "Now it is my turn to apologize to you, Mrs. Stanton, and *my* apology is sincere. That will not happen again. Until tomorrow, then." The phone clicked as he hung up.

Jessica slammed the phone down violently and stood for a minute tapping her foot in controlled temper, then her face cleared and she laughed aloud. He had certainly put her in her place! She began almost to look forward to this meeting with the notorious Nikolas Constantinos.

WHEN JESSICA DRESSED for the meeting the next day, she began early and allowed herself plenty of time to change her mind about what she would wear. She tried on several things and finally chose a severely tailored dull-gold suit that made her look mature and serious, and this she teamed with a cream-colored silk shirt. The muted gold picked up the gold in her tawny hair and lightly tanned skin, and she didn't realize the picture she made or she would have changed immediately. As it was, she looked like a golden statue come to life, with gleaming green jewels for eyes.

She was geared up for this meeting; when she walked into the outer office at two o'clock, her heart was pounding in anticipation, her eyes were sparkling, and her cheeks were flushed. At her entrance the secretary jumped to his feet with an alacrity that told her some stinging comments had been made concerning his conduct. Though his eyes were distinctly hostile, he escorted her into the inner office immediately.

"Mrs. Stanton, sir," he said, and left the office, closing the doors behind him.

Jessica moved across the office with her proud, graceful stride, and the man behind the desk rose slowly to his feet as she approached. He was tall, much taller than the average Greek, and his shoulders strained against the expensive cloth of his dark gray suit. He stood very still, watching her as she walked toward him, and his eyes narrowed to slits. She reached the desk and held out her hand; slowly her fingers were taken, but instead of the handshake she had invited, her hand was lifted and the black head bent over it. Warm lips were pressed briefly to her fingers, then her hand was released and the black head lifted.

Almost bemused, Jessica stared into eyes as black as night beneath brows that slashed across his face in a straight line. An arrogant blade of nose, brutally hard cheekbones, a firm lip line, a squared and stubborn chin, completed the face that was ancient in its structure. Centuries of Greek heritage were evident in that face, the face of a Spartan warrior. Charles had been right; this man was utterly ruthless, but Jessica did not feel threatened. She felt exhilarated, as if she was in the room with a tiger that she could control if she was very careful. Her heartbeat increased and her eyes grew brighter, and to disguise her involuntary response, she smiled and murmured, "Are you trying to charm me into voting my shares the way you want before you resort to annihilation?"

Amazingly, a smile appeared in response. "With a woman, I always try charm first," he said in the deep tones that seemed even deeper than they had last night over the phone.

"Really?" she asked in mock wonder. "Does it usually work?"

"Usually," he admitted, still smiling. "Why is it that I have the feeling, Mrs. Stanton, that you'll be an exception?"

"Perhaps because you're an unusually astute man, Mr. Constantinos," she countered.

He laughed aloud at that and indicated a chair set before his desk. "Please sit down, Mrs. Stanton. If we are to argue, let us at least be comfortable while we do it."

Jessica sat down and said impulsively, "Your accent is American, isn't it? It makes me feel so much at home!"

"I learned to speak English on a Texas oil field," he said. "I'm afraid that even Oxford couldn't erase the hint of Texas from my speech, though I believe it was thought by my instructors that my accent is Greek! Are you from Texas, Mrs. Stanton?"

"No, but a Texas drawl is recognizable to any American! How long were you in Texas?"

"For three years. How long have you been in England, Mrs. Stanton?"

"Since shortly before I married, a little over five years."

"Then you were little more than a child when you married," he said, an odd frown crossing his brow. "I'd assumed that you would be older, at least thirty, but I can see that's impossible."

Lifting her dainty chin, Jessica said, "No, I was a precocious eighteen when I married." She began to tense, sensing an attack of the type that she had endured so many times in the past five years.

"As I said, little more than a child. Though I suppose there are countless wives and mothers aged eighteen, it seems so much younger when the husband you chose was old enough to be your grandfather."

Jessica drew back and said coldly, "I see no reason

to discuss my marriage. I believe our business concerns stocks."

He smiled again, but this time the smile was that of a predator, with nothing humorous in it. "You're certainly correct about that," he allowed. "However, that issue should be solved rather easily. When you sold your body and your youth to an old man of seventy-six, you established the fact that monetary gain ranks very high on your list of priorities. The only thing left to discuss is: how much?"

CHAPTER TWO

YEARS OF EXPERIENCE had taught Jessica how to hide her pain behind a proud, aloof mask, and she used that mask now, revealing nothing of her thoughts and feelings as she faced him. "I'm sorry, Mr. Constantinos, but you seem to have misjudged the situation," she said distantly. "I didn't come here to accept a bribe."

"Nor am I offering you a bribe, Mrs. Stanton," he said, his eyes gleaming. "I'm offering to buy your stock."

"The shares aren't for sale."

"Of course they are," he refuted her silkily. "I'm willing to pay more than market value in order to get those stocks out of your hands. Because you are a woman, I've given you certain allowances, but there is a limit to my good nature, Mrs. Stanton, and I'd advise you not to try to push the price any higher. You could find yourself completely out in the cold."

Jessica stood and put her hands behind her back so he couldn't see how her nails were digging into her palms. "I'm not interested at any price, Mr. Constantinos; I don't even want to hear your offer. The shares aren't for sale, now or at any other time, and especially not to you. Good day, Mr. Constantinos."

But this man was no tame secretary and he did not intend to let her leave until he had finished with his business. He moved with a lithe stride to stop her and she found her path blocked by a very solid set of shoulders. "Ah, no, Mrs. Stanton," he murmured softly. "I can't let you leave now, with nothing settled between us. I've left my island and flown all the way to England for the express purpose of meeting you and putting an end to your asinine notions, which are wreaking havoc with this company. Did you think that I'd be put off by your high-and-mighty airs?"

"I don't know about my high-and-mighty airs, but your king-of-the-mountain complex is getting on my nerves," Jessica attacked, her voice sarcastic. "I own those shares, and I vote them as I think I should. The Dryden takeover was underhanded and stank to the heavens, and I voted against it. I would do it again if the issue arose. But a lot of other people voted against it as well, yet I notice that it's *my* stock you want to buy. Or am I only the first of the group to be brought into line?"

"Sit down, Mrs. Stanton," he said grimly, "and I will attempt to explain to you the basics of finance and expansion."

"I don't wish to sit down—"

"I said *sit!*" he rasped, and abruptly his voice was harsh with menace. Automatically Jessica sat down, then despised herself for not facing him and refusing to be intimidated.

"I am *not* one of your flunkies," she flared, but did not get up. She had the nasty feeling that he would push her down if she tried to leave.

"I am aware of that, Mrs. Stanton; believe me, if you were one of my employees, you would have learned long ago how to behave yourself," he retorted with heavy irony.

"I consider myself quite well-behaved!"

He smiled grimly. "Well-behaved? Or merely cunning and manipulative? I don't imagine it was very difficult to seduce an old man and get him to marry you, and you were smart enough to select a man who would die shortly. That set you up very nicely, didn't it?"

Jessica almost cried aloud with the shock of his words; only her years of training in self-control kept her still and silent, but she looked away from him. She could not let him see her eyes or he would realize how deeply vulnerable she was.

He smiled at her silence. "Did you think that I didn't know your history, Mrs. Stanton? I assure you, I know quite a lot about you. Your marriage to Robert Stanton was quite a scandal to everyone who knew and admired the man. But until I saw you, I never quite understood just how you managed to trap him into marriage. It's all very clear now; any man, even an old one, would jump at the chance to have your lovely body in his bed, at his convenience."

Jessica quivered at the insult and he noticed the movement that rippled over her skin. "Is the memory less than pleasing?" he inquired softly. "Did you find the payment more than you'd expected?"

She struggled for the composure to lift her head, and after a moment she found it. "I'm sure my private life is no concern of yours," she heard herself say coolly, and felt a brief flare of pride that she had managed that so well.

His black eyes narrowed as he looked down at her and he opened his mouth to say more, but the phone rang and he swore under his breath in Greek, then stepped away from her to lift the phone to his ear. He said something in harsh, rapid Greek, then paused. His eyes slid to Jessica.

"I have an urgent call from France, Mrs. Stanton. I'll only be a moment."

He punched a button on the phone and spoke a greeting, his language changing effortlessly to fluent French. Jessica watched him for a moment, still dazed with her inner pain, then she realized that he was occupied and she seized her chance. Without a word, she got to her feet and walked out.

SHE MANAGED TO control herself until she was home again, but once she was safely enclosed by her own walls, she sat down on the sofa and began to sob softly. Was it never to end, the nasty comments and unanimous condemnations of her marriage to Robert? Why was it automatically assumed that she was little more than a prostitute? For five years she had borne the pain and never let it be known how it knifed into her insides, but now she felt as though she had no defenses left. Dear God, if only Robert hadn't died!

Even after two years she could not get used to not sharing amusing thoughts with him, to not having his dry, sophisticated wisdom bolstering her. He had never doubted her love, no matter what had been said about their December-May marriage, and she had always felt the warmth of his support. Yes, he had given her financial security, and he had taught her how to care for the money he willed to her. But he had given her so much more than that! The material things he had bestowed on her were small in comparison to his other gifts: love, security, self-respect, self-confidence. He had encouraged her development as a woman of high intelligence; he had taught her of his world of stocks and bonds, to trust her own instinct when she was in doubt. Dear, wise Robert! Yet, for his marriage to her he had been laughed at and mocked, and she had been scorned. When a gentleman of seventy-six marries a gorgeous young girl of eighteen, gossips can credit it to only two things: greed on her part, and an effort to revive faded appetites on his.

It hadn't been that way at all. Robert was the only man she had ever loved, and she had loved him deeply, but their relationship had been more that of father to daughter, or grandfather to granddaughter, than of husband to wife. Before their marriage Robert had even speculated on the advantages of adopting her, but in the end he'd decided that there would be fewer legal difficulties if he married her. He wanted her to have the security she'd always lacked, having grown up in an orphanage and been forced into hiding herself behind a prickly wall of sullen passivity. Robert was determined that never again would she have to fight for food or privacy or clothing; she would have the best, and the best way to secure that way of life for her was to take her as his wife.

The scandal their marriage had caused had rocked London society; vicious items concerning her had appeared in the gossip columns, and Jessica had been shocked and horrified to read several accounts of men who had been "past lovers of the enterprising Mrs. S." Her reaction had been much the same as Robert's: to hold her head even higher and ignore the mudslingers. She and Robert knew the truth of the marriage, and Robert was the only person on earth whom she loved, the only person who had ever cared for her. Their gentle love endured, and she had remained a virgin throughout their marriage, not that Robert had ever given any indication that he wished the situation to be different. She was his only family, the daughter of his heart if not his flesh, and he schooled her and guided her and went about settling his financial affairs so they could never be wrested out of her control. And he trusted her implicitly.

They had been, simply, two people who were alone in the world and had found each other. She was an orphan who had grown up with a shortage of any type of love; he was an old man whose first wife had died years before and who now found himself without family in his last years. He took in the wary young girl and gave her every comfort, every security, even marrying her in an effort to make certain she never wanted for anything again. Jessica, in turn, felt a flood of love for the gentle, elderly man who gave her so much and asked for so little in return. And he had loved her for bringing her youth and beauty and bright laughter into the fading years of his life, and had guided her maturity and her quick mind with all the loving indulgence of a father.

While Robert had been alive, their scarcity of friends had not really bothered her, though she had suffered under the cuts she had received. There were a few real friends, like Charles, and they had been sufficient. But now Robert was gone and she lived alone, and the poisonous barbs she still received festered in her mind, making her ache and lie awake at night. Most women refused to speak to her and men acted as if she was fair game, and the fact that she kept quietly to herself was evidently not enough to change anyone's opinion of her. Thinking about it now, she acknowledged that, outside of Charles and Sallie, she had no friends. Even Sallie's Joel was a bit stiff with her, and she knew that he disapproved.

It wasn't until the shadows of early evening had darkened the room that she roused from her dejected seat on the sofa and went slowly upstairs to stand under the shower. She felt deadened, and she stayed under the needlelike spray for a long time, until the hot water began to go, then she got out, dried off, and dressed in a pair of faded old jeans and a shirt. Listlessly she brushed her hair out and left it loose on her shoulders, as it usually was when she was at home. Only when she was going out did she feel the need for the more severe hairstyle, to give her an older look, and she would not be going anywhere tonight. Like an animal, she wanted only to find a dark corner and lick her wounds.

When she went into the kitchen, she found Samantha moving about restlessly in her basket; as Jessica watched, frowning, the dog gave a sharp little whine of pain and lay down. Jessica went over and stroked the silky black head. "So, it looks like tonight is the night, my girl! Not before time, either. And if I remember correctly, it was on a Saturday that you ran away from me and got yourself in this fix, so I suppose it's poetic justice."

Samantha didn't care about philosophy, though she licked the gentle hand that stroked her. Then she laid her head down and began that sharp whining again.

Jessica stayed in the kitchen with the dog, and as time wore on and no puppies were born, she began to get worried, for Samantha appeared to be in distress. Was something wrong? Jessica had no idea what kind of four-legged Romeo Samantha had met; was it possible that she had mated with a larger breed and now the puppies were too big to be born? Certainly the little black dog was very swollen.

She rang over to Sallie's side of the house, but the phone rang endlessly and she hung up. Her neighbors were out. After chewing her lip indecisively for a moment, Jessica took the phone directory and began looking for the vet's number. She didn't know if Samantha could be moved while she was in labor, but perhaps the vet made house calls. She found the number and reached for the phone, which rang just as she touched it. She gave a startled cry and leaped back, then she grabbed up the receiver. "Mrs. Stanton."

"This is Nikolas Constantinos."

Of course it was, she thought distractedly. Who else had such a deep voice? "What do you want?" she demanded.

"We have unfinished business—" he began.

"It will just have to stay unfinished," she broke in. "My dog is having puppies and I can't talk to you. Good-bye, Mr. Constantinos." She hung up and waited a second, then lifted the receiver again. She heard a dial tone as she checked the vet's number again, then began dialing.

Half an hour later she was weeping in frustration. She could not get her vet, or any other, on the phone, probably because it was Saturday night, and she was sure that Samantha was going to die. The dog was yelping in agony now, squirming and shuddering with the force of her contractions. Jessica felt appallingly helpless, and grief welled up in her so that the tears streamed down her cheeks.

When the doorbell rang, she scrambled to answer

it, glad to have some company, even if the caller knew nothing about dogs. Perhaps it was Charles, who was always so calm, though he would be as useless as she. She jerked the door open and Nikolas Constantinos stepped in as if he owned the house, closing the door behind him. Then he swung on her and she had a glimpse of a grim, angry face before his expression changed abruptly. He took in her jean-clad figure, her mane of hair and tear-streaked face, and he looked incredulous, as if he didn't believe it was really her. "What's wrong?" he asked as he produced a handkerchief and offered it to her.

Without thinking, Jessica took it and scrubbed at her cheeks. "It—it's my dog," she said thinly, and gulped back fresh tears. "I don't think she can have her puppies, and I can't get a vet on the phone...."

He frowned. "Your dog is really having puppies?"

For answer, she burst into a fresh flow of tears, hiding her face in the handkerchief. Her shoulders shook with the force of her sobs, and after a moment she felt an arm slide about her waist.

"Don't cry," Constantinos murmured. "Where is she? Perhaps I can help."

Of course, why not? She should have thought of that herself; everyone knew billionaires were trained in animal husbandry, she told herself hysterically as she led the way into the kitchen.

But despite the incongruity of it, Nikolas Constantinos took off his jacket and slung it over the back of a chair, removed the gold studs from his cuffs and slid them into his pants pocket, then rolled up the sleeves of his white silk shirt. He squatted on his heels beside Samantha's bed and Jessica knelt next to him, because

Samantha was inclined to be snappy with strangers even
when she was in the best of moods. But Samantha did
not offer to snap at him, only watched him with plead-
ing, liquid eyes as he ran his hands gently over her swollen body and examined her. When he had finished, he
stroked Samantha's head gently and murmured some
Greek words to her that had a soft sound to them, then
he turned his head to smile reassuringly at Jessica. "Everything seems to be normal. We should see a pup any
minute now."

"Really?" Jessica demanded, her excitement spiral-
ing as her fears eased. "Samantha is all right?"

"Yes, you've worried yourself to tears for nothing.
Hasn't she had a litter before?"

Ruefully Jessica shook her head, explaining, "I've
always kept her in before. But this time she managed
to slip away from me and, well, you know how it goes."

"M'mmm, yes, I know how it goes," he mocked
gently. His black eyes ran over her slim build and made
her aware that he had a second meaning for his statement. He was a man and he looked on her as a woman,
with a woman's uses, and instinctively she withdrew
from his masculine appraisal. But despite that, despite
everything he had said to her that afternoon, she felt
better now that he was here. Whatever else he was, the
man was capable.

Samantha gave a short, sharp yelp and Jessica turned
anxiously to her dog. Nikolas put his arm about Jessica's
shoulders and pulled her against his side so that she felt
seared by the warmth of his body. "See, it's beginning,"
he murmured. "There's the first pup."

Jessica knelt there enthralled, her eyes as wide and
wondrous as a child's, while Samantha produced five

slick, squirming little creatures, which she nudged one by one against the warmth of her belly. When it became obvious that Samantha had finished at five, when all of the squeaking little things were snuggled against the furry black belly and the dog was lying there in tired contentment, Nikolas got to his feet and drew Jessica to hers, holding her for a moment until the feeling had returned to her numb legs.

"Is this the first birth you've witnessed?" he asked, tilting her chin up with his thumb and smiling down into her dazed eyes.

"Yes…wasn't it marvelous?" she breathed.

"Marvelous," he agreed. The smile faded from his lips and he studied the face that was turned up to him. When he spoke, his voice was low and even. "Now everything is fine; your tears have dried, and you are a lucky young woman. I came over here determined to shake some manners into you. I advise you not to hang up on me again, Jessica. My temper is"—here he gave a shrug of his wide shoulders, as if in acceptance of something he could not change—"not calm."

Half-consciously she registered the fact that he had used her given name, and that his tongue had seemed to linger over the syllables, then she impulsively placed her hand on his arm. "I'm sorry," she apologized warmly. "I wouldn't have done it if I hadn't been so worried about Samantha. I was trying to call the vet."

"I realize that now. But at the time I thought you were merely getting rid of me, and very rudely, too. I wasn't in a good mood anyway after you had walked out on me this afternoon. But when I saw you…" His eyes narrowed as he looked her up and down again. "You made me forget my anger."

She stared at him blankly for a moment before she realized that she hadn't any makeup on, her hair was tumbled about her shoulders, and worse than that, she was barefoot! The wonder was that he had even recognized her! He had been geared up to smash a sophisticated woman of the world, and instead he had found a weeping, tousled girl who did not quite reach his shoulder. A blush warmed her cheeks.

Nervously she pushed a strand of hair away from her face. "I—ummm—I must look a mess," she stammered, and he reached out and touched the streaked gold of her hair, making her forget in midsentence what she had been saying.

"No, you don't look a mess," he assured her absently, watching the hair slide along his dark fingers. "You look disturbingly young, but lovely for all your wet lashes and swollen lids." His black eyes flickered back to hers. "Have you had your dinner yet, Jessica?"

"Dinner?" she asked vaguely, before she mentally kicked herself for not being faster than that and assuring him that she had indeed already had her meal.

"Yes, dinner," he mocked. "I can see that you haven't. Slip into a dress and I'll take you out for dinner. We still have business to discuss and I think it would be wiser if the discussion did not take place in the privacy of your home."

She wasn't certain just what he meant by that, but she knew better than to ask for an explanation. Reluctantly she agreed. "It will take me about ten minutes," she said. "Would you like a drink while I'm dressing?"

"No, I'll wait until you can join me," he said.

Jessica ran upstairs and washed her face in cold water, which made her feel immensely better. As she applied her makeup, she noticed that her mouth was curved into a little smile and that it wouldn't go away. When she had completed her makeup, she took a look at herself and was disturbed by the picture she presented. Because of her bout of weeping, her lids were swollen, but with eye shadow and mascara applied, they looked merely sleepy and the irises gleamed darkly, wetly green, long Egyptian eyes that had the look of passions satisfied. Her cheeks bloomed with color, natural color, because her heart was racing in her breast, and she could feel the pulse throbbing in her lips, which were still smiling.

Because it was evening, she twisted her hair into a swirl atop her head and secured it with a gold butterfly clasp. She would wear a long dress, and she knew exactly which one she wanted. Her hands were shaking slightly as she drew it out of the closet, a halter-necked silk of the purest white, almost glittering in its paleness. She stepped into it and pulled the bodice up, then fastened the straps behind her neck. The dress molded itself to her breasts like another skin, then the lined silk fell in graceful folds to her feet—actually, beyond her feet, until she stepped into her shoes. Then the length was perfect. She slung a gold gauze wrap over her arm and she was ready, except for stuffing a comb and lipstick into a tiny evening bag—and remembering at the last minute to include her house key. She had to descend the stairs in a more dignified manner than she had gone up them, for the delicate straps of her shoes were not made for running, and she was only halfway down when Nikolas appeared from the living room and came to stand at the foot of the stairs, waiting for her. His gleaming eyes took in every inch of her in the shimmering white silk and she shivered under the expression she could see in them. He looked…hungry. Or…what?

When she reached the bottom step, she stopped and looked at him, eye to eye, but still she could not decide just what it was that glittered in those black depths. He put his hand on her arm and drew her down the last step, then without a word took the gold wrap and placed it about her bare shoulders. She quivered involuntarily under his touch, and his gaze leaped up to hers; this time it was all she could do to meet it evenly, for she was disturbed by her response to the lightest touch of his fingers.

"You are…more than beautiful," he said quietly.

What did that mean? She licked her lips uncertainly and his hands tightened on her shoulders; a quick glance upward revealed that his gaze had fastened on her tongue. Her heart leaped wildly in response to the look she saw, but he dropped his hands from her and stepped back.

"If we don't go now, we won't go at all," he said, and she knew exactly what that meant. He wanted her. Either that, or he was putting on a very good act, and the more she thought about it, the more such an act seemed likely. Hadn't he admitted that he always tried his charm on a woman in order to get his own way?

He certainly must want those shares, she mused, feeling more comfortable now that she had decided that he was only putting on the amorous act in order to get around her on the shares. Constantinos in a truly amorous mood must be devastating to a woman's senses, she thought, but her own leaping senses had calmed with the realization of what he was up to and she was once more able to think clearly. She supposed she would have to sell the shares; Charles had advised it, and she knew now that she would certainly not be able to continuously defy this man. She would tell him over dinner that she was willing to sell the shares to him.

He had turned out all of the lights except for a dim one in the kitchen for Samantha, and now he checked to make certain the door was locked behind them. "Haven't you any help living in with you?" he asked, frowning, his hand sliding under her elbow as they walked to his car.

"No," she replied, amusement evident in her voice. "I'm not very messy and I don't eat very much, so I don't need any help."

"But that means you're alone at night."

"I'm not frightened, not with Samantha. She sets up a howl at a strange footstep, and besides, Sallie and Joel Reese are in the other side, so I'm not really alone."

He opened the door of the powerful sports car he was driving and helped her into the seat, then went around to his side. She buckled her safety belt, looking with interest at the various dials and gauges. This thing looked like the cockpit of an airplane, and the car was at odds with what she had expected of him. Where was the huge black limousine with the uniformed chauffeur? As he slid into his seat and buckled up, she said, "Do you always drive yourself?"

"No, but there are times when a chauffeur's presence isn't desirable," he said, smiling a little. The powerful engine roared into life and he put the car into gear, moving forward with a smooth rush of power that pushed her back into her seat.

"Did you sell the country estate?" he asked from out of nowhere, making her wonder just how much he did know about her. More than just that vicious gossip, evidently; but he had known Robert before their marriage, so it was only natural that he should know about Robert's country home.

"Robert sold that a year before he died," she said steadily. "And after he died, I let the penthouse go; it was far too big and costly for just me. My half-house is just large enough."

"I would have thought a smaller apartment would have been better."

"I really don't like apartments, and then, there was Samantha. She needs room to run, and the neighborhood is friendly, with a lot of children."

"Not very glamorous," he commented dryly, and her ire rose a bit before she stifled it with a surge of humor.

"Not unless you think lines of drying laundry are glamorous," she agreed, laughing a little. "But it's quiet, and it suits me."

"In that dress, you look as if you should be surrounded by diamonds and mink, not lines of laundry."

"Well, what about you?" she asked cheerfully. "You in your silk shirt and expensive suit, squatting down to help a dog have puppies?"

He flashed her a look that glinted in the green lights from the dash. "On the island, life is much simpler than in London and Paris. I grew up there, running wild like a young goat."

She had a picture of him as a thin young boy, his black eyes flashing as he ran barefoot over the rough hills of his island. Had the years and the money and the layers of sophistication stifled the wildness of his early years? Then, even as she formed the thought in her mind, she knew that he was still wild and untamed, despite the silk shirts he wore.

Conversation died after that, each of them concerned with their own thoughts, and it wasn't until he pulled up before a discreetly lit restaurant and a doorman came to open the doors for them that Jessica realized where he had brought her. Her fingers tightened into fists at the curl of apprehension that twisted in her stomach, but she made her hands relax. He couldn't have known that she always avoided places like this—or could he? No, it was impossible. No one knew of her pain; she had always kept her aloof air firmly in place.

Taking a deep breath, she allowed herself to be helped out of the car, then it was being driven away and Nikolas had his hand on her elbow, escorting her to the door. She would not let it bother her, she told herself fiercely. She would talk with him and eat her meal and it would be finished. She did not have to pay any attention to anyone else they might meet.

After a few dinners out after their marriage, Robert had realized that it was intensely painful to his young bride to be so publicly shunned by people who knew him, and they had ceased eating out at the exclusive restaurants he had always patronized. It had been at this particular restaurant that a group of people had literally turned their backs on her, and Robert had gently led her away from their half-eaten dinner before she lost all control and sobbed like a child in front of everyone. But that had been five years ago, and though she had never lost her horror at the thought of eating in such a place—and this place in particular—she held her head proudly and walked without hesitation through the doors being held open by the uniformed doorman.

The maître d' took one glance at Nikolas and all but bowed. "Mr. Constantinos, we are honored!"

"Good evening, Swaine; we'd like a quiet table, please. Away from the crowd."

As they followed the maître d', winding their way between the tables, Jessica recovered herself enough to flash an amused glance up at the tall man beside her. "An isolated table?" she queried, her lips twitching in a suppressed smile. "So no one will notice the mayhem?"

The black head inclined toward her and she saw his flashing grin. "I think we can keep it more civilized than that."

The table that Swaine selected for them was as iso-lated as was possible on a busy Saturday night. It was partially enclosed by a bank of plants that made Jessica think of a jungle, and she half-listened for the scream of birds before she chided herself for her foolishness.

While Nikolas chose a wine, she glanced about at the other tables, half afraid that she would see a fa-miliar face; she had noticed the little silence that had preceded them as they made their way to their table, and the hiss of rapid conversation that broke out again in their wake. Had Nikolas noticed? Perhaps she was overly sensitive, perhaps the reaction was for Nikolas rather than herself. As a billionaire, he was certainly more noticeable than most people!

"Don't you like the table?" Nikolas's voice broke in on her thoughts and she jerked her eyes back to him, to find that he wore an irritated expression on his hard, dark face as he stared at her.

"No, the table's fine," she said hastily.

"Then why are you frowning?" he demanded.

"Black memories," she said. "It's nothing, Mr. Constantinos. I just had an…unpleasant experience in here once."

He watched her for a moment, then said calmly, "We can leave if it bothers you."

"It bothers me," she admitted, "but I won't leave. I think it's past time I got over my silly phobias, and what better time than now, when I have you to battle with and take my mind off old troubles?"

"That's twice you have alluded to an argument between us," he commented. He leaned closer to her, his hard brown hand reaching out to touch the low flower arrangement between them. "There won't be any arguments tonight. You're far too lovely for me to want to spend our time together throwing angry words about. If you start to argue, I'll simply lean over and kiss you until you're quiet. I've warned you now, so if you decide to spit defiance at me like a ruffled kitten, I can only conclude that you want to be kissed. What do you think about that, hmmm?"

She stared at him, trying to control her lips, but they parted anyway in a delicious smile and finally she laughed, a peal of laughter that brought heads swinging in their direction. She leaned over the table, too, and said confidentially, "I think, Mr. Constantinos, that I'll be as sweet and charming as it's possible for me to be!"

His hand left the flowers and darted out to capture her wrist, his thumb rubbing lightly over the delicate blue veins on the inside of her arm. "Being sweet and charming will also get you kissed," he teased huskily. "I think that I'll be the winner regardless! And I promise you that I'll kiss you hard if you call me mister again. Try to say Nikolas; I think you'll find it isn't that difficult. Or call me Niko, as my friends do."

"If you wish," she said, smiling at him. Now was the time to tell him about the shares, before he became too serious about his charming act. "But I want to tell you that I've decided to sell the shares to you, after all, so you don't have to be nice to me if you don't want to. I won't change my mind even if you're nasty."

"Forget the shares," he murmured. "Let's not talk about them tonight."

"But that's why you asked me to dinner," she protested.

"Yes, it was, though I haven't a doubt I could have come up with another good excuse if that one had failed." He grinned wickedly. "The little waif with the tear-streaked face was very fetching, especially as I knew a cool, maddeningly sophisticated woman was lurking behind the tears."

She shook her head. "I don't think you understand, Mr. Con—er—Nikolas. The shares are yours. There's no need to keep this up."

His lids drooped over the dark brilliance of his eyes for a moment and his hand tightened on her wrist. "Very well, let's discuss the damned shares and be finished with it, as you won't leave the subject alone. Why did you change your mind?"

"My financial advisor, Charles Welby, had already told me to sell rather than try to fight you. I was prepared to sell them, but your manner made me angry and I refused out of sheer contrariness, but as usual, Charles is right. I can't fight you; I don't want to become embroiled in boardroom politics. And there's no need for that outrageous price you mentioned, market value will do nicely."

He straightened, dropping her wrist, and he said

sharply, "I have already given you an offer; I won't go back on my word."

"You'll have to, if you want the shares, because I'll accept market value only." She faced him calmly despite the flare of temper she saw in his face.

He uttered something short and harsh in Greek. "I fail to see how you can refuse such a sum. It's a stupid move."

"And I fail to see how you'll remain a billionaire if you persist in making such stupid business deals!" she shot back.

For a moment his eyes were like daggers, then laughter burst from his throat and he threw back his head in sheer enjoyment.

Oblivious of the many interested eyes on them, he leaned forward once more to take her hand. "You are a gorgeous snow queen," he said huskily. "It was worth losing the Dryden issue to meet you. I don't think I will be returning to Greece as soon as I had planned."

Jessica's eyes widened as she stared at him. It seemed he was serious; he was actually attracted to her! Alarm tingled through her, warming her body as she met the predatory gaze of those midnight eyes.

CHAPTER THREE

THE ARRIVAL OF the wine brought her a welcome relief from his penetrating gaze, but the relief was only momentary. As soon as they were alone again, he drawled, "Does it bother you that I'm attracted to you? I would have thought you would find it commonplace to attract a man's desire."

Jessica tried to retrieve her hand, but his fingers closed firmly over hers and refused to let her go. Green sparks began to shoot from her eyes as she looked up at him. "I don't think you are attracted," she said sharply. "I think you're still trying to put me in my place because I won't bow down and kiss your feet. I've *told* you that the shares are yours, now please let go of my hand."

"You're wrong," he said, his hand tightening over hers until the grip was painful and she winced. "From the moment you walked into my office this afternoon, every nerve in my body has been screaming. I want you, Jessica, and signing those shares over to me won't get me out of your life."

"Then what will?" she demanded, tight-lipped. "What is your price for leaving me alone?"

A look of almost savage anger crossed his face; then he smiled, and the smile chilled her blood. The midnight eyes raked over her face and breasts. "Price?" he murmured. "You know what the price would be, to leave you alone...eventually. I want to sate myself with you, burn you so deeply with my touch that you will never be free, so that whenever another man touches you, you will think of me and wish me in his place."

The thought—the image it provoked—was shattering. Her eyes widened and she stared at him in horror. "No," she said thickly. "Oh, no! Never!"

"Don't be so certain," he mocked. "Do you think I couldn't overcome any resistance you might make? And I'm not talking about forcing you, Jessica; I'm talking about desire. I could make you want me; I could make you so hungry for my lovemaking that you'd beg me to take you."

"No!" Blindly she shook her head, terrified that he might really force himself on her. She wouldn't permit that, never; she had endured hell on earth because everyone saw her as a gold-digging little tart, but she would never let herself be reduced to the level of a kept woman, a mistress, all of the ugly things they had called her. "Don't you understand?" she whispered raggedly. "I don't want to get involved with you—with any man—on any level."

"That's very interesting," he said, his eyes narrowing on her face. "I can understand that you'd find your marriage duties to an old man to be revolting, but surely all of your lovers can't have been so bad. And don't try to pretend that you went into that marriage as pure as the driven snow, because I won't believe you. An innocent wouldn't sell herself to an old man, and besides, too many men claim to have...known you."

Jessica swallowed hard on the nausea that welled up in her and her head jerked up. White-faced, green eyes blazing, she spat at him, "On the contrary, Robert was an angel! It was the other men who left a bad taste in my mouth—and I think, Mr. Constantinos, that in spite of your money, you give me the worst taste of all."

Instantly she was aware that she had gone too far. His face went rigid and she had only a second of warning before the hand that held her fingers tightened and pulled, drawing her out of her chair until she was leaning over the table. He rose and met her halfway, and her startled exclamation was cut off by the pressure of his mouth, hot and hard and probing, and she had no defense against the intrusion of his tongue.

Dimly she could hear the swelling murmurs behind her, feel a flash of light against her lids, but the kiss went on and on and she was helpless to pull away. Panic welled in her, smothering her, and a whimper of distress sounded in her throat. Only then did he raise his punishing mouth, but he still held her over the table like that, his eyes on her white face and trembling lips, then he very gently reseated her and resumed his own seat. "Don't provoke me again," he said through his teeth. "I warned you, Jessica, and that kiss was a light one compared to the next one you will get."

Jessica didn't dare look up at him; she simply sat there and stared at her wine, her entire body shaking. She wanted to slap him, but more than that she wanted to run away and hide. That flash of light that she had noticed had been the flash of a camera, she knew, and she cringed inside to think of the field day the scandal sheets would have with that photo. Nausea roiled in her stomach and she fought fiercely against it, snatching up her wineglass with a shaking hand and sipping the cool, dry wine until she had herself under control again.

A rather uncomfortable-looking waiter appeared

with the menus and Jessica used every ounce of concentration that she possessed in choosing her meal. She had thought of allowing Constantinos to order for her; in fact, he seemed to expect her to do so, but it had become very important that she cling to that small bit of independence. She had to cling to something when she could feel the eyes boring into her from all corners of the room, and when across from her sat a man who made man-eating tigers seem tame.

"It's useless to sulk," he said now, breaking in on her thoughts with his smooth, deep voice. "I won't allow that, Jessica, and it was only a kiss, after all. The first of many. Would you like to go sailing with me tomorrow? The weathermen are predicting a warm, sunny day and you can get to know me as we laze about all day in the sun."

"No," she said starkly. "I don't ever want to see you again."

He laughed outright, throwing back his gleaming dark head, his white teeth flashing in the dimness like a wild animal's. "You're like an angry child," he murmured. "Why don't you scream that you hate me, and stamp your feet in a temper so I may have the pleasure of taming you? I'd enjoy tussling with you, rolling about until you tired yourself out and lay quietly beneath me."

"I don't hate you," she told him, regaining some of her composure despite his disturbing words. She even managed to look at him quite coolly. "I won't waste the energy to hate you, because you're just passing through. After the shares have been signed over, I'll never see you again, and I can't see myself shedding any tears over your absence, either."

"I can't let you continue to delude yourself," he

mocked. "I'm not merely passing through; I've changed my plans—to include you. I'll be in London for quite some time, for as long as it takes. Don't fight me, my dear; it's only a waste of time that's better spent in other ways."

"Your ego must be enormous," she observed, sipping at her wine. "You seem unable to believe that I simply don't fancy you. Very well, if that's what it takes to rid myself of you, when you take me home we'll go upstairs and you may satisfy your odd little urges. It won't take much effort, and it'll be worth it to see the back of you." Even as the words left her mouth, Jessica almost jumped in amazement at herself. Dear heaven, how did she manage to sound so cool and disinterested, and say such dreadful things? What on earth would she do if he took her up on it? She had no intention of going to bed with him if she had to scream her silly head off and make a scandal that would force both of them out of the country.

His face had turned to stone as she talked and his eyes had narrowed until they were mere slits. She had the urge to throw up her arms to protect her face, even though he didn't move a muscle. At last he spoke, grinding the words out between his teeth. "You cold little bitch, you'll pay for that. Before I'm finished with you, you'll regret opening your mouth; you'll apologize for every word. Go upstairs with you? I doubt I'll wait that long!"

She had to get out, she had to get away from him. Without thinking, she clutched her bag and said, "I have to go to the ladies—"

"No," he said. "You aren't going anywhere. You're

going to sit there until we've eaten, then I'll drive you home."

Jessica sat very still, glaring at him, but her hostility didn't seem to bother him. When their meal was served, he began to eat as if everything was perfectly calm and normal. She chewed on a few bites, but the tender lamb and stewed carrots turned into a lump in her throat that she couldn't swallow. She gulped at her wine, and there was a flash of a camera again. Quickly she set down her glass and paled, turning her head away.

He missed nothing, even when it seemed that he wasn't paying attention. "Don't let it upset you," he advised coolly. "The cameras are everywhere. They mean nothing; it's merely something to fill the space in their empty little tabloids."

She didn't reply, but she remembered the earlier flash, when he had been kissing her so brutally. She felt ill at the thought of that photo being splashed all over the gossip pages.

"You don't seem to mind being the target of gossip," she forced herself to say, and though her voice was a bit strained, she managed the words without gulping or bursting into tears.

He shrugged. "It's harmless enough. If anyone is really interested in who I had dinner with, or who stopped by our table for a moment's conversation, then I really have no objection. When I want to be private, I don't go to a public place."

She wondered if he had ever been the subject of such vicious gossip as she had endured, but though the papers were always making some mention of him closing a deal or flying here and there for conferences, sometimes with a vague mention of his latest "lovely," she could recall nothing about his private life. He had said that he lived on an island....

"What's the name of the island where you live?" she asked, for that was a subject as safe as any, and she dearly needed something that would allow her time to calm herself.

A wicked black brow quirked upward. "I live on the island of Zenas, which means Zeus's gift, or, more loosely translated, the gift of the gods. I'm using the Greek name for the god, of course; the Roman version is Jupiter."

"Yes," she said. "Have you lived there for long?"

The brow went higher. "I was born there. I own it."

"Oh." Of course he did; why should he live on someone else's island? And she had forgotten, but now she remembered, what he had said about growing up wild on the island. "Is it a very large island? Does anyone else live there, or is it just you alone on your retreat?"

He grinned. "The island is roughly ten miles long, and as much as five miles wide at one place. There is a small fishing village, and the people graze their goats in the hills. My mother lives in our villa year round now; she no longer likes to travel, and of course, there's the normal staff in the villa. I suppose there are some two hundred people on the island, and an assortment of goats, chickens, dogs, a few cows."

It sounded enchanting, and she forgot her troubles for a moment as she dreamed about such a quiet, simple life. Her eyes glowed as she said, "How can you bear to leave it?"

He shrugged. "I have many interests that require my time and attention, and though I'll always look on the island as my home, I'm not quite a hermit. The modern world has its attractions, too." He raised his wine-glass to her and she understood that a large amount of the world's attraction was in its women. Of course, on a small Greek island the young women would be strictly supervised until they wed, and a healthy man would want to relieve his more basic urges.

His gesture with the wineglass brought her attention back to her own wineglass, and she saw that it was nearly empty. "May I have more wine?"

"No," he refused smoothly. "You've already had two glasses, and you've merely pushed your food around on your plate instead of eating it. You'll be drunk if you continue. Eat your dinner, or isn't it the way you like it? Shall I have it returned to the kitchen?"

"No, the food is excellent, thank you." What else could she say? It was only the truth.

"Then why aren't you eating?"

Jessica regarded him seriously, then decided that he was a big boy and he should certainly be able to handle the truth. "I'm not exactly enjoying myself," she told him. "You've rather upset my stomach."

His mouth twitched in grim amusement. "You haven't upset mine, but you have without doubt upset my system in every other way! Since meeting you, I totally absolve Robert Stanton of foolishness, except perhaps in whatever overly optimistic expectations he may have had. You're an enchanting woman, even when you're insulting me."

She had never mentioned her relationship with Robert to anyone, but now she had the urge to cry out that she had loved him, that everyone was wrong in what they said of her. Only the years of practice in holding herself aloof kept her lips sealed on the wild cry of hurt, but she did allow herself to comment, "Robert was the least foolish man I have ever met. He knew exactly what he was about at all times."

Nikolas narrowed his eyes. "Are you saying that he knew you married him only for his money?"

"I'm saying nothing of the kind," she retorted sharply. "I won't discuss my marriage with you; it's none of your business. If you're finished with your meal, I'd like to go home now."

"*I've* finished," he said, looking pointedly at her plate. "However, you've hardly even begun to eat. You need food to absorb some of the wine you've had, and we won't leave here until you eat."

"I would bolt it down without chewing if that would free me from your company," she muttered as she lifted her fork and speared a morsel of meat.

He waited until she had the meat in her mouth and was chewing before he said, "But it won't. If I remember correctly, you have invited me upstairs when I take you home. To satisfy my 'odd little urges,' I think was how you phrased it. I accept your invitation."

Jessica swallowed and attacked another piece of meat. "You must have misunderstood," she said coldly. "I wouldn't let you inside my house, let alone my bedroom."

"My apartment will do just as well," he replied, his eyes gleaming. "Or the ground, if you prove difficult about the matter."

"Now see here," she snapped, putting her fork down with a clatter. "This has gone far enough. I want you to understand this clearly: I'm *not* available! Not to you, not to any man, and if you touch me, I'll scream until everyone in London hears me."

"If you can," he murmured. "Don't you imagine that I'm capable of stifling any screams, Jessica?"

"Oh?" she demanded with uplifted brows. "Are you a rapist? Because it would be rape, have no doubt about it. I'm not playing at being difficult; I'm entirely serious. I don't want you."

"You will," he said confidently, and she wanted to scream now, in frustration. Could he truly be so dense, his ego so invulnerable, that he simply couldn't believe that she didn't want to go to bed with him? Well, if he didn't believe that she'd scream, he'd certainly be surprised if he tried anything with her!

In one swift motion she stood up, determined not to sit there another moment. "Thank you for the meal," she said. "I believe it would be best if I took a taxi home, and I'll have Charles contact you Monday about the settlement of the shares."

He stood also, calmly laying his napkin aside. "I'm taking you home," he said, "if I have to drag you to my car. Now, do you want to make your exit in a dignified manner, or slung over my shoulder? Before you decide, let me assure you that no one will come to your aid. Money does have its uses, you know."

"Yes, I know," she agreed frigidly. "It allows some people to act like bullies without fear of retribution. Very well, shall we leave?"

He smiled in grim triumph and placed a bill on the table, and even in her anger she was startled at the amount he had laid down. She looked up in time to see him nod to the maître d', and by the time they had made their way across the room her wrap was waiting. Nikolas took the wrap and gently placed it about her shoulders, his hands lingering there for a moment as his fingers moved over her flesh. A blinding flash of light told her that this, too, had been photographed, and involuntarily Jessica shrank closer to him in an effort to hide. His hands tightened on her shoulders and he frowned as he looked down at her suddenly pale face. He looked around until he located the photographer, and though he said nothing, Jessica heard a muttered apology somewhere behind them. Then Nikolas had his arm firmly around her waist and he led her outside, where his car was just being driven up.

When the doorman and the young man who had brought the car had been settled with and Nikolas had seen that she was securely buckled into her seat, he said, "Why do you flinch whenever a flash goes off?"

"I dislike publicity," she muttered.

"It scarcely matters whether you like it or not," he said quietly. "Your actions have made certain that you will have it, regardless, and you certainly should be used to it by now. Your marriage made quite a lot of grist for the mill."

"I'm aware of that," she said. "I've been called a bitch to my face and a lot worse to my back, but that doesn't mean that I've ever become accustomed to it. I was eighteen years old, *Mr.* Constantinos"—she stressed the word—"and I was crucified by the press. I've never forgotten."

"Did you think no one would notice when you married a rich, elderly man of Robert Stanton's reputation?" he almost snarled. "For God's sake, Jessica, you all but begged to be crucified!"

"So I discovered," she said, her voice catching. "Robert and I ceased going out in public when it became obvious that I would never be accepted as his wife, though he didn't care on his own account. He said that he would find out who his true friends were, and there were a few. He seemed to cherish those few, and never said anything that indicated he wanted his life to be any different, at least in my hearing. Robert was endlessly kind," she finished quietly, for she found that even the memories of Robert helped to calm her. He had seen life so clearly, without illusions and with a great deal of humor. What would he think about this predatory man who sat beside her now?

He drove in silence and she leaned her head back and closed her eyes, tired and rather drained. All in all, it had been a long day, and the worst part was still to come, unless he decided to act decently and leave her alone. But somehow she doubted that Nikolas Constantinos ever acted in any way except to please himself, so she had best brace herself for war.

When he pulled up in the drive on her side of the house, she noticed thankfully that Sallie and Joel were home and were still awake, though her watch told her that it was ten-thirty. He cut off the engine and put the keys in his pocket, then got out and came around to open her door. He leaned in and helped her to gather her long skirt, then all but lifted her out of the car. "I'm not an invalid," she said tartly as his arm slid about her waist and pulled her against his side.

"That's why I'm holding you," he explained, his low laughter brushing her hair. "To prevent you from running."

Fuming helplessly, Jessica watched as he took the key from her bag and opened the door, ushering her inside with that iron arm at her back. She ignored him and marched into the kitchen to check on Samantha. She knelt and scratched the dog behind the ears, receiving a loving lick on the hand in return. A puppy squeaked at being disturbed and it too received a lick of the warm tongue, then Jessica was startled as two hard hands closed over her shoulders and pulled her to her feet.

She had had enough; she was tired of him and his arrogance. She exploded with rage, hitting at his face and twisting her body in his grasp as he tried to hold her against him. "No, damn you!" she cried. "I told you I won't!"

Samantha rose to her feet and gave a growl at seeing her mistress treated so roughly, but the puppies began to cry in alarm as she left them and she turned back to look at her offspring. By that time Nikolas had swept Jessica off her feet and into his arms and was back through the kitchen door with her, shouldering it shut behind him. He wasn't even breathing hard as he captured her flailing arms, and that made her even angrier. She arched her back and kicked in an effort to wiggle out of his arms; she hit out at that broad chest, and when that failed to stop him, she opened her mouth to scream. Swiftly he forced her head against his shoulder and her scream was largely muffled by his body. Blinded and breathless with fury, she gave a strangled cry as he suddenly dropped her.

Soft cushions broke her fall, then her body was instantly covered by his hard weight as he dropped down on her and pinned her. "Damn you, be still," he hissed, stretching a long arm up over her head. For a sickening moment she thought he would slap her, and she caught her breath, but no blow fell. Instead, he switched on the lamp at the end of the sofa and a soft light bathed the room. She hadn't realized where they were until he turned on the lamp and now she looked about her at the comfortable, sane setting of her living room. She turned her head to look up with bewilderment into the furious dark face above her.

"What's the matter with you?" he barked.

She blinked. Hadn't he been attacking her? He had certainly been manhandling her! Even now his heavy legs pressed down on hers and she knew that her skirt was twisted above her knees. She moved restlessly under him and he let his weight down more heavily on her in warning. "Well?" he growled.

"But...I thought...weren't you attacking me?" she asked, her brow puckering. "I thought you were, and so did Samantha."

"If I *had* been attacking you, the situation was reversed before I got very far," he snapped. "Damn you, Jessica, you don't know how tempting you are—and how infuriating—" He broke off, his black eyes moving to her lips. She squirmed and turned her head away, a breathless little "No" coming from her, but he captured her head with a hand on each side of her face and turned her mouth back to him. He was only a breath away and she tried to protest again, then it was too late. His hard mouth closed over her soft one, forcing her lips open, and his warm, wine-fragrant breath filled her mouth. His tongue followed, exploring and caressing her inner mouth, flicking at her own tongue, sending her senses reeling.

She was frightened by the pressure of his big, hard body over hers and for a moment her slim hands pushed uselessly at his heavy shoulders. But his mouth was warm and he wasn't hurting her now, and she had never before been kissed like this. For a moment—only one moment, she promised herself—she allowed herself to curve in his arms, to respond to him and kiss him back. Her hands slid over his broad shoulders to clasp about his neck, her tongue responded shyly to his; then she no longer had the option of returning his caresses or not. He shuddered and his arms tightened painfully about her and his mouth went wild, ravaging, sucking her breath hungrily from her body. He muttered something, thickly, and it took her dazed mind a minute to realize he had spoken in French and to translate the words. When she did, her face flamed and she tried to push him away, but still she was helpless against him.

He slid one hand under her neck and deftly unhooked the halter strap of her bodice. As his mouth left hers and trailed a fiery path down her neck, she managed a choked "No," to which he paid no attention at all. His lips moved the loosened straps of her bodice down as he planted fierce kisses along her shoulder and collarbone, licking the tender spot in the hollow of her shoulder until she almost forgot her rising fear and quivered with pleasure, clutching his ribs with helpless hands. He became impatient with the straps, still in the way of his wandering mouth, and jerked roughly at them, intent on baring her to the waist, and panic erupted in Jessica with the force of a volcano.

With a strangled cry she twisted frantically in his arms, holding her bodice up with one arm while, with the other, she tried to force his head away from her. He snarled in frustration and jerked her arm above her head, reaching for the material of her dress with his other hand. Her heartbeat came to a standstill and with superhuman effort she pulled her hand free, beating at his back. "No!" she cried out, nearly hysterical. "No, Nikolas, don't; I beg you!"

He stilled her words with the forceful pressure of his mouth, and she realized in a jolt of pure terror that she couldn't control him; he was bent on taking her. A sob erupted from her throat and she released her bodice to beat at him with both hands, crying wildly and choking out the muffled words, "No! No...." He raised his lips from hers and she moaned, "Please! Nikolas! Ah, don't!"

The savage movements of his hands stopped and he lay still, his breath heaving raggedly in his chest. She shook with sobs, her small face drenched with tears. He groaned deep in his throat and slid off the sofa, to kneel beside it and rest his black head on the cushion beside her. Silence fell on the room again and she tried to choke back her tears. Hesitantly she put her hands on his head, sliding her fingers through his thick hair, not understanding her need to comfort him but unable to resist the impulse. He quivered under the touch of her hands and she smelled the fresh sweat on his body, the maleness of his skin, and she realized how aroused he had been. But he had stopped; he hadn't forced her, after all, and she could feel all of her hostility draining away. For all her inexperience she knew enough about men to know that it had been quite a wrench for him to become so aroused and then stop, and she was deeply grateful to him.

At length he raised his head, and she gasped at the strained, grim expression on his face. "Straighten your dress," he said thickly, "or it may be too late yet."

Hastily she hooked her straps back into place and pushed the skirt down over her legs. She would have liked to sit up, but with him so close it would have been awkward, so she remained lying against the cushions until he moved. He ran his hand wearily through his hair. "Perhaps it's just as well," he said a moment later, getting to his feet. "We made no preparations, and I know I couldn't have— Was that what frightened you, Jessica? The thought of the risk we'd have been taking with an unwanted pregnancy?"

Her voice was husky when she spoke. "No, it…it wasn't that. You just…frightened me." She sat up and wiped at her wet cheeks with the palms of her hands. He looked at her and grimly produced the handkerchief that she had used earlier, to dry her eyes when he had first arrived—was it only a few hours ago? She accepted the square of linen and dried her face, then gave it back to him.

He gave a short, harsh laugh. "So I frightened you? I wanted to do a lot of things to you, but frightening you wasn't one of them. You're a dangerous woman, my dear, deadly in your charm. You leave a man aching and empty after you've pulled away." He inhaled deeply and began to button his shirt, and only then did she notice that somehow his jacket had been discarded and his shirt unbuttoned and pulled loose from his pants. She had no memory of opening his shirt, but only she could have done it, for his hands had been too busy on her to have accomplished it.

His face still wore that taut, strained look and she said in a rush, "I'm sorry, Nikolas."

"So am I, my dear." His dark gaze flickered to her and a tight little smile touched his mouth. "But you're calling me Nikolas now, so something has been accomplished." He tucked his shirt inside his pants and dropped down on the sofa beside her. "I want to see you again, and soon," he said, taking her hand. "Will you come sailing with me tomorrow? I promise that I won't rush you; I won't frighten you as I did tonight. I'll give you time to get to know me, to realize that you'll be perfectly safe with me. Whoever frightened you of men should be shot, but it won't be like that with me. You'll see," he said encouragingly.

Safe? Would she ever be safe with this man? She strongly doubted it, but he had been nicer than she would have expected and she didn't want to make him angry, so she tempered her words. "I don't think so, Nikolas. Not tomorrow. It's too soon."

His mouth pressed into an ominous line, then he sighed and got to his feet. "I'll call you tomorrow, and don't try anything foolish like trying to hide from me. I'd only find you, and you might not like the consequences. I won't be put off like that again. Do you understand?"

"I understand that you're threatening me!" she said spiritedly.

He grinned suddenly. "You're safe so long as you don't push me, Jessica. I want you, but I can wait."

Jessica tossed her head. "It could be a long wait," she felt compelled to warn.

"Or it could be a short one," he warned in his turn. "As I said, I'll call you tomorrow. Think about the sailing; you'd like it."

"I've never been sailing; I don't know the first thing about it. I could be seasick."

"It'll be fun teaching you what you don't know," he said, and he meant more than sailing. He leaned over and pressed a warm kiss to her mouth, then drew away before she could either respond or resist. "I'll let myself out. Good night, Jessica."

"Good night, Nikolas." It felt odd to be saying good night to him as if those moments of passion and terror had never happened. She watched as he picked up his jacket from the floor and walked out, his tall, lean body moving with the wild grace of a tiger. When he was gone, the house felt empty and too quiet, and she had a sinking feeling that Nikolas Constantinos was going to turn her life upside down.

CHAPTER FOUR

DESPITE FEELING EDGY when she went to bed, Jessica slept deeply and woke in a cheerful frame of mind. She had been silly to let that man work her into a state of nerves, but she would try to avoid him in the future. Charles could handle all the details of selling the stock.

Humming to herself, she fed Samantha and praised the puppies to their proud mother, then made toast for herself. She had not acquired the English habit of tea, so instead she drank coffee; she was lingering over the second cup when Sallie rapped on the window of the back door. Jessica got up to unlock the door and let her in, and she noticed the worried frown that marred Sallie's usually smiling face. Sallie held a folded section of newspaper.

"Is anything wrong?" asked Jessica. "But before you tell me, would you like a cup of coffee?"

Sallie made a face. "Coffee, my girl? You're not civilized yet! No, Jess, I think you should see this. It's a nasty piece, and just when all of that business was beginning to die down. I wouldn't have brought it over, Joel thought I shouldn't, but—well, you'll be hit with it when you go out, and I thought it would be better for you to see it privately."

Jessica held out her hand wordlessly for the paper, but she already knew what it was. Sallie had folded it to the gossip and society pages, and there were two photographs there. One, of course, was of Nikolas kissing her. She noticed dispassionately that it was a good picture, Nikolas so dark and strong, she much slighter in build, their mouths clinging together over the table. The other photo was the one taken when they had been leaving and Nikolas had had his hands on her shoulders, looking down at her with an expression that made her shiver. Raw hunger was evident in his face in that photo, and remembering what had happened when he brought her home made her wonder anew that he had stopped when she became frightened.

But Sallie was pointing to the column under the photos and Jessica sat down at the table to read it. It was a witty, sophisticated column, tart in places, but at one point the columnist became purringly vicious. Nausea welled in her as she skimmed over the lines of print:

London's notorious Black Widow was observed spinning her web over another helpless and adoring victim last night; the elusive Greek billionaire Nikolas Constantinos appeared to be completely captivated by the Widow's charm. Can it be that she had exhausted the funds left to her by her late husband, the esteemed Robert Stanton? Certainly Nikolas is able to maintain her in her accustomed style, yet from all reports this man may not be as easy to capture as she found her first husband. One wonders just who will be the victor in the end. The Widow seems to stop at nothing—but neither does her chosen prey. We will observe with interest.

Jessica dropped the paper onto the table and sat staring blindly across the room. She shouldn't let it bother her; she had been expecting this to happen. And certainly she should be accustomed to it, after five years, but it seemed that rather than becoming hardened, she was more sensitive now than she had been years ago. Then she had had Robert to buffer her, to ease the pain and make her laugh, but now she had no one. Any pain she suffered was suffered alone. The Black Widow—that phrase had been coined immediately after Robert's death, and it had stuck. Before that they had at least referred to her by name. The cutting little bits had always been nasty but stopped short of libel, not that she would ever have pursued the matter. The publicity involved in a suit would have been even nastier, and she would rather live a quiet life, with her few friends and small pleasures. She would even have returned to the States if it hadn't been for Robert's business interests, but she wanted to see to them and use the knowledge Robert had given her. Robert would have wanted that, too, she knew.

Sallie was watching her anxiously, so Jessica pulled a deep, shuddering breath into her lungs and forced herself to speak. "Well, that was certainly a vicious bit, wasn't it? I had almost forgotten how really rotten it can be.... But I won't make the mistake of going out again. It isn't worth it."

"But you can't hide away all your life," protested Sallie. "You're so young; it isn't fair to treat you like—like a leper!"

A leper—what an appalling thought! Yet Sallie wasn't so wrong, even though Jessica had yet to be stoned out of town. She was still welcome in very few homes.

Sallie cast about for a different subject, for although Jessica was trying to act casual about the whole matter, her face had gone pale and she looked stricken. Sallie jabbed the photo in the newspaper and said, "What about this dish, Jess? He's a gorgeous man! When did you meet him?"

"What?" Jessica looked down and two spots of color came back to her cheeks as she gazed at the photo of Nikolas kissing her. "Oh…actually, I only met him yesterday."

"Wow! He certainly is a fast worker! He looks the strong, masterful type, and his reputation is mind-boggling. What's he like?"

"Strong, masterful, and mind-boggling," Jessica sighed. "Just like you said. I hope I don't have to meet with him again."

"You've mush in your head!" exclaimed Sallie indignantly. "Honestly, Jess, you are unbelievable. Most women would give their right arm to go out with a man like that, rich *and* handsome, and you aren't interested."

"But then, I'm wary of rich men," Jessica replied softly. "You've seen an example of what would be said, and I don't think I could go through that again."

"Oh! I'm sorry, love," said Sallie. "I didn't think. But—just think! Nikolas Constantinos!"

Jessica didn't want to think of Nikolas; she wanted to forget the entire night. Looking at her friend's pale, closed face, Sallie patted her shoulder and slipped away. Jessica sat for a time at the table, her mind blank, but when she stood up to place her cup and saucer in the sink, it suddenly became more than she could handle and the tears fell freely.

When the bout of weeping ended, she was exhausted from the force of it and she wandered into the living room to lie down on the sofa, but that reminded her of Nikolas lying there with her, and instead she collapsed into a chair, pulling her feet up into the seat and wrapping her robe about her legs. She felt dead, empty inside, and when the phone rang, she stared at it dumbly for a long moment before she lifted the receiver. "Hello," she said dully.

"Jessica. Have you—"

She took the receiver away from her ear when she heard the deep voice, and listlessly let it drop back onto the cradle. No, she couldn't talk to him now; she hurt too deeply.

When the doorbell pealed some time later, she continued to sit quietly, determined not to answer it, but after a moment she heard Charles's voice call out her name and she got to her feet.

"Good morning," she greeted him while he eyed her sharply. She looked beaten.

"I read the paper," he said gently. "Go upstairs and wash your face and put on some clothes, then you can tell me about it. I intended to call you yesterday, but I had to go out of town, not that I could have done anything. Go on, my dear, upstairs with you."

Jessica did as she was told, applying cold water to her face and smoothing the tangles from her hair, then changing out of her nightgown and robe into a pretty white sundress with tiny blue flowers on it. Despite her numbness, she was glad that Charles was there. With his cool lawyer's brain he could pick at her responses until they were all neatly arranged where she could understand them, and he would analyze her feelings. Charles could analyze a rock.

"Yes, much better," he approved when she entered the living room. "Well, it is rather obvious that my fears for you were misplaced; Constantinos was obviously quite taken with you. Did he mention the Dryden issue?"

"He did," said Jessica, and even managed a smile for him. "I'm selling the stock to him, but don't imagine everything was sweetness and light. We get along like the proverbial cats and dogs. His comments on my marriage make that gossip column seem mild in comparison, and I have walked out on him and hung up on him once each—no, I've done it twice; he called this morning and I didn't want to talk to him. It would be best if I don't see him again, if you could handle all of the details of the stock transaction."

"Of course I will," replied Charles promptly. "But I feel certain you're underestimating your man. From that photo in the newspaper, he's attracted to more than your ConTech stock."

"Yes," admitted Jessica, "but there's no use. I couldn't live with that type of publicity again, and he attracts reporters and photographers by the dozens."

"That's true, but if he doesn't want something to be published, it isn't published. His power is enormous."

"Are you trying to argue his side, Charles?" Jessica asked in amazement. "Surely you understand that his attraction is only temporary, that he's only interested in an affair?"

Charles shrugged. "So are most men," he said dryly. "In the beginning."

"Yes, well, I'm *not* interested. By the way, the shares are going for market value. He offered much more than that, but I refused it."

"I see Robert's standards there," he said.

"I'll sell the stock to him, but *I* won't be bought."

"I never thought you would. I wished myself a fly on the wall during your meeting; it must've been diverting," he said, and smiled at her, his cool, aristocratic face revealing the dry humor behind his elegant, controlled manner.

"Very, but it stopped short of murder." Suddenly she remembered and she smiled naturally for the first time since reading that horrid gossip column. "Charles, Samantha had her puppies last night, five of them!"

"She took time enough," he observed. "What will you do with five yelping puppies about the house?"

"Give them away when they're old enough. There are plenty of children in the neighborhood; it shouldn't be that difficult."

"You think so? When have you last tried to give away a litter of unknown origin? How many females are there?"

"How should I know?" she demanded, and laughed. "They don't come with pink and blue bows around their necks, you know."

Charles grinned in return and followed her into the kitchen, where she proudly displayed the pups, all piled together in a little heap. Samantha watched Charles closely, ready to nip if he came too near her babies, but he was well aware of Samantha's tendencies and kept a safe distance from her. Charles was too fastidious to be an animal lover and the dog sensed this.

"I see you've no tea made," he commented, looking

at the coffeepot. "Put the water on, my dear, and tell me more about your meeting with Constantinos. Did it actually become hot, or were you teasing?"

Sighing, Jessica ran water from the tap into a kettle and put it on the stove. "The meeting was definitely unfriendly, even hostile. Don't let the photo of that kiss fool you, Charles; he only did that as a punishment and to make me shut up. I can't—" She started to say that she couldn't decide if she trusted him or not, but the ring of the doorbell interrupted her and she stopped in her tracks, a chill running up her spine. "Oh, glory," she gulped. "That's him now; I know it is! I hung up on him, and he'll be in a raging temper."

"I'll be brave and answer the door for you while you make the tea," offered Charles, searching for an excuse to get to Constantinos before he could upset her even more. That shattered look was fading from her eyes, but she was still hurt and vulnerable and she wasn't up to fending off someone like Constantinos. Jessica realized why Charles offered to get the door; he was the most tactful man in the world, she thought as she set out the cups and saucers for tea. And one of the kindest, always trying to shield her from any unpleasantness.

She stopped in her tracks, considering that. Why hadn't Charles offered to meet with Constantinos and work out the deal on the shares rather than letting her go herself? The more she thought about it, the more out of character it seemed. A wild suspicion flared and she dismissed it instantly, but it crept back. Had Charles deliberately thrown her into Nikolas's path? Was he actually *matchmaking?* Horrors! What had he been thinking of? Didn't he know that Nikolas Constantinos, while very likely to ask her to be his mistress, would never even consider marriage? And Charles certainly knew her well enough to know that she would never consider anything but!

Marriage? With Nikolas? She began to shake so violently that she had to put the tray down. What was wrong with her? She had only met the man yesterday, yet here she was thinking that she would never settle for less than being his wife! It was only that he was physically attractive to her, she told herself desperately. But Jessica was nothing if not honest with herself and she knew immediately that she was hiding from the truth. It wasn't only a physical attraction that she felt for Nikolas. She had seen a great many men who were handsome and physically appealing to her, but none that she had wanted as she had wanted Nikolas last night. Nor would she have been so receptive to Nikolas's caresses if her mind and emotions hadn't responded to him, too. He was brutal and ruthless and maddeningly arrogant, but she sensed in him a masculine appreciation for her femininity that tore down her barriers of hostility. Nikolas wanted her. That was fairly obvious, and she could have resisted that, had she not been aware that he delighted in her sharp mind and equally sharp tongue.

All in all, she was dangerously attracted to him, even vulnerable to falling in love with him, and that realization was a blow that surpassed the unpleasant shock of that vicious gossip column. White-faced, trembling, she stared at the kettle of boiling water, wondering what she was going to do. How could she avoid him? He was not a man to accept no for an answer, nor was she certain that she could say no to him, anyway. Yet to be in his company was to invite even greater pain, for he would not offer marriage and she would not be satisfied with less.

Eventually the shrill whistle of the kettle drew her mind back to the present and she hurriedly turned the heat off and poured the water over the tea. She had no idea if Nikolas would drink tea and decided that he wouldn't, so she poured coffee for him and also for herself; then, without allowing herself time to think about it, she picked up the tray and carried it through to the living room before she could lose all her courage.

Nikolas was lounging on the sofa like a big cat, while Charles had taken a chair; they both got to their feet as she entered, and Nikolas stepped forward to take the heavy tray from her hands and place it on the low table. She shot him a wary glance from under her lashes, but he didn't look angry. He was watching her intently, his gaze so penetrating that she shivered. He immediately noted her reaction and a sardonic half smile curved his mouth. He put his hand on her arm and gently forced her to a seat on the sofa, then took his place beside her.

"Charles and I have been discussing the situation," he said easily, and she started, shooting a desperate look at Charles. But Charles merely smiled and she could read nothing from his expression.

"What situation?" she asked, reaching for some hidden well of calmness.

"The position our relationship will put you in with the press," he explained smoothly as she handed Charles's tea across to him. By some miracle she kept from dropping the cup and saucer, though she felt her entire body jerk. When Charles had rescued his drink, she turned a pale face up to Nikolas.

"What are you saying?" she whispered.

"I think you know, my dear; you're far from stupid. I'll take certain steps that will make it plain to all observers that I don't feel I need the press to protect me from you, and that any long noses poked into my private life will rouse me to…irritation. You won't have to worry any longer about being the subject of a nasty Sunday-morning column; in fact, after I finish convincing the press to do as I want, all sympathy will probably swing to you."

"That's quite unnecessary," she said, lowering her lashes as she offered a cup of coffee to him. She felt confused; it had not occurred to her that Nikolas might use his influence to protect her, and rather than feeling grateful, she withdrew into a cool reserve. She didn't want to be indebted to Nikolas and drawn further into his sphere of influence. The paper had gotten it all wrong, he was the spider, not she! If she allowed it, he would weave silken threads all about her until she was helpless against him.

"I'll be the judge of that," Nikolas snapped. "If you'd told me last night why you were so upset about that damned photographer, I could have prevented both the column and the photos from being printed. Instead, you let your pride stand in the way, and look what you've endured, all for nothing. Now I know the extent of the situation and I'll act as I think best."

Charles said mildly, "Be reasonable, Jessica. There's no need for you to endure spiteful gossip. You've suffered it for five years; it's time that state of affairs was ended."

"Yes, but…" She halted, for she had been about to say, "But not by *him*," and she wasn't certain enough of Nikolas's temper to risk it. She took a deep breath and began again. "What I meant was, I don't see the need for any intervention, because there won't be another opportunity for this to happen. I'd have to be a fool to allow myself to get into that situation after what happened last night. I'll simply live here as quietly as possible; there's no need for me to frequent places where I'd be recognized."

"I won't allow that," Nikolas put in grimly. "From now on, you'll be by my side when I entertain or when I go out. People will meet you, get to know you. That's the only sure way of forever stifling the gossip, to let these people become acquainted with you and find out that they like you. You *are* a likable little wench, despite your damnable temper."

"Thank you!" she returned smartly, and Charles grinned.

"I could kick myself for missing your first meeting," he put in, and Nikolas gave him a wolfish grin.

"The first wasn't as interesting as the second," he informed Charles dryly. "And the third meeting isn't beginning all that well, either. It'll probably take me all day to convince her not to be obstinate over the matter."

"Yes, I can see that." Charles winked and replaced his empty cup on the tray. "I'll leave you to it, then; I've some work to do."

"Call me tomorrow and we'll settle about the shares," said Nikolas, getting to his feet and holding out his hand.

Jessica's warning sirens went off. "The shares are already settled," she said in fierce determination. "Market value only! I told you, Nikolas, I won't sign the papers if you try to buy me off with a ridiculously high price!"

"I shall probably break your neck before the day is out," returned Nikolas genially, but his eyes were hard. Charles laughed aloud, something very rare for him, and Jessica glared at him as he and Nikolas walked to the door. They exchanged a few low words and her suspicions flared higher. Then Nikolas let him out and returned to stand before her with his hands on his hips, staring down at her with an implacable expression on his hard face.

"I meant what I said," she flared, scrambling to her feet to stand before him and braving the volcanic heat of his eyes.

"So did I," he murmured, raising his hand and absently stroking her bare shoulder with one finger, his touch as light and delicate as that of a butterfly. Her breath caught and she stood very still until the caress of that one finger drove her beyond control and she began to tremble. The finger moved from her shoulder to her throat, then up to press under her chin and raise her face to his. "Have you decided if you want to go out on the boat with me?" he asked as his eyes slipped to her mouth.

"I—yes. I mean, yes, I've decided, and no, I don't want to go," she explained in confusion, and the corners of his mouth lifted in a wry smile.

"Then I suggest we go for a drive, something to keep me occupied. If we stay here all day, Jessica, you know what will happen, but the decision is yours."

"I haven't invited you to stay at all, much less all day!" she informed him indignantly, pulling away from him.

His arm dropped to his side and he watched sharply as the color rose in her cheeks. "You're afraid of me," he observed in mild surprise. Despite her brave, defiant front, there had been a flash of real fear in her eyes, and he frowned. "What is it about me that frightens you, Jessica? Are you afraid of me sexually? Have your experiences with men been so bad that you fear my lovemaking?"

She stared numbly at him, unable to formulate an answer. Yes, she was afraid of him, as she had never before feared any other human being. He was so lawless—no, not that. He made his own laws, his influence was enormous; he was practically untouchable by any known power. She already knew that her emotions were vulnerable to him and that she had no weapons against him at all.

But he was waiting for an answer, his strong features hardening as she moved involuntarily backward. She gulped and whispered wildly, "You—you wouldn't understand, Nikolas. I think that a woman would be in very good hands with you, so to speak, wouldn't she?"

"I like to think so," he drawled. "But if it isn't that, Jessica, what is it about me that makes you as wary as a frightened doe? I promise I won't slaughter you."

"Won't you?"

The whispered, shaking words had scarcely left her mouth before he moved, closing the distance between them with two lithe strides and capturing her as she gave an alarmed cry and tried to dart away. His left arm slid about her waist and pulled her strongly against him, while his right hand caught a fistful of her tawny hair and pulled firmly on it until her face was tilted up to his.

"Now," he growled, "tell me why you're afraid."

"You're hurting me!" she cried, anger chasing away some of her instinctive fear. She kicked at his shins and he gave a muffled curse, releasing her hair and scooping her up in his arms instead. Holding her captive, he sat down on the sofa and pinned her squirming body on his lap. The struggle was woefully unequal and in only a moment she was exhausted and subdued, lying quietly against the arm that was so hard and unyielding behind her back.

He chuckled. "Whatever you're afraid of, you're definitely not afraid to fight me. Now, little wildcat, tell me what bothers you."

She was tired, too tired to fight him right now, and she was beginning to understand that it was useless to fight him, in any event. He was determined to have everything his way. Sighing, she turned her face into his shoulder and inhaled the warm, earthy male scent of him, slightly sweaty from their struggle. What could she tell him? That she feared him physically because she had known no man, that it was a virgin's instinctive fear? He would never believe that; he would rather believe the tales that many men had made love to her. And she couldn't tell him that she feared him emotionally, that she was far too vulnerable to his power, or he would use that knowledge against her.

Then an idea struck her. He had given it to her himself. Why not let him believe that she had been so mistreated that she feared all men now? He had seemed receptive to that idea....

"I don't want to talk about it," she muttered, keeping her face turned into his shoulder.

His arms tightened about her. "You have to talk about it," he said forcefully, putting his mouth against her temple. "You have to get it out in the open, where you can understand it."

"I—I don't think I can," she said breathlessly, for his arms were preventing proper breathing. "Give me time, Nikolas."

"If I must," he said into her hair. "I won't hurt you, Jessica; I want you to know that. I can be very considerate when I get what I want."

Yes, he probably could, but he was thinking only of an affair while she was already beginning to realize that her heart was terrifyingly open, his for the taking—except that he didn't want it. He wanted only her body, not the tender emotions she could give him.

His hands were moving restlessly, one stroking over her back and bare shoulders, the other caressing her thigh and hip. He wanted to make love, *now,* she could feel the desire trembling in his body. She groaned and said, "No, Nikolas, please. I can't—"

"I could teach you," he muttered. "You don't know what you're doing to me; a man isn't a piece of rock!"

But he was, pure granite. Her slim body arched in his arms as she tried to slip away from him. "No, Nikolas! No!"

He opened his arms as if he was freeing a bird and she slid from his lap to the floor, sitting on it like a child, her head resting on the sofa. He sighed heavily. "Don't wait too long," he advised, his deep voice hoarse. "Run upstairs and do whatever you have to do before we go for a drive. I have to get out of here or there won't be any waiting."

He didn't have to tell her a second time. On trembling legs she ran upstairs, where she combed her hair and put on makeup, then changed her shoes for modest heels. Her heart was pounding wildly as she returned downstairs to him. She hardly knew him, yet he was gaining a power over her that was frightening. And she was helpless to prevent it.

When she approached him, he stood and pulled her

close with a masterful arm, and his hard warm mouth took hers lazily. When he released her, he was smiling, and she supposed he had reason to smile, for her response had been as fervent as it was involuntary.

"You'll be a blazing social success," he predicted as he led her to the door. "Every man will be at your feet if you continue to look so fetching and to blush so delightfully. I don't know how you can manage a blush, but the how really doesn't matter when the result is so lovely."

"I can't control my color," she said, miffed that he should think her capable of faking a blush. "Would you rather your kisses had no effect on me?"

He looked down at her and gave her a melting smile. "On the contrary, my pet. But if it's excitement that brings the flush to your cheeks, I shall know when you are becoming aroused and will immediately whisk you away to a private place. You must tell me all of your little signals."

She managed a careless shrug. "Before you whisk me away to be ravished, I suggest that you first make certain I'm not in the midst of a fight. Anger brings on the same reaction, I'm told. And I don't imagine that even your backing will smooth away all the rocks!"

"I want to know about any rocks that stub your toe," he said, and his voice grew hard. "I insist on it, Jessica. I won't have a repeat of the sort of trash I read this morning, not if I have to muzzle every gossip columnist in London!"

To her horror, it did not sound like an empty threat.

CHAPTER FIVE

WHEN THE DOORBELL rang, Jessica went very still. Nikolas put his hand on her waist and squeezed gently, then that hand urged her inexorably toward the door. Involuntarily she resisted the pressure and he looked down at her, his hard mouth curving into a dry smile. "Don't be such a little coward," he mocked. "I won't let the beasts eat you, so why not relax and enjoy it?"

Speechless, she shook her head. In the few days that she had known Nikolas Constantinos he had taken her life and turned it upside down, totally altered it. This morning he had given his secretary a list of people to call and invite to his penthouse that night, and naturally everyone had accepted. Who turned down Constantinos? At four o'clock that afternoon Nikolas had called Jessica and told her to dress for the evening, he would pick her up in two hours. She had assumed that they would be dining out again, and though she hadn't looked forward to it, she had realized the futility of resisting Nikolas. It wasn't until he had her at his penthouse that he had told her of his plans.

She was angry and resentful that he had done all of this without consulting her, and she had scarcely spoken to him since her arrival, which seemed to bother him not at all. But underneath her anger she was anxious and miserable. Though well aware that, with Nikolas backing her, no one would dare be openly cold or hostile, she was sensitive enough that it didn't really matter if their dislike was hidden or out in the open. She knew it was there, and she suffered. It didn't help that Nikolas's secretary, Andros, was there, his contempt carefully hidden from Nikolas but sneeringly revealed to her whenever Nikolas wasn't looking. It had developed that Andros was a second cousin to Nikolas, so perhaps he felt he was secure in his position.

"You're too pale," observed Nikolas critically, pausing with his hand on the handle to open the door. He bent and kissed her, hard, deliberately letting her feel his tongue, then straightened away from her and opened the door before she could react in any way other than the delicate flush that rose to her cheeks.

She wanted to kick him, and she promised herself that she would have his hide for his arrogant action, but for now she steeled herself to greet the small clusters of people who were arriving. Stealing a glance at Nikolas, she saw that his hard masculine lips wore a light coat of her lipstick and she blushed anew, especially when several of the sharp-eyed women noted it also, then darted their glances to her own lipstick as if matching the shades. Then he stretched out one strong hand and pulled her closer to his side, introducing her as his "dear friend and business partner, Jessica Stanton." The dear friend description brought knowing expressions to many faces, and Jessica thought furiously that he might as well have said *"chère amie,"* for that was how everyone was taking it. Of course, that was Nikolas's intention, but she did not plan to fall meekly in with his desires. When the second half of his introduction sank in, everyone immediately became very polite where for a moment she had sensed a direct snub. *Chère amie* was one thing, but business partner was another. He had made it obvious, with only a few well-chosen words, that he would take any insult to Jessica as an insult to himself.

To her surprise and discomfiture, Nikolas introduced one tall, smartly dressed blonde as a columnist, and by the pressure of his fingers she knew that this was the gossip columnist who had written that vicious little bit about her for the Sunday paper. She greeted Amanda Waring with a calm manner that revealed nothing, though it took all of her self-control to manage it. Miss Waring glared at her for a fraction of a second before assuming a false smile and mouthing all of the conventional things.

Her attention was jerked back to Nikolas by the spectacle of a stunning redhead sliding a silken arm about his muscular neck and stretching up against him to kiss him slowly on the mouth. It wasn't a long kiss, nor a deep one, but nevertheless it fairly shouted of intimacy. Jessica went rigid as an unexpected and unwelcome flame of jealousy seared her. How dare that woman touch him! She quivered and barely restrained herself from jerking the woman away from him, but if Nikolas himself hadn't released the woman's arm from his neck and stepped back from her, she might still have created a scene. The glance Nikolas gave her was as apologetic as one could expect from him, but the effect was ruined by the gleam of amusement in the midnight depths of his eyes.

Deliberately Nikolas drew his handkerchief out of his pocket and wiped the redhead's coral-beige lipstick from his mouth, something he hadn't done when he had kissed Jessica. Then he took Jessica's hand and said, "Darling, I'd like you to meet an old friend, Diana Murray. Diana, Jessica Stanton."

Lovely dark blue eyes turned on Jessica, but the expression in them was savage. Then the soft lips parted in a smile. "Ah, yes, I do believe I've heard of you," Diana purred.

Beside her, Jessica felt Nikolas turn as still as a waiting panther. She tightened her fingers on his hand and responded evenly, "Have you? How interesting," and turned to be introduced to Diana's escort, who had been watching with a guarded expression on his face, as if he didn't want to become involved.

Despite Nikolas's bombshell, or perhaps because of it, the room was fairly humming with conversation. Andros was moving from group to group, quietly taking over some of the duties of the host, thereby freeing Nikolas for the most part. For a while Nikolas steered Jessica about from one small knot of people to another, talking easily, bringing her into the conversations and making it obvious by his possessive hand on her arm or the small of her back that she was his, and had his support. Then, callously, she felt, he left her on her own and went off to talk business.

For a moment she was panic-stricken and she looked about, hunting for a corner seat. Then she met Andros's cold, smiling look and knew that he expected her to make a fool of herself. She took a firm grip on her wavering nerves and forced herself to approach a small group of women who were laughing and discussing a current comedy play. It wasn't until she had joined the group that she saw it contained Amanda Waring. Immediately a little silence fell over the women as they looked at her, assessing her position and wondering just how far good manners went.

She lifted her chin and said in a calm voice, "Isn't the lead role played by that actress Penelope something-or-other who was such a smash in America last year?"

"Penelope Durwin," supplied a plumpish, middle-aged woman after a moment. "Yes, she was nominated for their best-actress award, but she seems to like live theater better than films."

"Aren't you an American?" asked Amanda Waring in a velvet little voice, watching Jessica with her icy eyes.

"I was born in America, yes," said Jessica. Was this to become an interview?

"Do you have any plans to return to America to live?"

Jessica stifled a sigh. "Not at this time; I like England and I'm content here."

Conversation ceased for a stiff moment, then Amanda broke the silence again. "Have you known Mr. Constantinos long?" Whatever Amanda's personal feelings, she was first and foremost a columnist, and Jessica was good copy. More—Jessica was fantastic copy! Aside from her own notorious reputation, she was apparently the current mistress of one of the world's most powerful men, an elusive and sexy Greek billionaire. Every word that Jessica said was newsworthy.

"No, not for long," Jessica said neutrally, and then a different voice broke into the circle.

"With a man like Nikolas, it doesn't take long, does it, Mrs. Stanton?" purred a soft, openly hostile voice. Jessica quivered when she heard it and turned to look at Diana, meeting the woman's impossibly lovely blue eyes.

For a long moment Jessica looked at her quietly and the silence became so thick that it was almost suffocating as they all waited to see if a scene would develop. Jessica couldn't even summon up anger to help her; if anything, she pitied this gorgeous creature who watched her with such bright malice. Diana so obviously adored Nikolas, and Jessica knew how helpless a woman was against his charm, and his power. When the silence was almost unbearable, she replied gently, "As you say," and turned back to Amanda Waring. "We met for the first time this past Saturday," she said, giving the woman more information than she had originally intended, but she would be foolish to let the woman's antagonism live when she could so easily put it down.

Her ploy worked. Miss Waring's eyes lit, and hesitantly the other women rejoined the conversation, asking Jessica if she had any plans to visit Mr. Constantinos on his island. They had heard it was fabulous; was he leaving England soon; was she going with him? In the midst of answering their questions Jessica saw Diana leave the group, and she gave an inward sigh of relief, for she had felt that the woman was determined to provoke a scene.

After that, the evening was easier. The women seemed to unbend a little as they discovered that she was a rather quiet, perfectly well-behaved young woman who did not act in the least as if she coveted their husbands. Besides, with Nikolas Constantinos to control her, they certainly felt safe. Though he kept himself to the knot of men discussing business, every so often his black eyes would slide to Jessica's slim figure, as if checking on her. Certainly his alert gaze convinced any unattached male that it would be wise not to approach her.

Only once, when Jessica slipped away for a moment to check her hair and makeup, did she feel uneasy. She saw Diana talking very earnestly to Andros, and even as she watched, Andros flicked her a cool, contemptuous look that chilled her. She hurried away to Nikolas's bedroom and stood for a moment trying to calm her accelerated heartbeat, telling herself that she shouldn't be alarmed by a look. Heavens, she should be accustomed to such looks!

A knock on the door made her shake off her misgivings and she turned to open the door. Amanda Waring stood there. "May I disturb you?" she asked coolly.

"Yes, of course; I was just checking my hair," said Jessica, standing back for the woman to enter. She noticed Amanda looking around sharply at the furnishings, as if expecting black satin sheets and mirrors on the ceilings. In fact, Nikolas was rather spartan in his tastes and the large bedroom seemed almost bare of furniture. Of course, the huge bed dominated the room.

"I wanted to speak with you, Mrs. Stanton," began Amanda. "I wanted to assure you that nothing you said will be repeated in my column; Mr. Constantinos has made it clear that my job hangs in the balance, and I'm not a fool. I stand warned."

Jessica gasped and swung away from the mirror where she had been smoothing her hair. Horrified, she stared at Amanda, then recovered herself enough to say frostily, "He did *what?*"

Amanda's thin mouth twisted. "I'm sure you know," she said bitterly. "My editor told me this morning that if another word about the Black Widow appeared in my column, it would not only mean my job, I would be blacklisted. It took only a phone call from Mr. Constantinos to the publisher of the newspaper to accomplish that. Congratulations, you've won."

Jessica's lips tightened and she lifted her chin proudly. "I must apologize for Nikolas, Miss Waring," she said in calm, even tones, determined not to let this woman guess her inner turmoil. "I assure you that I didn't ask him to make the gesture. He has no use for subtlety, has he?"

In spite of the coldness in the woman's eyes, her lips quirked a bit in humor. "No, he hasn't," she agreed.

"I'm sorry he's been so nasty. I realize you have a job to do, and of course I'm fair game," Jessica continued. "I'll have to talk with him—"

The door opened and Nikolas walked in, staring coldly at Amanda Waring. "Miss Waring," he said forbiddingly.

Immediately Jessica knew that he had seen the columnist enter the room after her and had come to her rescue. Before he could say anything that would alienate the woman even more, she went to him and said coolly, "Nikolas, have you really threatened to have Miss Waring dismissed if she prints anything about me?"

He looked down at her and his lips twisted wryly. "I did," he admitted, and his glance slashed to Amanda. "I won't have her hurt again," he said evenly, but his tone was deadly.

"I'm perfectly capable of taking care of myself, thank you, Nikolas," Jessica said tartly.

"Of course you are," he said indulgently, as if she was a child.

Furious, Jessica reached out for his hand and dug her

nails into it. "Nikolas—*no*. I won't stand by and watch you throw your weight around for my benefit. I'm not a child or an idiot; I'm an adult, and I won't be treated as if I don't have any sense!"

Little gold flames lit the blackness of his eyes as he looked down at her, and he covered her hand with his free one, preventing her nails from digging into him any longer. It could have looked to be a loving gesture, but his fingers were hard and forceful and held hers still. "Very well, darling," he murmured, carrying her hand to his mouth. After pressing a light kiss on her fingers, he raised his arrogant black head and looked at Amanda.

"Miss Waring, I won't mind if your column mentions that the lovely Jessica Stanton acted as my hostess, but I won't tolerate any more references to the Black Widow, or to Mrs. Stanton's financial status. For your information, we have just completed a business deal that was very favorable to Mrs. Stanton, and she has not, is not, and never will be in need of funds from anyone else."

Amanda Waring was not a woman to be easily intimidated. She lifted her chin and said, "May I quote you on that?"

Suddenly Nikolas grinned. "Within reason," he said, and she smiled back at him.

"Thank you, Mr. Constantinos…Mrs. Stanton," she added after a moment, glancing at Jessica.

Amanda left the room and Nikolas looked down at Jessica with those little gold lights still dancing in his eyes. "You're a little cat," he drawled lazily. "Don't you know that now you'll have to pay?"

Not at all frightened, Jessica said coolly, "You deserved it, for acting like a bully."

"And you deserve everything you get, for being

such a provocative little tease," he said, and effortlessly pulled her into his arms. She tried to draw away and found herself helpless against his iron strength.

"Let me go," she said breathlessly, trying to twist away from him.

"Why?" he muttered, bending his head to press his burning lips into the hollow of her shoulder. "You're in my bedroom, and it would take only a slight tug to have this gown around your ankles. Jessica, you must have known that this gown would heat the blood of a plaster saint, and I've never claimed to be that."

She would have been amused at his statement if the touch of his mouth on her skin hadn't sent ripples of pleasure dancing through her veins. She was glad that he liked her gown. It *was* provocative; she knew it and had worn it deliberately, in the manner of a moth flirting with the flame that will singe its wings. It was a lovely gown, made of chiffon in alternating panels of sea green and emerald, swirling about her slim body like waves, and the bodice was strapless, held up only by the delicate shirring above her breasts. Nikolas was right, one tug would have the thing off, but then, she hadn't planned on being alone with him in his bedroom. She saw his head bend down again and she turned her mouth away just in time. "Nikolas, stop it! You have guests; you can't just disappear into the bedroom and stay there!"

"Yes, I can," he said, capturing her chin with one strong hand and turning her mouth up to his. Before she could reply again he had opened his mouth over hers, his warm breath filling her. His tongue probed, teasing her into response, and after a moment she forgot her protests, going up on tiptoe to strain against his hard body and offer him completely the sweetness of her mouth. Without hesitation he took it, his kisses becoming wilder and deeper as he hungrily tasted her. He groaned into her mouth and his hand began to slide up her ribs. It wasn't until his strong fingers cupped one soft breast that she realized his intentions and once again cold fear put out the fires of her own desire. She shuddered and began trying to twist out of his embrace; his arm tightened painfully about her and he arched her slim body against him, his mouth ravaging.

Jessica stiffened and cried out hoarsely, "No, please!"

He swore in Greek and pulled her back into his arms as she tried to get away from him, but instead of forcing his caresses on her, he merely held her tightly to him for a moment and she felt the thunderous pounding of his heart against her. "I won't force you," he finally said as he pressed kisses onto her temple. "You've had some bad experiences, and I can understand your fear. But I want you to understand, Jessica, that when you come to me, I won't leave you unsatisfied. You can trust me, darling."

Weakly she shook her head. "No, you don't understand," she muttered. "Nikolas, I—" She started to tell him that she had never made love, that it was fear of the unknown that made her shrink from him, but he laid a finger against her lips.

"I don't want to know," he growled. "I don't want to hear of another man's hands on you. I thought I could bear it, but I can't. I'm too jealous; I never want to hear you talk about another man."

Jessica shook her head. "Oh, Nikolas, don't be so foolish! Let me tell you—"

"No," he snapped, gripping her shoulders and shaking her violently.

Growing angry, Jessica jerked away from him and threw her head back. "All right," she rejoined tartly. "If you want to be such an ostrich, by all means go bury your head. It doesn't matter to me what you do!"

He glared at her for a moment, then his tense broad shoulders relaxed and his lips twitched with barely suppressed laughter. "It matters," he informed her mockingly. "You just haven't admitted it to yourself yet. I can see that I'll have to destroy your stubbornness as I'll destroy your fear, and in the same way. A few nights of lovemaking will turn you into a sweet, docile little kitten instead of a spitting wildcat."

Jessica stepped around him to the door, her tawny head high. As she opened the door, she turned and said coolly, "You're not only a fool, Nikolas, you're an arrogant fool."

His soft laughter followed her as she returned to the gathering, and she caught the knowing glances of several people. Diana looked furious, then turned her back in a huff. Sighing, Jessica wondered if Nikolas included Diana in many of his entertainments. She hoped not, but had the feeling that her hopes would be disappointed.

FROM THAT EVENING on, Nikolas completely took over her life. Almost every evening he took her to some small party or meeting, or out to dine in the poshest, most exclusive restaurants. She hardly had any free time to spend with Sallie, but that practical young woman was delighted that her friend was going out more and that no other vicious items about her had appeared in the press. Amanda Waring often mentioned Jessica's name

in tandem with Nikolas's, and even hinted that the prolonged presence of the Greek in London was due entirely to the charms of Mrs. Stanton, but she made no
mention of the Black Widow or of Jessica's reputation.

Even Charles was delighted that Nikolas had taken
over, Jessica often thought broodingly. She felt as if a
trusted friend had deserted her, thrown her into the
lion's den. Didn't Charles really understand what Nikolas wanted of her? Surely he did; men were men, after
all. Yet more and more it seemed that Charles deferred
to Nikolas in decisions concerning her assets, and even
though she knew that Nikolas was nothing short of a
financial genius, she still resented his intrusion into
her life.

She was bitterly disappointed but not really surprised
when, shortly after Nikolas's takeover of her affairs,
Charles gave her some papers to sign and told her they
concerned minor matters only. She had trusted him
implicitly before, but now some instinct made her read
carefully through the papers while Charles fidgeted.
Most of the papers did concern matters of little impor-
tance, but included in the middle of the stack was the
document selling her shares in ConTech to Nikolas for
a ridiculously high price and not the market price she'd
insisted on. Calmly she pulled the paper out and put it
aside. "I won't sign this," she told Charles quietly.

He didn't have to ask what it was. He gave her a wry
smile. "I was hoping you wouldn't notice," he admitted.
"Jessica, don't try to fight him. He wants you to have
the money; take it."

"I won't be bought," she told him, raising her head to
give him a level look. "And that's what he's trying to do,
buy me. Surely you have no illusions about his intent?"

Charles studied the tips of his impeccable shoes. "I have no illusions at all," he murmured. "That may or may not be a sad thing. Unvarnished reality has little to recommend it. However, being the realist I am, I know that you haven't a prayer of besting Constantinos in this. Sign the papers, my dear, and don't wake sleeping tigers."

"He's not sleeping," she mocked. "He's only lying in wait." Then she shook her head decidedly. "No, I won't sign the papers. I'd rather not sell the stock at all than let him think he's got me all bought and paid for—or I'll sell to a third party. At market price those shares will be snapped up in a minute."

"And so will you," Charles warned. "He doesn't want those stocks in anyone else's hands."

"Then he'll have to pay me market price." She smiled, her green eyes taking on a glint of satisfaction. Just once, she thought, she had the upper hand on Nikolas. Why hadn't she thought of threatening to sell the shares to a third party before now?

Charles left with the paper unsigned and Jessica knew that he would inform Nikolas immediately. She had an engagement with Nikolas that night to attend a dinner with several of his business associates, and she toyed with the idea of simply leaving town and standing him up rather than argue with him, but that would be childish and would only postpone the inevitable. She reluctantly showered and dressed, choosing with care a gown that didn't reveal too much of her; she knew that she could trust Nikolas's thin veneer of civilization only so far. Yet the modest gown was provocative in its own way, the stark severity of the black cloth against her pale gold skin a perfect contrast. Staring at her reflection in the mirror, she thought with wry bitterness of the Black Widow tag and wondered if anyone else would think of it.

As she had half-expected, Nikolas was a full half-hour early, perhaps hoping to catch her still dressing and vulnerable to him. When she opened the door to him, he stepped inside and looked down at her with such grimness in his black eyes that she was startled, even though she'd been expecting him to be angry.

The door was hardly closed behind him when he took her wrist and pulled her against him, dwarfing her with his size and strength. "Why?" he gritted softly, his head bent down so close to hers that his breath was warm on her face.

Jessica knew better than to struggle against him; that would only fan his anger. Instead, she made herself lie pliantly against him and answered him evenly, "I told you what I'd accept, and I haven't changed my mind. I have my pride, Nikolas, and I won't be bought."

The black eyes snapped angrily at her. "I'm not trying to buy you," he snarled, his hands moving to her slim back in a caressing movement that was the direct opposite of the anger she sensed in him. Then his arms wrapped about her, welding her to his hard frame, and he dipped his head even closer to press swift, light kisses on her upturned mouth. "I only want to protect you, to make you so secure that you'll never again have to sell your body, even in marriage."

Instantly she went rigid in his arms and she flashed him a glance that scorched. "Beware of Greeks bearing gifts," she retorted hotly. "What you mean is, you want to ensure that you're the only buyer!"

His arms tightened until she gasped for breath and

pushed against his shoulders in protest. "I've never had to buy a woman!" he ground out between clenched teeth. "And I'm not buying you! When we make love, it won't be because money has passed between us but because you want me as much as I want you."

Desperately she turned her head away from his approaching mouth and gasped out, "You're hurting me!" Instantly his arms loosened their hold and she gulped in air, her head dropping to rest on his chest. Was there nothing she could say that would make him understand her point of view?

After a moment he put her away from him and drew a folded paper from the inner pocket of his jacket. Spreading it open, he placed it on the hall table and produced a pen, which he held out to her. "Sign it," he ordered softly.

Jessica put her hands behind her back in the age-old gesture of refusal. "Market value only," she insisted, her eyes holding his calmly. She played her last ace. "If you don't want them, I'm certain there are other buyers who would be glad to get those shares at market value."

He straightened. "I'm sure there are," he agreed, still in that soft, calm voice. "And I'm also certain that if you sell that stock to anyone but me, you'll regret it later. Why are you being so stubborn about money? The amount of money you sell the stock for will in no way influence the outcome of our relationship. That's already been decided."

"Oh, has it?" she cried, clenching her small fists in fury at his arrogance. "Why don't you just go away and leave me alone? I don't want anything from you, not your money, nor your protection, and certainly not *you!*"

"Don't lie to yourself," he said roughly, striding forward to lace his arms about her and hold her to him. She flung her head back to deny that she was lying; that was the only chance he needed. He bent his black head, and his mouth closed over hers. His kiss wasn't rough but moved seductively over her lips, inviting her response and devastating her, sucking away her breath and leaving her weak in his arms. Her eyes closed, her lips opened helplessly to his mastering tongue, and she let him kiss her as deeply as he wished until she lay limply against him. His tenderness was even more dangerous than his temper, because her response to him was growing more passionate as she became accustomed to him and she sensed her own capitulation approaching. He was no novice when it came to women, and he knew as well as she did that the need he stirred in her was growing stronger.

"Don't lie to me, either," he muttered against her mouth. "You want me, and we both know it. I'll make you admit it." His mouth came down again to fit completely against her lips, and he took full possession of them, molding them as he wanted. He began to touch her breasts, deliberately asserting his mastery over her, trailing his fingertips lightly over the upper curves and leaving a growing heat behind. Jessica made a whimpering sound of protest, muffled by his mouth; she gasped under his onslaught, searching desperately for air, and he gave her his heated breath. Now his hand slid boldly inside her gown and cupped the round curves in his palm. At his intimate caress, Jessica felt herself drowning in the sensual need he aroused, and she gave in with a moan, twining her arms around his neck.

Swiftly he bent and slid his arm under her knees,

lifting her and carrying her to the lounge, where he placed her on the sofa and eased down beside her, never ceasing the drugging kisses which kept her under his sensual command. She moved restlessly, her hands in his hair, trying to get closer to him, aching with a need and emptiness which she didn't understand but couldn't ignore.

Triumph glittered in his eyes as he moved to cover her with his body, and Jessica opened her eyes briefly to read the look on his face, but she saw him through a haze of desire, her senses clouded. Nothing mattered right now, if only he would keep on kissing her....

His fingers had explored her satiny breasts, had teased the soft peaks into firm, throbbing proof of the effect he was having on her. Sliding his body down along hers, he investigated those tempting morsels with his lips and tongue, searing her with the heat of his mouth. Her hands left his head and moved to his shoulders, her fingers digging into the muscles which flexed with his every movement. Golden fire was spreading throughout her body, melting her, dissolving her, and she let herself sink into her own destruction. She wanted to know more, she wanted to have more of him, and she thought she would die from the pleasure he was giving her.

He left her breasts to move upward and kiss her mouth again, and now he let her feel the pressure of his entire body, the force of his arousal.

"Let me stay with you tonight," he breathed into her ear. "You want me, you *need* me, as much as I want and need you. Don't be afraid, darling; there's no need to be afraid. I'll take good care of you. Let me stay," he said again, though despite the soft words it wasn't a plea, but a command.

Jessica shuddered and squeezed her eyes tightly shut, her blood boiling through her veins in frustration. Yes, she wanted him—she admitted it—but he had some terrible ideas about her, and she found it hard to forgive him for that. As soon as he spoke, she began to recover her senses and remember why she didn't want to let him make love to her, and she turned her face away from his kisses.

If she let him make love to her, he would know as soon as he possessed her that he was wrong in his accusations; but she also knew in her bones that to go to him under those circumstances would lower her to exactly what he thought her to be now, and her standards were too high to allow that. He offered nothing but physical gratification and material gain, while she offered a heart that had been battered and was now overly sensitive to each blow. He didn't want her love, yet she knew that she loved him, against all logic and her sense of self-preservation.

He shook her gently, forcing her eyes open, and he repeated huskily, "Will you let me stay, darling? Will you let me show you how sweet it will be between us?"

"No," she forced herself to reply, her voice hoarse with the effort she was making. How would he react to a denial at this stage? He had a violent temper; would he be furious? She stared up into his black gaze, and her fear was plain for him to read, though he couldn't guess the cause. "No, Nikolas. Not…not yet. I'm not ready yet. Please."

He drew a deep breath, mastering his frustration, and she collapsed in intense relief as she realized that he wasn't angry. Roughly he drew her head against his shoulder and stroked her hair, and she breathed in the hot male scent of his skin and let him comfort her. "You don't have to be afraid," he insisted in a low tone. "Believe me. Trust me. It has to be soon; I can't wait much longer. I won't hurt you. Just let me show you what it means to be my woman."

But she already knew, she thought in despair. His confident masculinity lured her despite her better sense. His lovemaking would be sweet and fiery, burning away her control, her defenses, leaving her totally helpless in the face of his marauding mastery. And when he was finished, when his attention was attracted by another challenge, she would be in ashes. But how long could she hold him off, when every day increased her need of him?

CHAPTER SIX

HER HEELS CLICKING as she strode into the ConTech building, Jessica strove to control her temper until she was alone with Nikolas, but the determined clatter of her heels gave her away and she tried to lighten her step. Her soft lips tightened ominously. Just wait until she saw him!

"Good afternoon, Mrs. Stanton," said the receptionist with a friendly smile, and Jessica automatically returned the greeting. In a few short weeks, Nikolas had turned her world around; people smiled and greeted her now, and everyone connected with ConTech treated her with the utmost courtesy. But recognizing his enormous influence didn't make her feel more charitable toward him; she wanted to throttle him instead!

As she left the elevator, a familiar figure exited Nikolas's office, and Jessica lifted her chin as she neared Diana Murray. Diana paused, waiting for Jessica to approach her, and good manners forced Jessica to greet her.

"My, isn't Nikolas busy this afternoon?" purred Diana, her beautiful eyes watching Jessica sharply for any signs of jealousy.

"I don't know; is he?" countered Jessica coolly. "It doesn't matter; he'll see me anyway."

"I'm sure he will. But give him a minute," Diana ad-

vised in a sweet voice which made Jessica long to slap
her. She preferred unvarnished hostility to Diana's sac-
charine poison. Diana smiled and added, "Let him have
time to smooth himself down. You know how he is."
Then she walked away, her hips swaying with just the
right touch of exaggeration. Men probably found Diana
irresistible, Jessica thought savagely, and she promised
herself that if Nikolas Constantinos didn't walk carefully, he was going to find a storm breaking over his
arrogant head.

She thrust open the door, and Andros looked up from
his never-deserted post. As always when he saw her,
his eyes conveyed cold dislike. "Mrs. Stanton. I don't
believe Mr. Constantinos is expecting you."

"No, he isn't," agreed Jessica. "Tell him I'm here,
please."

Reluctantly Andros did her bidding, and almost as
soon as he had replaced the receiver, Nikolas opened
the doors and smiled at her. "Hello, darling. You're a
pleasant surprise; I didn't expect to see you until later.
Have you decided to sign the papers?"

This reference to his purchase of her shares only
served to fan higher the flame of her anger, but she
controlled herself until she had entered his office and
he had closed the doors firmly behind them. Out of
the corner of her eye, she saw him approaching, obviously intent on taking her in his arms, and she briskly
removed herself from his reach.

"No, I haven't decided to sign anything," she said
crisply. "I came here to get an explanation for this."
She reached into her purse and withdrew a slim packet
of papers attached with a paper clip to a creased enve-

lope. She thrust them at him and he took them, a frown wrinkling his forehead.

"What are these?" he asked, studying the darkened green of her eyes and gauging her temper.

"You tell me," she snapped. "I believe you're the responsible party."

He removed the paper clip and rapidly scanned the papers, flipping them one by one. It took only a minute; then he replaced the paper clip. "Is anything wrong? Everything looks in order."

"I'm certain everything is in perfect legal order," she said impatiently. "That isn't the problem, and you know it."

"Then exactly what is the problem?" he inquired, his lashes drooping to cover the expression in his eyes, but she knew that he was watching her and saw every nuance of her expression before she, too, shuttered her face.

He hooked one leg over the corner of the desk and sat down, his body relaxed. "I don't see why you're upset," he said smoothly. "Suppose you tell me exactly what you don't like about the agreement. It hasn't been signed yet; we can always make changes. I hadn't meant for you to receive your copy by mail," he added thoughtfully. "I can only suppose that my attorney tried to anticipate my wishes, and he'll certainly hear from me on that."

"I don't care about your attorney, and it doesn't make any difference how I received this piece of trash, because I won't sign it!" she shouted at him, her cheeks scarlet with anger. "You're the most arrogant man I've ever met, and I hate you!"

The amusement that had been lurking in his eyes

vanished abruptly, and when she spun on her heel and started for the door, too incensed even to yell at him, he lunged from his position on the desk to intercept her before she'd taken three steps. As his hand closed on her arm, she lashed out at him with her free hand. He threw his arm up to ward off the blow, then deftly twisted and caught that arm, too, and drew her against him.

"Let me go!" she spat, too infuriated to care if Andros heard her. She twisted and struggled, heaving herself against the iron band of his arms in an effort to break free; she was given stamina by her anger, but at last even that was exhausted. When she shuddered and dropped her head against his shoulder, he lifted her easily and stepped around the desk, where he sat down in his chair and cradled her on his lap.

Jessica felt faint, drained by her rage and the struggle with him, and she lay limply against him. His heart was beating strongly, steadily, under her cheek, and she noticed that he wasn't even breathing rapidly. He'd simply subdued her and let her tire herself out. He stretched to reach the telephone and dialed a single number, then spoke quietly. "Hold all calls, Andros. I don't want to be disturbed for any reason." Then he dropped the receiver back onto the cradle and wrapped both arms about her, hugging her securely to him.

"Darling," he whispered into her hair. "There's no need to be so upset. It's only a simple document—"

"There's nothing simple about it!" she interrupted violently. "You're trying to treat me like a high-priced whore, but I won't let you! If that's the way you think of me, then I don't want to see you again."

"I don't think of you as a whore." He soothed her. "You're not thinking clearly; all you're thinking now is that I've offered you payment for going to bed with me, and that isn't what I intended."

"Oh, no, of course it wasn't," she mocked in a bitter tone. She struggled to sit up and get away from the intimate heat of his body, but his enfolding arms tightened and she couldn't move. Tears sparkled in her eyes as she gave up and relaxed against him in defeat.

"No, it wasn't," he insisted. "I merely want to take care of you—thus the bank account and the house. I know you own the house where you live now, but admit it, the neighborhood isn't the best."

"No, it isn't, but I'm perfectly happy there! I've never asked for anything from you, and I'm not asking now. I don't want your money, and you've insulted me by asking me to sign a document swearing that I'll never make any demands against your estate for 'services rendered.'"

"I'd be extremely foolish if I didn't take steps to secure the estate," he pointed out. "I don't think you'd sue me for support, darling, but I have other people to consider and a responsibility to uphold. A great many people depend on me for their livelihood—my family as well as my employees—and I can't in good conscience do anything that might jeopardize their well-being in the future."

"Do all of your mistresses have to sign away any claims on you?" she demanded, angrily brushing away the single tear which dropped from her lashes. "Is this in the nature of a form letter, everything filled in except for the name and date? How many other women live in apartments or houses you've so kindly provided?"

"None!" he snapped. "I don't think I'm asking too much. Did you truly think I'd establish you as my mistress and leave myself vulnerable to any number of other claims? Is that why you're so angry, because I've made certain you can't get any money from me except what I freely give to you?"

He'd made the mistake of releasing her arm, and she swung wildly at him, her palm striking his face with enough force to make her hand tingle. She began to cry, tears flooding down her face while she gulped and tried to control them, and in an effort to get away from him she started fighting again. The results were the same as before: he simply held her and prevented her from landing any more blows, until she was breathless and worn out. Pain and anger mingled with her sense of helplessness at being held like that, her raw frustration at being unable to make him see how utterly wrong he was about her, and she gave up even trying to control her tears. With a wrenching sob she turned her face into his shoulder and gave in to her emotional storm.

"Jessica!" he ground out from between clenched teeth, but she barely heard him and paid no attention. A small part of her knew that he had to be furious that she'd slapped him—Nikolas wasn't a man to let anyone, man or woman, strike him and get away with it—but at the moment she just didn't care. Her delicate frame heaved with the convulsive force of her weeping. It would never end, the gossip and innuendo concerning her marriage; even though Nikolas wouldn't allow anyone else to talk about her, he still believed all of those lies himself. What he didn't seem to realize was that she could endure everyone else's insults, but she couldn't endure his, because she loved him.

"Jessica." His voice was lower now, softer, and the biting power of his fingers eased on her arms. She felt his hands touching her back, stroking soothingly up and down, and he cuddled her closer to his body.

With tender cajoling he persuaded her to lift her face, and he wiped her eyes and nose with his handkerchief as if she were a child. She stared at him, her eyes still luminous with tears, and even through her tears she could see the red mark on his cheek where she'd hit him. With trembling figures she touched the spot. "I—I'm sorry," she said, offering her apology in a tear-thick voice.

Without a word he turned his head and kissed her fingers, then bent his head and lifted her in the same motion, and before she could catch her breath he was kissing her, his mouth hot and wild and as hungry as an untamed animal's, tasting and biting and probing. His hand searched her breasts and moved downward to glide over her hips and thighs, on down to her knees, moving impatiently under the fabric of her dress. With a shock she realized that he was out of control, driven beyond the control of will by his own anger and the struggle with her, the softness of her body twisting and straining against him. He wasn't even giving her a chance to respond to him, and fear made her heartbeat speed up as she realized that this time she might not be able to stop him.

"Nikolas, no. Not here. No! Stop it, darling," she whispered fiercely, tenderly. She didn't try to fight him, sensing that at this stage it would only excite him more. He was hurting her; his hands were all over her, touching her where no man had ever touched before, pulling at her clothing. She reached up and placed her hands on both sides of his face and repeated his name softly, urgently, over and over until, abruptly, he was looking at her and she saw that she'd gained his attention.

A spasm crossed his face, and he ground his teeth, swearing beneath his breath. He slowly helped her to her feet, pushing her from his lap, and then got to his feet as if in pain. He stood looking at her for a moment as she swayed against the desk for support; then he cursed again and walked a few feet away, standing with his back to her while he wearily massaged the back of his neck.

She stared at his broad, muscular back in silence, too drained to say anything to him, not knowing if it was safe to do so. What should she do now? She wanted to leave, but her legs were trembling so violently that she doubted her ability to walk unaided. And her clothing was disheveled, twisted, and partially unbuttoned. With slow, clumsy fingers she restored her appearance, then eyed him uncertainly. His stance was that of a man fighting himself, and she didn't want to do anything that might annoy him. But the silence was so thick between them that she was uneasy, and at last she forced her unsteady legs to move, intending to retrieve her purse from where she'd dropped it and leave before the situation worsened.

"You aren't going anywhere," he said in a low voice, and she halted in her tracks.

He turned to face her then, his dark face set in weary lines. "I'm sorry," he said with a sigh. "Did I hurt you?"

His apology was the opposite of the reaction she had expected, and for a moment she couldn't think of a response. Then she dumbly shook her head, and he seemed to relax. He moved close to her and slid his arm around her waist, urging her close to him with gentle insistence. Jessica offered no resistance and pressed her head into the sheltering hollow of his shoulder.

"I don't know what to say," he muttered. "I want you to trust me, but instead I've frightened you."

"Don't say anything," she answered, having finally mastered her voice. "There's no need to go over it all again. I won't sign the paper, and that's that."

"It wasn't meant as an insult, but as a legal necessity."

"But I'm not your mistress," she pointed out. "So there's no need for the document."

"Not yet," he agreed. "As I said, my attorney anticipated my wishes. He was in error." His tone of voice boded ill for the poor attorney, but Jessica was grateful to the unknown man. At least now she knew exactly what Nikolas thought of her, and she preferred the painful truth to living in a dream.

"Perhaps it would be better if we didn't see each other anymore," she began, but his arm tightened around her and a scowl blackened his brow.

"Don't be ridiculous," he snapped. "I won't let you go now, so don't waste your breath suggesting it. I promise to control myself in the future, and we'll forget about this for the time being."

Lifting her head from his shoulder, Jessica gave him a bitter look. Did he truly think she could forget that he thought her the sort of woman who was available for a price? That knowledge was a knife thrust into her chest, but equally painful was the certainty that she didn't want him to vanish from her life. Whatever he had come to mean to her, the thought of never seeing him again made her feel desolate. She was risking her emotional well-being, flirting with disaster, but she could no more walk away from him now than she could stop herself from breathing.

SEVERAL WEEKS PASSED in a more restrained manner, as if he'd placed himself on his best behavior, and she managed to push away the hurt. He insisted that she accompany him whenever he went out socially, and she was his hostess whenever he entertained.

The strain on her was telling. At yet another party, she felt smothered and escaped into the coolness of the dark garden, where she sucked in deep lungfuls of fresh, sweet air; she had been unable to breathe in the smoke-laden atmosphere inside. In the weeks since she had met Nikolas, she had learned to be relaxed at social gatherings, but she still felt the need to be by herself occasionally, and those quiet times had been rare. Nikolas had the power of a volcano, spewing out orders and moving everyone along in the lava flow of his authority. She wasn't certain just where he was at the moment, but she took advantage of his lapse of attention to seek the quietness of the garden.

Just before leaving for the dinner party tonight, they'd had a flaming argument over her continued refusal to sell the stock to him, their first argument since the awful scene in his office. He wouldn't back down an inch; he was furious with her for defying him, and he had even accused her of trying to trick him into increasing his offer. Sick to death of his lack of understanding and tired of the running battle, Jessica had grabbed the paper and signed it, then thrown it to the floor in a fit of temper. "Well, there it is!" she had snapped furiously. It wasn't until he'd leaned down and picked up the paper to fold it and replace it in his pocket that she'd seen the speculative gleam in his eyes and realized that she'd made a mistake. Signing now, after he had accused her of holding out for a higher price and assured her that she wouldn't get it, had convinced him that she'd been doing exactly that all along, biding her time and hoping for a higher price. But it was too late now to do anything about it, and she had grimly conquered the tears that sprang to her eyes as the pain of his suspicions hurt her.

Strolling along the night-dewed path of white gravel, she wondered sadly if the sense of ease which had come into their relationship lately had been destroyed. He had ceased pressuring her to let him make love to her, had in fact become increasingly tender with her, as if he was at last beginning to care. The thought made her breathless, for it was like a dream come true. In a thousand ways, he spoiled her and curbed his impatient nature for her, and she no longer tried to fight her love for him. She didn't even want to any longer, so thoroughly had he taken her under his influence.

But all of that might be gone now. She should never have signed that agreement! She'd given in to his bullying tactics in a fit of temper, and all she had done was to reinforce his picture of her as a mercenary temptress. What ground she'd gained in his affections had been lost in that one moment.

Moving slowly along, her head down while she dreamed wistfully of marrying Nikolas and having his children—something not likely to happen now—it was some moments before she heard the murmur of voices. She was almost upon the couple before she realized it. She halted, but it seemed that they hadn't noticed her. They were only a dim shape in the darkness, the pale blur of the woman's gown blending into the darkness of the man's dinner jacket as they embraced.

Trying to move quietly, Jessica stepped back with

the intention of withdrawing without attracting attention to herself, but then the woman gave a sharp sigh and moaned, "Nikolas! Ah, my love..."

Jessica's legs went numb and refused to move as strength drained away from her. Nikolas? *Her* Nikolas? She was too dazed to feel any pain; she didn't really believe it. At last she managed to turn and look again at the entwined couple. Diana. Most assuredly Diana. She had recognized that voice. And—Nikolas? The bent black head, the powerful shoulders, *could* be Nikolas, but she couldn't be certain. Then his head lifted and he muttered in English, "What's wrong, Diana? Has no one been taking care of you, as lovely as you are?"

"No, no one," she whispered. "I've waited for you."

"Were you so certain I would return?" he asked, amusement coming into his voice as he raised his head higher to look into the gorgeous upturned face.

Jessica turned away, not wanting to see him kiss the other woman again. The pain had started when she saw for certain that Nikolas was the man holding Diana so passionately, but she determinedly forced it down. If she let go, she would weep and make a fool of herself, so she tilted her chin arrogantly and ignored the vise that squeezed her chest, the knife that stabbed her insides. Behind her, she heard him call her name, but she moved swiftly across the patio and into the protection of the house and the throng of people. People smiled at her now, and spoke, and she put a faint smile on her stiff lips and made her way very calmly to the informal bar.

Everyone was getting their own drinks, so she poured herself a liberal portion of tart white wine and sipped it as she moved steadily about the room, smiling, but not allowing herself to be drawn into conversation.

She could not talk to anyone just now; she would just walk about and sip her wine and concentrate on mastering the savage thrust of pain inside her. She wasn't certain how she would leave the party, whether she was strong enough to leave with Nikolas or if it would be best to call a taxi, but she would worry about that later. Later, after she had swallowed enough wine to dull her senses.

Out of the corner of her eye she saw Nikolas moving toward her with grim determination, and she swung to the left and spoke to the couple she nearly collided with, marveling that her voice could be so natural. Then, before she could move away, a strong hand closed on her elbow and Nikolas said easily, "Jessica, darling, I've been chasing you around the room trying to get your attention. Hello, Glenna, Clark…how are the children?"

With a charming smile he had Glenna laughing at him and telling him about her two young sons, whom it seemed Nikolas knew personally. All the time they talked, Nikolas kept a tight grip on Jessica's arm, and when she made a move to break away from him, his fingers tightened until she nearly gasped with pain. Then he was leading her away from Glenna and Clark and his fingers loosened, but not enough to allow her to escape.

"You're hurting my arm," Jessica said coldly as they wove through milling groups of laughing, chattering people.

"Shut up," he ground out between his teeth. "At least until we're alone. I think the study is empty; we'll go there."

As he literally pulled her with him, Jessica had a glimpse of Diana's face before they left the room behind, and the expression of pure triumph on the woman's face chilled her.

Pride stiffened her back, and when Nikolas closed the door of the study behind them and locked it, she turned to face him and lifted her chin to give him a haughty stare. "Well?" she demanded. "What do you want, now that you've dragged me in here?"

He stood watching her, his black eyes grim and his mouth set in a thin line that at any other time would have made her apprehensive but now left her curiously unmoved. He had thrust his hands into his pants pockets as if he didn't trust himself to control his temper, but now he took them out and his eyes gleamed. "It always amazes me how you can look like a queen, just by lifting that little chin."

Her face showed no reaction. "Is that all you brought me in here to say?" she demanded coolly.

"You know damned well it isn't." For a moment he had the grace to look uncomfortable, and a dull flush stained the brutal cheekbones. "Jessica, what you saw... it wasn't serious."

"That really doesn't matter to me," she thrust scornfully, "because our relationship isn't serious, either. You don't have to explain yourself to me, Nikolas; I have no hold on you. Conduct your little affairs as you please; I don't care."

His entire body jerked under the force of her words and the flush died away to a white, strained look. His eyes grew murderous and an instant before he moved she realized that she had gone too far, pushed him beyond control. She had time only to suck in her breath to cry out in alarm before he was across the room with a lithe, savage movement, his hands on her shoulders.

He shook her violently, so violently that her hair tumbled down about her shoulders and tears were jerked from her eyes before his mouth closed on hers and his savage kiss took her breath away. When she thought that she would faint under his onslaught, he lifted her slumping body in his arms and carried her to the soft, worn sofa where their host had obviously spent many comfortable hours. Fiercely he placed her on it and covered her body with his, holding her down with his heavy shoulders and muscular thighs. "Damn you!" he whispered raggedly, jerking her head back with cruel fingers tangled in her hair. "You have me tied in knots; I can't even sleep without dreaming about you, and you say you don't care what I do? I'll make you care, I'll break down that wall of yours—"

He kissed her brutally, his lips bruising hers and forcing a moan of protest from her throat, but he paid no attention to her distress. With his free hand he slid down the zipper of her dress and pulled the cloth from her shoulders, and only then did his mouth leave hers to press his sensual attack on the soft mounds of her breasts.

Jessica moaned in fright when her mouth was free, but as his hot lips moved hungrily down her body, a wanton need surged through her. She fought it fiercely, determined not to surrender to him after what had passed between them tonight, knowing that he thought her little better than a whore. And then he had gone straight into Diana's arms! The memory of the smugly victorious smile the woman had given her sent tears streaming down her face as she struggled against his overpowering strength. He ignored her efforts to free herself and moved to press completely over her, his hands curving her against his powerful, surging contours. He was feverish with desire and she was helpless against him; he would have taken her, but when he raised his head from her throbbing breasts, he saw her tear-drenched face and stopped cold.

"Jessica," he said huskily. "Don't cry. I won't hurt you."

Didn't he understand? He had already hurt her; he'd torn her heart out. She turned her head away from him with a jerky movement and bit her bruised lip, unable to say anything.

He eased his weight from her and pulled his handkerchief from his pocket to wipe her face. "It's just as well," he said grimly. "I don't want to make love to you for the first time on a sofa in someone else's house. I want you in a bed, *ma chère,* with hours in which I can show you how it should be between a man and a woman."

"Any woman," she said bitterly, remembering Diana.

"No!" he refuted fiercely. "Don't think of her, she means less than nothing to me. I was foolish—I'm sorry, darling. I wanted to ease myself with her, to relieve the tension that you arouse and won't satisfy, and instead I found that she leaves me cold."

"Really?" Jessica taunted, glaring at him. "You didn't look so cold to me."

He tossed the tear-wet handkerchief aside and captured her chin with one hand. "You think not? Did I act as if I was carried away by passion?" he demanded, forcing her to look at him. "Did I kiss her as I kiss you? Did I say sweet things to her?"

"Yes! You called her— No," she interrupted herself, becoming confused. "You said she was lovely, but you didn't—"

"I didn't call her darling, as I call you, did I? One kiss, Jessica! One kiss and I knew that she couldn't even begin to damp down the fires you've lit. Won't you forgive me for one kiss?"

"Would you forgive me?" she snapped, trying to turn her head away, but he held her firmly. Against her will she was softening, letting him talk her out of her resolve. The heavy weight of his limbs against her was comforting as he wrapped her in the security of his strength, and she began to feel that she could forgive any transgression so long as she could still touch him.

"I would have snatched you away from any man foolish enough to touch you," he promised her grimly, "and broken his jaw. I don't think I could control myself if I saw someone kissing you, Jessica. But I'd never walk away from you; I'd take you with me."

She shuddered and closed her eyes, recalling those awful moments when she had watched their embrace. "Neither can I control *my*self, Nikolas," she admitted hoarsely. "I can't bear to watch you make love to another woman. It tears me apart."

"Jessica!"

It was the first admission she had made that she cared for him, even a little. Despite their closeness over the past weeks, she had still resisted him in that, had refused to tell him that she cared. Now she could no longer hide it.

"Jessica! Look at me. *Look at me!*" Fiercely he shook her and her eyes flew open to stare into his blazing, triumphant eyes. "Tell me," he insisted, bending closer to her, his mouth poised above hers. His hand went to her heart, felt the telltale pounding, and lingered to tenderly stroke the soft womanly curves he found.

"Tell me," he whispered, and brushed his lips against hers.

Her arms went about his shoulders, clinging tightly to his strength as her own was washed away in the floodtide of her emotion. "I love you," she moaned huskily. "I've tried not to—you're so…arrogant. But I can't help it."

He crushed her to him so tightly that she cried out, and he loosened his hold immediately. "Mine," he muttered, pressing hot kisses over her face. "You're mine, and I'll never let you go. I adore you, darling. For weeks I've been half-mad with frustration, wanting you but afraid of frightening you off. You'll have no more mercy from me, you'll be my woman now!" And he laughed exultantly before he sat up and helped her to pull her gown back up. He zipped it for her, then his hard hands closed about her waist.

"Let's leave now," he said, his voice rough. "I want you so badly!"

Jessica shivered at the raw demand in his voice, elated but also frightened. The time had come when he would no longer allow her to draw away from him, and though she could feel her heart blooming at his admission of love, she was still wary of this man and the control he had over her.

Nikolas sensed her hesitation and pulled her close to him with a possessive arm. "Don't be frightened," he murmured against her hair. "Forget whatever has happened to you; I'll never do anything to hurt you. You said that you aren't frightened of me, but you are, I can tell. That's why I've suffered through these weeks of hell, waiting for you to lose your fear. Trust me now, darling. I'll take every care with you."

She buried her face against his shoulder. Now was the time to tell him that she had never made love before, but when she gathered her courage enough to raise her head and open her mouth, he forestalled her by laying his fingers gently across her bruised lips. "No, don't say anything," he whispered. "Just come with me, let me take care of you."

Her hair was a tumbled mass about her shoulders and she lifted her hands to try to twist it up again. "Don't bother," Nikolas said, catching her hand. "You look adorable, if anyone should see you, but we'll leave by the back way. Wait here while I make our excuses to our host; I'll only be a moment."

Left by herself, Jessica sat down and tried to gather her dazed and scattered thoughts. Nikolas loved her, he had admitted it. Love was the same as "adore," wasn't it? Certainly she loved him, but she was also confused and uncertain. She had always thought that a mutual declaration of love led to sweet plans for the future, but instead Nikolas seemed to plan only on taking her to bed. She tried to tell herself that he was an extremely physical man, and that afterward he would want to talk about wedding plans. It was just that she had always dreamed, in her heart, of going to her husband in white, and of deserving the symbol of purity. For a moment she toyed with the idea of telling Nikolas she didn't want to leave, but then she shook her head. Perhaps she had to prove her love for Nikolas by trusting him as he had requested and giving him the full measure of her love.

Then it was too late to worry, because Nikolas came back, and she drowned in the possessive glow of his dark eyes. Her nervousness was swamped by her automatic response to his nearness and she leaned pliantly against him as he led her out of the house by the back way and to his car parked down the narrow, quiet street.

London was a golden city by night, gleaming like a crown on the banks of the Thames, and it had never seemed more golden to her than it did tonight, sitting quietly beside Nikolas as he drove through the city. She looked at the familiar landmarks as if she had never seen them before, caught by the unutterable loveliness of the world she shared with Nikolas.

He didn't drive her home, as she had expected, but instead they went to his penthouse. That alarmed her, though she wasn't sure why, and she hung back, but he pulled her into the elevator and held her close, muttering hot words of love to her. When the elevator doors slid open, he took her hand and led her down the quiet, dim hallway to his door. Unlocking it, he let her inside and followed, locking the door behind him with a final-sounding click. She had gone a few steps forward and now stood very still in the darkness, and with a flick of his finger he switched on two lamps. Then he went over to his telephone console to make sure his automatic answering service was on.

"No interruptions tonight," he said, turning to her now. His eyelids drooped sensuously over his gleaming eyes as he came to her and drew her against his hard body. "Do you want anything to drink?" he asked, his lips moving against her temples.

She closed her eyes in ecstasy, breathing in the heady male scent of him, basking in his warmth. "No, nothing," she replied huskily.

"Nor do I," he said. "I don't want alcohol dulling my senses tonight; I want to enjoy every moment. You've obsessed me from the first moment I saw you, so forgive me if I seem to..." He paused, trying to find the word, and she smiled tenderly.

"If you seem to gloat?" she murmured.

"Gloat is too strong a word, but I do admit to a sense of triumph." He grinned.

She watched with a pounding heart as he shed his dinner jacket and draped it over a chair. His tie followed, and his satin waistcoat, then he came to her and she shrank back at the look on his face. So would the Spartan warriors of long ago have looked, proud and savage and lawless. He frightened her, and she wanted to run, but then he had her in his arms and his mouth covered hers and all thoughts fled as her senses were filled with him.

He lifted her and carried her along the corridor to his bedroom, shouldering the door closed behind them, then crossing to the huge bed and standing her before it.

Sanity fought with desire and she choked, "No, Nikolas, wait! I have to tell you—"

"But I can't wait," he interrupted huskily, his breathing ragged. "I have to have you, darling. Trust me, let me wipe out the touch of the others who have hurt you."

His mouth shut off anything else she might have said. He was far more gentle than she would ever have expected, his hands moving over her with exquisite tenderness, molding her to him as his lips drank greedily of hers. She gasped at the surge of pleasure that warmed her, and she curled her slender arms about his neck, arching herself against his powerful form and hearing his deep groan reverberating in her ears like music. With shaking hands he unzipped her gown and slid it down her hips to lie in a silky pool about her feet. He caught his breath at the slim, graceful delicacy of her body, then he snatched her close to him again and his mouth lost its gentleness as he kissed her hungrily. He muttered love words in French and Greek as his strong, lean fingers removed her underwear and dropped it carelessly to the floor, and she thrilled at the hoarse desire so evident in his voice. It was right, it had to be right, he loved her and she loved him....

Feverishly she unbuttoned his silk shirt, her lips pressing hot little kisses to his flesh as she revealed it. She had never caressed him so freely before, but she did so now, discovering with delight the curling hair that roughened his chest and ran in a narrow line down his abdomen. Her fingers flexed mindlessly in that hair, pulling slightly, then her hands dropped to his belt and fumbled awkwardly with the fastening.

"Ah...darling," he cried, his fingers closing almost painfully on hers. Then he brushed her hands aside and helped her, for she was trembling so badly that she couldn't manage to undo the belt.

Rapidly he stripped, and she caught her breath at the sight of his strong, incredibly beautiful body. "I love you," she moaned, going into his arms. "Oh, Nikolas, my love!"

He shuddered and lifted her, placing her on the bed and following her down, his mouth and hands all over her, rousing her to wilder, sweeter heights, then slowing and letting her drift back to awareness before he intensified his efforts again and took her to the brink of madness before drawing away. He was seducing her carefully, making certain of her pleasure, though he was going wild with his own pleasure as he stroked her lovely curves and soft hollows.

At last, aching with the need for his complete possession, Jessica moved her body urgently against him. She didn't know how to demand what she needed; she could only moan and clutch at him with frantic fingers. Her head moved mindlessly from side to side, rolling on the tawny pillow of her hair. "Nikolas—ah, beloved," she moaned, scarcely knowing what she said as the words tripped over themselves coming from her tongue. She wanted only his touch, the taste of his mouth on hers. "I never knew—oh, darling, please! Being your wife will be heaven." Her hands moved over his muscled ribs, pulling at him, and she called out to him with surrender plain in her voice. "Nikolas…Nikolas!"

But he had gone stiff, pulling away from her, and he rose up on his elbow to look at her. After a moment she realized that she had been deserted and she turned her head to look at him questioningly. "Nikolas?" she murmured.

The silence lengthened and thickened, then he made an abrupt, savage movement with his hand. "I've never mentioned marriage to you, Jessica. Don't delude yourself; I'm not that big a fool."

Jessica felt the blood draining from her face and she was glad of the darkness, of the dim lights that left only black-and-white images and hid the colors away. Nausea roiled in her stomach as she stared up at him. No, he wasn't a fool, but *she* was. Fiercely she fought back the sickness that threatened to overwhelm her, and when she spoke, her tone was even, almost cool.

"That's odd. I thought marriage was a natural result of love. But then, you've never actually said that you love me, have you, Nikolas?"

His mouth twisted and he got out of bed, walking to the window to stand looking out, his splendid body revealed to her in its nudity. He wasn't concerned with his lack of dress, standing there as casually as if he wore a suit and tie. "I've never lied to you, Jessica," he said brutally. "I want you as I've never wanted another woman, but you're not the type of woman I would ever take as my wife."

Jessica ground her teeth together to keep from crying out in pain. Jerkily she sat up against the pillows and drew the covers up over her nakedness, for she couldn't be as casual about it as he could. "Oh?" she inquired, only a slight strain revealed in her voice, for, after all, hadn't she had years of experience in hiding her feelings? "What type of woman am I?"

He shrugged his broad shoulders. "My dear, that's rather obvious. Just because Robert Stanton married you doesn't make it any less an act of prostitution, but at least he married you. What about all the others? They didn't bother. You've had some unpleasant experiences that have turned you against men, and I was prepared to treat you with a great deal of consideration, but I've never considered making you my wife. I wouldn't insult my mother by taking a woman like you home to be introduced to her."

Pride had always been a strong part of Jessica's character and it came to her rescue now. Lifting her chin, she said, "What sort of woman would you take home to Mama? A nun?"

"Don't get vicious with me," he snarled softly in warning. "I can deal with you in a way that will make your previous experiences seem like heaven. But to answer your question, the woman I marry will be a virgin, as pure as the day she was born, a woman of both character *and* morals. I admit that you have the character, my dear; it's the morals that you lack."

"Where will you find this paragon?" she mocked, not at all afraid of him now. He had already hurt her as badly as she could ever be hurt; what else could he do?

He said abruptly, "I have already found her; I intend to marry the daughter of an old family friend. Elena is only nineteen, and she's been schooled in a convent. I wanted to wait until she's older before we became betrothed; she deserves a carefree youth."

"Do you love her, Nikolas?" The question was torn from her, for here, after all, was an even deeper pain, to think that he loved another woman. By contrast to this unknown, unseen Elena, Diana seemed a pitiful rival.

"I'm fond of her," he said. "Love will come later, as she matures. She'll be a loving, obedient wife, a wife I can be proud of, a good mother to my children."

"And you can take her home to Mama," Jessica mocked in pain.

He swung away from the window. "Don't mock my mother," he hissed between his teeth. "She's a wonderful, valiant woman; she knew your late husband—are you surprised? When she heard of his disastrous marriage, she was shocked and dismayed, as most people were. Her friends here in London who wrote to her about you didn't ease her worries for an old friend. Should I insult her now by showing up with you in tow and saying, 'Mother, do you remember the gold-digger who took Robert Stanton for all he was worth and ruined the last years of his life? I've just married her.' Were you really such a fool as to think that, Jessica?"

Jessica flung aside the covers and stood up, her bearing erect and proud, her head high. "You're right about one thing," she said in a clipped voice. "I'm not the woman for you."

He watched silently as she went over to her gown and picked it up from the floor, slipping quickly into it. As she slid her feet into her shoes, she said, "Good-bye, Nikolas. It's been an interesting experience."

"Don't be so hasty, my dear," he jeered cruelly. "Before you walk out that door, you should consider that you could gain even more by being my mistress than you did by marrying Robert Stanton. I'm prepared to pay well."

Bitter pride kept her from reacting to that jibe. "Thanks, but no, thanks," she said carelessly, opening the door. "I'll wait for a better offer from another man. Don't bother seeing me out, Nikolas. You aren't dressed for it."

He actually laughed, throwing back his arrogant head. "Call me if you change your mind," he said by way of good-bye, and she walked out without looking back.

She called Charles early the next morning and told him that she would be out of town for several weeks. She hadn't cried, her eyes had remained dry and burning, but she knew that she couldn't remain in London. She would return only when Nikolas had left, flown back to his island. "I'm going to the cottage," she told Charles. "And don't tell Nikolas where I am, though I doubt that he'll bother to ask. If you let me down in this, Charles, I swear I won't ever speak to you again."

"Had a spat, did you?" he asked, amusement evident in his voice.

"No, it was really a rather quiet parting of the ways.

He called me a whore and said I wasn't good enough to marry, and I walked out," she explained coolly.

"My God!" Charles said something under his breath, then said urgently, "Are you all right, Jessica? Are you certain you should go haring off to Cornwall by yourself? Give yourself time to calm down."

"I'm very calm," she said, and she was. "I need a holiday and I'm taking it. You know where I am if anything urgent comes up, but other than that, I don't expect to see you for several weeks."

"Very well. Jessica, dear, are you certain?"

"Of course. I'm perfectly all right. Don't worry, Charles. I'm taking Samantha and the pups with me; they'll enjoy romping around Cornwall."

After hanging up, she made certain everything in the house was turned off, picked up her purse and walked out, carefully locking the door behind her. Her luggage was already in the car, as were Samantha and her wiggling, energetic family, traveling in a large box.

The rest in Cornwall would do her good, help her to forget Nikolas Constantinos. She had had a close call and she was grateful that she had escaped with her self-respect intact. At least she had prevented him from realizing how shattered she was.

Turning it over and over in her mind as she made the long drive to Cornwall, she wondered if she hadn't known all along just what Nikolas thought of her. Why else had she mentioned marriage at such a moment, when he was on the brink of making love to her? Hadn't she subconsciously realized that he would not let her think he intended marriage in order to seduce her?

She was glad that she hadn't told him that she was a virgin; he would have laughed in her face. She could have proved it to him, he would no doubt have demanded proof, but she was too proud. Why should she prove anything to him? She had loved Robert and he had loved her, and she would not apologize for their marriage. Somehow she would forget Nikolas Constantinos, wipe him out of her thoughts. She would not let his memory destroy her life!

CHAPTER SEVEN

FOR SIX WEEKS Jessica pored over the newspapers, searching for any notice, however small, to indicate that Nikolas had returned to Greece. He was mentioned several times, but it was always to say that he was flying here or there for a conference, and a day or so later she would read that he had returned to London. Why was he staying in England? He had never before remained for so long, always returning to his island at the first opportunity. She had no contact with Charles, so she couldn't ask him for any information, not that she would have anyway. She didn't want to know about Nikolas, she told herself fiercely time and again, but that didn't ease the ache in her heart that kept her lying awake night after night and turned food to ashes in her mouth.

She lost weight, her already slim figure becoming fragile. Instead of recovering, she was in danger of going into a Victorian decline, she told herself mockingly, but no amount of willpower could make her swallow more than a bite or two of food at any meal.

Long walks with Samantha and the gamboling puppies for company tired her out but did not reduce her to the state of exhaustion that she needed in order to sleep. After a while she began to feel haunted. Everything reminded her of Nikolas, though nothing was the same as it had been in London. She heard his voice, she remembered his devouring kisses, his fierce possessiveness. Perhaps he hadn't loved her, but he had certainly wanted her; he had been quite blatant about his desire.

Had he expected her to return to him? Was that why he was still in London? The thought was heady, but she knew that nothing had changed. He would take her on his terms, or not at all.

Still she lingered at the cottage, walking every day down to the beach, where the vacationers romped and children went into ecstatic fits over the five fat, prancing puppies. They had been weaned now, and mindful of their increasing size she gave them away one by one to the adoring children. Then there was only Samantha left with her, and the days trickled slowly past.

Then, one morning, she looked at herself in the mirror as she was braiding her hair, really looked at herself, and was stunned at what she saw. Had she really allowed Nikolas Constantinos to turn her into this pale, fragile creature with huge, dark-circled eyes? What was wrong with her? She loved him, yes; in spite of everything he had said to her, she still loved him, but she wasn't so weak in spirit that she would let him destroy her!

She began to realize that it solved nothing to hide away here in Cornwall. She wasn't getting over him; if anything, she was being eaten alive by the need to see him, to touch him.

Suddenly her chin lifted as an idea came to her. She still loved him, she could not rid herself of that, but it was no longer the pure, innocent love that she had offered him the first time. Bitter fires had scorched her heart. For the burned remains of that sweetness, physical love might be enough. Perhaps in his arms she might find that all of her love had been burned out and she would be free. And if not—if she found that in spite of everything she continued to love him—in the years to come, when he was married to his pure, chaste little Elena, she would have the memories and knowledge of his passion, passion such as Elena would never know.

Then she realized that when she became his mistress he would know that no other man had ever touched her. What would he think? Would he apologize, beg her forgiveness? The thought left her curiously unmoved, except for the bitterly humorous thought that the only way she could prove her virtue to him was by losing it. The situation was ironic, and she wondered if Nikolas would appreciate the humor of it when he knew.

Without consciously admitting it, her mind was made up. She would accept Nikolas on his terms, give up her respectability and chastity for the physical gratification that he could give her. But she would not let him support her; she would keep her independence and her pride, and when he married his pure little Greek girl, she would walk away and never see him again. She would be his mistress, but she would not be a party to adultery.

So she packed her clothing and closed up the cottage, put Samantha in the car and began the long drive back to London. The first thing she did was call Charles and tell him that she had returned, assuring him that she was fine. He had to go out of town that afternoon or he would have come over, and she was glad that their meeting was postponed. If Charles saw her now, so thin and wan, he would know that something was dreadfully wrong.

That same problem worried her the next morning

as she dressed. She couldn't get up the courage to call Nikolas; he might tell her that he was no longer interested, and she felt that she had to see him again even if he turned her down to her face. She would go to his office, be very calm and nonchalant about it—but could she carry it off when she looked so very fragile?

She used her makeup carefully, applying slightly more blusher than she normally used and taking extra care with her eyes. Her hair would have to be left down to hide the thin lines of her neck and soften the flesh-less contours of her cheekbones. When she dressed, she chose a floaty dress in a soft peach color, and was satisfied when she looked in the mirror. Nothing could quite disguise how delicate she had become, but she looked far from haggard.

As she drove to ConTech, she remembered the first time she had made this drive to meet Nikolas. She had been rushed, irritable, and not at all pleased. Now she was going to offer him what she had never thought to offer any man, the use and enjoyment of her body without benefit of marriage, and the only comfort she could find was that her body was all he would have. She had offered him her heart once, and he had scorned it. Never again would she give him the chance to hurt her like that.

Everyone recognized her now as she went up in the elevator, for she had often met Nikolas for lunch. Surprised murmurs of "Good morning, Mrs. Stanton" followed her, and she wondered for the first time if Nikolas was pursuing someone else now, but it really made no difference if he was. He could only turn her down if he was no longer interested, and any other rival would eventually have to give way to the precious, innocent Elena.

The receptionist looked up as she entered, and smiled warmly. "Mrs. Stanton! How nice it is to see you again!"

The greeting seemed genuinely friendly, and Jessica smiled in return. "Hello, Irena. Is Nikolas in today?"

"Why, yes, he is, though I believe he's planning a trip this afternoon."

"Thank you. I'll go in, if I may. Andros is here?"

"On guard as usual," Irena said, and wrinkled her nose in a private little communication that actually made Jessica laugh aloud. Evidently Andros had not endeared himself to the rest of the staff.

Calmly she walked into the office, and immediately Andros rose from his seat. "Mrs. Stanton!" he exclaimed.

"Hello, Andros," she returned as he eyed her with frank dislike. "I'd like to see Nikolas, please."

"I'm sorry," he refused in coolly neutral tones, though his eyes sparkled with delight at being able to turn her down. "Mr. Constantinos has someone with him right now and will be unable to talk to you for some time."

"And he's leaving on a business trip this afternoon," said Jessica dryly.

"Yes, he is," Andros said, his lips quirking in triumph.

Jessica looked at him for a moment, anger building in her. She was sick and tired of being treated like dirt, and from this moment on she planned to fight back. "Very well," she said. "Give him a message for me, please, Andros. Tell him that I'm willing to agree to his terms, if he's still interested, and he can get in touch with me. That's all."

She turned on her heel and heard Andros strangle in alarm. "Mrs. Stanton!" he protested. "I can't—"

"You will have to," she cut in as she opened the door, and had a glimpse of the consternation in his black eyes as she left the office. He had damned himself either way now, for if he passed on the message Nikolas would know that Andros had refused her entrance, and he would not dare withhold the message, for if Nikolas ever found out—and Andros knew that Jessica would make certain he did—there would be hell to pay. Jessica smiled to herself as she walked back to the elevator. Andros had had that coming for a long time.

The elevator took its time arriving, but she wasn't impatient. The way she figured it, Nikolas would hear from Andros in about ten minutes, and he would try to reach her on the phone when he had decided that she had enough time to get home. If she was late getting back, that was all to the good. Let Nikolas wait for a while.

Several other people were in the elevator when it finally did arrive, and it was necessary to stop at every floor before she finally reached the entrance level. She crossed to the glass doors, but as she reached out to push them open, a dark-clothed arm reached past her and opened it for her. She raised her head to thank the man for his courtesy, but the words stuck in her throat as she stared up into the leaping black eyes of Nikolas.

"You've terrified Andros out of ten years of his life," he said easily, taking her arm and ushering her through the door.

"Good. He deserved it," she replied, then eyed him

curiously. He was carrying his briefcase, as if he had left for the day. "But how did you get down so fast?"

"The stairs," he admitted, and grinned down at her. "I wasn't taking a chance of letting you get away from me today and not being able to find you before I have to leave this afternoon. That's probably the only reason Andros found the courage to give me your message so promptly; he knew I'd break his neck if he waited until later. You *were* serious, Jessica?"

"Perfectly," she assured him.

He still held her arm, his fingers warm and caressing, but his grip was unbreakable nonetheless. A limousine had drawn up to the curb and he led her to it. The driver jumped out and opened the back door and Nikolas helped her into the spacious backseat, then got in beside her. He gave the driver her address and then closed the sliding window between them.

"My car is here," she told him.

"It'll be perfectly safe until we return," he said, carrying her fingers to his lips for a light kiss. "Or did you think I could calmly leave on a dull business trip after receiving a message like that? No, darling, it's impossible. I'm taking you with me." And he gave her a look of such burning, primitive hunger that she shivered in automatic reaction to his sexuality.

"But I can't just leave," she objected. "Samantha—"

"Don't be silly," he interrupted softly. "Do you think I can't arrange to have a small dog looked after, or that I'd allow such a small thing to stand in my way? Samantha can be taken to an excellent kennel. I'll handle all the details; all you have to do is pack."

"Where are we going?" she asked, turning her head to look at the passing city streets. Evidently his desire had not waned, for there was no hesitation in his manner.

"To Paris, just for a couple of days. A perfect city to begin a relationship," he commented. "Unfortunately I'll be busy during the day with meetings, but the nights will be ours completely. Or perhaps I'll simply cancel the meetings and keep you in bed the entire time."

"Not good business practice," she said lightly. "I won't nag at you if you have to go off to your meetings."

"That's not very good for my ego," he teased, rubbing her wrist with his strong fingers. "I'd like to think that you burn for my touch as I do for yours. I'd nearly reached the limit of my patience, darling; another week and I'd have gone to Cornwall after you."

Startled, she looked at him. "You knew where I was?"

"Of course. Did you think I'd let you simply walk out on me? If you hadn't come back to me, I was going to force the issue, make you mine even if you bit and clawed, but I don't think you'd have resisted for long, h'mmm?"

It was humiliating to think that she hadn't been out of his reach even in Cornwall; he had known where she was and been content to let her brood. She turned her head again to stare blindly out the window, vainly trying to find comfort in the fact that he was, after all, still attracted to her. He might not love her, not as she understood love, but she did have some power over him.

He lifted her hand again and gently placed his lips on her soft palm. "Don't pout, darling," he said softly. "I knew that you'd come back to me when you decided to be realistic. I can be a very generous man; you'll want for nothing. You'll be treated like a queen, I promise you."

Deliberately Jessica pulled her hand away. "There are several things I want to discuss with you, Nikolas," she said in a remote tone. "There are conditions I want met; otherwise, I'm not interested in any sort of a relationship with you."

"Of course," he agreed dryly, his strong mouth curving into a cynical smile. "How much, my dear? And do you want it in cash, stocks or jewels?"

Ignoring him, she said, "First, I want to keep my own house. I don't want to live with you. You can visit me, or I'll visit you if you prefer that, but I want a life apart from yours."

"That's not necessary," he snapped, his straight brows pulling together over suddenly thunderous eyes.

"It's very necessary," she insisted evenly. "I don't delude myself that any relationship with you will be permanent, and I don't want to find myself forced to live in a hotel because I've given up my own home. And as I said, I'm not interested in living with you."

"Don't be so certain of that," he mocked. "Very well, I agree to that condition. You're always free to move in with me when you change your mind."

"Thank you. Second, Nikolas"—here she turned to him and fixed him with an even stare, her green eyes clear and determined, her soft voice nevertheless threaded with steel so that he knew she meant every word—"I will never, under any circumstances, accept any money or expensive gifts from you. As you told Amanda Waring, I don't need your money. I'll be your lover, but I'll never be your kept woman. And finally, on the day you become engaged to your Elena, I'll walk away from you and never see you again. If you're an unfaithful husband, it won't be with me."

A dark blush of anger had swept over his features as she spoke, then he became motionless. "Do you think my marriage would change the way you feel about me?" he demanded harshly. "You might feel now that you could walk away from me, but once you've known my touch, once we've lain together, do you truly think that you could forget me?"

"I didn't say I would forget you," she said, her throat becoming thick with anguish. "I said I'd never see you again, and I mean it. I believe very strongly in the marriage vows; I never looked at another man when I was married to Robert."

He shoved a hand roughly through his hair, disturbing the tidy wave and making it fall down over his forehead. "And if I don't agree to these last two conditions?" he wanted to know. He was obviously angry, his jaw tight, his lips compressed to a grim line, but he was controlling it. His eyes were narrowed to piercing slits as he watched her.

"Then I won't go with you," she replied softly. "I want your word that you'll abide by those conditions, Nikolas."

"I can make you go with me," he threatened almost soundlessly, his lips scarcely moving. "With one word from me, you can be taken away from England without anyone knowing where you are or how you left. You can be secluded, forced to live as I say you will live."

"Don't threaten me, Nikolas," she said, refusing to be frightened. "Yes, I know you can do all of those things, but you'll be defeating your own purpose if you ever resort to such tactics, for I won't be bullied. You *do* want a willing woman in your arms, don't you?"

"You damned little witch," he breathed, pulling her to him across the seat with an iron grip on her wrist. "Very well, I agree to your conditions—if you think you have the willpower to enforce them. You can probably refuse any gifts from me without being bothered by it, but when it comes to leaving me—we'll see. You're in my blood, and I'm in yours, and my marriage to Elena won't diminish the need I have to sate myself with your soft body, my dear. Nor do I think you could leave me as easily as you've planned, for haven't you come back to me now? Haven't you just offered yourself to me?"

"Only my body," she made clear. "*You* set those terms, Nikolas. You get only my body. The rest of me stays free."

"You've already admitted that you love me," he said roughly. "Or was that just a ploy to try to trap me into marriage?"

Despite the pain in her wrist where he held her so tightly, she managed a nonchalant shrug. "What do you know of love, Nikolas? Why talk about it? I'm willing to sleep with you; what more do you want?"

Abruptly he tossed her wrist back into her lap. "Don't make me lose my temper," he warned. "I might hurt you, Jessica. I'm aching with the need to possess you, and my patience is thin. Until tonight, my dear, walk softly."

From the look on his face, it was a warning to be taken seriously. She sat quietly beside him until the chauffeur stopped the limousine outside her house, then she allowed him to help her out. He leaned down and gave instructions to the chauffeur to pick up his luggage and return, then he and Jessica went up the walk. He took the key from her and unlocked the door, then opened it for her. "Can you be ready in an hour?" he asked, glancing at his watch. "Our flight leaves at noon."

"Yes, of course, but don't I need a booking?"

"You're taking Andros's seat," he replied. "Andros will be taking a later flight."

"Oh, dear, now he certainly will be cross with me," she mocked as she crossed to the stairway.

"He'll have to control his irritation," said Nikolas. "Go on; I'll arrange for Samantha and the pups."

"Just Samantha," she corrected. "I gave the pups away while we were in Cornwall."

"That should certainly make things easier," he said, grinning.

Jessica went up to her room and pulled her suitcases out again. All of this packing was becoming monotonous. Carefully she folded clothing and essentials into her leather cases, matching her outfits with shoes and accessories. Nikolas sauntered in when she was only half-finished and stretched out on the bed as if he had every right to be there, surveying her through half-closed eyes.

"You've lost weight," he said quietly. "I don't like it. What have you been doing to yourself?"

"I've been on a diet," she replied flippantly.

"Diet, hell!" He came off the bed and caught her arm, his other hand cupping her chin and turning her face up to his. Black eyes went sharply over her features, noting the shadows under her eyes, the defenseless quiver of her soft mouth. His hand quested boldly down her body, cupping her breasts and stroking her belly and hips. "You little fool!" he breathed sharply. "You're nothing but a shadow. You've nearly made yourself ill! Why haven't you been eating?"

"I wasn't hungry," she explained. "It's nothing to act up about."

"No? You're on the verge of collapse, Jessica." He put his arms about her and pulled her tightly to him, lowering his head to kiss her temples. "But I'll take care of you now and make certain that you eat enough. You'll need your strength, darling, for I'm a man with strong needs. If I were a gentleman, I would allow you a few days to regain your strength, but I'm afraid that I'm too selfish and too hungry for you to allow you that."

"I wouldn't want you to," she whispered against his chest, her arms moving slowly about him, feeling with growing desire his strong, hard body pressing to her. She had missed him so badly! "I need you, too, Nikolas!"

"I would take you now," he murmured, "but the car will be back soon and I really need more time than that to satisfy these weeks of frustration. But tonight—just wait until tonight!"

For a long moment she simply rested her head on his broad chest; she was tired and depressed, and glad to have his strength to rest upon. Though she had made her decision, it was against her basic nature to go against the morals of a lifetime, and sadly she realized that her love for Nikolas had not diminished despite her bitter pride. She would have to come to terms with that, just as she had accepted that, while he wanted her physically, he did not love her and probably never would. Nikolas had planned his life and he was not a man to allow anyone to upset his plans.

Only a few hours later, Jessica sat alone in the luxurious suite that Nikolas had reserved, staring about as if dazed. After their flight had landed at Orly, Nikolas had bundled her through customs at top speed and into a taxi; after a mad ride through the Paris traffic, he had deposited her in this hotel and left immediately for his meeting. She felt abandoned and desolate, and her nerves were beginning to quiver as feeling returned to them. For weeks she had been numbed, not feeling anything except the agony of rejection, but now, as she looked about her, she began to wonder just what she was doing here.

Vaguely she studied her surroundings, noting how exactly the pale green carpet picked out the green threads in the blue-green brocade of the sofa she sat upon and the heavy swag of the curtains. A lovely suite…even the flowers were color coordinated. A perfect setting for a seduction, when the lights were low and Nikolas turned his smoldering dark eyes on her.

Her mind shied away from the image of Nikolas, not wanting to think of the coming hours. She had agreed to be his lover, but now that the time was here, she felt rebellious. She thought of what he would say if she refused to go through with it and decided that he would be furious. She pushed the idea away, but as the minutes ticked away, the thought returned again and again, stronger each time, until at last she got up and paced the room in agitation as pain crawled along her nerves.

Had the pain of rejection unhinged her mind? Whatever had she been thinking of? She wouldn't be Nikolas Constantinos's mistress; she wouldn't be any man's mistress! Hadn't Robert instilled more self-respect into her than that? Nikolas didn't love her; he would never love her. His sole motivation was lust, and giving her virginity to him to prove her innocence would be her loss and mean nothing to him. Virginity wouldn't make him love her.

She remembered the tales from her teenage years, tales of girls whose boyfriends pressured them to "prove their love." Then, in a few weeks, the boyfriends were running after some other girl. She had been too withdrawn herself to get into such a situation; she had never really even dated, but she had thought at the time that the girls were such fools. Anyone could see that the boys were just after sex, any way they could get it. Wasn't it the same situation now? Oh, Nikolas was a far cry from a fumbling teenage boy, but all he wanted was sex. He might pretty it up with words like "want" and "need," and call her darling now and then and tell her that he adored her, but basically it was the same urge.

It was simply that she was a challenge to him, that was why he was so determined to make love to her. He couldn't accept defeat; he was far too fiery and arrogant. Everything about her challenged him, her coolness, her resistance to his lovemaking.

She had been standing at the window, looking out at the twinkling Parisian lights as they blinked on in the darkness, for some time when Nikolas returned. She didn't turn as he entered the room and he said softly, "Jessica? What's wrong, darling?"

"Nothing," she said flatly. "I'm just looking."

She heard the muffled thud as he dropped his briefcase and then he came to stand behind her, his warm hands sliding over her arms and crossing in front of her, pulling her back against his body. His head bent and his lips burned on the side of her neck. For a moment she went limp as a spark of desire arced across her nerve endings, then she twisted away from him in a rush of panic.

He frowned at her and took a step toward her; as he did, she retreated, holding her hands out to ward him off.

"Jessica?" he questioned, baffled.

"Don't come near me!"

"What do you mean?" he demanded, his brows snapping together. "What kind of game are you playing now?"

"I—I've changed my mind," she blurted. "I can't do it, Nikolas. I'm sorry, but I just can't go through with it."

"Oh, no, you don't!" he exploded, closing the distance between them with two long strides and catching her arm as she tried to whirl away from him. "Oh, no, you don't," he breathed savagely, jerking her to him. "No more waiting, no more putting me off. Now, Jessica. *Now.*"

She read his intent in his glittering black eyes as he bent down to lift her in his arms. Terror bloomed in her mind and she twisted madly in an effort to evade his lips, trying to throw herself out of his grasp. Tears poured out of her eyes and she began sobbing wildly, begging him not to touch her. Hysteria began to build in her as she realized she could not escape his brutal hold and her breath strangled in her chest.

Suddenly he seemed to realize that she was terrified; startled, he put her on her feet and stared down into her twisted, bloodless face.

CHAPTER EIGHT

"ALL RIGHT," HE said in a strained voice, backing away from her, his hands held up as if to show he was unarmed. "I won't touch you, I promise. See? I'll even sit down." He suited his actions to his words and stared at her, his black eyes somber. "But God in heaven, Jessica, *why?*"

She stood there on trembling legs, trying to control her sobs and find her voice to explain, but no words would come and she only returned his gaze dumbly. With a groan he brought his hands up and rubbed his eyes as if he was tired, and he probably was. When he dropped his hands loosely onto his knees, his expression was grim and determined. "You win," he said tonelessly. "I don't know what your hang-up about sex is, but I accept that you're too frightened to come to me without some assurance about the future. Damn it, if marriage is what it takes to get you, then you'll have your marriage. We can be married on the island next week."

Shock made her grope weakly for the nearest chair, and when she was safely sitting down, she said in a quavering voice, "No, you don't understand—"

"I understand that you have your price," he muttered angrily. "And I've been pushed as far as I can be pushed, Jessica, so don't start an argument now. You *will* sleep with a husband, won't you? Or do you have another nasty little surprise saved up for me after you have the ring on your finger?"

Anger saved her—clean, strength-giving anger spurting into her veins. It stiffened her spine and dried her tears. He was too arrogant and bullheaded to listen to her, and she was tempted for a minute to throw his offer back in his face, but her heart stopped her. Maybe he was proposing for all the wrong reasons, but it was still a proposal of marriage. And however angry he was now, at both her and himself, he would calm down and she would be able to tell him the truth. He would have to listen; she would make him. He was frustrated now and in no mood to be reasoned with; the best thing to do was not make him angry.

"Yes," she said almost inaudibly, lowering her head. "I'll sleep with you when we're married, no matter how frightened I get."

He heaved a sigh and leaned forward to rest his elbows on his knees in a posture of utter weariness. "Only that saved you tonight," he admitted curtly. "You really were frightened, you weren't faking it. You've really been treated roughly down the line, haven't you, Jessica? But I don't want to hear about it, I can't take it now."

"All right," she whispered.

"And stop looking like a whipped kitten!" he shouted, getting to his feet and pacing angrily to the window. He shoved his hands deeply into his pockets and stood staring out at the brightly lit streets. "I'll telephone Maman tomorrow," he said, reining in his temper. "And I'll try to get out of my meeting fairly early so we can shop for your wedding gown. Since we'll have to get married on the island, all of the trimmings will be expected," he explained bitterly.

"Why does it have to be on the island?" she questioned hesitantly.

"Because I grew up there," he growled. "The island belongs to me, and I belong to the island. The villagers would never forgive me if I got married anywhere but there, with all the traditional celebrations. The women will want to fuss over my bride; the men will want to congratulate me and give me advice on handling a wife."

"And your mother?"

He turned to face her and his eyes were hard. "She'll be hurt, but she won't question me. And let me warn you now, Jessica, that if you ever do anything to hurt or insult my mother, I'll make you wish you'd never been born. Whatever you've been through before will seem like heaven compared to the hell I'll put you through."

She gasped at the hatred in his eyes. Desperately she tried to defend herself and she cried out, "You know I'm not like that! Don't try to make me a villain because things haven't gone as you'd have liked them! I didn't want it to be this way between us."

"I can see that," he said grimly. "You'd have preferred it if I'd been as gullible as Robert Stanton, seeing only your angelic face and willing to give you anything you wanted. But I know you for what you are, and you won't take me to the cleaners like you did that old man. You had a choice, Jessica. As my mistress, you'd have been spoiled rotten and treated like a queen. As my wife, you'll have my name and very little else, but you made your choice and you'll live with it. Just don't expect any more generous settlements like I gave you for those stocks, and above all, remember that I'm Greek, and after the wedding you'll belong to me body and soul. Think about that, darling." He gave the endearment a sarcastic bite and she winced away from the savagery of his tone.

"You're wrong," she said in a trembling voice. "I'm not like that, Nikolas; you know I'm not. Why are you saying such awful things? Please, let me tell you how it was—"

"I'm not interested in how it was," he shouted suddenly, his face filled with the rage he could no longer control. "Don't you know when to shut up? Don't push me!"

Shaking, she turned away from him and crossed to the bedroom. No, she couldn't do it. No matter how much she loved him, it was plain that he'd never love her, and if she made the mistake of marrying him, he would make her life a misery. He'd never forgive her for bringing him to the point where he'd agreed to marriage. He was proud and angry, and as he had said, he was Greek. A Greek never forgot a grievance; a Greek went after vengeance.

It would be better to make a clean break, never to see him again. It would be impossible to forget him, of course, but she knew that any sort of marriage between them was impossible. She had lived with scorn and suspicion from strangers, but she couldn't take it from her husband. It was time she left England completely, returned to the States, where she could live in quiet seclusion.

"Put that suitcase back," he said in a deadly voice from the doorway as she lifted her case from the closet.

Paling, she cast him a startled glance. "It's the only

way," she pleaded. "Surely you see that marriage between us wouldn't work. Let me go, Nikolas, before we tear each other to pieces."

His mouth twisted cynically. "Backing out, now that you know you won't be able to twist me around your little finger? It won't work, Jessica. We'll be married next week—unless you want to pay the price for walking out of this hotel without me?"

She knew what he meant and her chin went up. Without a word, she shoved her suitcase back onto the shelf and closed the door.

"I thought so," he murmured. "Don't get any more ideas about running out on me, or you'll regret it. Now come back in here and sit down. I'll order dinner sent up and we'll work out the details of our arrangement."

He was so cold-blooded about it that the last thing she wanted to do was talk to him, but she went ahead of him and took a seat on the sofa, not looking at him.

He ordered dinner without asking her preference, then he called Andros, who was on the floor below them, and told him to come to the suite in an hour, he wanted him to take some notes. Then he replaced the receiver and came to take a seat on the sofa beside her. Uneasily Jessica edged away from him and he gave a short bark of laughter.

"That's odd behavior for a prospective bride," he mocked. "So standoffish. I won't let you get away with that, you know. I'm paying for the right to touch you when I please and however I please, and I don't want any more playacting."

"I'm not playacting," she denied shakily. "You know I'm not."

He eyed her thoughtfully. "No, I suppose you're not.

You're afraid of me, aren't you? But you'll do what I want, if I marry you first. Too bad that kills any sense of mercy I might have possessed."

There was no convincing him. Jessica fell silent and tried to draw together the shreds of her dignity and composure. He was furious, and her attempts to establish her innocence were only making him that much angrier, so she decided to go along with him. If nothing else, she could salvage her pride.

"Nothing else to say?" he jeered.

She managed a cool shrug. "Why waste my time? You'll do what you want anyway, so I might as well go along for the ride."

"Does that mean you've agreed to marry me?" The tone was mocking, but she sensed the seriousness underlying the mockery and she realized that he wasn't certain that she'd stay.

"Yes, I'll marry you," she replied. "On the same conditions that I agreed to be your mistress."

"You backed out of that," he pointed out unkindly.

"I won't back out of this."

"You won't get a chance to. The same conditions, eh? I seem to remember that you didn't want to live with me; needless to say, that condition doesn't stand."

"The part about the money does," she said, turning her green eyes on him, opaque and mysterious with the intensity of her thoughts. "I don't want your money. Anything that I want, I'll pay for myself."

"That's interesting, even if it isn't convincing," he drawled, putting one strong brown hand on her throat and lightly stroking her skin. "If you're not marrying me for my money, why are you marrying me? For myself?"

"That's right," she admitted, meeting his gaze squarely.

"Good, because that's all you're getting," he muttered, leaning toward her as if drawn irresistibly by her mouth.

His lips fastened angrily on hers; his hands were hard and punishing and he pulled her close to him, but she didn't struggle. She rested pliantly against him and let him ravage her mouth until the anger began to fade and the hungry desire in him became stronger. Then she kissed him back, tentatively, and the pressure of his hard mouth lessened.

The long kiss provided an outlet for his black anger and she could sense him growing calmer even as his passion flared. He was prepared to wait now; he knew that she would be his within a week. He drew back and stared down into her pale face with its soft, trembling lips, then he kissed her again, hard.

The arrival of their dinner interrupted them and he released her to get to his feet and open the door. He seemed in a calmer frame of mind now, and as they ate, he even made small talk, telling her about his meeting and the problems that had been discussed. She relaxed, sensing that the worst of his temper had passed.

Andros arrived right on cue just as they were finishing the meal, and his dark eyes flashed at her in silent hostility before he gave his attention to Nikolas.

"Jessica and I are going to be married," Nikolas announced casually. "Next week, on the island. Tuesday. Make all the arrangements and notify the press that an engagement has been announced, but give them no details about when the wedding will take place. I'll call Maman myself, early tomorrow morning."

Andros's astonishment was plain, and though he didn't look at Jessica again, she sensed his dismay. No doubt his nose was more than a little out of joint to learn that the woman he actively disliked was going to marry his employer!

"We'll also have a prenuptial agreement drawn up," Nikolas continued. "Take all of this down, Andros, and have it on Leo's desk tomorrow morning. Tell him I want it back the day after tomorrow at the latest. It will be signed before we go to the island."

Andros sat down and opened his pad, his pen at the ready. Nikolas gave Jessica a considering stare before he started speaking again.

"Jessica renounces in advance all monetary claims against my estate," he drawled, sitting down and stretching his long legs out before him. "Should we be divorced, she will be entitled to no alimony and no property except such gifts as I have made to her, which will be her personal property."

Andros flashed Jessica a startled look, as if expecting her to disagree, but she sat quietly, watching Nikolas's dark, brooding face. She felt calm now, though she knew that her entire future was at stake. Nikolas had agreed to marriage when she had thought that he never would, so it was a start.

"While we're married," Nikolas continued, leaning his black head back against the sofa, "Jessica will conduct herself with strict propriety. She's not to leave the island without my personal escort, or with my permission and a substitute escort that I've chosen. She will also turn over the handling of all her income from her first husband to me." Now he, too, looked at Jessica, but still she made no protest. Her business affairs would be in marvelously competent hands with Nikolas, and she had no fears of him cheating her.

Then a thought occurred to her, and before she could halt herself, she said evenly, "I suppose that's one way of getting back the money you paid for my stocks."

Nikolas's jaw went rigid and she wished that she'd held her tongue rather than make him even angrier. She wasn't even protesting letting him have control of the money; she hadn't wanted it anyway. He wanted to have her completely under his power and she was willing to go along with him. It was a chance she was taking, but she had to hope that when he found out how wrong he was, he would soften his stand.

After a tense moment Nikolas delivered his final condition. "Last of all, I shall have final authority over any children that we should have. In case of divorce, I'll retain custody, though of course Jessica will be permitted visitation rights if she wants to come to the island. Under no circumstances will she be permitted to take the child or children away from the island or to see them without my permission."

Pain twisted her heart at that last and she hastily turned her head away so they couldn't see the welling of tears in her eyes. He seemed so hard! Perhaps she was being a fool; perhaps he'd never come to love her. Only the thought that he would know beyond a doubt that she came to him an innocent gave her the courage to agree to his conditions. He would at least realize that she wasn't going to corrupt their children.

If only there would be children! Nikolas seemed to take it for granted that their marriage wouldn't last, but already she knew that for her it was forever. No matter what he did, she would always be married to him in her heart. She wanted to have his children, several children, miniature replicas of him with black hair and black, flashing eyes.

"No comments, Jessica?" Nikolas asked softly, the jeering tone plain in his voice.

Jerking her thoughts back from a delightful vision of herself holding a tiny black-eyed baby in her arms, she stared at him for a moment as if she didn't recognize him, then she gathered herself and replied almost inaudibly, "No. I agree to everything you want, Nikolas."

"That's all," he said to Andros, and when they were alone again, he snapped, "You won't even make a token protest to keep any children, will you? Or are you hoping that I'll pay you to stay away from them? If so, disillusion yourself. You won't get a penny from me under any circumstances!"

"I agreed to your conditions," she cried shakily, her control broken by a heavy pain in her chest. "What more do you want? I've learned that I can't fight you, so I won't waste my breath. As for any children we might have, I want children—I want *your* children—and the only way I'll ever leave them will be if you physically throw me off the island. And don't insult me by insinuating that I won't be a good mother."

He stared down at her, a muscle in his jaw jerking out of control. "You say you can't fight me," he muttered hoarsely, "but you still deny me."

"No, no," she moaned, despairing of ever making him understand. "I'm not refusing you. Can't you see, Nikolas? I'm asking more from you than you're offering, and I'm not talking about money. I'm talking about yourself. So far you've offered me only the same part of yourself that you gave Diana, and I want more than that."

"And what about you?" he growled, getting to his feet and pacing restlessly about the room. "You won't even give me that much; you hold yourself away and demand that I give in to you in every respect."

"You don't have to marry me," she pointed out sharply, abruptly weary of their bickering. "You can let me walk out that door, and I promise you that you'll never see me again, if that's what you want."

His mouth twisted savagely. "You know I can't do that. No, you've got me so twisted inside that I've got to have you; I'll never be worth a damn if I can't satisfy this ache. It's not a wedding, Jessica, it's an exorcism."

His words still rang in her ears the next day as she paced the suite, waiting for him to return from his meeting. Andros was there; he had been there all morning, watching her, not talking, and his silent vigilance rasped painfully on her nerves. It had been a hellish night, sleeping alone in the big bed that Nikolas had intended to share with her, listening to him turn restlessly on the sofa. She had offered to take the sofa and let him have the bed, but he had glared at her so fiercely that she hadn't insisted. They had both slept very little.

Earlier, he had phoned his mother and Jessica had shut herself in the bathroom, determined not to listen to the conversation. When she came out of the bathroom, Nikolas had gone and Andros was there.

Just when she thought she couldn't stand the silence any longer, Andros spoke, and she nearly jumped out of her skin. "Why did you agree to all of Niko's conditions, Mrs. Stanton?"

She looked at him wildly. "Why?" she demanded. "Do you think he was in any mood to be reasonable? He was like a keg of dynamite waiting for some fool to set him off."

"You're not afraid of him, though," Andros observed. "At least, you're not afraid of his temper. Most people are, but you've always dared him to do his worst. I've been turning it over and over in my head, and I can think of only one reason why you'd let him make those insulting conditions."

"Oh? What have you decided?" she asked, pushing her heavy hair away from her eyes. She had been too upset that morning to put it up and now it tumbled untidily over her shoulders.

"I think you love him," Andros said quietly. "I think you're willing to marry him under any conditions because you love him."

She gulped at hearing it put into words. Andros was watching her with a different light in his dark eyes, a certain acceptance and the beginnings of understanding. "Of course I love him," she admitted in a tight whisper. "The only problem is making him believe it."

Suddenly Andros smiled. "You don't have a problem, Mrs. Stanton. Niko is besotted with you. When he calms down, he'll realize, as I did, that under the conditions he set, the only reason you had for marrying him is love. It's only because he's so angry now that it hasn't already occurred to him."

Andros didn't know the whole of it, but still his words gave her hope. He said that Nikolas was besotted with her. That was a little hard to believe; Nikolas was always so much in control, but it was true that he was willing to marry her if he couldn't have her any other way.

Nikolas arrived then, preventing her from talking with Andros any longer, but she felt better. The two men conferred over a sheaf of papers that Nikolas took out of his briefcase, then Andros took the papers to return to his room and Nikolas turned to Jessica.

"Are you ready?" he asked remotely.

"Ready?" She didn't understand.

He sighed impatiently. "I told you that we'd shop for your wedding dress. And you'll have to have rings, Jessica, they'll be expected."

"I'll have to put up my hair," she said, turning to the bedroom, and he followed her.

"Just brush it and leave it down," he ordered. "I like it better down."

Wordlessly she obeyed him and took out her lipstick. "Wait," he said, catching her wrist and pulling her around to him. She knew what he wanted and her heart lightened as she leaned against him and lifted her mouth for his kiss. His lips pressed on hers and his hot breath filled her mouth, making her dizzy. He wanted more; he wasn't content with kisses, but with a quiver of his body he pulled away from her and once again the look in his eyes bordered on the murderous.

"Now you can put on your lipstick," he muttered, and slammed out of the bedroom.

With a shaking hand she applied the lipstick. His temper hadn't improved, and she was afraid that to deny him even her kisses would make him that much worse. No, nothing would satisfy Nikolas but her full surrender, and she wished fervently that the next week would fly past.

But how could an entire week fly by when even the afternoon dragged? She could feel the tension building up in her as they sat at the quiet, exclusive jewelers and examined the trays of rings that he set out. Nikolas was no help at all; he merely sat back and told her to pick out what she liked, he didn't care. Nothing he could have said would have been better calculated to demolish any joy Jessica might have felt in the proceedings. On the other hand, the jeweler was so nice and tried to be so helpful that she hated to disappoint him with her disinterest, so she forced herself to carefully examine each and every ring that he thought she might like. But try as she might, she couldn't choose one. The brightly winking diamonds might have been glass for all she cared; she wanted only to find a quiet corner and weep her eyes out. At last, with tension cracking in her voice, she said, "No—no! I don't like any of them!" and made as if to get to her feet.

Nikolas stopped her with an iron grip on her wrist and he forced her back into her chair. "Don't get upset, darling," he said in a gentler tone than he had used all day. "Calm down; you mustn't weep or it will upset Monsieur. Shall I pick one out for you?"

"Yes, please," she said in a stifled voice, turning her face away so he couldn't see her eyes brimming with the tears he had said she mustn't shed.

"I don't care for the diamonds either, Monsieur," Nikolas was saying. "Her coloring needs something warmer…yes, emeralds to match her eyes, in a gold setting."

"Of course—I have just the thing!" Monsieur said excitedly, taking the trays of diamonds away.

"Jessica?"

"What?" she asked, still not turning around to face him.

She should have known that he'd never allow her to keep her head turned away from him. One long forefinger stroked along her jaw, then gently forced her face to turn to him. Black eyes took in her pallor, her tense expression, noted the wetness that threatened to overflow from her eyes.

Without a word, he took out his handkerchief and wiped her eyes as if she were a child. "You know I can't bear for you to cry," he whispered. "If I promise not to be such a beast, will you smile for me?"

It wasn't in her to deny him anything when he was being so sweet, even if he had been as cold as ice only a moment before. Her lips parted in a gentle smile and Nikolas touched her mouth with his finger, tracing her lip line. "That's better," he murmured. "You understand why I won't kiss you here, but I want to, very much."

She kissed his fingers in answer, then he saw the jeweler returning and he straightened up, taking his hand away, but his brief attentions had put color in her cheeks and she was smiling hazily.

"Ah, this is more like it," Nikolas said, pouncing on a ring as soon as the jeweler set the tray down before them. He took Jessica's slender hand and slid the ring onto it; it was too big, but she caught her breath at the sight of it.

"What a lovely color," she breathed on a sigh.

"Yes, this is what I want," Nikolas decided. The square-cut emerald was not so big that it looked awkward on her graceful hand, and the rich, dark green looked better on her than a thousand diamonds would have. Her golden skin and tawny hair were a perfect setting for her mysterious Egyptian green eyes, and the emerald ring was only an echo of her own coloring. Brilliant diamonds surrounded the emerald, but they were small enough that they didn't detract from the deep color of the gem. He removed it gently from her finger and gave it to the jeweler, who carefully put it aside and measured Jessica's finger. "And a wedding ring," Nikolas added.

"Two," inserted Jessica bravely, meeting his eyes. After a moment he gave in, nodding his permission.

"I don't like wearing rings," he said as they left the jewelers, his arm hard about her waist.

"We're going to be married, Nikolas," she said, turning to face him and putting both hands on his chest. "Shouldn't we try as hard as we can to make a success of our marriage? Or are you going into it with divorce already on your mind?" Her voice quivered at that thought, but she met his dark gaze squarely.

"I don't have anything on my mind except having you," he said bluntly. "Rings aren't important to me. If you want me to wear a wedding ring, then I'll wear one. A ring won't stop me if I want to be free of you."

She nearly choked on the pain that welled up in her chest and she turned abruptly away, fighting for composure. By the time he caught up with her she had managed to pull her cool mask in place again and she revealed nothing of her inner hurt.

When they were in the taxi, she heard him give the address of a well-known couturier and she said quietly, "I don't know what you have in mind, Nikolas, but there isn't time to have a gown made. A ready-to-wear gown will be fine with me."

He didn't even glance at her, and after his gentle-

ness in the jewelry shop, the chill was that much colder.
"You're forgetting who I am," he snapped. "If I want a
gown ready for you by tomorrow afternoon, the gown
will be ready."

There was nothing to say to that, because it was true,
but she thought of the people who would be sitting up
all night to do the delicate stitchery that had to be done
by hand and she knew that it wasn't worth it. But Nikolas had a set to his jaw that dissuaded her from arguing
with him, and she sat back in miserable silence.

So far as Jessica knew, Nikolas was not inclined to
personally select clothing for his women, but he was
recognized the instant he stepped into the cool foyer
of the salon. Immediately a tall, slender woman with
severely styled ash-blond hair was gliding across the
dove-gray carpet toward them, welcoming them to the
salon, and if Monsieur Constantinos wished to see anything in particular...

Nikolas was all charm, raising the woman's fingers
to his lips, his wolfish black eyes bringing a wave of
color to her cheeks that owed nothing to artificiality.
Nikolas introduced Jessica, then said smoothly, "We're
to be married next week in Greece. I managed to convince her only yesterday, and I want to have the wedding immediately, before she can change her mind. But
this leaves very little time for the gown, you understand,
as we are leaving for Greece the day after tomorrow."

The woman snapped to attention and assured him
that a gown could indeed be ready, if they would like
to see some models....

A parade of models appeared, some wearing white,
but the majority in pastel colors, delicately flattering
colors that were nevertheless not virginal white. Niko-

las looked them all over carefully and finally chose a gown with classically simple lines and requested it in a shade of pale peach. Jessica suddenly frowned. This was her wedding gown, and she was entitled to wear the traditional white.

"I don't like peach," she said firmly. "In white, please, Madame."

Nikolas glared at her and the woman looked startled, but Jessica stood her ground. It was to be white or nothing. At last Nikolas gave in, for he didn't want to make a scene in front of extremely interested witnesses, and Jessica was taken into the dressing room to be measured.

"You made a fool of yourself, insisting on white," Nikolas said curtly on the way back to the hotel. "Your name is recognized even in France, Jessica."

"It's my wedding, too," she said stubbornly.

"You've already been married, my sweet; it should be old hat to you by now."

Her lower lip trembled at that cut and she quickly firmed it. "Robert and I were married in a civil ceremony, not a religious one. I'm entitled to a white gown, Nikolas!"

If he caught her meaning, he ignored it. Or perhaps he simply didn't believe it. He said grimly, "After your history, you should count yourself lucky I'm marrying you at all. I have to be the world's biggest fool, but I'll worry about that afterward. One thing is for certain, as my wife you'll be the most well-behaved woman in Europe."

She turned her head in frustration, staring out the window at the chic Parisian shoppers, the elegant cafés. She had seen nothing of Paris except fleeting glimpses through the window of the taxi and the gay, mocking lights of the night winking up into her hotel window.

It was too late to back out now, but she was aware of the awful, creeping knowledge that she had made a mistake in agreeing to the marriage. Nikolas was not a man to forgive easily, and not even the knowledge that she was not promiscuous would make him forget that, to his way of seeing it, she had sold herself to him for a price—marriage.

CHAPTER NINE

"THERE!" ANDROS SHOUTED to Jessica above the roar of the helicopter blades. "That is Zenas."

She leaned forward to watch eagerly as the small dot in the blue of the Aegean began to grow bigger, then it was rushing toward them and they were no longer over the sea but over the stark, barren hills with the shadow of the helicopter flitting along below them like a giant mosquito. Jessica glanced at Nikolas, who was at the controls, but he didn't acknowledge her presence by so much as the flicker of an eyelash. She wanted him to smile at her, to point out the landmarks on his island, but it was only Andros who touched her arm and directed her attention to the house they were approaching.

It was a vast, sprawling house, built on the cliffside with a flagstone terrace enclosing three sides of the house. The roof was of red tile; the house itself was white and cool amid the shade of orange and lemon trees. Looking down, she could see small figures leaving the house and walking up to the helipad, which was built off to the right of the house on the crest of a small hill. A paved drive connected the house to the helipad, but Andros had told her that there was only one vehicle on the island, an old army jeep owned by the mayor of the village.

Nikolas set the helicopter down so lightly that she

didn't even feel a bump, then he killed the engine and pulled off his headset. He turned a grim, unsmiling face to Jessica. "Come," he said in French. "I will introduce you to Maman—and remember, Jessica, you're not to upset her."

He slid open the door and got out, ducking his head against the wind whipped up by the still-whirling rotors. Jessica drew a deep breath to steady her pounding heart and Andros said quietly, "Not to worry. My aunt is a gentle woman; Nikolas is not at all like her. He is the image of his father, and like his father before him he is protective of my aunt."

She gave him a grateful smile, then Nikolas beckoned impatiently and she clambered out of the helicopter, holding desperately to the hand Nikolas had extended to help her. He frowned a little at the coldness of her fingers, then he drew her forward to the group that had gathered at the edge of the helipad.

A small woman with the erect bearing of a queen stepped forward. She was still beautiful despite her white hair, which she wore in an elegant Gibson Girl style, and her soft, clear blue eyes were as direct as a child's. She gave Jessica a piercing look straight into her eyes, then she looked swiftly at her son.

Nikolas bent down and pressed a loving kiss on the delicately pink cheek, then another on her lips. "Maman, I've missed you," he said, hugging her to him.

"And I've missed you," she replied in a sweet voice. "I'm so glad you're back."

With his arm still about his mother, Nikolas beckoned to Jessica, and the look he gave her as she stepped closer warned her to behave. "Maman, I'd like you to meet my fiancée, Jessica Stanton. Jessica, my mother, Madelon Constantinos."

"I'm happy to meet you at last," Jessica murmured, meeting that clear gaze as bravely as possible, and she discovered to her astonishment that she and Madame Constantinos were nearly the same size. The older woman looked so fragile that Jessica had felt like an Amazon, but now she found their eyes on the same level and it was a distinct shock.

"And I'm happy to meet you," Madame Constantinos said, moving out of Nikolas's embrace to put her own arms around Jessica and kiss her on the cheek. "I was certainly surprised to receive Niko's phone call announcing his intentions! It was…unexpected."

"Yes, it was a sudden decision," Jessica agreed, but her heart sank at the coolness of the old woman's tone. It was obvious that she was less than happy over her son's choice of a bride. Nevertheless, Jessica managed a tremulous smile, and Madame Constantinos's manners were too good to permit her to exhibit her displeasure any more openly. She had spoken in English, very good English with a slight drawl that she could only have picked up from Nikolas, but as she turned to introduce Jessica to the other people she switched to French and Greek. Jessica didn't understand any Greek, but all of the people spoke some French.

There was Petra, a tall, heavyset woman with black hair and eyes and the classic Greek nose, and laughter shining in her face. She was the housekeeper and her employer's personal companion, for they had been together since Madame Constantinos had come to the island. There was a natural grace and pride about the big woman that made her beautiful despite her almost manly proportions, and a motherly light gleamed in her eyes at the barely concealed fear and nervousness on Jessica's face.

The other woman was short and plump, her round face as gentle as any Jessica could remember. She was Sophia, the cook, and she patted Jessica's arm with open affection, ready to accept immediately any woman that Kyrios Nikolas brought home to be his bride.

Sophia's husband, Jason Kavakis, was a short, slender man with solemn dark eyes, and he was the groundskeeper. He and Sophia lived in their own cottage in the village, but Petra was a widow and she had her own room in the villa. These three were the only staff at the villa, though the women from the village were all helping with the preparations for the wedding.

The open, unrestrained welcome that she received from the staff helped Jessica to relax and she smiled more naturally as Madame Constantinos linked arms with Nikolas and began organizing the transfer of their luggage to the villa. "Andros, please help Jason carry the bags down." Then she removed her arm and gave Nikolas a little push. "And you, too! Why should you not help? I will take Mrs. Stanton to her room; she is probably half-dead with fatigue. You've never learned to take a trip in easy stages."

"Yes, Maman," he called to her retreating back, but his dark eyes looked a warning at Jessica.

Despite the coolness of her welcome from Madame Constantinos, Jessica felt better. The old lady was not an autocratic matriarch, and Jessica sensed that beneath her restraint she was a pert, gentle old woman who treated her son as if he was simply her son, rather than a billionaire. And Nikolas himself had immediately softened, becoming the Niko who had grown up here and who had known these people since babyhood. She couldn't imagine him intimidating Petra, who had probably diapered him and watched his first toddling steps, hard as it was for Jessica to picture Nikolas as an infant or a toddler. Surely he had always been tall and strong, with that fierce light in his dark eyes.

The villa was cool, with the thickness of its white walls keeping out most of the brutal Greek sun, but the quiet hum of central air-conditioning told her that Nikolas made certain his home was always at a comfortable temperature.

She had already realized that Nikolas's tastes were Greek, and the villa bore that out. The furnishings were sparse, with vast amounts of open floor space, but everything was of the highest quality and built to last for years. The colors were of the earth, soft brick tones for the tiles of the floor, over which were scattered priceless Persian rugs, muted greens and natural linen for the furniture upholstery. Small statues in different shades of marble were set in niches, and here and there were vases of incredible delicacy, sitting comfortably in the same room with pottery that had surely been produced by the villagers.

"Your bedroom," said Madame Constantinos, opening the door of a square white room with graceful arched windows and furnishings done in shades of rose and gold. "It has its own bath attached," she continued, crossing the room to open a door and indicate a tiled bath. "Ah, Niko, you must show Jessica about the villa while Petra unpacks for her," she said without pause when Nikolas appeared with Jessica's luggage and set it in the middle of the floor.

Nikolas smiled, his eyes twinkling. "Jessica would probably like a bath instead; I know I would! Well, darling?" he asked, turning to Jessica with the smile still lingering in his eyes. "You have your choice, shall it be a guided tour or a bath?"

"Both," she said promptly. "Bath first, though."

He nodded and left the room with a careless "I'll be along in half an hour, then," thrown over his shoulder. Madame Constantinos took her leave soon after, leaving Jessica standing in the middle of the floor looking about the charming room and feeling deserted. She pulled off her travel-worn clothing and took a leisurely bath, returning to the room to find that Petra had efficiently unpacked for her in the meantime. She dressed in a cool sundress and waited for Nikolas, but the time passed and after a while she realized that he didn't mean to return for her. He had simply offered to give her a tour to please his mother; he had no intention of spending that much time in her company. She sat quietly on the bed and wondered if she had a prayer of ever winning his love.

It was much later, after a light dinner of fish and *soupa avgolemono,* which was a lemon-flavored chicken soup Jessica found delicious, that Nikolas approached her as she stood on the terrace watching the waves roll onto the beach so far below. She would have liked to avoid him, but that would have looked odd, so she remained at the wall of the terrace. His hard fingers clasped her shoulders and drew her back against him; his head bent down to hers and it must have looked as though he was whispering sweet nothings in her ear, but what he said was, "Have you said anything to Maman to upset her?"

"Of course not," she whispered vehemently, giving in to the force of those fingers and leaning against his chest. "I haven't seen her at all from the time she took me to my room until dinner. She doesn't like me, of course. Isn't that what you wanted?"

"No," he said, his mouth curving bitterly. "I didn't want you here at all, Jessica."

Her chin rose proudly. "Then send me away," she dared him.

"You know I can't do that, either," he snapped. "I'm living in torment, and I'll either crawl out of it or I'll pull you down with me." Then he released her and walked away, and she was left with the bitter knowledge of his hatred.

THE DAY OF her wedding dawned clear and bright with the remarkable clarity that only Greece had. She stood in the window and looked out at the barren hills, every detail as sharp and clear as if she had only to reach out her hand to touch them. The crystalline sunlight made her feel that if she could only open her eyes wide enough she would be able to see forever. She felt at home here, on this rocky island with its bare hills and the silent company of thousands of years of history, the warm and unquestioning welcome of the dark-eyed people who embraced her as one of their own. And today she would marry the man who owned all this.

Though Nikolas's hostility was still a barrier between them, she felt more optimistic today, for today the terrible waiting was over. The traditional ceremony and the exuberant celebrations that followed would soften him; he would have to listen to her tonight, when they were alone in his bedroom, and he would know the final truth when she gave him the unrivaled gift of her chastity. Smiling, she turned away from the window to begin the pleasant ritual of bathing and dressing her hair.

In the few days that she had been on the island she had already become steeped in the traditions of the people. She had imagined that they would be married in the small white church with its arched windows and domed roof, the sunlight pouring through the stained glass, but Petra had set her right about that. The religious ceremony was seldom performed in the church, but rather in the house of the groom's godfather, or *koumbaros,* who also provided the wedding entertainment. Nikolas's godfather was Angelos Palamas, a rotund man of immense, gentle dignity, his hair and eyebrows white above eyes as black as coal. An improvised altar had been set in the middle of the largest room of Kyrios Palamas's house, and she and Nikolas would stand before the altar with the priest, Father Ambrose. She and Nikolas would wear wreaths of orange blossoms on their heads, the wreaths blessed by the priest and linked by a ribbon, as their lives would be blessed and linked.

With measured, dreamy movements, she braided her hair in a fat single braid and coiled it on her head in the hairstyle that signified maidenhood. In a little while Madame Constantinos and Petra would come in to help her dress, and she went to the closet and took down the zippered white plastic bag that held her wedding gown. She hadn't looked at it before, exercising a childish delight in saving the best for last, and now her hands were tender as she laid the bag on the bed and unzipped it, being careful not to catch any of the material in the zipper.

But when she drew the delicate, lovely dress out, her

heart and breathing stopped, and she dropped it as if it had turned into a serpent, turning blindly away with hot tears pouring down her cheeks. He had done it! He had countermanded her instructions while she was in the dressing room being measured, and instead of the white dress she had dreamed of, the creation that lay crumpled on the bed was a pale peach in color. She knew that the salon hadn't made a mistake; she had been too positive in her request for white for that. No, it was Nikolas's doing, and she felt as if he had torn out her heart.

Wildly she wanted to destroy the dress, and she would have if she had had anything else suitable, but she hadn't. Neither could she bring herself to pick it up; she sat in the window with the scalding tears blinding her and sticking in her throat, and that was how Petra found her.

Strong, gentle arms went about her and she was drawn against the woman's bosom and rocked tenderly. "Ah, it is always so," Petra crooned in her deep voice. "You weep, when you should laugh."

"No," Jessica managed in a strangled voice, pointing in the direction of the bed. "It's my gown."

"The wedding gown? It is torn, soiled?" Petra went over to the bed and picked up the gown, inspecting it.

"It was supposed to be *white*," Jessica whispered, turning her small, drowned face back to the window.

"Ah!" Petra exclaimed, and left the room. She returned in only a moment with Madame Constantinos, who went at once to Jessica and put her arm about her shoulders in the first warm gesture she'd made.

"I know you're upset, my dear, but it's still a lovely gown and you shouldn't let a mistake ruin your wedding day. You'll be beautiful in it—"

"Nikolas changed the color," Jessica explained tautly, having conquered the rush of tears. "I insisted on white—I was trying to make him understand, but he wouldn't listen. He let me think the dress would be white, but while I was in the dressing room, he changed the color."

Madame Constantinos caught her breath. "You insisted—what are you saying?"

Wearily Jessica rubbed her forehead, seeing that now she would have to explain. Perhaps it was just as well for Madame Constantinos to know the whole story. She searched for a way to begin and finally blurted out, "I want you to know, Madame—none of the things you've heard about me are true."

Slowly Madame Constantinos nodded, her blue eyes sad. "I think I had already realized that," she said softly. "A woman who had traveled as many roads and known as many lovers as have been attributed to you would have had some of that knowledge in her face, and your face is innocent of any such knowledge. I had forgotten how gossip can spread like a cancer and feed on itself, but you have reminded me and I promise I won't forget again."

Encouraged, Jessica said hesitantly, "Nikolas told me that you were a friend of Robert's."

"Yes," Madame Constantinos acknowledged. "I had known Robert Stanton for most of my life; he was a dear friend of my father's, and beloved of the entire family. I should have remembered that he saw things far more clearly than the rest of us. I've thought many harsh things about you in the past, my dear, and I'm deeply ashamed of myself. Please, can you possibly forgive me?"

"Of, of course," Jessica cried, jumping to her feet to hug the older woman and wipe at the tears that welled anew. "But I want to tell you how it was, how I came to marry Robert. After all, you have a right to know, since I'm going to marry your son."

"If you'd like to tell me, please do so, but don't feel that you owe an explanation to me," Madame Constantinos replied. "If Niko is satisfied, then so am I."

Jessica's face fell. "But he isn't satisfied," she said bitterly. "He believes all of the tales he's heard, and he hates me almost as much as he wants me."

"Impossible," the older woman gasped. "Niko couldn't be that much of a fool; it's so plain that you're not a scheming adventuress!"

"Oh, he believes it, all right! It's partly my fault," she admitted miserably. "At first, when I wanted to hold him off, I let him think that I—I was frightened because I'd been mistreated. I've tried since then to explain to him, but he simply won't listen; he refuses to talk about my 'past affairs' and he's furious because I won't go to bed with him—" She stopped, aghast at what she had blurted out to his mother, but Madame Constantinos gave her a startled look, then burst into a peal of laughter.

"Yes, I can imagine that would make him wild, because he has his father's temperament." She chuckled. "So, you must convince my blind, stubborn son that your experience is wholly fictional. Do you have any idea how you might accomplish such a thing?"

"He'll know," Jessica said quietly. "Tonight. When he realizes that I have a right to a white wedding dress."

Madame Constantinos gasped as at last she realized the significance of the dress. "My dear! But Robert—

no, of course not. Robert was not a man to wed a young girl for physical gratification. Yes, I think I must hear how this came about, after all!"

Quietly Jessica told her of how she had been young and alone and Robert had wanted to protect her, and of the vicious gossip she had endured. She left out nothing, not even how Nikolas had come to propose to her, and Madame Constantinos was deeply troubled when the tale ended.

"There are times," she said slowly, "when I would like to smash a vase over Niko's head, even if he is my son!" She looked at the wedding gown. "Have you nothing else to wear? Nothing white?"

Jessica shook her head. "No, nothing. I'll have to wear it."

Petra brought crushed ice and folded it in hand towels to make compresses for her eyes, and after half an hour all traces of her tears had gone, but she was unnaturally pale. She moved slowly, all vitality gone from her, all sparkle killed. Gently Madame Constantinos and Petra dressed her in the peach gown and set the matching veil on her head, then they led her from the room.

Nikolas wasn't there; he was already at the home of his godfather, but the villa was filled with relatives, aunts and uncles and cousins who smiled and chattered and patted her as she passed. None of her friends were there, she realized with a start, but then, there were only two: Charles and Sallie. That made her feel more alone, chilled as if she would never again be warm.

Andros was to escort her down the path that led to the village, and he waited for her now, tall and dark in a tuxedo, and momentarily looking so much like Nikolas that she gasped. Andros smiled and gave her his arm;

his manner had warmed over the past few days and now he was frankly solicitous as he discovered how she trembled, how cold her hands were.

Nikolas's female relatives rushed outside to form an aisle from the top of the hill down to the village, standing on both sides of the path. As she and Andros reached them, they began to toss orange blossoms down on the path before her, and the village women were there in traditional dress, tossing small, fragrant white and pink blossoms. They began to sing, and she walked on flowers down the path to join the man she would marry, but still she felt frozen inside.

At the door of Kyrios Palamas's house Andros gave her over to the arm of Nikolas's godfather, who led her to the altar, where Nikolas and Father Ambrose waited. The altar, the entire room, danced with candles, and the sweet smell of incense made her feel as if she was having a dream. Father Ambrose blessed the wreaths of orange blossoms that were set on their heads as they knelt before the altar, and from that moment on it was all a blur. She had been coached on what to say and she must have made the proper responses; when Nikolas made his vows, his deep, dark voice reverberated inside her head and she looked around a little wildly. Then it was over, and Father Ambrose joined hands with them and they walked around the altar three times while little Kostis, one of Nikolas's innumerable cousins, walked before them waving a censer, so they progressed through clouds of incense.

Almost immediately the crowded room burst into celebration, everyone laughing and kissing each other, while cries of "The glass! The glass!" went up. The newly married couple was laughingly shoved to the hearth, where a wineglass was turned upside down. Jessica remembered what she should do but her reactions were dulled by her misery and Nikolas easily beat her, his foot smashing the wineglass while the villagers cheered that Kyrios Constantinos would be the master in his house. As if it could ever be any other way, Jessica thought numbly, turning away from the devilish gleam in Nikolas's black eyes.

But he caught her back to him, his hands hard on her waist and his eyes glittering as he forced her head up. "Now you're legally mine," he muttered as he bent his head and captured her lips.

She didn't fight him, but the response that he had always known was lacking. He raised his head, frowning when he saw the tears that clung to her lashes. "Jessica?" he asked questioningly, taking her hand, his frown deepening when he felt its iciness, though the day was hot and sunny.

Somehow, though afterward she wondered at her stamina, she made it through the long day of feasting and dancing. She had help in Madame Constantinos and Petra and Sophia, who gently made it clear that the new Kyria was weak with nerves and not able to dance. Nikolas threw himself into the celebration with an enthusiasm that surprised her until she remembered that he was Greek to the bone, but even with all the laughing and dancing and the glasses of ouzo he consumed, he returned often to his bride and tried to entice her appetite with some delicacy he had brought. Jessica tried to respond, tried to act normally, but the truth was that she couldn't make herself look at her husband. No matter how she argued with herself, she couldn't escape the fact that she was a woman, and her woman's heart was easily bruised. Nikolas had destroyed all of her joy in her wedding day with the peach gown and she didn't think she would ever be able to forgive him.

It was late; the stars were already out and the candles were the only illumination in the house when Nikolas approached her and gently swung her up into his arms. No one said anything; no jokes were made as the broad-shouldered man left the house of his godfather and carried his bride up the hill to his own villa, and after he had disappeared from view, the celebration began again, for this was no ordinary wedding. No, the Kyrios had finally taken a bride, and now they could look forward to an heir.

As Nikolas carried her up the path with no visible effort, Jessica tried to gather her scattered wits and push her unhappiness aside, but still the cold misery lay like a lump in her chest. She clung to him with her arms around his neck and wished that it was miles and miles to the villa and perhaps then she would be more in control of herself by the time they arrived. The cool night air soothed her face and she could hear the rhythmic thunder of the waves as they pounded against the rocks, and those seemed more real to her than the flesh-and-blood man who carried her in his arms.

Then they were at the villa and he carried her around the side of the terrace until he reached the double sliding glass doors of his bedroom. They opened silently at his touch and he stepped inside, letting her slide gently to the floor.

"Your clothes have been brought in here," he told her softly, kissing the hair at her temple. "I know you're frightened, darling; you've been acting strange all day. Just relax; I'll fix myself a drink while you're changing into your nightgown. Not that you'll need a night-gown, but you do need some time to calm down," he said, grinning, and suddenly she wondered just how many glasses of ouzo he'd had.

He left her and she stared wildly around the room. She couldn't do it; she couldn't share that big bed with him when she felt as she did. She wanted to scream and cry and scratch his eyes out, and in a sudden burst of tears and sheer temper she tore the peach gown off and looked around for scissors to destroy it. There were no scissors to be found in the bedroom, however, so she tore at the seams until they ripped apart, then she threw the gown on the floor and kicked it.

She drew a deep, shuddering breath into her lungs and wiped the furious tears off her cheeks. The gesture had been childish, she knew, but she felt better for it. She hated that gown, and she hated Nikolas for ruining her wedding day!

He would be returning soon, and she didn't want to face him while wearing nothing but her underwear, but neither did she have any intention of putting on a seductive nightgown for his benefit. She threw open the closet door and grabbed the one pair of slacks she had with her and a pullover top. Hastily she snatched the top over her head just as the door opened.

Thick silence reigned as Nikolas took in the tableau of her standing there clutching a pair of slacks and staring at him with anger and fear plain in her wide eyes. His black gaze wandered to the tattered wedding gown on the floor, then back to her.

"Settle down," he said softly, almost in a whisper. "I'm not going to hurt you, darling, I promise—"

"You can keep your promises," she cried hoarsely,

dropping the slacks to the floor and pressing her hands to her cheeks as the tears began to slide from her eyes. "I hate you, do you hear? You—you *ruined* my wedding day! I wanted a white gown, Nikolas, and you had them use that horrible peach! I'll never forgive you for that! I was so happy this morning, then I opened the bag and saw that ugly peach thing and I—I— Oh, damn you, I've cried enough over you; I'll never let you make me cry again, do you hear? I hate you!"

Swiftly he crossed the room to her and put his hands on her shoulders, holding her in a grip that didn't hurt but nevertheless held her firmly. "Was it so important to you?" he murmured. "Is that why you haven't looked at me all day, all over a silly gown?"

"You don't understand," she insisted through her tears. "I wanted a white one, and I wanted to keep it and give it to our daughter for *her* wedding—" Her voice broke and she began to sob, trying to turn her head away from him.

With a muttered curse he pulled her to him and held her tightly in his arms, his dark head bent to rest atop her tawny one. "I'm sorry," he whispered into her hair. "I didn't understand. Don't cry, darling; please don't cry."

His apology, so unexpected, had the effect of startling her out of her tears, and with a caught breath she raised her tear-wet eyes to stare at him. For a moment, their eyes held; then his midnight gaze slipped to her mouth, and as quickly as that he was kissing her, pulling her even closer to his powerful frame as if he could make her a part of himself, his mouth hungrier and more devouring than it had ever been before. She tasted the ouzo he had been drinking, and it made her drunk, too, so that she had to cling to him even to stand upright.

Impatiently he scooped her up in his arms and carried her to the bed, and for a moment she stiffened in alarm as she remembered that she still hadn't told him the truth. "Nikolas...wait!" she cried breathlessly.

"I've been waiting," he said thickly, his restless mouth raining kisses across her face, her throat. "I've waited for you until I thought I would go mad. Don't push me away tonight, darling—not tonight."

Before she could say anything else, his mouth closed over hers again. In the sweet intoxication sweeping over her at the touch of his lips, she momentarily forgot her fears, and then it was too late. He was beyond listening to her, beyond the reach of any plea as he responded only to the force of his passion.

Still she tried to reach him. "No, wait!" she said, but he ignored her as he pulled her top over her head, momentarily smothering her in the folds of material before he freed her from it and tossed the garment aside. His eyes were glittering feverishly as he stripped her underwear away, and her pleas for patience stuck in her throat as he dropped his robe and covered her with his powerful body. Panic bloomed in her, and she tried to control it, forcing herself to think of other things until she regained some small measure of self-control, but it was useless. A thin sob tore out of her throat as Nikolas drew her down into the fathomless well of his desire, and blindly she clung to him as the only tower of strength in a wildly shaking world.

CHAPTER TEN

JESSICA LAY IN the darkness listening to Nikolas's even breathing as he slept, and her flesh shrank when he moved in his sleep and his hand touched her breast. Slowly, terrified of waking him, she inched away from his hand and off the bed. She couldn't just lie there beside him when every nerve in her body screamed for release; she'd go for a walk, try to calm herself down and sort out her tangled emotions.

Silently she pulled on the discarded slacks and top and let herself out through the sliding doors onto the terrace. Her bare feet made no sound as she walked slowly around the terrace, staring at the faint glow of the breakers as they crashed onto the rocks. The beach drew her; she could walk down there without taking the risk of waking anyone, though she doubted that anyone would still be up now. It had to be nearing dawn; or perhaps it wasn't, but it seemed as though she had spent hours in that bedroom with Nikolas.

Depression weighed on her shoulders like a rock. How silly and stupid she had been to think she would be able to control Nikolas even for a moment. If he had loved her, it might have been possible, but the raw truth of the matter was that Nikolas felt nothing for her except lust, and now she had to live with that knowledge.

She walked slowly along the rim of the cliff, hunting

for the narrow, rocky path that led down to the beach, and when she found it, she began a careful descent, well aware of the treacherously loose rocks along the path. She gained the beach and found that only a thin strip of sand was above the tide and that the incoming waves washed about her ankles as she walked. The tide must be coming in, she thought absently; she'd have to keep watch on it and climb up before the water got too deep.

For just a moment she had managed to push away thoughts of Nikolas, but now they returned, swooping down on her tired mind like birds of prey. She had wagered her happiness in the battle with him and she had lost. She had given her innocence to a man who didn't love her, all for nothing. Nothing! In the dark, savage hours of the night it had been forced into her consciousness that she had gained nothing, and he had gained everything. He had wanted only the release he could find with her flesh, not her virginity or her love. She felt used, degraded, and the bitterest knowledge of all was that she had to see it through. He'd never allow her to leave him. She had learned to her cost that mercy was not a part of Nikolas's character.

She almost choked on her misery. It hadn't been at all as she had imagined. Perhaps if Nikolas had been tender, adoring, easy with her, she wouldn't feel so shocked and shattered now. Or perhaps if he hadn't been so frustrated, if he hadn't drunk so much ouzo, he would have been more patient, better able to cope with her fright. If, if! She tried to excuse him by telling herself that he had been pushed past control; she told herself over and over that it was her own fault; she should have made him listen before. But after a day of unbroken pain and unhappiness, it was too much for her to handle just now.

A wave suddenly splashed above her knees and with a start she looked about. The tide was still coming in, and the path was a long way down the beach. Deciding that it would be easier to climb over the rocks than to resist the tide, she clambered up on the jagged rocks that lined the beach and began picking her way over them. She had to watch every step, for the moonlight was treacherous, making her misjudge distances. Several times she wrenched her ankles, despite taking all the care in the world, but she persisted and at last, when she looked up, she saw that she was only a few feet from the path.

In relief she straightened and stepped onto a flat rock; but the rock was loose and she dislodged it, sending it skittering down, to splash into the water. For a moment she teetered, trying to regain her balance, but another rock slipped under her foot and with a cry she fell sideways. Her head banged against a rock and instant nausea boiled in her stomach; only instinct kept her clawing at the rocks, trying to catch herself before she fell the entire distance. Her hands tore other rocks loose and she fell painfully, the loose rocks bouncing down onto her and knocking others loose in their turn. She had started a small avalanche and they piled up against her.

When the hail of rocks had stopped, she raised her head and gasped painfully for breath, not certain what had happened. Her head throbbed alarmingly, and when she put her hand up, she felt the rapidly swelling knot under her hair. At least she wasn't bleeding, as far as she could tell, and she hadn't fallen into the water. She sat for a moment trying to still the alarming sway of her vision and the nausea that threatened. The nausea won, and she retched helplessly, but afterward she didn't feel any better. Slowly she realized that she must have hit her head harder than she had first thought, and her exploring fingers told her that the swelling now extended over almost the entire side of her head. She began to shiver uncontrollably.

She wasn't going to get any better sitting here; she needed to get to the villa and wake someone to call a doctor. She tried to stand and groaned aloud at the pain in her head. Her legs were like dead weights; they didn't want to move. She tried again to stand, and it wasn't until another rock was dislodged by her struggles that she saw the rocks lying across her legs.

Well, no wonder she couldn't stand, she told herself fuzzily, pushing at the rocks. She could move some of them, despite the dizziness that made her want to lay her head down and rest, and she pushed those into the sea where it boiled only a few feet below her.

But some of the rocks were too heavy, and her lower legs were securely pinned. She had made a mess of her midnight walk, just as she had made a mess of her marriage; it seemed she couldn't do anything right! Helplessly she began to laugh, but that hurt her head and she stopped.

She tried shouting, knowing that no one would hear her above the booming of the tide, especially as far away as she was from the villa, and shouting hurt her head even worse than laughing had. She fell silent and tilted her head back to stare at the two moons that swung crazily in the sky. Two moons. Two of everything.

A wave hit her in the face and it cleared her senses for a moment. The tide was still coming in. How high did the tide get here? She couldn't remember noticing.

Was it nearly high tide now? Would the water soon start dropping? Smiling wearily, she leaned over and rested her throbbing head on her curled-up arm.

A long time later she was roused by the sound of someone shouting her name. Oddly, she couldn't raise her head, but she opened her eyes and stared through the dim gray light of dawn, trying to see who had called her. She was cold, so cold, and it hurt to keep her eyes open. With a sigh, she closed them again. The shout came again, and now the voice was strangled. Perhaps someone was hurt and needed help. Gathering her strength, she tried to sit up, and the explosion of pain in her head sent her reeling into a tunnel of darkness.

NIGHTMARES TORMENTED HER. A black-eyed devil kept bending over her, hurting her, and she screamed and tried to push him away from her, but he kept coming back when she least expected it. She wanted Nikolas, he would keep the devil from hurting her, but then she would remember that Nikolas didn't love her and she knew she had to fight alone. And there was the pain in her head, her legs, that stabbed at her whenever she tried to push the devil away. Sometimes she cried weakly to herself, wondering when it would end and someone would help her.

Gradually she realized that she was in a hospital. She knew the smells, the sounds, the starchy white uniforms that moved around. What had happened? Oh, yes, she had fallen on the rocks. But even when she knew where she was, she still cried out in fear when that big, black-eyed man leaned over her. Part of her knew now that he wasn't a devil; he must be a doctor, but there was something about him...he reminded her of someone....

Then at last she opened her eyes and her vision was clear. She lay very still in the high hospital bed, mentally taking stock of herself and discovering what parts worked, what parts didn't work. Her arms and hands generally obeyed commands, though a needle was taped to the inside of her left arm and a clear plastic line attached it to an upside-down bottle that hung over her head. She frowned at the apparatus until that became clear in her mind and she knew it for what it was. Her legs worked also, though every movement was painful and she was stiff and sore in every muscle.

Her head. She had banged her head. Slowly she raised her right arm and touched the side of her head. It was still swollen and tender, but her hair was still there, so she knew that the injury hadn't been serious enough to warrant surgery. All in all, she was extremely lucky, because she hadn't drowned, either.

She turned her head and discovered immediately that it wasn't a smart move; she closed her eyes against the bursting pain, and when it had subsided to a tolerable ache, she opened her eyes again, but this time she didn't move her head. Instead, she looked about the hospital room carefully, moving nothing but her eyes. It was a pleasant room, with curtains at the windows, and the curtains were drawn back to let in the golden crystal of the sunshine. Comfortable-looking chairs were set about the room, one right beside her bed and several others against the far wall. An icon was set in the corner, a gentle little statue of the Virgin Mary in colors of blue and gold, and even from across the room Jessica could make out the gentle, glowing patience on her face. She sighed softly, comforted by the delicate Little Mother.

A sweet fragrance filled the room, noticeable even

above the hospital smells of medicine and disinfectant. Great vases of flowers were set about the room, not roses as she would have expected, but pure white French lillies, and she smiled as she looked at them. She liked lillies; they were such tall, graceful flowers.

The door opened slowly, almost hesitantly, and from the corner of her eye Jessica recognized the white of Madame Constantinos's hair. She wasn't foolish enough to turn her head again but she said, "Maman," and was surprised at the weakness of her own voice.

"Jessica, love, you're awake again," Madame Constantinos said joyously, coming into the room and closing the door behind her. "I should tell the doctor, I know, but first I want to kiss you, if I may. We've all been so worried."

"I fell on the rocks," Jessica said by way of explanation.

"Yes, we know," Madame Constantinos said, brushing Jessica's cheek with her soft lips. "That was three days ago. To complicate the concussion you had, you developed an inflammation in your lungs from the soaking you received, all on top of shock. Niko has been frantic; we haven't been able to make him leave the hospital even to sleep."

Nikolas. She didn't want to think about Nikolas. She thrust all thoughts of him out of her tired mind. "I'm still so tired," she murmured, her eyelashes fluttering closed again.

"Yes, of course," Madame Constantinos said gently, patting her hand. "I must tell the nurses now that you're awake; the doctor will want to see you."

She left the room and Jessica dozed, to be awakened some unknown time later by cool fingers closing around her wrist. She opened her eyes to drowsily study the dark, slightly built doctor who was taking her pulse. "Hello," she said when he let her wrist down onto the bed.

"Hello, yourself," he said in perfect English, smiling. "I am your doctor, Alexander Theotokas. Just relax and let me look into your eyes for a moment, h'mmm?"

He shone his little pencil flashlight into her eyes and seemed satisfied with what he found. Then he listened intently to her heart and lungs, and at last put away his chart to smile at her.

"So, you've decided at last to wake up. You sustained a rather severe concussion, but you were in shock, so we postponed surgery until you had stabilized, and then you confounded us by getting better on your own," he teased.

"I'm glad," she said, managing a weak smile. "I don't fancy myself bald-headed."

"Yes, that would have been a pity," he said, touching a thick tawny strand. "Until you consider how adorable you would have been with short baby curls all over your head! Nevertheless, you've been steadily improving. Your lungs are almost clear now and the swelling is nearly gone from your ankles. Both legs were badly bruised, but no bones were broken, though both ankles are sprained."

"The wonder is that I didn't drown," she told him. "The tide was coming in."

"You were soaking wet anyway; the water reached at least to your legs," he told her. "But you've improved remarkably; I think that perhaps in another week or ten days you may go home."

"So long?" she questioned sleepily.

"You must wait until your head is much better," he said, gently insistent. "Now, you have a visitor outside who is pacing a trench in the corridor. I will light a candle tonight in thanks that you have recovered consciousness, for Niko has been a wild man and I was at my wits' end trying to control him. Perhaps after he has talked to you he will get some sleep, eh, and eat a decent meal?"

"Nikolas?" she asked, her brow puckering with anxiety. She didn't feel up to seeing Nikolas now; she was so confused. So many things had gone wrong between them....

"No!" she gasped, reaching out to clutch the doctor's sleeve with weakly desperate fingers. "Not yet—I can't see him yet. Tell him I've gone back to sleep—"

"Calm down, calm down," Dr. Theotokas murmured, looking at her sharply. "If you don't want to see him, you don't have to. It's simply that he has been so worried, I thought perhaps you might tell him at least to go to a hotel and get a good night's sleep. He has been here for three days, and he's scarcely closed his eyes."

Madame Constantinos had said much the same thing, so it must be true. Taking a deep breath, she steadied her wildly tingling nerves and breathed out an assenting murmur.

The doctor and his retinue of nurses left the room, and immediately the door was pushed open again as Nikolas shouldered his way past the last nurse to leave. After one shocked glance, Jessica looked away. He needed to shave and his eyes were hollow and red with exhaustion. He was pale, his expression strained. "Jessica," he said hoarsely.

She swallowed convulsively. After that one swift

glance, she knew that the devil who had tormented her in her nightmares was Nikolas; the devil had had those same dark, leanly powerful features. She remembered him bending over her that night, her wedding night, and she shuddered.

"You—you look terrible," she managed to whisper. "You need to sleep. Maman and the doctor said you haven't slept—"

"Look at me," he said, and his voice sounded as though he was tearing it out of his throat.

She couldn't. She didn't want to see him; his face was the face of the devil in her nightmares, and she still lingered halfway between reality and that dream world.

"Jessica, my God, look at me!"

"I can't," she choked. "Go away, Nikolas. Get some sleep; I'll be all right. I just—I just can't talk to you yet."

She sensed him standing there by her side, willing her to look at him, but she closed her eyes again on an acid burning of tears, and with a smothered exclamation he left the room.

It was two days before he visited her again and she was grateful for the respite. Madame Constantinos had carefully explained that Nikolas was asleep, and Jessica believed it. He had looked totally exhausted. According to his mother, he slept for thirty-six hours, and when she reported with satisfaction in her voice that Niko had finally woken up, Jessica began to brace herself. She knew that he would be back, and she knew that this time she wouldn't be able to put him off. He had given in to her the last time only because she was still so groggy and he had been tired; she wouldn't have that protection now. But at least now she could think clearly, though she still had no idea what she would do.

She only knew her emotions; she only knew that she bitterly resented him for ruining her wedding day, childish though she knew she was being about that. She was also angry, with him and with herself, because of the fiasco of their wedding night. Anger, humiliation, resentment and outraged pride all warred within her, and she didn't know if she could ever forgive him.

She had improved enough that she had been allowed out of bed, even though she went no farther than the nearest chair. Her head still ached sickeningly if she tried to move rapidly, and in any case her painful ankles did not yet permit much walking. She found the chair to be marvelously comfortable after lying down for so long, and she talked the nurses into leaving her there until she tired; she was still sitting up when Nikolas came.

The afternoon sun streamed in through the windows and caught his face, illuminating starkly the strong bone structure, the grim expression. He looked at her silently for a long moment, and just as silently she stared back, unable to think of anything to say. Then he turned and hung the DO NOT DISTURB sign on the door, or at least she thought that was what it said, as she couldn't read Greek.

He closed the door securely behind him and came around the foot of the bed to stand before her chair, looking down at her. "I won't let you run me out this time," he said grimly.

"No," she agreed, looking at her entwined fingers.

"We have a lot to talk about."

"I don't see why," she said flatly. "There's nothing to say. What happened, happened. Talking about it won't change anything."

His skin tightened over his cheekbones and suddenly he squatted down before her so he could look into her face. His chiseled lips were pulled into a thin line and his black eyes burned over her face. She almost flinched from him; fury and desire warred in his eyes, and she feared both. But she controlled herself and gave him back look for look.

"I want to know about your marriage," he demanded curtly. "I want to know how you came to me still a virgin, and damn it, Jessica, I want to know why in hell you didn't tell me!"

"I tried," she replied just as curtly. "Though I don't know why. I don't have to explain anything to you," she continued, unable to give in to his anger. She had endured too much from Nikolas; she couldn't take any more.

A vein throbbed dangerously in his temple. "I have to know," he muttered in a low tone, his voice becoming strained. "God in heaven, Jessica—please!"

She trembled to hear that word from him, to hear Nikolas Constantinos saying please to anyone. He, too, was under a great deal of tension; it was revealed in the rigid set of his shoulders, the uncompromising lines of his mouth and jaw. She let out her breath on a shuddering sigh.

"I married Robert because I loved him," she finally muttered, her fingers picking unconsciously at the robe she wore. "I still do. He was the kindest man I've ever known. And he loved me!" she asserted with a trace of wildness, lifting up her tangled tawny head to glare at him. "No matter how much filth you and people like you throw at me, you can't change the fact that we loved each other. Maybe—maybe it was a different kind of love, because we didn't sleep together, didn't try to have sex, but I would have given my life for that man, and he knew it."

His hand lifted, and even though she shrank back in the chair, he put his hand on her throat, caressing her soft skin and letting his fingers slide warmly to her shoulder, then downward to cup a breast where it thrust against her robe. Despite the tingle of alarm that ran along her skin, she didn't object to his touch, because she had learned to her cost that he could be dangerous when he was thwarted. Instead, she watched the raw hunger that leaped into his eyes.

His gaze lifted from where his thumb teased and aroused her flesh to probe her face. "And this, Jessica?" he asked hoarsely. "Did he ever do this to you? Was he incapable? Did he try to make love to you and fail?"

"No! No to all of it!" Her voice wobbled out of control and she took a deep breath, fighting for poise, but it was hard to act calm when the mere touch of his thumb on her breast was searing her flesh. "He never tried. He said once that love was much sweeter when it wasn't confused by basic urges."

"He was old," Nikolas muttered, suddenly losing patience with the robe and tugging it open, exposing the silky nightgown underneath. His fingers slid inside the low neckline to cup and stroke the naked curves under the silk, making her shudder with mingled response and rejection. "Too old," he continued, staring at her bosom. "He'd forgotten the fires that can burn away a man's sanity. Look at my hand, Jessica. Look at it on your body. It drove me mad to think of an old man's spotted, shriveled hand touching you like this. It was even worse than thinking of you with other men."

Involuntarily she looked down and a wild quiver ran through her at the contrast of his strong, dark fingers on her apricot-tinted flesh. "Don't talk about him like that," she defended shakily. "I loved him! And one day you, too, will be old, Nikolas."

"Yes, but it will still be *my* hand doing the touching." He looked up again and now two spots of color were spreading across his cheekbones as he became more aroused. "It wouldn't have made any difference how old he was," he admitted raggedly. "I couldn't bear the thought of any other man touching you, and when you wouldn't let me make love to you, I thought I'd go mad with frustration."

She couldn't think of anything to say and she drew back so that his hand was dislodged from her breast. Temper flared in his eyes and she realized that Nikolas would never be able to accept her will over his, even in the matter of her own body. The thought killed the tiny heat of response in her and she threw out coolly, "None of that matters now; it's over with. I think it would be best if I returned to London—"

"No!" he snapped savagely, rising to his feet and pacing about the small room with the restless stride of a panther. "I won't let you run away from me again. You ran away the other night and look what happened to you. Why, Jessica?" he asked, his voice suddenly husky. "Were you so frightened of me that you couldn't stay in my bed? I know that I— My God, why didn't you tell me? Why didn't you make me listen? By the time I realized, it was impossible for me to stop. It won't be like that again, sweet, I promise. I felt so guilty; then, when I saw you lying across those rocks, I thought that you'd—" He stopped, his face grim, and suddenly Jessica remembered the voice she thought had been pure imagination, calling out her name. So it had been Nikolas who had found her.

But his words froze her emotions in her breast. He felt *guilty*. She could think of a lot of reasons he could have given her for wanting her to stay, but few of them would have so insulted her sense of pride. She'd *swim* back to England before she'd stay with him merely to let him assuage his sense of guilt! She wanted to rage at him in her hurt and humiliation, but instead she pulled a mantle of deceptive calm about her and strove instinctively for her mask of cool disdain, so carefully cultivated over the years. "Why should I have told you?" she asked in a remote little voice, ignoring the fact that she had tried to do that very thing for weeks. "Would you have believed me?"

He made a slashing movement with his hand, as if that wasn't important. "You could have had a doctor examine you, given me proof," he growled. "You could have let me find out for myself, but in a manner much less brutal than what you endured. If you'd told me, if you hadn't fought…"

For a moment she merely stared at him, astonished at his unbelievable arrogance. Regardless of his billions and his surface sophistication, underneath he was Greek to the core of him and a woman's pride counted for nothing.

"Why should I prove anything to you?" she jeered out of the depths of her misery. "Were you a virgin? Who set you up to judge my character?"

Dark anger washed into his face and he took one long stride toward her, reaching out as if he longed to shake her, but then he remembered her injuries and he let his arms fall. She glared at him stonily as he drew a deep breath, obviously trying to control his temper. "You brought it on yourself," he finally snapped, "if that is your attitude."

"Is it my fault you're a bully and a tyrant?" she challenged, hearing her voice rise with temper. "I tried to tell you from the day we met that you were wrong about me, but you categorically refused to listen, so don't try to throw it all back on me! I should never have come back from Cornwall."

He stood looking down at her, his hard face unreadable, then his mouth twisted bitterly. "I'd have come after you," he said.

She pushed away the disturbing words and sought for control over her temper. When she could speak without any heat, she said distantly, "It's all over, anyway; it's no use crying about what might have been. I suggest a quiet, quick divorce—"

"No!" he gritted murderously. "You're my wife, and you'll stay my wife. I'm a possessive man, and I don't let my possessions go. You're mine, Jessica, in fact as well as in name, and you'll stay on the island even if I have to make you a prisoner."

"What a charming picture!" she cried in sudden desperation. "Let me go, Nikolas. I won't stay with you."

"You'll have to," he told her, his black eyes gleaming. "The island is mine, and no one leaves without my permission. The people are loyal to me; they won't help you to escape no matter how you charm them."

Impotently she glared at him. "I'll make you a laughingstock," she warned.

"Try it, my dear, and you'll find out the extent of a Greek husband's authority over his wife," he warned.

"I won't look such a laughingstock when you're sitting on pillows."

"You'd better not lay a hand on me!" she said furiously. "You may be Greek, but I'm not, and I won't be punished by you."

"I doubt if it will be necessary," he said, drawling now, and she knew that he was once more in command of the situation and aware of what he was going to do. "You'll be more cautious now about pushing me, won't you, love?"

"Get out!" she shouted, rising to her feet in a temper that made her forget her tender head, and she was forcefully reminded of her injuries as nauseating pain crashed into her skull and she wobbled on her unsteady feet. Instantly he was beside her, lifting her in his arms and placing her on the bed, easing her down onto the pillows. Through a haze of pain she said again, "Go away!"

"I'll go, until you've calmed down," he told her, leaning over her like the devil in her dreams. "But I'll be back, and I'll take you back to the island with me. Like it or not, you're my wife now and you'll stay my wife." On those final words he left her, and she stared through a mist of tears at the ceiling, wondering how she could endure such open warfare in the place of marriage.

CHAPTER ELEVEN

BUT IT WASN'T open warfare. Nikolas wouldn't allow that, and she was helpless to fight him. The only weapon she had was her coldness, and she used that relentlessly, not giving an inch to him when he came to visit her. He ignored her lack of response and talked to her pleasantly, telling her of the day-to-day happenings on the island and the people who asked about her. Everyone sent their love and wanted to know when she would be out of the hospital, and she found it extraordinarily difficult to keep from responding to that. In the few short days she had been on the island she had been made so welcome that she missed the people there, especially Petra and Sophia.

It was on the morning that she was released from the hospital that Nikolas shredded her self-possession, and he did it so easily that afterward she realized he had only been waiting until she was stronger to take action. When he sauntered into her room and found her already dressed and ready to leave, he kissed her casually before she could draw back, then released her before she could react to that, either.

"I'm glad you're ready," he commented, picking up the small suitcase containing the few clothes he had brought for her stay in the hospital. "Maman and Petra gave me strict orders to bring you back as soon as possible, and Sophia has cooked a special dinner for you. Would you like to have *soupa avgolemono,* eh? You liked that, didn't you?"

"Why don't you save yourself the trouble of taking me back and just put me on a plane for London?" she asked coolly.

"And what if you did go to London?" he returned, looking down at her with exasperation in his eyes. "You'd be alone, the butt of more cruelty than you can imagine, especially if you're pregnant."

Stunned, she looked up at him and he said mockingly, "Unless *you* took precautions? No? I didn't think so, and I confess that the thought never entered my mind."

Impotently she glared at him. She wanted to hit him, and at the same time she melted oddly inside at the thought of having his baby. Damn him, in spite of everything, she knew with a bitter sense of resignation that she still loved him. It wasn't something she would recover from, yet she wanted to hurt him because he had hurt her. She was shocked at the violence of her feelings and she tore her gaze away from him, looking down at her hands.

It took every ounce of her willpower to keep the tears from falling and she said defeatedly, "All right. I'll stay until I know if I'm going to have a baby or not."

"That could take a while," he told her, smiling smugly. "After your fall, your entire system could be out of balance. And I intend to do everything I can to make you pregnant if that's what it takes to keep you on the island."

"Oh!" she cried, drawing away from him, shattered

at the thought. Her panic was plain in her eyes as she stared at him. "Nikolas, no. I can't take that again."

"It won't be like that again," he assured her, reaching out to catch her arm.

"I won't let you touch me!"

"That's another right husbands have over wives." He grinned, pulling her to him. "Make up your mind to it now, pet; I'm going to be exercising my marital rights. That's why I married you."

She was so upset that she went without protest to the taxi he had waiting, and she didn't talk to him at all on the drive through Athens to the airport. At any other time she would have been enchanted with the city, but now she was frightened by his words and her head had begun to ache.

Nikolas's own helicopter was at the airport, fueled up and ready for flight, and through a haze of pain Jessica realized that he must have brought her to the hospital in the helicopter. She had no memory of anything after the last time she fainted on the rocks, and suddenly she wanted to know what had happened.

"Nikolas, you found me, didn't you? When I fell?"

"Yes," he said, frowning. He slanted a look down at her and his gaze halted, surveying her pale, strained face.

"What happened then? After you found me, I mean."

He took her arm and led her across the tarmac to the helicopter, walking slowly and letting her lean on him. "At first I thought you were dead," he said remotely, but the harsh breath he drew told her that the memory wasn't something he could handle easily, even now. "When I got down to you, I found that you were still alive and I dug you out from under those rocks, then carried you back up to the villa. Sophia was already up; she was beginning to cook when she saw me coming up the path with you, and she ran to help me."

They had reached the helicopter and he opened the door, then lifted her onto the seat and closed the door securely. He walked around and slid his long frame onto the seat in front of the controls and reached for the headset. He looked at it in his hand, frowning absently. "You were soaked, and shivering," he continued. "While Andros contacted the hospital and made arrangements for transportation from the airport to the hospital, Maman and I stripped you and wrapped you in blankets, then we flew here. You were in deep shock and surgery was postponed, though the doctors were concerned, but Alex told me that you almost certainly wouldn't survive major surgery at that time; your condition had to stabilize before he could even consider it."

"Then I got better," she finished for him, smiling wanly.

He didn't smile in return. "Your responses were better," he muttered. "But you developed a fever, and your lungs were inflamed. Sometimes you were unconscious; sometimes you were delirious and screamed whenever I or any of the doctors came near you." He turned his head to look at her, his eyes flat and bitter. "At least it wasn't just me; you screamed at every man."

She couldn't tell him that it had been him she had feared, and after a moment of silence he put the headset on and reached for the radio controls. Jessica leaned her head back and closed her eyes, willing the throb in her temples to go away, but when the rotors began turning, it increased the pain and she winced. A hand on her knee brought her eyelids fluttering open and at Nikolas's concerned, questioning gaze she put her hands over her ears to let him know what was wrong. He nodded and patted her leg sympathetically, which made her want to cry. She closed her eyes again, shutting out the vision of him.

Unbelievably, she slept on the flight back to the island. Perhaps there was something in the medication she was still taking that made her drowsy, but Nikolas had to wake her when the flight was over and she sat up in confusion to see what seemed like the entire population of the island turned out for her arrival. Everyone was smiling and waving and she waved back, touched to tears by the warmth she felt from the islanders. Nikolas jumped from the helicopter, yelling something that made everyone laugh, then he reached her side as she released her seat belt and he slid the door open.

With an ease that both frightened and elated her, he reached in and lifted her against his chest. "I can walk," she protested.

"Not down the hill," he said. "You're still too wobbly. Put your arms around me, love; let everyone see what they want to see."

It was true that when she slid her arms around his muscular neck it seemed to please everyone, and several jocular-sounding remarks were made to him, to which he responded with grins and several remarks of his own. Jessica promised herself that she would learn Greek without delay; she wanted to know what he was saying about her.

He carried her down to the villa and straight to his bedroom, for she couldn't think of it as theirs. As he placed her on the bed, she looked around wildly, and before she could choke the words back, she cried out, "I can't sleep here, Nikolas!"

With a sigh he sat down on the edge of the bed. "I'm sorry you feel that way, darling, because you'll have to sleep here. Rather, you'll have to sleep with me, and that's what has you worried, isn't it?"

"Can you blame me?" she questioned fiercely.

"Yes, I can," he returned calmly, his black eyes implacable. "You're an intelligent, adult woman, and you should be capable of realizing that future lovemaking between us will be nothing like our wedding night. I was half-drunk, frustrated, and I lost control. You were frightened and angry and you fought me. The result was predictable and you got hurt. It won't be like that again, Jessica. The next time I take you, you'll enjoy it as much as I will."

"Can't you understand that I don't want you?" she flashed, unreasonably angry that he should so calmly plan on making love to her when she had said he couldn't. "Really, Nikolas, your conceit must be colossal if you imagine that I'd want to sleep with you after that night."

Temper flared in his eyes. "You can thank God that I know you so well, Jessica, or I'd make you regret those words!" he snapped. "But I *do* know you, and I know that when you're hurt and frightened you strike back like a spitting, clawing kitten, and you have years of practice in putting on that cold mask of yours. Oh, no, darling, you don't fool me. No matter how your pride tells you to resist me, I remember a night in London when you came to me and whispered that you loved me. You were sweet and shy that night; you weren't acting. Do you remember it, too?"

Jessica's eyes closed in horror. That night! How could she forget? And how like Nikolas to remember the secret she had said aloud, thinking that he'd return the sweet words and admit to loving her. But he hadn't, not then and not since. Words of passion had come from his lips, but never words of love. Shaking, she cried out, "Remember? How can I forget? Like a fool I let you get too close to me, and the words were barely out of my mouth when you slapped me in the face with your true opinion of me. At least you opened my eyes, jerked me out of my silly dream. Love isn't immortal, Nikolas. It can die."

"Your's didn't die," he murmured confidently, a smile curving his hard, chiseled lips. "You married me, and you wanted your white gown for the wedding. You wore your hair in the style of a virgin; yes, I noticed. Everything you did shouted that you were marrying me forever, and that's how it will be. I've hurt you, darling, and I've made you unhappy, but I'll make it up to you. By the time our first baby is born, you'll have forgotten that I ever made you shed a tear."

That remark almost made her leap off the bed, and to prove him wrong she promptly burst into tears, which played havoc with her headache. With a comforting murmur Nikolas took her in his arms and lay down on the bed with her to hold her close and whisper soothingly to her, and perversely his nearness did calm her. At last she hiccupped into silence and nestled closer against him, her face buried in his shirt. Out of that doubtful sanctuary she said hesitantly, "Nikolas?"

"Yes, darling?" he muttered, his deep voice rumbling under her ear.

"Will—will you give me a little time, please?" she asked, raising her tear-stained face to him.

"I'll only give you time to recover completely," he replied, brushing her hair back from her temples with gentle fingers. "Beyond that, I won't wait. I can't. I still want you like mad, Mrs. Constantinos. Our wedding night was a mere appetizer."

She quivered in his arms at the sudden vision she had of being devoured by him, as if he were a hungry animal. She felt torn by indecision, loving him but unable to give in to him, to trust him or know what he was about. "Please don't rush me," she whispered. "I'll try; I really will. But I—I don't know if I'll ever be able to forgive you."

One corner of his mouth jerked before he firmed his lips together and said, "Forgive me or not, you're still mine, and I'll never let you go. I'll repeat it as many times as I have to to make you believe me."

"We've made a mess of it, Niko," she whispered painfully, tears filling her eyes again as she used the shortened, affectionate version of his name for the first time.

"Yes, I know," he muttered, his eyes going bleak. "We'll just have to try to salvage something and make our marriage work."

After he had gone, Jessica lay on the bed trying to quiet her confused emotions; she felt so many things at once that she was helpless to sort them out. With part of herself she wanted to melt into his arms and give in to the love which she still felt for him in spite of everything that had happened; the other part of her was bitterly angry and resentful and wanted to get as far away from him as possible. For years, she had suppressed pain and loneliness, but Nikolas had ripped away the barrier of her self-control and she could no longer push away or ignore the aches. Her long-controlled emotions were boiling out of her in a bitter release, and she resented the way he had torn away her defenses.

What a mockery of a marriage, she thought tiredly. A woman shouldn't require defenses against her husband; a marriage should be based on mutual trust and respect, and even now Nikolas felt neither of those things for her. She had thought that when he realized how wrong his assumptions concerning her had been, his entire attitude would change, but she'd been wrong. Perhaps he no longer resented her so bitterly, but he still would not allow her any authority concerning her own life. He wanted to control her, make her every movement subject to his whim, and Jessica didn't think she could tolerate a life like that.

After a time she dozed, and woke to the long shadows of late afternoon. Her headache had eased; in fact, it was gone, and she felt better than she had since the accident. Getting out of bed, she walked carefully to the bathroom, fearing an onset of her headache, but it didn't return and gratefully she stripped off her wrinkled clothing and ran water in the huge, red-tiled sunken tub. Petra had supplied the bathroom with an assortment of toiletries that surely Nikolas had never used, unless he had a hidden passion for perfumed bubble bath, and she poured the liquid liberally into the tub until it had mountains of foam in it.

After pinning her hair up, she stepped into the tub and sank down until the bubbles tickled her chin. She reached for the soap, then gave a frightened squeal as the door opened without warning. Nikolas stepped through, a worried frown creasing his brow, but the frown turned into a grin as he surveyed her where she lay, all but submerged in the bubbles. "Sorry, didn't mean to startle you," he said.

"I'm taking a bath," she said indignantly, and his grin spread wider.

"So I see," he agreed, dropping his tall frame onto the floor by the tub and sprawling out to lean on his elbow. "I'll keep you company, since this is the first time I've been privileged to witness your bath and wild horses couldn't drag me away."

"Nikolas!" she wailed, her cheeks flushing red.

"Now, calm down," he soothed, reaching out to run a finger over her nose. "I promised you that I wouldn't make a pass at you, and I won't, but I didn't promise that I wouldn't get to know my wife and let her become accustomed to me."

He was lying. Suddenly she knew that he was lying and she jerked away from his hand, tears springing to her eyes. "Get away from me!" she cried hoarsely. "I don't believe you, Nikolas! I can't stand it. Please, please go away!" If he stayed, he would take her to bed and make love to her, regardless of his promise. He had only told her that to catch her off guard, and she couldn't submit to him again. Shuddering sobs began to quake through her body, and with a muffled curse he got to his feet, his face darkening with fury.

"All right," he said through gritted teeth. "I'll leave you alone. God, how I'll leave you alone! A man can take only so much, Jessica, and I've had it! Keep your empty bed; I'll sleep elsewhere." He stormed out of the bathroom, slamming the door behind him with a force that jarred it on its hinges, and a second later she heard the bedroom door slam, too.

She winced and drew a shuddering breath, trying to control herself again. Oh, it was useless; this marriage would never work. Somehow she'd have to convince Nikolas to set her free, and after tonight that shouldn't be too difficult.

NIKOLAS, HOWEVER, PROVED himself unyielding in his refusal to let her leave the island. She was aware that he looked at the situation as a battle he had every intention of winning, despite her constant maneuvering to keep a comfortable distance between them. She also saw that his anger at her in the bathroom had been largely staged, for what reason she didn't know. He was irritated that she didn't fall into his arms whenever he touched her, the way she had prior to their marriage, but he had no intention of denying himself the pleasures of her body if he could find the slightest weakness in her resistance. He was simply waiting, watching her carefully, ready to pounce.

The strain of keeping up a front of calmness and serenity before everyone else was telling on her, but she didn't want to distress Nikolas's mother, or even Petra or Sophia. Everyone had been so kind to her—after her release from the hospital she had been coddled shamelessly by the entire household—that the last thing she wanted was to worry them with a warlike atmosphere. By silent, mutual consent, she and Nikolas let it be assumed that he slept in another room because her head still ached and his restlessness interfered with her sleep. As she was still plagued by headaches if she tried to exert herself in any way, the explanation was accepted without question.

Without making a big production out of it, she pretended that she was not recovering as rapidly as she really was, using her physical condition as a weapon against Nikolas. She rested frequently and would sometimes slip away without comment to lie down with a cold, damp cloth over her eyes and forehead. Someone would usually check on her before too long, and in that manner she made certain the entire household was aware of her delicacy. She hated to trick them like that, but she had to protect herself, and she was aware that she would have to take whatever chance presented itself if she was to escape from the island. If everyone thought her weaker than she actually was, she had a better chance of succeeding.

The opportunity presented itself the next week when Nikolas informed them at the dinner table that he and Andros were flying to Athens the following morning; they would spend the night and return to the island the next day. Jessica was careful not to look up, certain that her expression would give her away. This was it! All she had to do was to hide onboard the helicopter, and once they had landed in Athens and Nikolas and Andros had left to attend their meeting, she could slip out of the craft, walk into the terminal building, and purchase a ticket for a flight out of Athens.

She spent the evening making her plans; she retired early and packed the essentials she would take with her in the smallest suitcase she had, then replaced the case in the closet. She checked her purse to make certain that the money she had brought was still in her wallet; it was, as Nikolas no doubt felt certain that no one on the island was susceptible to a bribe, and in that he was probably correct. But she hadn't even thought of that, and now she was glad that she hadn't, as he would probably have taken the money away from her if she had tried something like that.

She counted the money carefully; when she had left England to travel to Paris with Nikolas, she had provided herself with enough cash to buy anything she might want, or to cover any emergency she was likely to encounter. Every penny was still there. She wasn't certain that it was enough to purchase a ticket to London, but she could certainly get out of Greece. Even if she could only get as far as Paris, she could telephone Charles and have him wire extra funds to her. Nikolas had control of her business concerns, but she hadn't emptied her bank account, and those funds were still available to her.

Later, when everyone had retired, she would take the suitcase and hide it in the helicopter. From her previous trips in it, she knew that there was a small space behind the rear seats, and she thought that there was enough room for both herself and the suitcase. To be certain, she would take a dark blanket and huddle under it on the floor if she couldn't get behind the seats. Remembering the construction of the helicopter, she thought it would be possible for someone to hide in that manner. The helicopter was built to carry six passengers, and the seats were broad and comfortable. Nikolas would pilot the craft himself, and Andros would be in the seat next to him; there would be no reason for them to look behind the rear seats.

As a plan, it had a lot of drawbacks, relying too heavily on chance and happenstance, but it was the only plan she had and probably the only chance she would have, as well, so she had to take the risk. It wasn't in her mind to disappear forever, but only until she'd had the chance to become certain within herself how she felt about Nikolas, and whether or not she wanted to continue with their marriage. All she asked was a little time and a little distance, but Nikolas wouldn't willingly give her what she needed. Jessica felt that she had been pushed and pulled more than she could stand. From the moment she had met Nikolas, he had maneuvered and manipulated her until she felt more like a doll than a woman, and it had become essential to her that she regain control of her own life.

Once, naïvely, she had thought that love could solve any problem, but that was another dream that had been shattered. Love didn't solve anything; it merely complicated matters. Loving Nikolas had brought her a great deal of pain and very little in the way of happiness. Some women could have been content with the physical gratification that he offered and accepted that he didn't love them in return, but Jessica wasn't certain that she possessed the sort of strength that required. That was what she had to discover about herself: whether she loved Nikolas enough to live with him regardless of the circumstances, whether she could make herself accept the fact that she had his desire but not his love. A lot of marriages were based on less than love, but she had to be certain before she let herself be maneuvered once again into a corner with nowhere to turn.

She knew her husband; his plan was to get her pregnant, thereby tying her irrevocably to the island and to him. She also knew that she had very little time left before he began putting his plan into action. He'd left her alone thus far, but she was nearly fully recovered now, and she sensed with sharpened instincts that he was now entirely unconvinced by her charade and would come to her bed at any time. She knew that she had to escape now if she was to have that time by herself to decide on a calm, reasonable level whether she could continue living with him.

After putting her purse away, she prepared for bed and turned out the lights, not wanting to do anything suspicious. She lay quietly in bed, her body relaxed but her mind alert to every sound in the villa.

The bedroom door opened, and a tall, broad-shouldered form threw a long shadow over her. "Are you awake?" Nikolas asked quietly.

For answer, Jessica reached out and switched on the lamp. "Is something wrong?" She struggled up to prop herself on her elbow, her eyes wide and wary as she watched him enter the room and close the door behind him.

"I need a few things from the closet," he informed her, and her heart stopped as she watched, paralyzed, while he crossed to the closet and slid the doors open. What if he should take the suitcase that contained the clothing she had packed? Why hadn't she insisted that he take his things out of the closet? But that would have looked odd to his mother, and in all honesty he hadn't taken advantage of the situation. What clothing he needed, he took from the closet sometime during the day, and never at times when he might find her undressed.

He took down one of his own suitcases made of dark brown leather, and she drew a shuddering breath of relief. He looked at her sharply. "Are you feeling all right? You look ill."

"Just the usual headache." She forced herself to answer calmly, and before she could stop herself she blurted out, "Do you want me to pack for you?"

A grin slashed the darkness of his face. "Do you think I'll make an unholy mess of folding my shirts? I manage well enough, but thank you for the offer. When I return," he added thoughtfully, "I think I'll take you back to Dr. Theotokas for another examination."

She didn't want that, but as she planned to be gone before then she made no protest. "Because of the headaches? Didn't he say that it would take time for them to go away?"

He took a shirt from the clothes hanger and folded the garment neatly before placing it in the opened suitcase. "Yes, but I think you should be making a better recovery than you are. I want to make certain there aren't any other complications."

Like a pregnancy? The thought sprang without warning into her mind, and she began to tremble. It was possible, of course, but surely too early to tell. She didn't have any idea herself as yet. But wouldn't it be ironic if she managed to escape Nikolas's clutches and found that she was already pregnant? She wasn't certain what she would do if those circumstances arose, so she pushed the thought from her mind.

Conversation lapsed, and she propped herself higher on the pillow and watched as he completed his packing. When he closed the case and set it aside, he came to sit beside her on the bed. Uneasy at his nearness, she didn't say anything, her eyes unwavering as she watched him. A crooked little smile twitched at his lips. "I'll be leaving at dawn," he murmured, "so I won't wake you up. Will you give me a good-bye kiss tonight?"

She wanted to refuse, yet part of her yielded, held her motionless as he bent down and lightly pressed his mouth to hers. It wasn't a demanding kiss, and he straightened away from her almost immediately. "Good night, darling," he said softly, and putting his hands on her ribcage he eased her down beneath the light covers and began to tuck them in around her. She raised her eyes to meet his and gave him a small, timid smile, but it was enough to still his hands in their occupation.

He caught his breath, and his dark eyes began to gleam as the muted glow of the lamp caught their expression. "Good night," he said again, and leaned over her.

This time his mouth lingered, moving over her lips and molding them to meet the pressure of his. The pressure wasn't intense, but still the contact remained, warm and enticing, his breath sweet and heady with the wine they had had with dinner. Unconsciously she put her hand on his arm and stroked her fingers upward to clasp his shoulder, then on to curve about his neck. He deepened the kiss, his tongue meeting hers and exploring, making exciting forays against the sensitive places he found, and Jessica felt herself drifting into the red haze of sensual pleasure, not yet alarmed by his touch.

With a slow movement he folded the covers down far enough to let the soft curves of her breasts become visible to his avid gaze. He lifted his head from hers and watched as his long fingers slid beneath the thin silk of her nightgown and curved over the rich flesh, then moved up again to catch the strap and draw it down her arm. Jessica made a small gesture of fear, but he was being so slow and gentle that she didn't struggle; instead her lips sought his flesh eagerly, tasting the slightly salty taste of the skin along his cheekbone, the curve of his jaw. He turned his head and their mouths met again, and her eyelashes fluttered closed. The leisurely movement of his hand urged the pink silk slowly lower, baring the upper curve of one breast. Then the delicate rosy nipple was free and his hand left the strap to capture her exposed beauty.

"Now I'll kiss you good night," he whispered and he shifted so that his mouth slid down the arched curve of her throat. He paused, and his tongue explored the sensitive hollow between her neck and shoulder blade, making her shiver with a delight which was rapidly growing beyond her control. She didn't care. If he had only been this slow and tender on their wedding night, perhaps none of their problems would still exist. She lay quietly under his wandering touch, enjoying the delicate sensations and the spreading heat in her body.

Then his lips continued their journey and moved down the satin slope to close hotly over the throbbing bud. She moaned aloud and arched her back, her hand clenched in the rich thickness of his hair as she held his head to her. The gently pulling motions of his mouth set sharp twinges of pure physical desire shooting along her nerve endings. Her trembling intensified, and she started to reach for him; then he released her flesh and lifted his head, drawing back from her.

He was smiling, but the smile was sharp with triumph. "Good night, darling," he murmured, drawing the strap onto her shoulder again. "I'll see you in two days." Then he was gone, taking the suitcase and closing the door silently behind him, and Jessica lay on the bed, biting her lips to keep from screaming in both fury and frustration. He'd done that deliberately, seducing her with his gentleness until she forgot her fear, then not taking her to fulfillment. Were his actions motivated by revenge for the way she'd refused his advances before, or was it all a calculated maneuver to bring her to heel? She rather thought it was the latter, but she was more determined than ever not to give in to him. She would *not* be his sexual slave!

The thought of her escape gave her grim pleasure. He was so certain of his victory; let him wonder what had gone wrong when he found that his wife had fled rather than sleep with him. Nikolas was far too selfish and self-confident; it would do him a world of good to have someone stand up to him every so often.

She set the alarm on the clock for 2:00 a.m., then settled down in the bed, hoping she could sleep. She did, eventually, but had had only a few hours of rest when the alarm went off. She silenced it quickly and got out of bed, then used the flashlight that was always in the drawer of the table by the bed to find her jeans, shirt, and a pair of crepe-soled shoes. She inched the closet door open and removed the small suitcase, then went over to the sliding glass doors that led to the terrace. She released the lock with only a faint click, her hands steady as she slid the door open just enough to allow her to slip through the opening. Hastily she switched off the flashlight, hoping no one was up at this hour to see the betraying light.

There was no moon, but the faint starlight was enough to guide her as she avoided the furniture set about the terrace and made her way silently around to the front of the house. She left the terrace and followed the flagstone path which led up the hill to the helicopter pad. She had gone only a short distance when her legs began to ache and tremble with fatigue, an unwelcome reminder that she truly wasn't completely recovered. Her heart was hammering in her chest when she finally reached the helicopter, and she paused for a moment, breathing rapidly.

The door of the aircraft opened easily, and she crawled inside, banging her hip painfully with the suitcase and muttering an imprecation at the unwieldy luggage. She switched the flashlight on again to pick her way between the seats to the rear. The space behind the rear seats was a mere two feet deep, and she found immediately, by trying to curl up inside it, that it could not accommodate both herself and the suitcase. She placed the suitcase on the floor between the last two sets of seats, but decided that it could be seen too easily in that location.

She studied the interior of the helicopter for a minute, then folded herself once again into the hiding place and stood the suitcase between herself and the back of the seat; the seat was tilted forward a little, but not enough to be noticeable, she hoped. The position was cramped, and she wouldn't be able to move at all until they had landed in Athens and Nikolas and Andros had left, but it was the best she could manage. She left the suitcase in position and crawled out, her legs and arms already stiff from the short time she had been crouching there. She had intended to bring a blanket but had forgotten it, and now she promised herself that when she hid herself prior to takeoff she would have a blanket to cushion the hardness of the cold metal.

Elated, she carefully crept down the hill and into her

bedroom and closed the sliding door behind her. She could have waited in the helicopter, but she had a cautious hunch that Nikolas might look in on her before he left, and she intended to be snug in her bed; underneath the nightgown, though, she would still have on her clothes.

Then she saw that she would have to remove her shirt if she didn't want it to be visible above the nightgown, and she wouldn't have a chance to put it on again. She would have very little time in which to reach the helicopter ahead of the two men, and she didn't want to waste any of it in dressing. She would keep the shirt on, and pull the covers up under her chin.

She kicked her shoes off and stood them beside the bed on the side away from the door, then lay down to rest. She wasn't even tempted to nap; her blood was racing through her veins in excitement, and she waited impatiently for the faint sounds in the silent house that would indicate that someone was moving around.

The sky was just beginning to lighten when she caught the sound of water running and knew that she hadn't long to wait now. She turned on her side to face the door and pulled the covers up snugly under her chin. Forcing herself to breathe deeply and steadily, she waited.

She didn't hear his footsteps; he moved as silently as a big cat, and the first indication she had of his presence was when the door opened almost without a sound and a thin sliver of light fell across the bed. Jessica concentrated on her breathing and peeped through her lashes at him as he stood in the doorway watching her. The seconds ticked away and panic began to coil in her stomach; why was he waiting? Did he sense that something was out of the ordinary?

Then he closed the door with a slow movement, and she drew a deep, shuddering breath of relief. She threw back the covers and slid her feet into the waiting shoes, then snatched up the dark brown blanket that she had gotten out earlier but forgotten to take with her, and let herself out the sliding doors.

Her heart was in her throat, interfering with her breathing as she ran as silently as she could around the house and up the hill. How long did she have? Seconds? If they left the house before she was inside the helicopter, they would see her. Had Nikolas been dressed? She couldn't remember. Panting, she gained the crest of the hill and threw herself at the helicopter, wrenching at the door. It had opened so easily before, but now it was stubborn, and she fumbled at it for several agonizing seconds before the handle turned and the door opened. She scrambled in and closed the door, throwing a hasty look at the house to see if they were coming. No one was in sight yet, and she slumped in the front seat, limp with relief. She hadn't known that escaping would be so nerve-racking, she thought tiredly. Her entire body ached from the unaccustomed exertion, and her head had begun to throb.

Her movements were slower as she crawled to the back of the helicopter and tilted the seat forward to allow her into her hiding place. She spread the blanket and curled up in the small space, her head pillowed on her arm. She was so tired that, despite the uncomfortable position, she felt herself begin to drift into sleep, and it wasn't until Nikolas and Andros boarded the helicopter that she jerked herself back to awareness.

They had noticed nothing unusual, it seemed, but she held her breath.

They exchanged a few words in Greek, and she gnawed her lip in frustration that she couldn't understand them. Madame Constantinos and Petra had taught her a few words, but she hadn't made much progress.

Then she heard the whine of the rotor as it began turning, and she knew that her plan had worked.

The vibration of the metal made her feel as if her skin were crawling, and already she had a cramp in her left calf. She cautiously moved her arm to rub the painful cramp, glad that the beating roar of the blades drowned out all sound. The noise reached a peculiar whine, and they lifted off, the aircraft tilting forward as Nikolas turned it away from the house and toward the sea that lay between the island and Athens.

Jessica had no idea how long the flight lasted, for her head was aching so badly that she closed her eyes and tried to lose herself in sleep. She didn't quite succeed, but she must have dozed because it was the cessation of noise as the blades slowed that alerted her to the fact that they had landed. Nikolas and Andros were talking, and after a moment they both left the helicopter. Jessica lay there listening to the dying whir of the blades. She was afraid to get out immediately in case they were still in the area, so she counted slowly to one thousand before she left her hiding place.

She was so stiff that she had to sit in a seat and rub her protesting legs before they would obey her, and her feet tingled as the circulation was restored. Retrieving the suitcase from behind the seat, she peered out, but could see no one who resembled her husband; so she took a deep breath, opened the door, and climbed out of the helicopter.

It surprised her that no one paid any attention to her as she walked casually across the tarmac and entered the terminal building. She knew from her own experiences that comings and goings at air terminals were carefully watched, and the very fact that no one stopped her to ask her business made her uneasy. It was still early, and though there were a good many people in the building it lacked the crush of the later hours; the women's restroom was almost empty, and none of the women there noticed her as she slipped into one of the stalls and locked the door, then opened her suitcase and took out her purse and the dress she was going to wear. Marveling at the modern fabrics which didn't wrinkle, she stripped off her jeans and shirt and folded them into the open case, then struggled into panty hose and pulled the dress over her head. The smooth, silky fabric felt good against her skin, and she settled the ice blue garment into place, then contorted her arms behind her back to do up the zipper. Comfortable, classic pumps completed the outfit. She placed her other shoes in the suitcase, then fastened it and picked it up in one hand, together with her purse, and left the cubicle.

She did a quick job on her hair, twisting it up and securing it loosely with a few pins, and added glossy coral color to her mouth. Her eyes stared back at her from the mirror, wide and filled with alarm, and she wished that she had sunglasses to hide behind.

Leaving the security of the restroom, she approached the ticket counter and asked the cost of a tourist class ticket to London. Luckily the fare was well within her means, and she purchased a ticket for the next available flight, but there she was stalled. The next flight wasn't until after lunch, and Jessica quailed at the thought of waiting that long. She would be missed on the island long before that; probably even now it had been noticed that she wasn't to be found. Would they search the island first, or notify Nikolas that his wife had disappeared? If only she'd thought to leave a note telling them that she'd gone with Nikolas! That way, no one would have known that she was missing, until Nikolas returned without her.

Her stomach protested its emptiness; so she went to the restaurant and ordered a light breakfast, then sat at the small table trying to force the food down her tight throat. The thought of something going wrong at this late stage was horrifying.

Leaving most of her meal on the plate, she purchased a fashion magazine and tried to ignore her anxiety as she flipped through the glossy pages, noting the newest styles. A glance at her watch increased her anxiety; surely Nikolas had been notified by now. What would he do? He had endless resources; he could tighten security to make certain that she didn't leave the country. She had to be on that jet before he discovered that she had left the island.

The clock ticked slowly, laboriously on. She forced herself to sit quietly, not wanting to draw attention to herself by pacing or in any way betraying her nervousness. The terminal was crowded now as tourists poured into Athens, and she tried to concentrate on the stream of people. How much longer? It was almost noon now. An hour and a half and she would be on her way, provided that there were no delays in takeoff.

When she felt someone at her elbow, she didn't respond immediately, hoping that it was a stranger, but the utter stillness told her that this was a forlorn hope. Fatalistically, Jessica turned her head and gazed calmly into the stony black eyes of her husband.

Though his face was expressionless, she could feel the force of his anger, and she knew that he was livid. Never before had she seen him this angry, and it took more courage than she had known she possessed to stand before him and give him back look for look, but she did it, lifting her chin defiantly. A savage glitter lit his eyes for a brief second, then he disciplined himself and leaned down to pick up her suitcase. "Come with me," he uttered between clenched teeth, and his long fingers wrapped around her arm to ensure that she did as he had ordered.

CHAPTER TWELVE

HE TOOK HER out to the parking area, where a dark blue limousine waited; to her embarrassment, Andros sat in the back. He moved to the opposite end of the seat, and Nikolas helped Jessica in, then climbed in beside her. He spoke sharply to the driver, and the vehicle was set in motion.

It was an utterly silent drive. Nikolas was grim, unspeaking, and she had no intention of unleashing his temper if she could avoid it. In a way, she decided that she was grateful for Andros's presence, as it forced her husband to restrain himself. She couldn't even think about later, when they would be alone.

The limousine stopped at the front entrance of a hotel so modern it would have fit in in the middle of Los Angeles more than in a city which had existed for thousands of years. Dragged along like a child in tow, she was forced to match Nikolas's long strides as they entered the hotel and took the elevator up to the penthouse. He probably owned the hotel, she thought wryly.

She was braced for the worst, and it was an anticlimax when he opened the door and ushered her inside the luxurious apartment, said tersely to Andros, "Don't let her out of your sight," and then left without even glancing at her.

When the door had closed behind him, Andros whistled soundlessly between his teeth. He looked at Jessica ruefully. "I've never seen him so angry before," he told her.

"I know," she said, letting out her breath in a long sigh. "I'm sorry you had to be involved."

He shrugged. "He won't be angry with me unless I let you escape from me, and I don't intend to do that. I'm attached to my neck, and prefer to remain so. How did you leave the island?"

"I hid on the helicopter," she explained, sitting down in one of the extremely comfortable chairs and running her fingers over the royal-blue upholstery. "I had it all planned, and it worked like a charm—except that the flight to London wasn't until after lunch."

He shook his head. "It wouldn't have made any difference. Don't you know that Niko would have traced you long before your flight landed, and you would have been met as you left the plane? Met and detained?"

She hadn't thought of that, and she sighed. If only she had left that note! "I wasn't leaving him for good," she explained, her voice troubled. "But I need some time by myself to think…" She halted, unwilling to discuss her marriage with Andros. He was much friendlier than he had been before he discovered that she loved Nikolas, but some basic reserve made it difficult for her to be so open.

Andros sat down across from her, his lean, dark face anxious. "Jessica, please remember that Niko isn't a man of compromises; yet he has constantly compromised his own rules since he met you. I don't know what has gone wrong between you. I thought that after the wedding things would be better. Would it make you feel more confident to know that Nikolas must care for you, or he wouldn't act as he does?"

No, that didn't help. Sometimes she thought that Nikolas was capable of feeling nothing but lust for her, and guilt that their wedding night had been such a fiasco for her. Their relationship was so tangled that she wondered if anything could save it now.

"Where did he go?" she asked, her spirit draining from her as she remembered how he had refused to look at her. She had insulted him, deceived him, and he wouldn't easily forgive her.

"Back to the meeting he was attending," answered Andros. "It was urgent, or he wouldn't have returned."

Another black mark against her. He had left an important meeting to collect her, and he would be furious that others knew his wife was attempting to leave him.

"No one else knew," said Andros, guessing her thoughts. "He told me only when we were on the way to the airport."

Thank heaven for small favors, she thought, though she doubted that it would make much difference to Nikolas's temper.

There was nothing to do but wait for him to return; though there were books aplenty in the apartment, she couldn't settle down to read. Andros ordered lunch for both of them, and again she had to force herself to eat. After that, time dragged. She put records on the stereo and tried to relax, a useless effort; instead she paced the room, rubbing her arms as if she were chilled.

The magnificent sun was setting when the door finally opened and Nikolas entered, his dark face still a mask which revealed nothing. He didn't say a word to Jessica but conversed with Andros in rapid Greek. Finally Andros nodded and left the apartment, and she was alone with Nikolas.

Her stomach tightened in anticipation, but still he didn't look at her. Pulling his tie loose from his neck, he muttered, "Order dinner while I shower. And don't even try to leave; the staff will stop you before you reach the street."

She believed him and bit her lip in consternation as he disappeared into one of the rooms that opened off the lounge area. She hadn't explored the apartment, having been too nervous to have any interest in her surroundings, so she had no idea of what the different rooms were. Obediently she lifted the telephone and ordered dinner from someone who spoke excellent English, subconsciously choosing those foods that she had noticed Nikolas particularly liked. Was it a feminine instinct, to soothe away male ire by an offering of food? she wondered. When she realized what she had done, she smiled wryly at herself, feeling a strange kinship with cavewomen from thousands and thousands of years ago.

The food arrived as Nikolas reentered the lounge, his black hair still damp from his shower. He was simply dressed in black pants and a white silk shirt, which clung to his body in patches where his skin was wet, leaving his dark skin visible beneath the thin fabric. She watched his face, trying to gauge the extent of his anger, but it was like trying to read a blank wall.

"Sit down," he said remotely. "You've had a busy day; you need to replenish your strength."

The lamb chops and artichoke hearts were the best she had ever tasted, and she was able to eat with an improved appetite despite his hostile presence across from her. She was nearly finished before he spoke again, and she realized that he had waited until then to keep from upsetting her and ruining her appetite.

"I called Maman," he said, "and told her that you were with me. She was frantic, of course; they all were. You'll apologize for your thoughtlessness when we return home, though I managed to gloss over it by telling Maman that you had smuggled yourself to Athens in order to be with me. She was glad that you felt well enough to pursue me so romantically," he finished sarcastically, and Jessica flushed.

"I didn't think of leaving a note until it was too late," she confessed.

He shrugged. "No matter. You'll be forgiven."

She placed her fork carefully beside the plate and gathered her courage. "I wasn't leaving you," she offered in explanation. "At least—"

"It damned well looked as though you were!" he snapped.

"Not permanently," she persisted.

"You're right about that. I would have had you back within two days at the most." He appeared to be on the verge of saying something else, but he bit back the words and said instead, "If you've finished, it would probably be wise if you took your bath now. I'll probably break your neck if I have to listen to your excuses right now!"

For a moment, Jessica sat there defiantly; then she pressed her lips together and did as he had directed. He was in no mood to be reasonable right now, and if she listened to very much more of his sarcasm she was likely to lose her own temper, and she didn't want that to happen. Scenes between herself and Nikolas could quickly become violent and always ended in the same manner, with him making love to her.

She locked herself in the giant bathroom and took a shower, not being in the mood for a long, relaxing bath in the tub. As she toweled herself dry, she noticed a dark blue robe hanging on a hook on the door, and as she hadn't brought a nightgown with her she borrowed the robe and tied it about her. It was enormous, and she had to roll the sleeves up before her hands peeped out. She had to lift the hem in order to walk, and she held the gathered material in her hand as she left the bathroom.

"Very fetching," Nikolas drawled from his reclining position on the bed.

Jessica stopped cold, glaring at him. He had turned off all the lights except for the bedside lamp, and the covers on the bed were turned back. He had also undressed.

She didn't pretend to misunderstand his intentions. Nervously she pushed her hair back from her face. "I don't want to sleep with you."

"That's good, because I have no intention of sleeping."

Her face flamed with temper. "Don't play word games with me! You know very well what I mean."

His black eyes were narrowed as he surveyed her from her bare feet to her disheveled hair. "Yes, I know very well that you have an aversion to sharing a bed with me, but I'm your husband, and I'm tired of my empty bed. It's obvious that if you're well enough to smuggle yourself to Athens, you're well enough to fulfill your wifely obligations."

"You're strong enough that I can't fight you off," she said fiercely. "But you know that I'm not willing.

Why can't you listen to me? Why do you refuse to let me decide for myself how I feel?"

He merely shook his head. "Don't try to throw up a smoke screen of words; it won't work. Take off the robe and come here."

Defiantly she crossed her arms and glared at him. "I wasn't leaving you!" she insisted. "I just wanted some time by myself to—to think and get myself on an even keel again, and I knew you'd never loosen the chains and let me go if I asked you."

"I'm sorry you feel that way about our marriage," he replied in a silky voice, his expression dangerous. "Jessica, darling, are you going to come here, or am I going to have to fetch you?"

"I expect you'll have to fetch me," she stated, not giving in an inch. She tensed all over at the thought of a repeat of his earlier lovemaking, and her face must have revealed the fear she felt because some of the sternness left his expression.

"You don't have to be afraid," he said, uncoiling his length from the bed with a wild grace. Her breath caught in her throat at the untamed beauty of his naked male body, but at the same time she stepped back in alarm.

"No. I don't want to," she said childishly, putting up a hand to ward him off. He merely caught it and used it to pull her close to him, the male scent of him enveloping her and making her feel surrounded by him.

"Don't fight me," he whispered, opening the robe with his free hand and pushing it away from her shoulders to let it drop about her feet in a blue pool. "I promise you won't be hurt, darling. It's time you learned about being my wife, and it's a lesson you'll enjoy."

Jessica shivered, rigid with anxiety, and goose bumps roughened her skin as he leaned down to press his hot mouth into the tender hollow of her shoulder. She remembered the night before, when he had roused her gently into desire, then left her unfulfilled, a calculated move that had left her feeling both insulted and frustrated. His physical desires were hot and demanding, but his brain always remained alert and cool, unaffected by the wildly shifting emotions that kept her so unsettled. Was this merely another calculated maneuver as he tried to break her spirit, tame her into accepting his authority?

She wrenched away from him, shaking her head in denial. "No," she said again, though she had no hope that he would accept her refusal.

He moved swiftly, lifting her into his arms and carrying her the few steps to the bed. He placed her on the cool sheet and followed her down, his arms and legs securing hers and holding her motionless. "Just relax," he crooned, trailing soft kisses over her shoulder and neck, then up to her trembling lips. "I'll take care of you, darling; there's nothing to be afraid of this time."

Violently Jessica turned her head away from him, and he pressed his lips instead to the line of her jaw, the sensitive shell of her ear. She made a strangled sound of protest, and he murmured soothingly to her, continuing the light kisses as he trailed his fingers over her body, learning the soft slopes and curves and reassuring her that this time he wasn't going to be impatient with her.

She tried to hold herself away from the seductive quality of those light, elusive touches on her skin, but she wasn't cold by nature, and eventually her sense of awareness began to dim and grow hazy. Imperceptibly she began to relax in his arms, and her skin warmed, taking on the flushed glow of a woman who was awakening to desire. Still he lingered over her, stroking and petting her almost as if she were a cat, and finally she let her breath out in a tremulous sigh and turned her head to seek his mouth with hers.

His kiss was slow and deep, passionate without being demanding, and he continued until at last her control broke and she moved eagerly against him, her arms winding around his neck. Excitement coursed through her veins and she felt on fire, her skin burning, and only the touch of his hands and body gave her any relief.

Finally she could stand it no longer and clutched at him with desperate hands, and he moved over her and possessed her soft body with the urgent masculinity of his. Jessica caught her breath on a sob and arched herself beneath him, glorying in the sensation of oneness with him, intent on nothing but the growing, pulsing need of her body that he gently satisfied.

But he wasn't that easily satisfied; she had wounded his arrogant Greek pride in trying to leave him, and he spent the long hours of the night making her admit time and again that he was her physical master. He wasn't brutal; at no time did he lose control. But he aroused her with his insistent, prolonged caresses and forced her to plead with him for release. At the time, she was so submerged in sensuality that nothing mattered to her except being in his arms and accepting his lovemaking. It wasn't until she woke the next morning and looked over at her sleeping husband that a chill ran over her, and she wondered at his motivation.

Had the night been only a demonstration of his mastery of her? Not once, even in the depths of his own passion, had he uttered a word of love. She began to feel that his lovemaking had been as calculated as before, designed only to make her accept his domination; there was also his stated intention of making her pregnant.

She turned her head restlessly on the pillow, aware of a cold knot of misery in her stomach. She didn't want to believe any of that; she wanted him to love her as she loved him; yet what else could she think? Tears slipped down her cheeks as she stared at the ceiling. Charles had warned her from the beginning not to challenge Nikolas Constantinos. His instinct was to conquer; it was part of his nature, and yet she had thrown her own will into opposition to his at every turn. Was it any wonder that he was so determined to subdue her?

Since she had met him, she had been on an emotional seesaw, but suddenly the never-ending strain had become too much. She was crying, soundlessly, endlessly, and she couldn't stop, the pillow beneath her head becoming wet with the slow rain of her tears.

"Jessica?" she heard Nikolas ask sleepily, lifting himself onto his elbow beside her. She turned her head and looked at him, her lips trembling, her eyes desolate. A concerned frown puckered his brow as he touched his fingers to her wet cheek. "What's wrong?"

She couldn't answer; she didn't know what was wrong. All she knew was that she was so miserable she wanted to die, and she wept softly.

SOME TIME LATER, a stern Dr. Theotokas gave her an injection and patted her arm. "It's only a mild sedative; you won't even go to sleep," he assured her. "Though it's my opinion that rest and time are all that are required to make you well again. A severe concussion isn't something one recovers from in a matter of days. You've overexerted yourself, both physically and emotionally, and now you're paying the price."

"I know," she managed to say, giving him a weak smile. Her tears had slowed, and already the sedative was making itself felt in the form of a creeping relaxation. Was her weeping a form of hysteria? Probably so, and the doctor wasn't a fool. She was nude in her husband's bed; he'd have had to be blind not to know how they had spent the night—therefore the discreet warning about overexerting herself.

Nikolas was talking to Dr. Theotokas in Greek, his voice hard, rough, and the doctor was being very positive in his replies. Then the doctor was gone, and Nikolas sat down on the bed beside her, putting one arm on the other side of her and propping himself up on it. "Are you feeling better?" he asked gently, his dark eyes examining her closely.

"Yes. I'm sorry," she sighed.

"Shhh," he murmured. "It's I who should be apologizing. Alexander has just cursed me for being seven kinds of fool and not taking better care of you. I won't tell you what he said, but Alexander knows how to make a point," he finished wryly.

"And…now?" she asked.

"Now we return to the island, and you're to spend your time doing nothing more tiring than lying on the beach." His gaze met hers squarely. "I've been forbidden to share your bed until you've completely recovered, but we both know the concussion isn't the only problem. You win, Jessica. I won't bother you again until it's what you want, too. I give you my word on that."

SEVEN WEEKS LATER, Jessica stood on the terrace and stared absently at the gleaming white yacht anchored out in the bay; unconsciously her hand went to her stomach, her fingers drifting over the flatness. His promise had been scrupulously kept, but it had been given too late. It would still be some time yet before her condition began to show, but already she had seen the little smiles that Petra and Sophia exchanged whenever she was unable to eat any breakfast yet raided the kitchen later with a ravenous appetite. In a thousand ways, she had betrayed herself to the women, from her increased sleepiness to the way she had learned to move slowly to prevent the dizziness which swept over her if she stood abruptly.

A baby! She wavered between a glowing contentment that she was actually carrying Nikolas's child, and a deep depression that the relationship between them hadn't improved at all since they had returned to the island. He was still restrained, cool. She knew that it distressed Madame Constantinos, but she couldn't bring herself to make up to Nikolas, and he wasn't doing any making up, either. He'd made it plain that she would have to take the next step, and she had backed off. If anything, she was more confused than before, with the knowledge of her pregnancy weighing on her. The yo-yo effect the pregnancy had on her emotions kept her unsettled, unable to decide on any course of action. But right now, she was just recovering from a bout of nausea and feeling resentful that Nikolas should have made her pregnant so easily, and she glared at the yacht below.

Andros had brought the yacht in yesterday. Nikolas had worked like a demon these past weeks, both to catch up on his work and to divert himself, but he had decided that a cruise would be a welcome change, and he had sent Andros to the marina where the yacht was berthed to bring it to the island. Nikolas had planned to leave in two days, with Jessica and his mother along, and Jessica was beginning to suspect that he meant to settle things between them whether she liked it or not once he had her on the yacht. He had given his word that he wouldn't bother her, but he had probably never thought that the situation would last this long.

She resentfully turned away from the sight of the graceful ship and met Sophia's smiling dark eyes as she held out a glass of cool fruit juice. Jessica took the glass without protest, though she wondered how Sophia always knew just when her stomach was upset. A tray with dry toast and weak tea was also brought to her every morning now, and she knew that the coddling would intensify as her pregnancy advanced. The women hadn't said anything yet, knowing that she hadn't informed Nikolas of his impending fatherhood, but she would have to tell him soon.

"I'm going for a walk," she told Sophia, giving the empty glass back to her, and their ability to communicate had improved to the extent that Sophia understood her the first time and beamed at her.

Walking slowly, careful to avoid the sun whenever she could, Jessica picked her way cautiously down the steep path that led to the beach. She was joined by a leaping, prancing Samantha. Nikolas had even had the small dog brought over, and Samantha was having the time of her life, romping with unlimited freedom. The village children spoiled her terribly, but she had attached herself to Nikolas, and now Jessica made a face at her. "Traitor!"

she told the dog, but Samantha barked so happily that she had to smile.

She found a piece of driftwood and amused herself by throwing it for Samantha to retrieve, but halted the game when the dog showed signs of tiring. She suspected that Samantha had managed to get in the family way again; Nikolas had reported, laughingly, that he'd seen her being very friendly with a native dog. She sat down on the sand and stroked the dog's silky head. "Both of us, my girl," she said ruefully, and Samantha whined in pleasure.

At length, she began retracing her steps up the path, concentrating on her footing to make certain she didn't fall. She was taken totally by surprise when a gruff voice behind her barked playfully, "What are you doing?" She shrieked in alarm, whirling about, and the sudden movement was too much. She had a glimpse of Nikolas's dark, laughing face before it swam sickeningly away from her, and she flung out both hands in an effort to catch herself as she pitched forward. She didn't know if she hit the ground or not.

When she woke, she was in her bedroom, lying on the bed. Nikolas was sitting on the edge of the mattress, washing her face with a cold wet cloth, his dark face set in stern lines.

"I—I'm sorry," she apologized weakly. "I can't think why I fainted."

He gave her a brooding glance. "Can't you?" he asked. "Maman has a very good idea, as do Petra and Sophia. Why haven't you told me, Jessica? Everyone else knows."

"Told you what?" She delayed, pouting sulkily, trying to put off the moment when she actually had to tell him.

His jaw tightened. "Don't play games with me," he said harshly, leaning over her with determination. "Are you having my baby?"

In spite of everything, a certain sweetness pierced her. There were only the two of them in the room, and this moment would never happen again. A slow smile, mysterious in its contentment, curved her lips as she reached for his hand. With a timeless gesture she placed his palm over her still-flat abdomen, as if he could feel his tiny child growing there. "Yes," she admitted in perfect serenity, lifting her glowing eyes to him. "We've made a baby, Nikolas."

His entire body quivered, and his black eyes softened incredibly, then he stretched out on the bed beside her and gathered her into his arms. His hand stroked her tawny mane of hair, the strong fingers trembling. "A baby," he murmured. "You impossible woman, why haven't you told me before? Didn't you know how happy you would make me? Why, Jessica?"

The heady sensation of his warm body lying against her so dazed her mind that she forgot to think of anything else. She had to gather her thoughts before she could answer. "I thought you'd gloat," she said huskily, running the tip of her tongue over her dry lips. "I knew you'd never let me go if you knew about the baby...."

His gaze went to her mouth as if drawn by a magnet. "Do you still want to go?" he muttered. "You can't, you know; you're right in thinking that I'll never let you go. Never." His tone thickened as he said, "Give me a kiss, darling. It's been so long, and I need your touch."

It had been a long time. Nikolas had been strict about

not touching her, perhaps doubting his control if he allowed himself to kiss and caress her. And once Jessica had recovered from her shock, she had missed his touch and his hungry kisses. Trembling slightly at the memory, she turned to him and lifted her face.

His mouth touched hers lightly, sweetly;

this was not the type of kiss she had received from Nikolas before. She melted under the petal-soft contact, nestling closer to him and lifting her hand to his neck. Automatically her lips opened and her tongue darted out to touch his lips and move within to seek the caress of his own tongue. Nikolas groaned aloud and abruptly the kiss changed; his mouth became ravenous as the pressure increased. Instantly heat rose in Jessica's middle, the same mindless desire he had roused in her before pride and anger had forced them apart. She ached for him; she felt as if she would die without his touch. Her body arched to him, seeking relief that only he could give.

With a deep moan, Nikolas lost control. Every muscle in his big body was shaking as he opened her dress and removed it. The wild light in his eyes told her that he might hurt her if she resisted, reminding her for a stricken moment of their wedding night, but then that frightening vision faded and she moved against him. Her own shaking fingers unbuttoned his shirt, her lips searching across his hairy chest and making his breath catch. By the time she reached for his belt, his hand was there to help her and impatiently he shed his pants and moved over her.

His mouth was drink to a woman dying of thirst; his hands created ecstasy wherever they touched. Jessica gave herself to him simply, sweetly, pliant to his every whim, and he rewarded her tenfold with his care of her, his hungry enjoyment of her. She loved this man, loved him with all her heart, and suddenly that was all that mattered.

When she floated back to earth, she was lying in his arms, her head pillowed on his shoulder while he lazily stroked her body as one would a cat. Smiling, Jessica lifted her head to look at him and found that he was smiling, too, a triumphant, contented smile. His black eyes were sleepy with satiation as he met her gaze. "I had no idea pregnant women were so erotic," he drawled, and a fiery blush burned her face.

"Don't you dare tease me now!" she protested, not wanting anything to spoil the golden glow that still enveloped her.

"But I'm not teasing. You were desirable before, God knows, but now that I know you have my child inside you, I don't want to turn you loose for even a moment." His deep voice went even deeper, became thick. "I don't think I can stay away from you, Jess."

Silently she played with the curls of hair on his chest. This afternoon had changed everything, not least of all her own attitude toward him. She loved him, and she was helpless before that fact. She had to put away her resentment and concentrate on that love, or she wouldn't have a life worth living, because she was bound mind and body to this man. Perhaps he didn't love her, but he was certainly not indifferent toward her. She would give him her love, wrap him about so tightly with the tender bonds of her heart that someday he would come to love her, too. And she had a powerful weapon in the child she carried; Nikolas would adore the baby.

A gnawing worry had been lifted from her mind.

Since their return to the island, she had been terrified that he would make love to her, haunted by her contradictory but still bitter memories of their wedding night and the one other night she had spent with him. This afternoon, in the golden sunlight, he had proved to her that lovemaking could be sweet, too, and he had satisfied her with all the skill of an experienced lover. She knew now that with time those bitter memories would fade, lost in the newer memories of nights in his arms.

"No more empty nights," he growled, echoing her thoughts. He leaned over her, and his dark face was hard, almost brutal with a resurgence of his desire; unfortunately she was still thinking of their wedding night, and she gasped in alarm when she saw his face looking so much as he had looked then. Before she could stop herself, her hands were pushing at his shoulders, and she had cried out, "Don't touch me!"

He jerked back as if he had been slapped, his face going pale.

"Don't worry about that," he said tightly, swinging off the bed and grabbing up his pants. "I've done everything I can think of to make it up to you, and you've thrown it all back in my face. I have no more arguments, Jessica, no more persuasions. I'm tired, damn it, tired of—" He broke off and jerked his pants on, and Jessica came out of her frozen horror at what she had done.

"Nikolas, wait—it isn't—"

"I don't give a damn what it isn't!" he ripped out savagely, his jaw set like granite. "I won't bother you again." He slammed out of the bedroom without looking at her again and Jessica lay on the bed, stunned by the violence of his reaction and by the raw emotion that had been in his voice. She had hurt him, something she hadn't thought possible. Nikolas had always seemed so tough, so impervious to anything she said or did, except to be angry when she defied him. But he had his pride, too; perhaps he had finally tired of a woman who resisted him at every turn. The thought made her shrink inside, thinking of being without his absorbing interest in everything she did, his open appreciation of her body.

She left the bed, too, and pulled on her robe. Restlessly, miserably, she paced the room. How *could* she have done that to him? Just when she had admitted that she needed him, she had let her silly fears drive him away and she was totally lost without him. What would she do without his arrogant strength to bolster her when she was depressed or upset? From the day they had met he had supported her, protected her.

Her head had begun to throb and she rubbed her temples abstractedly. At last she gathered up her courage and pulled on her clothing with trembling hands. She had to find Nikolas and make him listen, explain why she had pushed him away.

When she entered the living room, Madame Constantinos was there and she looked up from her book as Jessica entered. "Are you all right, my dear?" she asked in her soft French, her sweet face worried.

"Yes," Jessica muttered. "I— Do you know where Nikolas is, Maman?"

"Yes, he and Andros have locked themselves in the study with strict orders not to be disturbed. Andros is flying to New York tomorrow and they are finalizing a merger."

Andros was handling that? Jessica passed a shaking hand over her eyes. Nikolas should have been handling that merger, she knew, but he was delegating the responsibility to Andros so he could take time to be with her on the yacht. How could she have been so blind?

"Is anything wrong?" Madame Constantinos asked worriedly.

"Yes—no. Yes, there is. We've had a quarrel," Jessica confessed. "I need to see him. He misunderstood something that I said."

"M'mmmm, I see," said his mother. She looked at Jessica with those clear blue eyes. "You told him of the child, then?"

Evidently her condition was well-known to all the women of the household, she reflected. She sat down and sighed wearily. "Yes. But that isn't why he's angry."

"No, of course not. Nikolas would never be angry at the thought of becoming a father," mused Madame Constantinos, smiling a little. "He is undoubtedly as proud as a peacock."

Yes," Jessica admitted huskily, remembering the look on his face when she had told him of the baby.

Madame Constantinos was looking out the glass doors of the terrace, smiling a little. "So Niko is angry and upset, is he? Let him alone for tonight, my dear. He probably wouldn't listen to you anyway, right now, so let him stew in his own misery for a little while. That is a small-enough punishment for the misery he has caused you. You've never said why you were on the beach so early in the morning, my dear, and I haven't liked to ask, but I do have a fairly accurate picture of what happened that night. Yes, let Niko worry for tonight."

Tears welled in Jessica's eyes. "It wasn't all his fault, Maman," she defended Nikolas. She felt as if she would die. She loved him, and she had driven him away.

"Don't fret," Madame Constantinos advised serenely.

"You cannot think clearly now. Tomorrow everything will be better, you'll see."

Yes, thought Jessica, gulping back her tears. Tomorrow she would try to make up to Nikolas for her past coldness, and she didn't dare think what she would do if he turned away from her.

CHAPTER THIRTEEN

By the time morning came, Jessica was pale with her own unhappy thoughts. She wanted only to heal the breach between her and Nikolas, and she was unsure how to go about it or if he even wanted to mend things between them. She was in agony from the need to see him and explain, to touch him; more than anything she needed to feel his arms about her and hear his deep voice muttering love words to her. She loved him! Perhaps there was no rhyme or reason to it, but what did that matter? She'd known from the first that he was the only man who could conquer the defenses she'd built about herself and she was tired of denying her love.

She dressed hurriedly, without regard for how she looked, and merely brushed her hair, then left it hanging down her back. As she rushed into the living room she saw Madame Constantinos sitting on the terrace and she went through the glass door to greet her. "Where is Niko, Maman?" she asked in a trembling voice.

"He's on board the yacht," the older woman answered. "Sit down, child; have your breakfast with me. Sophia will bring something light. Have you been ill this morning?"

Surprisingly she hadn't. That was the only good thing about this morning that she could see. "But I must see Nikolas as soon as possible," she insisted.

"All in good time. You cannot talk to him now, so you might as well have your breakfast. You must take care of the baby, dear."

Reluctantly Jessica sat down, and in just a moment Sophia appeared with a tray. Smiling, she set out a light breakfast for Jessica. In the halting Greek that Jessica had acquired in the weeks she'd been on the island she thanked Sophia and was rewarded by a motherly pat of approval.

Gulping, Jessica chewed at a roll, trying to force it past the lump in her throat. Far below them she could see the white gleam of the yacht; Nikolas was there, but he might as well be a thousand miles away. There was no way she could get out to him unless one of the fishermen would take her, and for that she would have to walk to the village. It wasn't such a long walk, and before, she would have done it without a second thought, but her pregnancy had badly undermined her stamina and she was hesitant about making it that far in the fierce heat. As Madame Constantinos had said, she had to take care of the precious life inside her. Nikolas would hate her if she did anything that could harm his child.

After she'd eaten enough to satisfy both her mother-in-law and Sophia, and had pushed the tray away, Madame Constantinos said quietly, "Tell me, dear, do you love Niko?"

How could she ask? wondered Jessica miserably. It must be evident in every word she'd said since Nikolas had stormed out of her bedroom the day before. But Madame Constantinos's soft blue eyes were on her and she admitted in a strained whisper, "Yes! But I've ruined it—he'll never forgive me for what I said to him! If he loved me, it might be different—"

"How do you know that he doesn't love you?" demanded the older woman.

"Because all he's been concerned with since we met was going to bed," Jessica confessed in deep depression. "He says he wants me—but he's never said that he loves me."

"Ah, I see," said Madame Constantinos, nodding her white head knowingly. "Because he's never told you the sky is blue, you know that it can't possibly be that color! Jessica, my dear, open your eyes! Do you truly think Niko is so weak in character that he would be a slave to his lust? He wants you, yes—physical desire is a part of love."

Jessica didn't dare hope that it could be true that Nikolas loved her; on too many occasions he had totally ignored her feelings and she said as much to Madame Constantinos.

"I never said he is an amiable man," the other woman retorted. "I'm speaking from personal experience. Niko is the image of his father; they could be one and the same man. It wasn't always comfortable, being Damon's wife. I had to do everything his way or he would fly into a rage, and Niko is the same. He is so strong that sometimes he fails to understand that most people do not have that same strength, that he needs to soften his approach."

"But your husband loved you," Jessica pointed out softly, her eyes trained on the remote gleam of the yacht on the crystalline sea.

"So he did. But we had been married for six years before he told me so, and then only because I was suffering from the loss of our second child, a still-birth. When I asked him how long he had loved me, he looked at me in amazement and said, 'From the first. How can a woman be so blind? Never doubt that I love you, even when the words aren't said.' And so it is with Niko." Quietly, her clear blue eyes on Jessica, Madame Constantinos said again, "Yes, Niko loves you."

Jessica went even paler, shaken at the wild surge of hope that shot through her. Did he love her? Could he *still* love her, after yesterday?

"He loves you," reassured his mother. "I know my son, as I knew my husband. Niko lost his head over you; I have seen him look at you with such yearning in his eyes that it took my breath away, for he is a strong man and he doesn't love lightly."

"But—but the things he's said," protested Jessica shakily, still not daring to let herself hope.

"Yes, I know. He's a proud man, and he was angry with himself that he couldn't control his need for you. It is partly my fault, this trouble between you and Niko. He loves me, and I was upset when I thought my dear friend Robert had married a gold-digger. Niko wanted to protect me, but he couldn't make himself leave you alone. And you, Jessica, were too proud to tell him the truth."

"I know," said Jessica softly, and tears welled in her eyes. "And I treated him so badly yesterday! I've ruined it, Maman; he'll never forgive me now." The tears dripped from her lashes as she remembered the look that had been in Nikolas's eyes as he'd left her bedroom. She wanted to die. She felt as if she'd smashed paradise with her own hands.

"Don't fret. If you can forgive him for his pride, my dear, he'll forgive you for yours."

Jessica gasped at the thrust, then admitted to herself

the truth of it. She had used her pride to hold Nikolas away, and now she was paying for it.

Madame Constantinos placed her hand on Jessica's arm. "Niko is leaving the yacht now," she said gently. "Why don't you go to meet him?"

"I—yes," gulped Jessica, getting to her feet.

"Be careful," called Madame Constantinos after her. "Remember my grandchild!"

Her eyes on the small rowboat steadily narrowing the gap between it and the beach, Jessica made her way down the path that led to the water. She went down it with a hammering heart, wondering if Madame Constantinos was right that Nikolas truly loved her. Thinking back, it seemed to her that he did—or had. If only she hadn't ruined it!

Nikolas had beached the rowboat and was securing it against the tide when she walked across the sand up to him. He wore only a pair of blue cut-off jeans and his nearly nude, muscular body rippled with lithe grace as he moved. She caught her breath in sheer admiration and stopped in her tracks.

Nikolas straightened and saw her. His black eyes were impossible to read as he stood there looking at her, and she drew in a quivering breath. He wouldn't make the first move, she knew; she'd have to do it. Taking her courage in both hands, she said quietly, "Nikolas, I love you. Can you possibly forgive me?"

Something flickered in the black depths of his eyes, then was gone. "Of course," he said simply, and walked toward her.

When he was so close that she could smell the clean sweat of his body, he stopped and asked, "Why?"

"Your mother opened my eyes," she said, swallowing with some difficulty. Her heart was lodged in her throat and was pounding so hard she could barely speak. He wasn't going to make it easy for her, she could see. "She made me realize that I've been allowing my pride to ruin my life. I—I love you, and even if you don't love me, I want to spend the rest of my life with you. I hope you love me; Maman thinks you do, but even if you c-can't love me, it doesn't matter."

He shoved his fingers through his black hair, his face suddenly grim and impatient. "Are you blind?" he demanded roughly. "All of Europe knew I took one look at you and went mad. Do you think I'm such a slave to lust that I'd have pursued you so single-mindedly if I'd only wanted you for sex?"

Her heart leaped wildly as he spoke words that were so similar to those his mother had used. So Madame Constantinos did know her son! And as she'd said, Niko was much like his father. She reached out shaking hands and her fingers clutched at the warm skin that covered his ribs. "I love you," she whispered shakily. "How can you ever forgive me for being so blind and stupid?"

A quiver ran through his entire body, and with a deep groan, he snatched her to him, burying his face in her tangled hair. "There's no question of forgiving you," he muttered fiercely. "If you can forgive me, if you can still love me after the way I've hounded you so mercilessly, how can I hold a grudge against you? Besides, my life won't be worth living if I let you go. I love you." Then he lifted his head and repeated, "I love you."

Her entire body began to quiver as she heard his deep voice at last saying those words, and once he had admitted it, he kept on saying it, over and over, while she clung to him with desperate strength, her face buried in the warm, curly hair that covered his chest. He cupped her chin in his palm and turned her face up to his and she was engulfed in his hungry, possessive kiss. Wild little tingles began to shoot along her nerves and she stood on tiptoe to press herself against him, her arms sliding up to twine about his neck. His firm, warm skin beneath her fingers made her feel drunk and now she no longer wanted to resist him; she responded to him without reserve. At last she could indulge her own need to touch him; to stroke his darkly tanned skin and bite sensuously at his lips. A deep groan came from his chest as she did exactly that, and the next moment he had scooped her up in his arms and was striding across the sand.

"Where are you taking me?" she whispered, trailing her lips across his shoulder, and he answered her in a strained voice.

"Over here, to where the rocks hide us from view." And in a moment they were surrounded by the rocks and he carefully placed her on the sun-warmed sand. Despite the urgency she sensed in him, he was gentle as he made love to her, holding himself back, as if he feared hurting her. His skilled, patient attention carried her to rapture, and when she floated back to earth, she knew that their lovemaking had been clean and healing, wiping out all of the pain and anger of the past months. It had sealed the pact of their confessed love, made them truly man and wife. Clasped tightly in his arms, her face buried against his heaving chest, she whispered, "All of this time wasted! If only I'd told you—"

"Shhh," he interrupted, stroking her hair. "No self-recriminations, darling, because I'm not free from guilt either, and I'm not good at admitting when I'm wrong."

His strong mouth curved into a wry smile and he moved his hand to her back, the stroking motion continuing as if she was a cat. "I understand now why you were so wary of me, but at the time every rejection was like a slap in the face," he continued softly. "I wanted to leave you alone; you'll never know how much I wanted to be able to walk away and forget about you, and it made me furious that I couldn't. I'm not used to anyone having that kind of power over me," he confessed in self-mockery. "I couldn't admit that I'd finally been defeated; I did everything I could to get the upper hand again, to try to manage my emotions, but nothing worked, not even Diana."

Jessica gasped at his audacity in even mentioning that name to her and she raised her head from his chest to glare at him jealously. "Yes, what about Diana?" she asked sharply.

"Ouch," he winced, flicking the tip of her nose with a long brown finger. "I've opened my bloody mouth when I should've kept it shut, haven't I?" But his black eyes sparkled and she knew that he was enjoying her jealousy.

To get back at him, she refused to be put off. "Yes, you did," she agreed. "Tell me about Diana. That night you said you'd only kissed her once, is that true?"

"Within reason," he hedged.

Furious, she clenched her fist and struck him in the stomach with all her strength, which wasn't enough to really hurt him but which made him grunt. "Hey!" he protested, grabbing her fist and holding it. But he was laughing, a carefree laugh that she'd never heard from him before. He looked exultant, he looked happy, and that made her even more jealous. "Niko," she bit out, "tell me!"

"All right," he said, his laughter fading to a faint smile. His black eyes watched her sharply as he admitted, "I meant to take her. She was willing, and she was balm to a battered ego. Diana and I had a brief affair some months before I met you, and she made it clear that she wanted to resume our relationship. You had me so confused, so frustrated, that I couldn't think of anything but trying to break the hold you had on me. You wouldn't let me have you, but I kept coming back for more of that delicate cold shoulder and I was furious with myself. You acted as if you couldn't stand my touch, while Diana made it obvious that she wanted me. And I wanted a responsive woman in my arms, but when I began kissing her, it just wasn't right. She wasn't you, and I didn't want her. I wanted only you, even if I couldn't admit to myself just then that I loved you."

His explanation hardly mollified her, but as he still held her fist and her other arm was effectively pinned to her side by his encircling arm, she couldn't take out her anger on him physically. She still glared at him as she ordered, "You're not to kiss another woman again, do you hear? I won't stand for it!"

"I promise," he murmured. "I'm all yours, darling; I have been from the moment you walked across my office toward me, if you'd only wanted me. But I admit that I like that green fire in your eyes; you're beautiful when you're jealous."

His words were accompanied by a wickedly charming grin that accomplished its purpose, for she melted at the look of loving ownership he gave her. "I suppose it tickles your ego that I'm jealous?" she asked, letting herself relax against him.

"Of course. I went through torture, I've been so jealous of you; it's only fair that you be a little jealous, too."

He followed his admission with a searching kiss that had her flowing against him; it was as if her desire for him, so long denied, had burst out of control and she couldn't hold back her pleasure. Like an animal he sensed that and took advantage of it, deepening his kiss, stroking her body with sure, knowing hands. "You're beautiful," he whispered raggedly. "I've dreamed so many times of having you like this; I don't want to let you go for even a minute."

"But we have to," Jessica replied dreamily, her green eyes sleepy with love and need. "Maman will be waiting for us."

"Then I suppose we'd better return," Nikolas growled, sitting up and raising her with an arm behind her back. "I wouldn't like for her to send someone looking for us. And you *are* sleepy, aren't you?"

"Sleepy?" she asked, startled.

"You won't be able to stay awake, will you?" he continued, his black eyes sparkling. "You'll have to take a nap."

"Oh!" she exclaimed, her eyes widening as understanding dawned. "I believe you're right; I'm so sleepy I won't be able to stay awake until lunch."

He laughed and helped her dress, and hand in hand they walked up the path. Holding his strong hand tightly, Jessica felt the golden glow of love inside her expand until it included the whole world. For the first time in her life everything was as it should be; she loved Nikolas and he loved her, and already she carried his child. She would tell him the full story of her marriage, explain why she had hidden behind the lies others had told, even from him, but it would make no difference to their love, she knew. In deep contentment she asked, "When did you admit to yourself that you love me?"

"When you were in Cornwall," he admitted gruffly, his fingers tightening. He stopped and turned to face her and his dark face had a grim expression as he remembered. "It was two days before Charles deigned to tell me where you'd gone, and I was on the verge of insanity before he decided I'd been punished enough. I'd spent two days trying to get you on the phone, waiting hours outside your house for you to come home. I kept thinking of the things I'd said to you, remembering the look in your eyes as you left, and I was in a cold sweat thinking I'd lost you. That was when I knew I loved you, because the thought of not seeing you again was agony."

She looked at him in surprise. If he'd loved her that early, why had he insisted on those insulting conditions in the prenuptial agreement? She asked him as much, her voice troubled, and in response to the echo of pain he saw in her eyes, he pulled her into his arms and laid his cheek on her head.

"I was in pain, and I lashed out," he muttered. "I'm sorry, darling, I'll have that damned thing torn up. But I kept thinking that you were holding out for a ring so you could get your hands on my money, and it drove me wild because I loved you so much I had to have you, even thinking all you wanted was money."

"I've never wanted your money. I'm even glad you took control of my money, because I was furious with you for bullying me into taking such a large sum for the shares of ConTech when I didn't want it."

"I know that now, but at the time I thought that that was *exactly* what you wanted. My eyes were opened on our wedding night, and when I woke up and you were gone—" He broke off the sentence and closed his eyes, his expression tormented.

"Don't think of that," she said gently. "I love you."

His eyes opened and he looked at her, the clear depths of her eyes shining with the love she felt. "Even when I'm mad with jealousy and frustration, I still have a spark of sanity left," he said, his mouth curving in amusement. "I still had the sense to make you my wife." He leaned down and swept her up in his arms. "Maman is waiting for us. Let's give her the good news, then take that nap. I'll take you home, love"—and he started up the path to their home, his stride long and effortless as he carried her. Jessica curled her arms about his neck and rested against him, knowing she was safe in the strength of his love.

* * * * *

AN INDEPENDENT WIFE

CHAPTER ONE

THE PHONE ON her desk rang but Sallie didn't look up from her typewriter or otherwise indicate that she'd even noticed the noise. With a sigh Brom got to his feet and leaned across his desk to reach the phone and put the receiver to his ear. Sallie typed on, her brow puckered with concentration.

"Sal! It's for you," said Brom dryly, and Sallie looked up with a start to see Brom lying stretched across his desk holding her telephone out to her.

"Oh! I'm sorry, Brom, I didn't hear it ring," she apologized, grinning at him as she took the receiver from his hand. He often ribbed her about being in another world, and it was nothing less than the truth; he often answered her calls as well as his own because usually she was concentrating so hard she didn't hear the phone ring.

He grinned back at her as he regained his seat and said, "It's Greg."

"Sallie," said Sallie into the mouthpiece by way of greeting.

And Greg Downey, the news editor, drawled, "Come see me, kid."

"I'm on my way," she said enthusiastically and hung up the phone.

As she switched off her electric typewriter and

reached for the cover, Brom questioned, "Off again, birdie?"

"I hope so," replied Sallie, flipping her long braid back over her shoulder. She loved foreign assignments; they were like bread and butter to her. She thrived on them. Other reporters got jet lag—Sallie got her second wind. Her energy and good humor seemed inexhaustible, and as she rushed off to Greg's office she could already feel the adrenalin flowing through her system, making her heart pump faster and her whole body tingle with anticipation.

Greg looked up as she knocked on his open door and a smile softened his hard face when he saw her. "Did you run?" he asked dryly as he got up and crossed to her, closing the door behind her. "I just hung up the phone."

"Normal speed," said Sallie, laughing at herself with him. Her dark blue eyes sparkled with laughter and dimples peeped out of her cheeks. Greg looked down at her glowing little face and passed a hard arm about her to hug her briefly to him before releasing her.

"Do you have anything for me?" she asked eagerly.

"Nothing for right now," he replied, returning to his chair, and he laughed at the way her face fell.

"Cheer up, I've got good news for you anyway. Have you ever heard of the Olivetti Foundation?"

"No," said Sallie bluntly, then frowned. "Or have I? *Who* Olivetti?"

"It's a European charity organization," Greg began, and Sallie pounced in triumph.

"Oh-ho! I place it now. The world's blue bloods sponsor an enormous charity ball every summer, right?"

"Right," concurred Greg.

"Am I interested?" asked Sallie. "America doesn't have any blue blood, you know, only hot red blood."

"You're interested," Greg drawled. "The shindig is being held this year in Sakarya."

Sallie's face lit up. "Greg! Marina Delchamp?"

"Yeah," he grinned. "How about that, eh? I'm practically giving you a vacation. Interview the dashing wife of the finance minister, attend the ritziest party you've ever imagined, and all on the payroll. What more could you want?"

"Great!" she said enthusiastically. "When is it?"

"End of next month," he grunted, lighting a slim cigar. "That leaves plenty of time for you to buy any new gear if you don't have anything suitable for attending a charity ball."

"Smarty," she teased, wrinkling her pert little nose at him. "I'll bet you think I don't have anything in my closet except pants. For your information, I own quite a few dresses."

"Then why don't you ever wear them around here?" he demanded.

"Because, boss dear, you have a habit of sending me out to the wilds without a minute's notice, so I've learned to be prepared."

"And you're so afraid that you'll miss an assignment that you keep a packed bag under your desk," he returned, not at all fooled by her retort. "But I really do want you to dress up, Sallie. Sakarya could be an important ally, especially since the oil fields on the northern border are producing so heavily now. It helps that Marina Delchamp is an American and her husband is so influential with the King, but it never hurts to look your best."

"Umm, yes, the State Department will be relieved to know that I'm on their side," she said with perfect sincerity, keeping her face straight with an effort, and Greg shook his fist at her.

"Don't laugh," he warned her. "The boys in Washington are going all out with Sakarya. The King knows the power he has with those oil fields. Through Marina's influence with her husband Sakarya has become more pro-Western, but it's still an iffy thing. This charity ball will be the first time such an event has been held in an Arab country and it's going to be covered by all the news agencies. Television will be there, too, of course. I've even heard that Rhydon Baines will interview the King, but it hasn't been confirmed yet." Greg leaned back in his chair and clasped his hands behind his head. "There's a rumor going around that Baines is quitting television anyway."

Sallie's bright eyes dimmed a fraction. "Really?" she asked. "I never thought Rhy Baines would quit reporting."

Greg narrowed his gaze on her, his attention caught by her tone. "Do you *know* Rhydon Baines?" he asked incredulously. It didn't seem likely. Rhydon Baines was in a class by himself with his hard-hitting documentaries and interviews, and Sallie hadn't been a top-flight reporter for that long, but the girl did get around and she knew a lot of people.

"We grew up together," Sallie said casually. "Well, not really together, he's older than I am, but we come from the same town."

"Then I've got more good news for you," Greg said, leaning back in his chair and eyeing her sharply. "But keep it close. It's not supposed to be general knowledge yet. The magazine has been sold. We've got a new publisher."

Sallie's heart jolted. She wasn't sure if that was good news or not. A turnover at the top could mean a turnover at the lower levels, too, and she loved her job. *World in Review* was a first-class publication; she would hate to see it ruined.

"Who's the new head knocker?" she questioned warily.

"Didn't you guess?" He looked surprised. "Rhydon Baines, of course. That's why it's not definite about the interview with the King of Sakarya. I heard that the network offered him anchor man to get him to stay, but he turned them down."

Sallie's eyes became huge. "Rhy!" she repeated in a dazed tone. "My God, I never thought he'd come out of the field. Are you certain? Rhy loved reporting more than—more than anything else," she finished, her heart almost stopping in alarm as she realized what she'd nearly said: Rhy loved reporting more than he loved me! What would Greg have said if she'd blurted that out? She could see her job going down the drain anyway, without anticipating the event.

"The way I understand it," Greg expanded, puffing on his cigar and not noticing the slight hesitation in her speech, "he's signed with the network to do a certain number of documentaries over the next five years, but other than that he's coming out of the field. Maybe he's bored."

"Bored?" Sallie muttered, as if the idea was incomprehensible. "With reporting?"

"He's been on top of the heap for a long time," Greg replied. "And maybe he wants to get married, settle down. God knows he's old enough to have all of his wild oats sowed."

"He's thirty-six," Sallie said, struggling for control. "But the idea of Rhy settling down is ridiculous."

"Frankly, I'm glad he's coming in with us. I look forward to working with him. The man's a genius in his field. I thought you'd be happy with the news, but you look like someone's spoiled your Christmas."

"I—I'm stunned," she admitted. "I never thought I'd see the day. When will the news be made public?"

"Next week. I'll try to see that you're here when he comes in, if you like."

"No, thanks anyway," she refused, smiling ruefully at him. "I'll see him soon enough."

Returning to her desk several minutes later Sallie felt as if she'd been kicked in the gut and, rather than face Brom's questions, she detoured to the ladies' room and collapsed on the sofa. Rhy! Of all the news magazines, why did he have to choose *World in Review?* It would be almost impossible for her to find another job she liked nearly as well. It wasn't that Rhy would fire her, but she knew that she didn't want to work with him. Rhy was out of her life now and she had no room for him; she didn't want to be around him even on a professional basis.

What had Greg said? That perhaps Rhy wanted to marry and settle down? She almost laughed aloud. Rhy was already married—to her, and they'd been separated for seven years, during which time she had seen him only on television. Their marriage had broken up precisely because Rhy *couldn't* settle down.

Breathing deeply, Sallie stood up and smoothed her expression. Worrying about it now would interfere with her work and she was too much of a professional to allow that. Tonight would be plenty of time to plan what she'd do.

THAT NIGHT AS she dawdled over the grapefruit half that constituted her supper, her face brightened. The possibility was strong that Rhy wouldn't even recognize her; she'd changed a lot in seven years, lost weight, let her hair grow, even her name was different. And the publisher wouldn't exactly be rubbing shoulders with the reporters; she might go for weeks at a time without even glimpsing him. She was out of the country for long stretches, too.

Besides, would Rhy even care if he discovered that one of his reporters was his estranged wife? Seven years was a long time, and there had been no contact at all between them. The break had been final, absolute. Somehow neither one of them had gotten around to filing for a divorce, but there really hadn't been a need for one. They had gone their separate ways, built separate lives, and it was as if the year they'd been married never existed. The only result of that year was the drastic change in Sallie. Why couldn't she carry on with her job like always, even if Rhy did recognize her?

The more she thought about it, the more it seemed possible. She was good at her job and Rhy wasn't a man to let his private life interfere with work, as she knew better than anyone else. If she did her job and kept out of his way he would never let out any hint of their personal connection. After all, it was all over for Rhy, just as it was for her.

Usually Rhy never entered her thoughts unless she saw him on television, but now that his presence loomed so large in her life again she found the past crowding in on her. She tried to concentrate on other things and managed fairly well until she went to bed that night, when memories of that year swamped her.

Rhy. Sallie stared upward through the darkness at the ceiling, recalling his features and forming them into his face. She could do that easily, for she'd seen him on television any number of times these past seven years. At first she'd been left sick and shaking whenever she glimpsed his face and she would rush to turn the set off, but gradually that reaction had left her, turned into numbness. Her system had protected itself against such intense grief, allowing her to pick up the pieces of her shattered life and try to build again. The numbness had turned into determination and the determination into indifference as she learned to live without Rhy.

Looking back at the timid, insecure girl she had been, Sallie felt as if that girl had been a stranger, someone to be pitied but not really worth wasting any grief over. The wonder wasn't that Rhy had left her, but rather that he'd ever been attracted to her in the first place. No matter how she considered it she just couldn't find any reason why a dynamic man like Rhy Baines would have wanted to marry a mousy little nonentity like Sarah Jerome. She hadn't been the gay, daredevil Sallie then, but Sarah. Quiet, plump, malleable Sarah.

Unless Rhy had married her just because she was malleable, someone he could control, push into the background when he wanted her out of the way, yet someone who would provide home and hearth when he did wander back home? If so, he'd been sadly disappointed, for she'd been malleable on every point except his job. Sarah wanted her husband at home every night, not flying off to report on wars and revolutions and drug smuggling, the very stuff that was the wine of life to Rhy Baines. She had sulked and nagged and wept, terrified that each time he left her would be the last, that he'd come home in a coffin. She wanted only to hold that strong man to her because she lived only through him.

In the end it had been too much for Rhy and he had walked out after only a year of marriage, and she hadn't heard from him since. She'd known that he wouldn't call her because his last words to her had been, "When you think you're woman enough for me, give me a call!"

Cynical, hurting words. Words that had clearly revealed his contempt of her. Yet those words had changed her life.

Sighing at the sleep that evaded her, Sallie rolled onto her stomach and clutched the pillow into a ball against her chest. Perhaps tonight was a good time to dredge up all the memories and give them an airing. After all, she might shortly be seeing her long-absent husband.

They had been acquainted for years, as far back as Sallie could remember. Rhy's aunt had lived next door to the Jeromes, and as Rhy had been her favorite nephew it was nothing unusual for him to stop by at least once a week when he was growing up. The visits became fewer when he left town, but he never let too long go by without calling in on his aunt. By then he was beginning to make a name for himself as a reporter, and he had been hired by a television station in New York City. Occasionally he would walk across to the white picket fence that separated the two houses and talk to Sallie's father, and if Sallie or her mother were about he would speak to them, sometimes lightly teasing Sallie about growing up so fast.

Shortly after she turned eighteen Sallie's parents were killed in a car crash and she lived alone in the small, tidy house she had inherited. It was paid for and the insurance money was enough to keep her going until she had recovered from her grief enough to begin looking for a job, so she let the days drift by, dreading the time when she would have to go out on her own. She became closer to Aunt Tessie, Rhy's aunt, for each lived alone. Aunt Tessie died in her sleep just two months after the death of Sallie's parents and Rhy returned home for the funeral.

He was twenty-eight, devilishly good-looking, with a dangerous quality about him that took her breath away. He was a man who lived on his nerve and his wits and thoroughly enjoyed it, and he'd just been snapped up by one of the major television networks, working as a foreign correspondent. He saw Sallie at his aunt's funeral and called the next day to ask her out. She had thought then that he must be bored, used to as he was to so much glamour and excitement, but she had known when she looked in the mirror that he wouldn't find any glamour or excitement with her. She was short, pretty enough in a quiet way, but a bit on the plump side. Her short mop of rich, dark hair was a good color, dark sable, but it lacked style and did nothing for her small face with its round cheeks. But Rhy Baines had asked her out and she went, her heart thumping half in fear and half in exhilaration at actually being alone with such a gorgeous, sexy man.

Rhy was a sophisticated adult; he probably meant nothing by the kiss he pressed lightly on her lips when he said good-night after that first date. He didn't even put his arms around her but merely tilted her face up with a finger under her chin. To Sallie, however, it was an explosion of her senses and she had no idea how to control it or mask her response to him. Simply, openly, she had melted against him, her soft mouth fused to his. Long minutes later, when he dragged his head back, he was breathing raggedly and, to her surprise, he asked her out again.

On their third date only his self-control preserved her innocence. Sallie was helpless against her attraction to him, having fallen head over heels in love, yet she was taken by surprise when he abruptly asked her to marry him. She had expected him to take her to bed, not to propose, and she humbly accepted. They were married the next week.

For six glorious days she was in ecstasy. He was a marvelous lover, patient with her inexperience, tender in his passion. He seemed amazed at the fiery passion he could arouse in his quiet little wife and for the first few days of their married life they devoted themselves to lovemaking. Then came that phone call, and before she knew it Rhy was throwing some clothing in his suitcase and rushing out the door with only a hasty kiss for her and a terse "I'll call you, baby," thrown at her over his shoulder.

He was gone for just over two weeks and she discovered by watching the evening news that he was in South America, where a particularly bloody revolution had slaughtered just about everyone in the previous government. Sallie spent the entire time he was gone crying herself to sleep at night and vomiting up her meals whenever she tried to eat. Just the thought of Rhy in danger made her cringe. She had just found him after the nightmare of losing her parents and she adored him. She wouldn't be able to bear it if anything happened to him.

He returned looking brown and fit and Sallie screamed her rage and fear at him. He retaliated and the quarrel that followed kept them from speaking for two days. It was sex that brought them together again, his surging appetite for her wildly responsive little body and her helpless yielding to him. That became the pattern of their marriage, with him gone for longer and longer periods even though she promptly became pregnant.

They had even quarreled over her pregnancy, with Rhy bitterly accusing her of becoming pregnant deliberately in an attempt to make him stay at home. She knew he didn't want children just now and that he had no intention of changing his job. Sallie hadn't even attempted to defend herself, for even worse than being accused of becoming pregnant as part of some scheme was the shameful knowledge that she had been too ignorant to take precautions. She had simply never thought of it and she knew that Rhy would be disgusted with her if he knew the truth.

When she was six months pregnant Rhy was wounded in a border skirmish between two developing African nations and he came home on a stretcher. She had thought that his close brush with death would bring him to his senses and for once she hadn't raged and nagged at him when he returned; she was too elated at the thought of having him with her permanently. Within a month, however, he was gone on another assignment even though he hadn't fully recovered from his wound, and he was still gone when she went into premature labor. The network brought him home, but by the time he arrived she was already out of the hospital and their stillborn son had been buried.

He stayed with her until she was recovered physically from giving birth, but she was grief stricken at losing her baby and bitter with him because he had been absent during the crisis. When he left again the atmosphere between them was still cold and silent. Perhaps she should have realized then how indifferent Rhy had become to her, but it still came as a shock that he could so easily leave her forever, as he did on his next trip home. She had returned from buying groceries and found him sprawled on the sofa in the living room, his suitcase by the door where he had dropped it. His face was drawn with weariness, but his charcoal-gray eyes had still held that characteristic bite as he looked her up and down, his manner one of waiting.

Unable to stem the words that jumped to her lips, Sallie began berating him for his inconsiderate behavior, his total lack of feeling for her after the trial she had undergone, the pain she had suffered. If he truly loved her he would get another job, one that would let him stay with her when she needed him so badly. In the middle of this, Rhy got to his feet and picked up his suitcase. As he walked out the door he had said sarcastically, "When you think you're woman enough for me, give me a call."

She hadn't seen him since.

At first she had been devastated. She had cried for days and leapt for the telephone every time it rang. Checks arrived from him every week for her support, but there were never any notes included. It was as if he would do his duty and support her, but had no interest in seeing her or talking to her. She wasn't woman enough for him.

At last, desperately, knowing only that her life wasn't worth living without Rhy, Sallie decided to *make* herself into a woman who was woman enough for Rhy Baines. With feverish determination she enrolled in the local college and set about gaining the knowledge that would transform her into a more sophisticated person. She signed up for language classes and crash courses in every craft she could think of, forcing herself out of her shyness. She got a job, a low-paying job as a clerk at the local newspaper office, but it was her first job and it was a start. With that paycheck every week, her very own paycheck, came something she could hardly recognize at first, but which became larger with each succeeding check: a sense of self-reliance.

She found that she was doing well in her language classes, was, in fact, at the top of her class. She had a natural aptitude for words and languages and she enrolled in a creative writing class. The time that this consumed forced her to give up her courses in crafts, but her interest in writing grew by leaps and bounds and she didn't miss puttering about with paints and straw.

Like a snowball, her forced activities grew in size and scope until she didn't have an idle hour in her day. Once she began making friends she discovered that it was easy, that she liked being with people. Slowly she began to emerge from the shell that had encased her for all of her life.

With all of her activities, Sallie was seldom still and often forgot meals. Pounds melted from her petite frame and she had to replace her entire wardrobe. She went from slightly plump to almost too thin, and as her face slimmed the exotic bone work of her skull was revealed. Without the roundness of her cheeks to balance them her dark blue eyes became huge in her face and underneath them her high, chiseled cheekbones gave her an almost Eastern quality. She had been attractive before, but now she became something more, a young woman who was striking and unusual. Never classically lovely, not Sallie, but now she stood out in a crowd. As her hair grew she simply pulled it back out of her way, not bothering to keep it cut, and the sable-colored mass began to stream down her back in a thick mane.

As she changed physically her entire manner changed. Her self-confidence soared; she became outgoing and found that she had a keen mind and an appreciation of the absurdities of life that made people seek her out. She was enjoying herself, and thoughts of Rhy became fewer and fewer.

They had been separated for almost a year when she realized that as she had grown up, she had also grown away. The weekly check from Rhy was like a revelation, for as she stared at his bold, sprawling signature on the check she was stunned to find that the crippling pain was gone. Not only that, if Rhy came back to her now it would curtail the exciting new life she'd built for herself and she didn't want that. She had made herself over, made herself into a woman who was woman enough for Rhy Baines—and now she found that she didn't need him. She no longer needed to live through him; she had herself.

It was like being released from prison. The knowledge that she was self-sufficient and independent was like a heady wine, making her giddy. Now she understood why Rhy had put his job over her; like him, she had become hooked on excitement, and she wondered how he had lived with her as long as he had.

With a great sense of relief she mailed Rhy's check back to his address at the network, enclosing a note explaining that she had a job and was trying to support herself, therefore his support was no longer needed, though she did appreciate the thought. That was the last communication between them and that had been rather one-sided as Rhy had never replied to her note. The checks had simply ceased to arrive.

Then fate stepped into Sallie's life. A bridge she was driving across collapsed, and though she was far enough across that her car didn't slide into the river below, several behind her weren't so lucky. Without really thinking about what she was doing she helped in the rescue of the people who had survived the plunge into the river and obtained interviews with everyone involved. Afterwards she went to the newspaper office where she worked, typed up a report of the accident, including her own colorful eyewitness description, and gave it to the editor. It was printed, and she was given a new job as a reporter.

Now, at the age of twenty-six, she had completed her degree and was a reporter for one of the better weekly news magazines and her zest for new experiences had not waned. Now she fully understood why danger hadn't kept Rhy from his job, for she enjoyed the danger, the heart-pounding excitement of taking off in a helicopter while ground troops sprayed automatic fire at the aircraft, the exhilaration of coming down in a plane with only one good engine, the satisfaction of a difficult job well-done. She had rented out her house and now lived in a neat two-room apartment in New York, a mere stopping place between assignments. She had no plants and no pets, for who would take care of them while she was halfway around the world? She had no romantic interests, for she was never in one place for long, but she had scores of friends and acquaintances.

No, she reflected sleepily as she finally began to doze off, she didn't want Rhy back in her life now. He would only interfere with the things she enjoyed. But, thinking about it, she didn't think that he would care what she did if by some chance he did recognize her, and that wasn't likely. After all, he hadn't thought about her in seven years. Why should he start now?

CHAPTER TWO

SALLIE STOOD BEFORE her mirror and studied the photograph she held in her hand of herself at the age of eighteen. Then she looked back at her reflection and studied the differences. The most obvious change was that now she had cheekbones instead of cheeks. The hair, too, of course, grown from a short mop that barely covered her ears into the thick braid that hung to her waist. The only thing that hadn't changed was her eyes, large, dark blue eyes. However, if she wore dark glasses whenever she thought she might run into Rhy she could continue indefinitely to keep her identity from him.

She had thought about it from all angles and decided not to rely on Rhy's good nature, which was a chancy thing at best. Rhy was hair-triggered, volatile, never predictable. The best thing to do was to avoid him whenever possible and try to keep Greg from introducing her to her own husband as an old friend from his hometown!

Rhy was supposed to arrive that morning; the news had been broken yesterday that the magazine had been sold to Rhydon Baines, who had resigned as a network foreign correspondent and would hereafter devote his time and talents to the publishing of news, except for occasional documentary specials. The entire building had hummed with the news. Veteran reporters had suddenly become uneasy, checking their credits, reviewing their work and comparing it to Rhy's direct, slashing style of reporting. And if Sallie had heard one comment from an excited woman about how handsome Rhydon Baines was she had heard a hundred. Even women who were happily married were thrilled to be working with Rhy. He was more than a top reporter—he was a celebrity.

Sallie was already bored with the entire business. First thing this morning she was going to ask Greg for an assignment, anything to get away until things calmed down. She'd already been three weeks between assignments so no one would think it odd that she was becoming restless. It was more than a month until the charity ball in Sakarya and she didn't think she'd be able to sit still that long.

Suddenly noticing the time, she cast a last quick glance over her slender form, neat and capable in dark blue slacks and a blue silk shirt. Her hair was pulled back and braided into one long fat rope and, as the final touch, she had added a pair of dark glasses. She could tell anyone who asked that she had a headache and the light hurt her eyes; the glasses weren't so dark that she couldn't work with them on if necessary.

Then she had to rush, and as the elevator in her apartment building was notoriously slow in arriving she used the stairs, running down them two at a time and reaching her bus stop just as the bus was closing its doors. She yelled and pounded on the doors and they slid open and the driver grinned at her. "Wondered where you were," he said jokingly. In actual fact, she was a regular bus door pounder.

She made it to the office with a minute to spare and collapsed into her chair, wondering how she had made it across the street without being hit at least six times. The blood was racing through her veins and she grinned. It was time for some action when her usual method of getting to work was beginning to seem exciting!

"Hi," Brom greeted her. "Ready to meet the man?"

"I'm ready to do some traveling," she retorted. "I've been here too long. I'm growing cobwebs. I think I'll beard Greg in his den and see if I can't get some action."

"You're nuts," Brom informed her bluntly. "Greg's quick today. You'd be better off to wait until tomorrow."

"I'll take my chances," Sallie said blithely.

"Don't you always? Hey, why the glasses? Are you trying to hide a black eye?" Brom pounced, his eyes lighting up at the possibility that Sallie had gotten involved in a brawl somewhere.

"Nope." To convince him she raised the glasses to let him see for himself that her eyes were normal, then set them back in place on her nose. "I've got a headache and the light is bothering me."

"Do you have migraines?" Brom asked in concern. "My sister has 'em and the light always bothers her."

"I don't think it's a migraine," she hedged. "It's probably just a nervous reaction to sitting still for so long."

Brom laughed, as she had meant him to, and she made her escape to talk to Greg before Rhy arrived and all chance was lost.

As she neared Greg's open door she heard him on the phone, his voice curt and impatient, and Sallie's eyebrows rose as she listened. Greg was by nature an impatient man, one of the doers of the world, but he wasn't usually unreasonable but his attitude now didn't strike her as being reasonable. Brom was right, Greg was "quicker" than usual, edgy and irascible, and she had no doubt that it was all due to Rhy's impending arrival.

When she heard the phone crash down into the cradle she poked her head around the door and inquired, "Would a cup of coffee help?"

Greg's dark head jerked up at the sound of her voice and his mouth moved into a wry grimace. "I'm swimming in coffee now," he grunted in reply. "Hell's bells, I didn't know there were so many idiots working in this building. I swear if one more fool calls me—"

"Everyone's nervous," she soothed.

"You're not," he pointed out. "Why the glasses? Are you so famous now that you've got to travel incognito?"

"There's a reason for the glasses," Sallie retaliated. "But because you're being nasty I won't tell you."

"Suit yourself," he growled. "Get out of my office."

"I need an assignment," she pointed out. "I'm at the snapping stage myself."

"I thought you wanted to be here to meet your old hometown pal," Greg shot back. "Anyway, I don't have anything to give you right now."

"Come on," she pleaded. "You've got to have a little something. No riots, no natural disasters, no political kidnappings? There's bound to be a story for me somewhere in the world!"

"Maybe tomorrow," he replied. "Don't be in such a hurry. For God's sake, Sal, I may need you around in case the Man gets testy. An old friend is nice to have around—"

"To throw to the lion?" she interrupted dryly.

Abruptly Greg grinned. "Don't worry, doll, he won't tear you to pieces, only maul you around a bit."

"Greg, you're not listening to me," she groaned. "I've

been stagnating here for three weeks. I need to earn my keep."

"You don't have any sense," he observed.

"You don't have any sense of mercy," she retorted. "Greg, *please.*"

"What's the damned hurry?" he suddenly yelled. "Dammit, Sal, I've got a new publisher coming in and he's not exactly a babe in the woods. I don't expect to have any fun today, so get off my back, will you? Besides, he may *ask* to see you, and I sure as hell want you here if he does."

Sallie collapsed into a chair, groaning aloud as she realized that she would have to tell Greg the truth. That was the only way he would give her an assignment, and perhaps it wouldn't be such a bad thing if Greg knew. At least then he wouldn't keep trying to throw her at Rhy. And realistically Greg had a right to know the circumstances and be aware of the complications that could arise from her very presence.

Gently she said, "Greg, I think you should know that Rhy might not be so glad to see me."

He was instantly alert. "Why not? I thought you were friends."

She sighed. "I can't say if we're friends or not. I haven't seen him in seven years, except on television. And there's something else. I wasn't going to tell you, but you'll need to know. Do you know that I'm married, but that I've been separated from my husband for years?"

Greg nodded, a sudden stillness coming over his features. "Yes, I know, but you've never said who your husband is. You go by your maiden name, don't you?"

"Yes, I wanted to do everything completely on my

own, not capitalize on his name. He's very well-known. As a matter of fact, my husband is…umm…Rhydon Baines."

Greg swallowed audibly, his eyes growing round. He gulped again. Sallie didn't lie, he knew, she was brutally honest, but—Rhydon Baines? That tough, hard-as-nails man and this fragile little fairy with her laughing eyes? He said roughly, "My God, Sallie, the man's old enough to be your father!"

Sallie burst into a peal of laughter. "He is not! He's only ten years older than I am. I'm twenty-six, not eighteen. But I wanted you to know why I want an assignment. The further away I am from Rhy, the better it is. We've been separated for seven years but the fact remains that Rhy is still my husband and personal relationships can get sticky, can't they?"

Greg stared at her in disbelief, yet he believed her. He just couldn't take it in. Sallie? Little Sallie Jerome and that big, hard man? She looked like a kid, dressed all in blue and with that fat braid hanging to her waist. He said softly, "I'll be damned. What happened?"

She shrugged. "He got bored with me."

"Bored with you?" chided Greg. "C'mon, doll!"

She laughed again. "I'm nothing like I was then. I was such a cowardly little snit, no wonder Rhy walked out on me. I couldn't stand the separations caused by his job. I made myself sick with worry and nagged him to death, and in the end he walked out. I can't say I blame him. The wonder is that he lasted as long as he did."

Greg shook his head. It was impossible to imagine Sallie as a timid person; he sometimes thought that she hadn't a nerve in her body. She was willing to take on anything, and the more dangerous it was the more she enjoyed it. It wasn't an act, either. Her eyes would sparkle and the color glow in her cheeks whenever the going got difficult.

"Let me get this straight," he muttered. "He doesn't know that you work here?"

"I wouldn't think so," she replied cheerfully. "We haven't been in touch in six years."

"But you're still married. Surely he sends you support checks—" He stopped at the outraged look on her face, and sighed. "Sorry. You refused support, right?"

"After I could support myself, yes. When Rhy left I had to fend for myself and somewhere along the way I acquired a backbone. I like doing for myself."

"You've never asked for a divorce?"

"Well…no," she admitted, her nose wrinkling in puzzlement. "I've never wanted to remarry and I don't suppose he's ever wanted to, either, so we just never got around to a divorce. He probably finds it convenient, having a legal wife who's never around. No ties, but it keeps him safe from other women."

"Would it bother you? Seeing him again?" Greg asked roughly, more disturbed than he cared to admit by the idea of Sallie being married to Rhydon Baines.

"Seeing Rhy? No," she said honestly. "I got over him a long time ago. I had to, to survive. Sometimes it doesn't even seem real, that I was—that I *am*—married to him."

"Will it bother him, seeing you again?" persisted Greg.

"Certainly not emotionally. It has to be over for him, too. After all, he was the one who walked. But Rhy *does* have a temper, you know, and he might not like the idea of his wife working for him, even under a different name. And he might not want me around to cramp his style. I have no intention of interfering in his private life, but he doesn't know that. So you see, it would be a good idea to send me on assignment and keep me away from him, at least at first. I don't want to lose my job." She topped all of this off with a sunny smile and Greg shook his head.

"All right," he muttered. "I'll find something for you. But if he ever notices that you're his wife I know nothing about it."

"About what?" she asked, playing dumb, and he wasn't able to stifle a chuckle.

Sallie knew better than to push her luck with Greg, so she left him with a quick, heartfelt "Thanks!" and went back to her desk. Brom was gone and she was relatively alone, though only a partition separated their little cubicle from the others, and the clatter of typewriters and hum of voices were as plain as if there was nothing between her and the rest of the office.

By the time Brom returned with a steaming cup of coffee she felt more relaxed, her anxiety eased by Greg's promise to help keep her out of Rhy's sight. She finished the article she was writing and felt pleased with the end product; she liked putting words together to form ideas and felt an almost sensuous satisfaction when a sentence turned out as she had planned.

At ten o'clock the buzz of the office ceased momentarily, then resumed at a lower hum and without raising her eyes Sallie knew that Rhy had entered. Cautiously she turned her head away and pretended to search for something in the drawer of her desk. After a moment the buzz resumed its high pitch, which meant that Rhy had left after taking a quick look over the office.

"Oh, God!" a female voice cried over the others. "Just think, a hunk like that is *single!*"

Sallie grinned a little, recognizing the voice as that of Lindsey Wallis, an exuberant office sexpot with more mouth than brains. Still, there was no doubting that Lindsey was serious in her appreciation of Rhy's dynamic good looks. Sallie knew as well as anyone the effect her husband could have on a woman.

Fifteen minutes later her phone rang and she jumped on it, an action that raised Brom's eyebrows. "Get the hell out of the building," Greg muttered in her ear. "He's on his way to meet everyone. Go home. I'll try to get you out of town tonight."

"Thanks," she said and hung up. Standing, she collected her purse and said, "See ya," to Brom.

"Flying off, little birdie?" he asked, as he always did.

"It looks that way. Greg said to pack." With a wave she left, not wanting to linger, since Rhy was on his way down.

She stepped into the corridor and her heart nearly failed her when the elevator doors slid open and Rhy stepped out, flanked by three men she didn't know and the previous publisher, Mr. Owen. Rather than walk straight toward them she turned and went to the stairs, being careful to keep her eyes lowered and her head slightly averted, but she was still aware that Rhy had stopped and was looking after her. Her pulse thudded in her veins as she darted down the stairs. What a close call!

Waiting at the apartment for Greg to call nearly drove her mad with impatience. She paced the floor for a while; then excess energy drove her to clean the refrigerator out and rearrange her cabinets. That didn't take much time as she hadn't accumulated a lot of either food or utensils. At last she hit on the perfect way to pass the time: she packed her bags. She loved packing, going through her essentials and putting them in their proper place; she had her notebooks and assorted pens and pencils, a tape recorder, a dog-eared dictionary, several paperbacks, a pencil sharpener, a pocket calculator, replacement batteries and a battered flashlight, all of which traveled with her wherever she went.

She had just finished arranging them neatly when the phone rang and she answered it to hear Greg's terse voice giving her the welcome news that he had an assignment for her.

"It's the best I could do, and at least it'll get you out of town," he grunted. "You're on a flight to D.C., in the morning. A senator's wife is making big noises about a general leaking classified information at a drunken party."

"Sounds pretty," Sallie commented.

"I'm sending Chris Meaker with you," Greg continued. "Talk with the senator's wife. You won't be able to even get close to the general. Chris will have a brief on it for you. Meet him at JFK at five-thirty."

Now that she knew her destination Sallie was able to complete her packing. She chose conservative dresses and a tailored pants suit, not her favorite clothes, but she felt that the restrained clothing would help her with the interview, making the senator's wife more trusting.

As usual, she could hardly sleep that night. She was always restless the night before she left on assignment if Greg gave her any warning of it. She preferred having to rush straight from the office to the airport, without having time to think, without wondering if everything would work out, without wondering what would happen if Rhy ever recognized her....

CHRIS MEAKER, THE photographer, was waiting for her at the airport the next morning and as she approached him with a grin and a wave he got to his feet, his tall, lanky body unfolding slowly. He gave her a sleepy smile in return and bent down to kiss her on the forehead. "Hi, doll," he said, his quiet, lazily deep voice making her grin grow wider. She liked Chris. Nothing ever upset him; nothing ever hurried him. He was as calm and deep as a sheltered lagoon. He was even peaceful to look at, with his thick sandy hair and dark brown eyes, his brow broad and serene, his mouth firm without being stubborn. And most important of all, he never made a pass at her. He treated her affectionately, like a little sister, and he was protective in his quiet way, but he never made any suggestive statements to her or in any way acted as if he was attracted to her. That was a relief, because Sallie just didn't have the time for romantic ties.

Now he looked her up and down and his level brows rose. "Ye gods, a dress," he said, mild surprise evident in his voice, which meant he was astonished. "What's the occasion?"

Sallie had to grin again. "No occasion, just politics," she assured him. "Did Greg send that envelope he promised me?"

"Got it," he replied. "Have you already checked your luggage?"

"Yes," she nodded. Just then their flight was called over the loudspeaker and they walked over to the boarding area and through the metal detector, then on to the waiting jet.

On the flight to the capital Sallie carefully read the brief Greg had prepared. Considering how little time he'd had, he had included a lot of detail and she became absorbed in the possibilities. This wasn't the type of reporting she usually did but Greg had given her what he had, and she'd return the favor by doing her best.

When they reached Washington and checked into their hotel it looked as if doing her best wouldn't be good enough. While Chris lounged in a chair and leafed through a magazine Sallie called the senator's wife to confirm the appointment Greg had made for an interview that afternoon. She was told that Mrs. Bailey was sorry but she was unable to see any reporters that day. It was a polite, final brush-off, and it made her angry. She had no intention of failing to get the story Greg had sent her after.

It took an hour of phone calls to a chain of contacts but when the hour was up she had interviewed, over the phone, the hostess of the "drunken party" where the general had supposedly revealed the classified material. Everything was vehemently denied, except for the presence of both the general and Mrs. Bailey on the night in question, but when the indignant hostess muttered in passing that "Hell hath no fury" Sallie began to get the idea that Mrs. Bailey was a woman scorned.

It was a possibility. The general was a trim, distinguished man with metallic gray hair and a good-humored twinkle in his eyes. After talking it over with Chris, who agreed with her theory, they decided to pursue that angle.

Forty-eight hours later, tired but satisfied, they

caught a plane back to New York. Though her theory hadn't been verified by either of the two principals, the general or Mrs. Bailey, she was content that she knew the reason behind Mrs. Bailey's denouncement of the general. Once they had been checking they had found several restaurants in the capital area where the general had been seen dining with an attractive woman of Mrs. Bailey's general description. Senator Bailey had suddenly canceled a trip overseas to stay with his wife. The general's wife, who had shed twenty pounds and turned her graying hair into a flattering soft blond, was suddenly more in evidence at her husband's side. There was also only Mrs. Bailey's accusation against the general; no one else had added their word to hers and, moreover, the general had not been relieved of his post despite the furor in the press.

Sallie had telephoned all of that in to Greg the night before and he had agreed with her. The article would be placed in that week's issue, and she had barely gotten it in under the deadline.

He was cryptic on the subject of Rhy, commenting only that the man was a mover, and by that she deduced that changes were being made. She would have preferred going on another assignment immediately, but Greg had nothing available and there were always expense sheets to complete and a report to type out. Thankfully, the weekend had arrived and she had a bit more time before she had to go in to the office.

On Monday morning, she reported to work with butterflies in her stomach, but to her relief and surprise the entire day went by without so much as a glimpse of her husband, though the floor buzzed with speculation on the changes he was making in the format of the magazine. She avoided the upper floors, no longer going up to see Greg when an idea came to her; she called him instead, and Brom commented that he'd never seen her stay in one place for so long before.

Tuesday was the same, except that that was the day the magazine hit the newsstands and Greg called to offer his congratulations. "I've just received a call from Rhy," he said gruffly, having picked up the shortened version of Rhy's name from her. "Senator Bailey called him at home this morning."

"Am I being sued?" Sallie questioned.

"No. The senator explained the entire situation and his wife is giving us a retraction of her previous statement concerning the general. You were right on target, doll."

"I thought I was," she agreed cheerily. "Do you have anything else I can do?"

"Just watch your back, doll. Several editors I know are mad as the devil that you're the only one who caught on to what was under everyone's noses."

She laughed and hung up, but the knowledge that her instincts had been right gave her a lift for the rest of the day. Chris came by at lunch and asked if she wanted to share a sandwich with him and she accepted. There was a small cafeteria in the building offering nothing more sophisticated than soup, sandwiches, coffee and cold drinks for those who couldn't get out for lunch, but the meager fare was more than enough for her. She and Chris shared a postage-stamp table and talked shop over cups of strong black coffee.

Just as they were finishing there was a stir among the other people eating lunch and the back of Sallie's neck prickled in warning. "It's the boss," Chris informed her casually. "With his girlfriend."

Sallie sternly resisted the urge to turn around, but out of the corner of her eye she watched the two figures move down the cafeteria line selecting their lunch. "I wonder what they're doing here," she murmured.

"Testing the food, at a guess," Chris replied, turning his head to stare openly at the woman by Rhy's side. "He's checked into everything else. I don't see why he should overlook the food. She looks familiar, Sal. Do you know her?"

Sallie narrowed her eyes in concentration, examining the woman with relief, because that kept her from staring at Rhy. "You're right, she is familiar. Isn't she Coral Williams, the model?" She was almost certain of the woman's identity, that classic golden perfection could belong to no one else.

"So it is," Chris grunted.

Rhy turned then, balancing his tray as he moved to a table, and Sallie hastily lowered her eyes, but not before her heart gave a breath-stopping lunge at his appearance. He hadn't changed. He was still lithe and muscular, and his hair was still the same midnight black, his strong-boned face still hard and sardonic, tanned from long exposure to the sun. By contrast the woman at his side was a graceful butterfly, his exact opposite in coloring.

"Let's go," she said in a low tone to Chris, sliding out of her chair. She sensed Rhy's head turning in her direction and she carefully turned her back to him without any show of hurry. Chris followed her out of the cafeteria, but she was burningly conscious of Rhy's gaze on her as she left. That was twice he had stared at her. Did he recognize her? Was her walk familiar to him? Was it her hair? That long braid was distinctive enough in itself, but she didn't want to have her hair cut because he would certainly recognize her then.

She was still shaken when she returned to her desk, due in large part to her reaction to Rhy's appearance. No other man had ever attracted her the way he did and she found to her dismay that the situation was still the same. Rhy had a raw virility, an aura of barely leashed power that set her heart to pounding and forcibly reminded her of the nights she had once spent in his arms. She might be free of him emotionally, but the old physical ties seemed to be as strong as ever and she felt vulnerable.

Out of habit she picked up the phone and called Greg, but he was out to lunch and she dropped the receiver back into the cradle with a ragged sigh. She couldn't just sit there; her nature demanded that she take some sort of action. At last she scribbled a note to Brom asking him to notify Greg that she'd taken ill with a headache and was going home for the rest of the day. Greg would see through the excuse, but Brom wouldn't.

She hated to run away from anything, but she knew that she needed to think about her reaction to Rhy, and once she was home she did exactly that. Was it only because he was her husband, because she knew him as she knew no other man? He was her only lover; she'd never even been attracted to another man as she had been to Rhy. Old habits? She hoped that was it, and when she realized that she hadn't felt the least flicker of jealousy over Coral Williams she was relieved, because that proved she was over Rhy. All she felt for him was the basic urge between a man and a woman who found each other sexually alluring, nothing more. Certainly she was old enough to control those feelings, as the past seven years had proved to her.

The phone rang late that afternoon and when she answered it Greg said curtly, "What happened?"

"Rhy and Coral Williams came into the cafeteria at lunch while Chris and I were there," she explained without hesitation. "I don't think Rhy recognized me, but he kept staring. That's the second time he's stared at me like that, so I thought I'd better clear out." That wasn't exactly the reason, but it was a good excuse and she used it. Why tell Greg that seeing Rhy had upset her?

"You thought right," Greg said, sighing. "He was in my office not long after Brom brought your note up. He wanted to meet you, since you're the only reporter he hasn't met personally. Then he asked me to describe you, and he got a funny look on his face when I did."

"Oh, no," she groaned. "He's latched on to something—he *would!*" she said in swift disgust. "He's as fast as a snake. Did he ask where I'm from?"

"Be prepared, doll. He didn't ask that, but he got your phone number."

"Holy cow," she groaned again. "Thanks for doing what you could, Greg. If Rhy does find out I'll cover our tracks."

Greg hung up and she began pacing the floor, waiting for the phone to ring again. What should she say? Should she try to disguise her voice? But afternoon faded into evening and still the expected call didn't come, so at last she bathed and went to bed. But she slept restlessly, falling into a deep sleep only in the early hours of the morning.

It was the phone that woke her in the morning, the insistent ringing intruding slowly into her consciousness. At first she thought it was the alarm clock and she tried to shut it off but the ringing continued. When she realized it was the phone she grabbed it and in her haste dropped it to the floor. She hauled it up by the cord and at last got the receiver to her ear. "Hello," she muttered sleepily, her voice sounding thick.

"Is this Miss Jerome?" a deep, husky voice asked. There was a husky quality to that voice that tingled her nerves, but she was too sleepy to pick it up.

"Yes, this is she," she acknowledged, stifling a yawn. "Who is this?"

"I'm Rhydon Baines," the voice said and Sallie's eyes popped open. "Did I wake you?"

"Yes, you did," she said baldly, unable to think of any polite assurance to give him, and a deep chuckle made her shiver with reaction. "Is anything wrong, Mr. Baines?"

"No, I just wanted to congratulate you on the job you did in Washington. That was a good piece of reporting. Sometime when you're free come up to my office for a talk. I think you're the only reporter on my staff I haven't met personally and you're one of my best."

"I—I will," she stammered. "Thank you, Mr. Baines."

"Rhy," he corrected. "I prefer to be on first-name basis with the staff. And by the way, I apologize for waking you up, but it's time you were up anyway if you're going to be at work on time." With another chuckle he said goodbye and hung up and Sallie gasped as she looked at the clock. She *was* going to be late if she didn't hurry, but Rhy would wait a long time if he was waiting for her to put in an appearance in his office!

CHAPTER THREE

THE MORNING WENT by without anything happening, though she kept a weather eye out for any sign of Rhy. She had to trust Greg to warn her if she should disappear into the ladies' room, but her phone remained silent. Brom was sent out on an assignment to L.A. and their little cubicle was silent after he left; her nerves began to fray under the strain. She ate an apple at her desk for lunch, not daring to risk going to the cafeteria or even venturing outside the building on the chance she might run into Rhy. She was beginning to feel like a prisoner!

Shortly after lunch Greg called and said, "Come up here, Sal. I don't want to talk over the phone."

Her heart leapt into her throat and she rushed up the stairs to the next floor. Greg's door was open, as usual, and she went in. Greg looked up from the papers he was reading and his expression was grim. "Rhy's secretary just called. He wants your file. I had to send it up. I had no choice. He hasn't returned from lunch yet, so you've got a few minutes of grace. I just thought I'd warn you."

She swallowed the lump in her throat. "Thanks for trying," she said, and managed a whimsical little smile. "It was a dumb idea, anyway, trying to hide from him. He probably won't care one way or the other."

Greg smiled in return, but his eyes were narrowed with worry as she left his office.

Deep in thought and facing the fact that Rhy would know her identity very shortly, she punched the elevator button instead of taking the stairs. She took a deep breath and braced herself.

Abruptly she realized that she was waiting for the elevator and the lights showed that it was coming up. Muttering to herself for her stupidity she turned on her heel and headed for the stairs, but just as she reached them the elevator doors slid open and a voice called, "Sallie Jerome! Wait a minute!"

Her head jerked around and she stared at Rhy for several seconds, frozen in her tracks with horror, then she pulled the heavy door open and took a step, intending to run before she realized the futility of it. Rhy had taken a good look at her and the arrested expression on his face told her that she'd been recognized. She couldn't avoid it any longer; he now knew who she was and he wasn't a man to let the matter drop. She released the door and swung back to face him, her delicate jaw tilting upward pugnaciously. "You wanted to see me?" she challenged.

He moved from his stance in front of the elevator and strode the few short yards that separated them. He looked taut, his skin pulled over his cheekbones, his mouth compressed into a thin line. "Sarah," he whispered savagely, his gray eyes leaping furiously.

"Sallie," she corrected, flipping her braid over her shoulder. "I'm called Sallie now."

His hand shot out and he gripped her wrist, his long fingers wrapping about the fragile bones as if to measure them. "You're not only called Sallie instead of Sarah, you're Jerome again instead of Baines," he hissed, and she shivered with alarm. She knew Rhy's voice in all of his moods, the well-remembered husky quality made it distinctive. It was a voice that could sound whispery and menacing when he was angry, rasping when he was hammering out a point on television, or low and incredibly seductive when he was making love. A wild little frisson ran along her nerves at the tone she could detect in his voice now. Rhy was in a dangerous temper and it paid to be wary of him when he was angry.

"I think you'd better come with me," he murmured, sliding his fingers from her wrist to her elbow and moving her to the elevator. "We've got a lot to say and I don't want to say it in the hallway."

He retained his light but firm hold on her as they waited for the elevator to return to the floor and a copyboy stared at them as he walked down the hall to disappear into one of the offices. "Let go of me," she whispered.

"No way, Mrs. Baines," he refused in a soft tone. The bell sounded as the elevator reached their floor and the doors slid open. He moved forward with her into the box and the doors slid closed, leaving her totally alone with him in that small space. His forefinger jabbed the number for the administrative floor and the elevator lurched into movement.

Sallie summoned all of her poise and gave him a polite little smile, determined to hide the sudden coiling of fear in her stomach. "What do we have to talk about? It's been seven years, after all."

He smiled, too, but his smile wasn't polite; the savagery of it sent shivers down her spine. "Then let's talk about old times," he said between his teeth.

"Can't it wait?"

"No," he said softly. "Now. I've got a lot of questions and I want answers to them."

"I've got work to do—"

"Just shut up," he warned, and she did.

The elevator lurched to a halt and her stomach lurched with it. Rhy's manner made her uneasy and she didn't want to be alone with him, much less go through the inquisition she knew she was in for.

He ushered her out of the elevator and down the corridor to his private office. His secretary looked up and smiled when she saw them, but the words she started to say were halted when Rhy hurled "No interruptions" over his shoulder as he followed Sallie into his office and closed the door firmly behind them.

Sallie stood only a few feet away from him and blinked, trying to adjust herself to the reality of his presence. She had been forced to accept his absence and now she just could not accept his presence. He was a mirage, a figment of her imagination, far too virile and forceful to be real.

But he stood by the door, watching her with those unnerving gray eyes, and he was very real and solid. Rather than meet those eyes she let her gaze drift over his body and she noted automatically the way his dark brown suit fit him impeccably, the trousers molding themselves to the muscled length of his legs. Her pulse began to beat a bit faster and she caught her lower lip with her teeth.

"Rhy…" Her voice quavered and she cleared her throat, then began again. "Rhy, why are you acting like this?"

"What do you mean?" he asked, his eyes glinting

dangerously. "You're my wife and I want to know what's going on here. You've obviously been avoiding me. Should I have ignored your presence, as you seem prepared to do with mine? Forgive me if I was slow on the uptake, baby, but I was surprised to see you and you caught me off-balance. I didn't think to pretend that I didn't know you."

She caught her breath in relief. "Oh, that," she said, sighing, weak now that she knew what he wanted. "Yes, I was avoiding you. I didn't know how you'd take the idea of my working for you and I didn't want to risk losing my job."

"Have you told anyone that we're married?" he barked.

She shook her head. "Everyone knows me as Sallie Jerome. I went back to my maiden name because I didn't want to use the influence of your name."

"That's big of you, Mrs. Baines," he murmured sarcastically, moving to his desk. "Sit down, I won't bite."

She took a chair, more than ready now to answer his questions. If he had been going to fire her he would already have done so; her job was safe and she relaxed visibly.

Rhy didn't sit down but instead leaned against his desk, crossed his long legs at the ankle and folded his arms across his chest. He was silent while his glittering gray eyes looked her over thoroughly from head to foot and Sallie began to tense again. She didn't know why, but he made her feel threatened even when he wasn't moving. Then his silence irritated her and she said tartly, "What did you want to talk about?"

"You've changed, Sarah—Sallie," he corrected himself. "It's a drastic change, and I don't mean just your name. You've grown a mane of hair and you've lost so much weight a good wind would blow you away. And most of all, you're doing a damned good job at something I would've sworn you'd never touch. How did you get to be a reporter?"

"Oh, that was just luck," she said cheerfully. "I was driving on a bridge when it collapsed and I wrote it up and turned it in to the editor of the newspaper and he changed my job from clerk to reporter."

"You make it sound almost logical for you to be one of the top correspondents for a first-class news magazine," he said dryly. "I gather you like your job?"

"Oh, yes!" she said, leaning forward eagerly. Her big eyes sparkled and she tripped over her words in her enthusiasm. "I love it! I never could understand why you were always so anxious to get back to work, but then I was bitten by the same bug. It gets in your blood, hooks you, doesn't it? I suppose I've become an excitement junkie, I only feel half-alive when I'm stuck here in the office."

"Your eyes haven't changed," he muttered almost to himself, his gaze locked on her face. "They're still as dark blue as the sea and so big and deep a man could drown in them. Why did you change your name?" he demanded abruptly.

"I told you, I didn't want to trade on your name," she explained patiently. "I wanted to stand on my own feet for a change and I found that I liked it. As for Sallie, somehow Sarah was changed to Sallie at college and I've been Sallie ever since then."

"College?" he asked, his eyes sharpening.

"Yes, I *finally* got my degree," she said, laughing a little. "After you left I took a lot of courses—languages and creative writing—but when I began reporting it took up so much time that I had to get my degree in fits and spurts."

"Did you go on a diet, too? You've changed everything else in your life, why not get a new figure?" He sounded almost resentful and she stared at him in bewilderment. Surely he didn't mind that she'd lost a little weight? It hadn't even been that much.

"No, I didn't go on a diet, losing weight just happened," she said, her tone reflecting her lack of understanding of the question. "I became so busy that I didn't have time to eat and that still holds true."

"Why? Why did you change yourself so drastically?"

A sudden tingle told her that this was not a casual conversation, a catching-up on old times, but that Rhy had deliberately brought her around to this question. For what reason she didn't know, but she didn't mind telling him the truth. After all, the laugh was on her. She raised her eyes to his. "When you left, Rhy, you told me to call you when I thought I was woman enough for you. I nearly died. I wanted to die. Then I decided to fight for you, to make myself into a woman you'd want, so I took a lot of courses and learned how to do a lot of things, and along the way I also learned how to do without you. End of story."

"Not quite," he said sardonically. "Your rascally husband has reentered and another chapter has started, and to make the plot really interesting he's now your boss. Let's see," he mused, "is there a company policy against employing relatives?"

"If there is," she returned clearly, "I was here first."

"But I'm the boss," he reminded her, a wolfish grin moving across his face. "Don't worry about it, baby. I don't intend to fire you. You're too good a reporter for me to let you go to someone else." He got to his feet and so did she, but he said, "Sit down, I'm not finished." Obediently she resumed her seat and he walked around to take his own chair, leaning back in it as he picked up a file.

Sallie recognized the file as belonging to personnel and she realized that it held her own records. But she had no reason to keep Rhy from reading it, so she watched as he leafed through it.

"I'm curious about your application," he said. "You said no one knows we're married, but what did you put down as your marital status?" he questioned. "Ah, here it is. You've been very honest. You admitted to being married. But your husband's name is, SEPARATED—CONFIDENTIAL INFORMATION."

"I told you no one knew," she replied.

He looked over the application and his brows abruptly snapped together. "Next of kin—none?" he demanded harshly. "What if you'd been hurt, even killed? That does happen, you know! How could I have been notified?"

"I didn't think you'd care," she defended herself. "Actually, I didn't think about it at all, but I can see where you'd want to know. You might want to get married again someday. I'm sorry, that was thoughtless of me."

A vein began throbbing in his temple and she watched it in fascination. It meant that he was furious, as she remembered all too well, but she couldn't think why he should be so angry. After all, she hadn't been killed, so she didn't see anything to worry about.

He closed the file and tossed it back onto his desk, his lips pressed into a grim line. "Get married again!"

he suddenly shouted. "Why would I be fool enough to do that? Once was enough!"

"It certainly was," she agreed with heartfelt sincerity.

His eyes narrowed and he seemed to force his temper down. "You don't think you'd like to remarry?" he asked silkily.

"A husband would interfere with my job," she said, and shook her head. "No, I'd rather live by myself."

"You don't have any…er…close friends who object when you take off for days, even weeks, at a time?" he probed.

"I have a lot of friends, yes, but they're mostly in the business themselves so they understand if I go on assignment," she answered calmly and ignored the inference he made. It was none of his business if she had any lovers or not, and suddenly she felt it was important for her pride that he not know he was the only man who had ever made love to her. After all, he certainly hadn't lived the life of a monk, as witness the gorgeous Coral Williams!

"I've read a lot of your articles," he commented, switching to a different tack. "You've been in some tight places—Lebanon, Africa, South America. Don't your *friends* mind that you could get hurt?"

"Like I said, they're in the business themselves. Any of us could come back dead," she returned dryly. "It was the same with you, but you kept going. Why *have* you grounded yourself? You could pick your own assignments, and we heard you were offered the anchor job?"

"Maybe it's a sign of old age, but I got tired of being shot at," he said abruptly. "And I was getting bored, I wanted a change. I'd made some good investments through the years and when *Review* came up for sale

I decided to make the change, so I bought it. I'm still signed with the network to do four documentaries for next year and that's always interesting. I have time to do more research, to build a background on my subject."

Sallie looked doubtful. "I think I'd prefer foreign assignments."

He started to say something when the phone on his desk buzzed. In swift irritation he punched the intercom line and snapped, "I said no interruptions!"

Simultaneously the door opened and a soft voice said, "But I knew you wouldn't consider me an interruption, darling. If you have some poor reporter on the carpet I'm sure you've already said all that needs to be said."

Sallie turned her head to stare in amazement at Coral Williams, who was breathtaking in a severe black dress that merely served to flatter her blond perfection. The model was a picture of self-confidence as she smiled at Rhy, fully expecting him to welcome her with open arms.

Rhy said evenly, "I see your problem, Miss Meade," and replaced the receiver. To Coral he said in the same even tone, "It had better be important, Coral, because I've got a lot on my mind."

Such as stumbling over his long-lost wife, Sallie thought to herself, involuntarily smiling as she got to her feet. "If that's all, Mr. Baines...?"

He looked frustrated and ill-tempered. "We'll talk about it later," he snapped, and she took it that she was dismissed. She made her exit with a triumphant grin at a visibly puzzled Coral and gave Rhy's secretary the same grin on her way out.

The first thing she had to do was relieve Greg's

mind, so she stopped by his office on her way down. "He knows," she told him matter-of-factly, sticking her head through the door. "It's okay, he didn't fire me."

Greg shoved his fingers roughly through his hair, rumpling the prematurely gray strands into untidy peaks. "You've aged me ten years, doll." He sighed. "I'm glad he knows, that's a weight off me. Is it going to be common knowledge?"

"I wouldn't think so," she hedged. "He didn't mention that. Coral is in his office now, and I don't think he'd want anyone fouling up *that* relationship."

"What a wonderfully understanding wife you are," he mocked, and she stuck her tongue out at him.

With all of the tension behind her she attacked the article she was writing with renewed vigor and finished it that afternoon. Again Chris stopped by her desk, this time to tell her that he was leaving that night for Miami. "Want to see me off?" he invited, and she readily accepted.

Sometimes it was nice to see a familiar face in the crowd when you got on a flight in the middle of the night, so she saw nothing unusual about Chris wanting her company. It wasn't until they were on their way to the airport that Sallie realized that Chris had sought out her company several times lately. She liked Chris, he was a good, steady friend, but she knew that it would never develop into anything more serious on her part. Rather than let the situation stew, she asked him frankly, "Just for the record, why are you asking me to lunch, to see you off, et cetera? Is it for a reason I should know?"

"I'm using you," he admitted just as frankly. "You're good company and you don't expect anything more than friendship. You keep my ego built up, too, because you're a great-looking woman."

She had to chuckle; in her opinion great-looking women were not petite dynamos with more energy than fashion sense. But it was still nice to have a man voice that opinion. "Thanks," she told him cheerfully, "but that still doesn't tell me why."

He raised his sandy eyebrows. "Because of another woman, of course. What else could it be?"

"Anyone I know?" she asked.

"No, she's not in this business. She lives in my apartment building and she's the nesting type. She wants a nine-to-five husband, and I can't see myself settling down into that routine. It's a standoff. She won't back down and neither will I."

"So what will you do?"

"Wait. I'm a patient man. She'll either come around or we won't get together, it's that simple."

"Why should she do all the giving?" Sallie asked indignantly, amazed that even reasonable Chris should expect the woman to make all of the adjustments.

"Because I know I can't," he mocked, smiling a little. "I know my limitations, Sal. I only hope she's stronger than I am and can make some changes."

Then he deftly changed the subject and Sallie realized that he had revealed as much as he was going to. They talked shop for the rest of the time, and she waited with him for his flight to be called, sensing that he felt vulnerable. Leaving for a long trip in the middle of the night with no one to see you off was a lonely experience, and she was willing to give him at least one familiar face to wave goodbye to.

It was after ten when she finally got back to her

apartment and she quickly showered and got ready for bed. Just as she turned out the lamp the phone rang and she switched the light back on to answer it.

"Sallie? Where in hell have you been?" Rhy demanded impatiently, and as always his husky voice made her spine tingle.

"At the airport," she found herself answering automatically.

"Meeting someone?" he asked, and his voice became sharper.

"No, seeing someone off." She had recovered her poise, and she quickly asked, "Why are you calling?"

"You left this afternoon before we got anything settled," he snapped.

Mystified, she echoed, "Settled? What's there to settle?"

"Our marriage, for one thing," he retorted sarcastically.

Abruptly she understood and tried to reassure him that she wouldn't cause any trouble in the termination of their marriage. "We shouldn't have any trouble getting a divorce, considering how long we've been separated. And getting a divorce is a good idea. We should have done it sooner. Seven years is a long time. It's obvious that our marriage is over in every respect except legally. I see no reason why it shouldn't be terminated on paper, too."

"You talk too much," he observed, the rasp coming into his voice that warned of his rising temper.

Confused, Sallie fell silent. What had she said to make him angry? Why had he brought up the subject if he didn't want to talk about it?

"I don't want a divorce," he said a moment later. "I've

found it very convenient, having a little wife tucked away somewhere."

She laughed and sat up in bed, pushing a pillow behind her back for support. "Yes, I can see where it would come in handy," she dared to tease him. "It keeps the husband-hungry women effectively at bay, doesn't it? Still, we've reached the point where to remain married is foolish. Shall I file or would you rather?"

"Are you being deliberately stupid?" he barked. "I said I don't want a divorce!"

Sallie fell silent again, stunned by his insistence. "But, Rhy!" she finally protested incredulously. "Whyever not?"

"I told you," he said with the manner of one explaining the obvious. "I find it convenient to have a wife."

"You could always lie!"

"Why should I bother? And there's always the chance of a lie being found out. No, thank you for the offer, but I think I'll keep you, regardless of who you have waiting in the wings to take my place."

Abruptly Sallie was angry. Why had he called her at all if he didn't want a divorce, and who was he to make snide remarks about anyone waiting in the wings? "You're just being obnoxious!" she charged furiously. "What's wrong, Rhy? Is Coral crowding you a bit? Do you need your convenient wife for protection? Well, you can hide behind someone else, because I don't need your cooperation for a divorce! You deserted me, and you've been gone for seven years, and any judge in the state will give me a divorce!"

"You think so?" he challenged, laughing aloud. "Try it. I've made a lot of friends and divorcing me could be harder than you think. You'd better have a lot of money and a lot of time before you start, and you'd better have a more reliable job. You're in a rather vulnerable position, aren't you? You can't afford to make your boss angry."

"My boss can go straight to—to hell!" she shouted furiously and slammed the receiver down. The phone began ringing again immediately and she glared at it for a moment, then when it continued its irritating noise she reached over and unplugged it, something she rarely did in case Greg needed to reach her.

Then she turned out the lamp and pounded her pillow into shape, but any chance for sleep was now remote. She lay in the darkness and fumed, wishing she could take her temper out on Rhy's head. Why had he called at all if he didn't want to talk about a divorce? If he wanted to use her to keep Coral at a distance he could just find someone else to do his dirty work for him! Personally, she thought Coral was just his type, someone poised and sophisticated who wouldn't care if her husband was more interested in his job than in his wife.

Then, as if someone had turned on a light in a dark room, she knew why Rhy was so stubborn about not getting a divorce, why he had asked all of those prying, suggestive questions about her friends. If she had learned anything at all about Rhy during the year they had been together it was that he was a possessive man. He didn't want to give up anything that belonged to him, and that included his wife. It obviously didn't bother him that thousands of miles might separate them, that they hadn't seen each other in years, his attitude was that once his wife, always his wife. *He* might not want her anymore, but he was too stubborn to give her up if he thought anyone else might want to marry her. What he didn't realize was that her attitude was much the same as his: once was enough.

She admitted honestly to herself that she would never love another man as she had loved Rhy, and even though she had now recovered from the emotional damage he'd inflicted she didn't think she'd ever be able to love so passionately, so demandingly again. Neither was she willing to settle for a lukewarm, comfortable relationship after having known such a love.

Of course, there'd be no convincing him that she didn't want a divorce in order to marry another man. He'd never understand the need she felt to be free of him. While he'd been only a distant figure it hadn't bothered her, but now that he was going to be around permanently she felt stifled. Rhy's character was too forceful, too possessive, and if he thought he had any legal authority over her he wouldn't hesitate to use it in any way he wanted.

For the first time Sallie seriously faced the possibility that she might have to hunt for another job. She loved her job, she liked working for *World in Review,* but there were other publications. And with Rhy threatening to fire her if she tried to divorce him the best thing she could do was spike that weapon before he had a chance to use it.

CHAPTER FOUR

SALLIE STARED MOROSELY at the keys of her typewriter, trying to force words into a reasonable sentence, but her mind stayed stubbornly blank and so did the white paper rolled into the machine. She had always been so enthusiastic about her work, the words pouring from her in swift, flowing sentences, that this block she was experiencing was tying her nerves into king-size knots. She'd never had this trouble before and she was at a loss. How could she write about something that bored her to tears? And this article *was* boring!

Brom had been summoned to Greg's office and now he returned. "I'm off," he announced, clearing the top of his desk. "Munich."

Sallie swiveled in her chair to face him. "Anything interesting?"

"A Common Market meeting. There's some trouble that could break it up. I'll see you when I get back."

"Yeah, okay," Sallie said, and tried to smile.

Brom paused by her desk and his hand touched her shoulder. "Is anything wrong, Sal? You've been acting under the weather for a couple of weeks now. Have you seen a doctor?"

"It's nothing," she assured him, and he left. When she was alone again she turned back to the typewriter and scowled at it. She hadn't seen a doctor; there was nothing to cure boredom. Why was she being kept in the office? Greg knew that she did her best work in the field, but it had been three weeks since she'd returned from Washington and she hadn't been on a single assignment since then, not even a small one. Instead she'd been flooded with "suggestions" for articles that anyone could have written. She'd done her best, but she'd come up against a stone wall now and suddenly she was angry. If Greg wasn't going to use her she wanted to know why!

In determination she switched off her typewriter and made her way to Greg's office. He wasn't there, so she sat down to wait, and as she waited her temper faded, but her resolve didn't. The natural tenacity that kept her on a lead when she wanted a story also kept her firm in her decision to get to the bottom of why suddenly Greg was ignoring her. They'd always had the best of working relationships, respect mixed with affection, and now it was as if Greg no longer trusted her to do her job.

She had to wait almost forty minutes before Greg returned, and when he opened the door and saw her sitting there, a wary, concerned expression crossed his face before he quickly smoothed it away. "Hi, doll, how's the article going?" he greeted her.

"It isn't. I can't do it."

He sighed at the blunt announcement and sat down behind his desk. After toying with a pencil for a minute he said easily, "We all have problems occasionally. What's wrong with the article? Anything you can put your finger on?"

"It's boring," she said baldly and Greg flinched. "I don't know why you've been throwing all the garbage at me, so I'm asking you, why? I'm good at my job, but you aren't letting me do it. Are you trying to force me to resign? Has Rhy decided that he doesn't want his wife working for him, but he doesn't want to make things look bad by firing me?"

Greg ran his fingers through his gray-brown hair and sighed, his hard, firm-jawed face tense. "You're putting me on the spot," he muttered. "Can't you just let things rest for a while?"

"No!" she exploded, then calmed herself. "I'm sorry. I think I know that it isn't your fault, you've always given me the assignments you thought I could handle. It's Rhy, isn't it?"

"He's taken you off foreign assignments," Greg affirmed.

Though Sallie had braced herself for something like that, to hear the words actually spoken and her suspicions confirmed was a worse blow than she had anticipated. She paled and visibly shrank in her seat. Taken off assignment! It was a deadly blow. All of the passion she'd offered to Rhy had been transferred to her job when he walked out and through the years she'd learned that a satisfying job had enriched her life. She didn't doubt that a psychologist would tell her that her job was merely a substitute for what she really wanted, a man, and perhaps it had been at first. But she was no longer the same person she'd been seven years before; she was a mature, independent adult, and she felt as a musician might if his hands were crippled, as if her life had been blighted.

Through a throat thick with horror she murmured, "Why?"

"I don't know why," Greg replied. "Look, honey, all I know is he took you off foreign assignment. You can still cover anything in the States and several things have come up but I kept you here because anyone could have covered the others and I wanted you available in case something more important developed. Maybe I was wrong. I was trying to do what was best for the magazine, but I know how you are about being in one place for too long. If anything comes up, regardless of what it is, do you want it? Just say the word and it's yours."

"It doesn't matter," she said wearily, and he frowned. Defeat wasn't something he expected from Sallie. Then she looked up and her dark blue eyes were beginning to spark with anger. "On second thought, yes, I do want it. Anything! If you can keep me gone for six months straight, that will be fine, too. The only way I'm going to keep from killing Rhy is if I'm kept away from him. Was this supposed to be kept secret, that I'm off foreign assignment?"

"I wouldn't think so," Greg denied. "I just didn't tell you because I kept hoping I could keep you satisfied on other jobs, but nothing came up. Why?"

"Because I'm going to ask Rhy that same question," she said, and a feline smile curved her mouth at the thought of engaging in battle with her arrogant husband.

Greg leaned back in his chair and studied the suddenly glowing little face, alight with the anticipation of a struggle. For a minute he'd been worried about her, afraid that vibrant energy had been snuffed, but now he grinned in appreciation. Sallie came alive when the going was roughest and that was one of the characteristics that made her one of his best reporters. "Give it all you've got," he said gruffly. "I need you back in the field."

Amanda Meade, Rhy's secretary, smiled at Sallie

when she entered. Amanda had also been the secretary of the former publisher and she knew all of the staff; proof of her discretion was that no talk had circulated about Sallie's private interview with Rhy, for which Sallie was grateful. She didn't want any gossip starting about them or Rhy might take it into his head to jettison her entirely in order to halt the talk.

"Hi, Sallie," Amanda greeted her. "Is there anything I can help you with, or do you need to see the boss?"

"The boss, if he's available," Sallie replied.

"He's available for the minute," Amanda confirmed, "but he's got a lunch date with Miss Williams at twelve, so he'll be leaving shortly."

"I won't be long," Sallie promised. "Ask if he'll see me."

Amanda buzzed the inner office on the private line and Sallie listened as she explained the reason for the interruption. After only a few seconds she hung up and smiled again. "Go on in, he's free—and he's been in a very good mood lately, too!"

Sallie had to laugh. "Thanks for the information, but I don't think I'll ask for a raise, anyway!"

Crossing to Rhy's office she entered and firmly closed the door behind her, wanting to make certain that none of their conversation was overheard. Rhy was standing by the huge plate-glass window, staring down at the hordes of people below as they surged up and down the street. He was in his shirt sleeves, with the cuff links removed and lying on his desk and the cuffs rolled back to reveal muscular forearms. When he turned she saw that he'd also removed his tie; he looked more like a reporter than a publisher and he exuded an air of virility that no other man could quite match.

"Hello, baby," he drawled, his rough-velvet voice containing an intimate note that made her pulses leap. "It took you long enough to get here. I was beginning to think you were playing it safe."

What did he mean? Had Greg called to warn Rhy that she was coming? No, she'd just left Greg's office, and in any case he wanted her free to go on assignment. Printer's ink ran in Greg's veins, not blood.

"I don't understand," she said curtly. "What do you mean, it took me long enough?"

"For you to realize you'd been grounded," he replied, smiling as he approached her. Before she had a chance to avoid him he was standing before her, his hard, warm hands clasping her elbows and she quivered at his touch. She tried to move away and his grip tightened, but only enough to hold her. "I was going to tell you the night I called, but you hung up on me," he continued, still smiling. "So I waited for you to come to me."

Sallie was blessed with acute senses and now she wished that they weren't so acute, because she could smell the warm male scent of his body under the quiet aftershave he wore. He was close enough for her to notice that he still, after all these years, didn't wear an undershirt, because she could see the dark curling hairs on his chest through the thin fabric of his shirt. She tore her gaze away from his chest and lifted it higher to his cleanly shaven jaw, to his lips, relaxed and smiling, then higher still, to the direct gaze of those dark gray eyes under level black brows.

With supreme willpower she forced her attention away from his physical attractions and said in a half whisper, "Why? You know how much I love foreign assignments. Why did you take me off?"

"Because I'm not that much of a newsman," he answered dryly, and she stared at him in bewilderment. He released her elbows and slid his hands warmly up her arms, drawing her with him to the desk, where he leaned against its edge and pulled her forward until she stood between his legs. He was more on her level in that position, and the mesmerizing gray eyes looking directly into hers prevented her from protesting at his closeness.

"What do you mean?" she managed, her voice no stronger this time than it had been before. His fingers were massaging the bare skin of her upper arms and involuntarily she began to tremble.

"I mean that I couldn't stand the thought of sending you into potentially dangerous situations," he explained softly. "South America, Africa, the Middle East are all political time bombs and I didn't want to take the chance that you might be caught in one of them if they explode. Europe—even in Europe there are kidnappings, terrorist groups, bombings in air terminals and on the streets. For my own peace of mind I took you off foreign assignment, though Downey nearly had a stroke when I told him. He thinks you're one of the best, baby. I could wring his neck when I think of the situations he's sent you into!"

"Greg's a professional," Sallie defended huskily. "And so am I. I'm not helpless, Rhy. I've taken weapons training and self-defense courses. I can take care of myself. Staying here is driving me crazy! I feel as if I've been put out to pasture!"

He laughed and reached behind her for her braid, pulling it over her shoulder and settling the thick rope over her breast. He began playing with the braid, running his fingers over the smooth twists of hair and the corners of his mouth moved into another smile. "This is quite a mane," he murmured. "I'd like to see it out of this braid and spread across my pillow while I make love to you."

Sallie was rocked on her heels by his words and her cheeks paled. Of all the things he might have said she certainly hadn't expected that! She raised stunned eyes to him and saw his pupils dilated with desire; then he jerked her forward and she lay against him, trapped by the pressure of his powerful legs clasping hers and his arms as they slid around her.

She gasped at the contact of his hard, warm body and, as they always had, her senses began swimming when he touched her. Fighting for control, she turned her head to him to demand that he turn her loose and he took advantage of the opportunity, fitting her more tightly into the curve of his body with the pressure of his arms, and bending his head down. His mouth was hot and forceful and drugging, and she began wriggling in his grasp, trying to escape from her inevitable response to him as much as she was trying to escape from the man himself. By stretching her willpower to its limits she managed to resist the probing of his tongue between her lips, keeping her teeth tightly clenched. After a moment he lifted his head and his breathing was faster, his eyes still eager.

"Open your mouth," he commanded huskily. "You know how I want to kiss you. Let me feel your sweet little tongue against mine again."

He lowered his head again, and this time her willpower wasn't up to the demands she made on it. Her senses exploded with pleasure at the touch of his lips on hers and when his tongue moved demandingly she let her lips and teeth part and he gained possession of the sweet interior of her mouth. With a groan he tightened his arms and in response her hands slid up his arms and shoulders to climb about his neck. Her slim body quivered at the wild storm his kiss was causing, and helplessly she arched against him, gasping her need into his mouth as she realized just how strongly he was aroused.

It had always been like that. From the first kiss they had shared to the last time he'd made love to her, their physical responses to each other had been strong and immediate. She'd never wanted another lover because she'd known instinctively that no other man could arouse her as Rhy did, even now, despite all of the perfectly good reasons she had for not wanting to respond to him. Her body simply did not listen to her mind, and after a few moments she stopped wanting to protest. She felt wildly alive and drowning at the same time, straining against him even as her senses were overwhelmed by the countless pleasure signals her nerves were giving out.

When he lifted his mouth from hers she was so weak and trembly that she had to cling to him for support. Triumph gleamed hotly in his eyes as he held her up with one arm about her waist and with his free hand he cupped her chin and held it still while he pressed swift light kisses across her face and lips.

"Mmm," he groaned deep in his throat, "that still hasn't changed. It's still dynamite."

His words brought a measure of sanity to her fevered brain, and she struggled to put a little space between them. Yes, it *was* still dynamite, and it had nearly blown up in her face! She was a fool if she allowed Rhy to use his physical attractions to make her forget the reason she'd come up here.

"Rhy—don't!" she protested, turning her face away as his lips continued to nibble at her skin. "Let me go. I came up here to talk to you—"

"We've talked," he interrupted huskily, his voice going even lower and rougher, a signal which told her he didn't want to stop. "I'd rather make love now. It's been a long time, but not long enough for me to forget what it was like between us."

"Well, *I've* forgotten," she lied, once again avoiding his kiss. "Stop fooling around! I'm serious about my job and I don't like being grounded because you think that a woman can't take care of herself in a crisis."

He ceased trying to kiss her, but his eyes were impatient as he stared down at her. "All right, we'll talk about the job, then I want the subject dropped. I didn't say that I don't think a woman can take care of herself. I said that I didn't want *you* in a dangerous situation because I didn't think *I* could stand it."

"Why should you care?" Sallie demanded in surprise. "You certainly haven't exhibited much concern for my welfare since you walked out, so don't ruin my job by acting concerned now."

Abruptly he released her and she moved several feet away from him. She was glad of the distance; she needed all of her wits about her in order to handle Rhy, and his closeness clouded her brain with erotic fever. "My decision is final," he informed her curtly. "You're off foreign assignment, permanently."

She stared at him and her stomach lurched sickeningly at his words. Permanently? She could more easily stop eating than she could give up the dangerous excitement of the job she loved! He couldn't have thought of anything that would hurt her more if he'd planned this for years. "Do you hate me so much?" she murmured, her dark blue eyes turning almost to black with pain. "What have I ever done to you to make you treat me like this?"

"Of course I don't hate you," he denied impatiently, thrusting a long-fingered hand through his black hair. "I'm trying to protect you. You're my wife and I don't want you hurt."

"Drivel!" she cried, her small fists clenching at her side. "Being tied down is worse than anything that's likely to happen to me on assignment! I'm only half-alive here. I'm going crazy staring at that blasted type-writer hour after hour with nothing coming in my head to put down on paper! And don't say I'm your wife! The extent of our relationship was that we slept together off and on for about a year, then you went your way and I went mine, and I'm a lot happier now than I ever was with you. You were an even bigger flop as a husband than I was as a wife!" She stopped and drew a trembling breath, trying to control the urge to break something, to hit out at him with her fists. Though she had a temper she wasn't usually so uncontrolled and she knew that frustration had strained her nerves.

"Flop or not, you're my wife and you'll stay my wife," he stated coldly, dropping the words like stones on her head. "And my wife will not go on foreign assignments!"

"Why don't you just shoot me?" she demanded furiously, her voice rising. "That would be more merciful than driving me mad with boredom! Blast you, Rhy,

I don't know why you married me anyway!" she concluded in acute frustration.

"I married you because I felt sorry for you," he informed her bluntly, and the simple statement left her gaping at him in outrage.

"You—you felt *sorry* for me?" she cried, and she thought she'd explode with rage. Of all the humiliating things to say to her!

"You were such a lonely little thing," he explained calmly, as if every word didn't lash at her raw nerves. "And so starved for affection, for a human touch. I thought, Why the hell not? I was twenty-eight years old. It was time I got married. And here was an added bonus."

"Yes," she snapped, stalking to the window to stare down at the street below, anything to keep from looking at the mocking dark face, the sardonic eyes. "You got protection from all of your pursuing girlfriends!" With relish she contemplated planting a fist right in his mouth, except that Rhy wouldn't let her get away with that. She knew that he'd retaliate.

He grinned at her temper and walked up behind her, so close that his breath stirred the hair at her temple. "No, baby, the added bonus was the way you went wild whenever I touched you. You looked so quiet and tame, a plump little dove, but in bed you turned into a wildcat. The contrast was fascinating."

"I can see you've had a lot of laughs over it!" she blurted, her face going crimson with humiliation.

"Oh, no, I never laughed," he replied, his voice suddenly becoming soft and whispery. "The loving between us was too good. No other woman ever quite matched you. Everything else about you has changed, but not the way you respond."

Her pride stung, she retorted sharply, "Forget about that. It didn't mean anything."

"I think it did. It means I've found my wife again. I want you back, Sallie," he informed her silkily.

Astonishment spun her around to face him, and she stared up at him with eyes grown huge in her small face. "You're joking!" she accused, her voice shaking. "It's impossible!"

"I don't think it's so impossible," he murmured, catching her close to him and pressing his face into her hair. "I never meant to let you go, anyway," he continued, his voice growing low and seductive. She knew that he was consciously using the erotic power of his voice to disarm and attract her, but recognizing his weapons didn't necessarily give her the strength to fight them. She shivered and tried to pull away, but his grip tightened.

"I thought you'd back down and call me. I was fed up with your nagging and determined to teach you a lesson," he said, raising his head and looking down into her astounded face. "But you didn't call, and I had my career to see to and time got away from me. Seven years is a long time to be separated, but we've both matured in that length of time, and I intend to pull on that leash you still have around your neck, sweetheart!"

"Don't be silly!" she said, shaking her head to deny his casual assumption that she had no choice in the matter, that she would tamely let him lead her about. He had a lot to learn about her! "It wouldn't work out, Rhy. We're two different people now. I'm no longer content to putter around a house. There are so many things I want to do that I may never get around to them all. I have to be on the move."

"I'll be traveling quite a bit with the documentaries I've signed to do. You could always quit your job and travel with me," he pointed out, and she recoiled from that suggestion as if he had thrown a snake at her.

"Give up my job?" she echoed, aghast. "Rhy, are you crazy? I don't want to spend my life tagging after you! This isn't just a job to me, it's *my* career, too. If you want us to be together so badly you quit *your* job." She drew her mouth into a hard line and glared her challenge at him.

"I make more than you do," he drawled. "It would be stupid for me to quit. Besides, I own this magazine."

"The entire idea of us trying to live together is stupid," she blasted him. "Why not just obtain a quiet divorce? You won't have to worry that I'll ask for alimony, I like supporting myself—"

"No," he interrupted, his jaw hardening as temper began to flicker in his eyes. "No divorce, under any circumstances."

"All right, maybe you can make it difficult for me to get a divorce," she acknowledged. "But I don't have to live with you and I don't have to work for you. There are other magazines, newspapers and wire services, and I'm good at my job. I don't need you or your magazine."

"Don't you? Like I've told before, I have a lot of friends and if I put the word out that I don't want you working, believe me, you won't be reporting. Maybe you could get a job in a restaurant or driving a cab, but that'll be it, and I can stop that too if I want." His eyes narrowed on her and a grin split his dark face. "And in the meantime, you're still my wife, and I intend to treat you as such."

The threat was implicit in his words and she sucked in her breath. Alarm rioted along her nerves as she realized that he intended to resume his marital rights. "I'll get a court order forcing you to stay away from me!" she ground out, too angry now to back down even though she knew that, if dared, Rhy would go to any lengths to get what he wanted.

"A court order might be difficult to obtain if the right pressure is brought to bear," he mocked, enjoying his power over her. "And after a little while you just might decide that you like having me around, you did before. If I remember correctly, and I do, that was the basis of all your complaints, that I was never there. Let's try the whole bit again, hmm?" he murmured cajolingly. "And you wanted kids. We'll have kids, all you want. As a matter of fact, I'm willing to start on that project right now."

Sallie ground her teeth in rage, more upset than he could know by his reference to having children. The beast! "I've had a baby, thank you!" she choked, lashing out in her raging need to hurt him as she'd been hurt, as she still hurt. "And if *I* remember correctly, Mr. Baines, you didn't want him! I carried him alone, and I had him alone and I buried him alone! I don't need you or anything about you!"

"I don't care whether or not you need me," he said, his mouth tightening into a grim line at her reckless words. "I can make you want me, and that's all that matters. You can spit fire at me all you want, but you and I both know that if I want you I can have you. Make up your mind to it, you're mine and I'm not about to let you go. I'm ready to settle down now, for real this time. You're my wife, and I wouldn't mind a couple of kids before we're too old."

She strangled on the hot words that bubbled in her throat and jerked away from him. "No," she refused savagely. "No to everything. No to you and no to your kids. Let someone else have the honor! I'm sure Coral would be more than eager to take on the job. And since she's waiting for you now I won't keep you any longer!"

His roar of laughter followed her as she stormed out of his office and Amanda Meade stared at her with round eyes. Without a word Sallie slammed the door and stood in the hallway, shaking with temper. The most galling thing of all was that she was helpless. Rhy had the power to destroy the career she'd so carefully, lovingly created for herself and he'd do it without a moment's thought if he wanted her.

She returned to her desk and sank into her chair, trembling inside. Why was he doing this to her? He couldn't be serious—could he? The memory of his hot kisses returned vividly and blood surged into her cheeks. *That* hadn't changed! Was it just sex that he wanted from her, that and the challenge she now represented to his male ego? She had been his once and she might have guessed that he'd be unable to endure the thought that now she didn't want him.

The only thing was, she wasn't so certain now that she didn't want him. Making love with him was fantastic, and she'd never forgotten the heated magic of his caresses. For just a minute she sank into a delicious daydream of what it would be like to be his wife again, to live with him and sleep beside him and make love with him; then cold reality intruded. If she went back to

him, then what? He'd already grounded her. He'd take
her away from her job entirely, perhaps even get her
pregnant again. Sallie thought longingly of a baby, but
she knew Rhy well enough to think beyond that. She
could see herself with a child and Rhy growing bored
and restless as he had before, resentful that she'd become pregnant. He wouldn't be faithful; he wasn't now,
so why should he be later?

He'd tire of her and she'd be both without a job and
hampered by a baby. Top jobs in the reporting field
were hard to come by and required more than dedica-
tion; they required a reporter's whole life. If she left
the field she'd have a difficult time returning, carving
another niche for herself, and if there was a baby, what
would she do then?

The thought of what could happen if she returned to
Rhy frightened her and she knew that if she had a choice
she would take her job. It had never let her down as Rhy
had. And she loved what she was doing. She knew just
how precious her independence was, and she wasn't
about to sacrifice it for physical gratification.

She couldn't think what to do. Her nature was to act,
but in this situation there was nothing she *could* do. Rhy
would block any effort she made to get another job unless she disappeared and took another name, moved to
another section of the country. The thought shook her;
it seemed so drastic, but even before her nerves had settled she was making plans. Why should a little thing like
creating another identity stop her? Hadn't she learned
that she could handle almost anything? She would hate
to give up her job, this particular job, but she could find
another if she had to. The important thing was to stay
away from Rhy.

It was still a few minutes before lunchtime, but she jerked the cover over her typewriter and slung her purse over her shoulder. If she knew Rhy he would start maneuvering immediately to hem her in, and she had a lot of things to do to protect herself.

She caught a taxi to the bank where she kept her checking and savings accounts and closed both of them out. She didn't know if Rhy could block any withdrawals if she needed money in a hurry, but it seemed wise not to take the chance. Over the years she had managed to save several thousand dollars, enough that she would be able to support herself while she looked for another job, and she felt more secure with the cashier's check in her purse. Rhy would find that she was no longer a helpless little ninny for him to intimidate!

She was rarely hungry, but she'd burned a lot of calories that morning and her stomach was beginning to protest. On impulse she stopped at the bar and grill just around the corner from the *World in Review* building and found an empty booth in a dark corner. It was like going into a cave until her eyes adjusted to the dimness, then she recognized several of the staff either sitting at the bar or tucking into lunch in one of the dark booths. She ordered a grilled cheese sandwich and coffee and was waiting for her food when Chris dropped his lanky form into the seat opposite her. It was the first time she'd seen him since he'd returned from Florida, and she noticed how tanned he looked, even in the dimness of the bar.

"Florida suits you," she commented. "How have you been?"

He shrugged, his quiet face wry. "I'm still at a standoff, if that's what you're asking. What about you, doll? I've heard a rumor that you've been grounded."

"It's true," Sallie admitted, frowning. "Orders from the top."

"Baines himself? What'd you do?"

"It's not what I did, it's what I am. He thinks foreign assignment is too dangerous for me."

Chris snorted in disbelief. "C'mon, Baines is too good a newsman to ground you for a stupid reason like that. Level with me, Sal. What's going on? I saw him staring at you that day in the cafeteria."

"Oh, it's true that he thinks foreign assignment is too dangerous for me," she insisted. "But that's only part of the reason. He thinks I'd be a nice addition to his personal scalp collection, if you get my meaning. Unfortunately, I don't agree."

Chris whistled soundlessly through his teeth. "Big boss is after you, eh? Well, I agree with him that you're a fetching little witch. The only difference is, I never had the guts to tackle you."

Sallie exploded into laughter, knowing that while Chris might like her well enough he'd never been attracted to her romantically. Though he was the footloose type he was attracted to nesting women; he wanted someone who could provide a stable base for him when he returned from his wanderings. Sallie was too much of a wanderer herself for Chris to be interested. He kept a straight face while she rocked with laughter, holding her sides, but his brown eyes danced with amusement.

Afterward they returned to work together, and as they entered the lobby Chris had his arm affectionately around her waist. The first person Sallie saw was Rhy, waiting for the elevator, and as he looked at them and saw Chris with his arm about her his eyes flared, then narrowed to furious slits.

"Uh-oh, trouble," Chris muttered to her, then gave her a grin. As the elevator opened and Rhy stepped in Chris compounded his sins by hugging her close and kissing the top of her head. In the last glimpse Sallie had of Rhy before the doors closed and hid him from view he looked murderous.

CHAPTER FIVE

"YOU FOOL," SALLIE whispered to Chris, torn between laughter and genuine concern. Rhy was a dangerous man when he was angry. He was strong enough and wild enough and mean enough to handle just about anyone he wanted to handle, and he'd taken a lot of specialized training. Underneath his perfectly tailored three-piece suits Rhy was a half-civilized commando and he could hurt Chris badly. "Are you trying to get yourself killed? Rhy has a hair-trigger temper!"

"I didn't want him to take you for granted," Chris explained lazily. He gave her a crooked grin. "Feel free to use me any time you need the safety of numbers, the least I can do is return the favors you've done me. I use you, you use me in return."

Sallie drew in her breath. The idea was tempting, to pretend to Rhy that she was wildly in love with Chris, except that she didn't think she could act well enough to make it convincing and she would hate to push Rhy far enough that he lost his temper and hurt Chris.

"Thanks for the offer, but I don't think it'd be very smart to act out our charades in front of him," she declined. "I like your face as it is. But if you don't mind I'll throw up your name as a smoke screen to hide behind."

"Okay by me." He regarded her seriously. "Why are

you trying to get away from him? He's got everything a man—or a woman—could want."

"I knew Rhy before he bought the magazine," Sallie explained with caution, not wanting to tell him too much. "He wants to renew the relationship and I don't. It's that simple."

"Except for the feeling that you're leaving a lot untold, I believe you," Chris mused almost to himself and left her with a smile.

After returning to her desk Sallie waited all afternoon for a call summoning her to Rhy's office, but the call didn't materialize and she finally realized that he was more subtle than that. He'd let her worry about it, become anxious and vulnerable. She'd show him!

With a flourish she pushed aside the article she'd been working on and rolled a clean sheet of paper into the typewriter. If Rhy wanted to play dirty, then she had no scruples about not doing her work. Instead of concentrating on that stupid article she'd begin her memoirs! If she wrote her life story down as it happened, when she got old it would be finished and she wouldn't have to try to remember all of the details!

Adrenalin flowed through her veins and her fingers flew over the typewriter keys. For the first time in weeks words spilled out of her brain and she scarcely paused to get them in order. She felt elated, alive again. Enthusiasm pulsed through her body.

Suddenly she dropped her hands, staring at what she'd written. Why play around with her memoirs? Why not take her own experiences and weave them into a novel? She'd always wanted to write a book but she'd never had the time. Now she had the time, and she wanted to laugh aloud at the thought of using Rhy's time and money to begin a new career for herself.

Feverishly she put a fresh page in the typewriter, then sat for several minutes, stumped by her first problem—what name should she use for her heroine? Could she just leave a blank space and insert the name later? Then she realized that she had to have a name before she could visualize her character, and that thought led her to ponder the physical attributes of her creation. Writing a book was different from writing an article of an eyewitness report. Then she had facts to deal with, but with fiction she had to create the details herself. Except for that first creative writing course she was trained in facts and this was harder than she'd imagined.

But before the day was over she had sweated eight pages out of her imagination and she glared impatiently at the clock, which insisted that it was time she left. She slid her precious eight pages into a folder and tucked it under her arm. She would work on them at home, on her own typewriter.

Seldom had anything held her concentration in such a tight grip and when she finally went to bed that night the plot and scenes kept darting around in her mind. This was a challenge that equaled the most dangerous of assignments, and she felt the same enthusiasm, the same drive to get it accomplished. She almost resented the hours she was forced to waste sleeping, but at last she drifted off into a deep, dreamless sleep, the most restful she'd had in weeks.

For a week she worked on the manuscript during every spare moment, taking it to work with her, sitting up late at night and typing until she was so tired that she had to sleep. Rhy didn't call her and she was so caught up in her project that she ceased waiting for him to make a move. She was aware of his silence only with the outer edge of her consciousness, and she didn't worry about it. So long as he didn't try to resume their relationship she was content to let time slide by and, judging by the number of times she saw Coral Williams either entering or leaving the building, Rhy felt no sense of urgency either.

She was ready to leave one afternoon when her phone rang, which startled her, as that had become a rarity. Since Brom was still away she snatched it up and heard Rhy's gravelly voice say tersely, "Get up here, Sallie. We have a problem."

Staring at the phone after he'd hung up, Sallie wondered about the nature of the "problem." Did he mean that they personally had a problem—if so, she had to agree—or did he mean that the magazine had a problem? Had something come up that required her personal qualifications? Was Rhy backed into a corner where he would have to use her or lose a story? She relished that thought as she made her way up to Rhy's office, wondering just how he would handle that situation.

Amanda waved her into Rhy's office with an urgent "They're waiting for you!" and when she entered she saw that Greg was also present, prowling restlessly about the office while Rhy was sprawled back in his big chair with his feet propped on his desk; he looked physically relaxed, but the glitter of his eyes revealed his mental alertness.

Greg turned as she entered and glared at her, his jaw belligerent. He always looked like that when he was upset and Sallie caught her breath in alarm.

Without greeting Rhy she said huskily to Greg,

"What's wrong? Has anyone been hurt?" Two years ago one of her closest friends had been killed in South America while covering a revolution, and the tragedy had made her highly sensitive to the risks they all took. She never worried about herself, but now she braced herself to receive the news that another reporter had been wounded, perhaps killed. Her tension was evident in her low-toned voice and Greg picked it up immediately.

"No, no one's been hurt," he assured her gently, remembering the only time he'd ever seen her break down, when he had told her that Artie Hendricks had been killed.

She sighed in relief and sank into a chair, glancing at Rhy to find his face still, his eyes furious.

Puzzled, she looked back at Greg. "Then what's wrong?"

"The Sakaryan charity ball is next week," Greg informed her, crossing the office to sit down beside her.

"Yes, I know. I was supposed to cover it," she said dryly and shot a scathing look at Rhy. "Who're you sending in my place?"

"I *was* sending Andy Wallace and Patricia King," Greg snapped. "But Marina Delchamp has refused to grant a personal interview. Dammit!" he exploded in frustration, pounding his fist on the arm of the chair. "It was all set up and now she refuses!"

"That doesn't sound like Marina," Sallie protested. "She's not at all snobbish. There must be a reason."

"There is," Rhy drawled the answer from his relaxed position. "She won't talk to anyone but you, or so she says. Why does it have to be you? Do you know her personally?"

Sallie grinned as she realized that her wishful thinking had come true—Marina had placed Rhy between a rock and a hard place, and he wasn't enjoying the situation.

"Yes, she's a friend of mine," she admitted, and if Rhy thought it strange that she knew the gorgeous ex-model he said nothing. Now Marina was the wife of one of the most powerful men in Sakarya and in charge of the charity ball, and she could choose any reporter she wanted.

"Talk to her, convince her to talk to Patricia King instead of you," Rhy ordered. "Or get the interview over the phone." The satisfaction in his tone revealed that he thought he'd just solved the entire problem and she bristled, but struggled to hide her temper.

"I suppose when you're the wife of the finance minister you can give interviews or not, whichever you want," she said casually.

"Sallie," Rhy informed her with deadly calm, "I'm ordering you to get that interview over the phone."

"But it won't work!" she said, widening her eyes in innocence. "Marina can talk to me whenever she'd like if that's all she wants. She wants to *see* me. And I have an invitation to the ball anyway," she finished smugly. She had been intending to take on part of her vacation next week and fly to Sakarya at her own expense, but now she saw a way of defeating Rhy and it was all she could do to stop herself from laughing aloud.

"It won't work," Rhy warned softly. "I said no foreign assignments and I meant it. You can't go."

Beside her, Greg cursed beneath his breath in frustration and got to his feet, shoving his fists into his pockets. "She's the best reporter I've got!" he said in restrained violence. "You're wasting her!"

"I'm not wasting her," Rhy snarled, coming out of his chair with a lithe twist of his body that had him instantly poised, ready to react. In that instant Sallie read danger in his narrowed eyes. "I've told you before, Downey, she's off anything that even smells like it might be dangerous, and that includes any damned party in an oil-rich desert where every power in the world is jockeying around trying to figure out how to get control of that oil!"

"Are you blind?" Greg bellowed. "She thrives on danger. She carries it around with her! Dammit, man, she can't even catch a bus in a normal manner! Her everyday life would turn a sane person's hair gray!"

Deftly Sallie put herself between the two big, angry men and tilted her delicate jaw at Rhy. "If Marina refuses to see Patricia I suppose you just won't get an interview," she said, bringing the conversation back to its original subject. Triumph gleamed in her dark blue eyes. "It's me or no one. How much of a newsman are you?"

His jaw clenched in anger, but he shot a look at Greg. "Get out of here," he ordered harshly, jerking his eyes back to her. "My answer is still no."

"Suit yourself." She left the office with more poise than she would have thought possible, but chuckled to herself as she collected her belongings and left the building.

She wasn't surprised the next morning when she was directed to Rhy's office as soon as she entered the building. She stalled for a few moments, enjoying making him wait while she put up her shoulder bag and locked the manuscript in her desk, then she carefully wiped all traces of amusement from her expression as she went to meet him.

Instead of the frustrated anger she'd expected to see on his face he wore a look of intense satisfaction, and she felt a twinge of uneasiness. "I've solved our problem," he almost purred, moving close to her and reaching out to stroke her hair.

Diverted, she slapped his hand away in irritation. "I'm going to cut my hair!" she said curtly. "Maybe then you'll keep your hands to yourself."

"Don't cut it," he advised. "You wouldn't like the consequences."

"I'll cut my hair if I feel like it. It's nothing to you!"

"We won't argue that now, but I'm warning you, don't cut your hair or I'll turn you over my knee." With that threat he left the subject and quirked an inquiring eyebrow at her. "Don't you want to hear about my solution?"

"No. If you like it that well I know I'll hate it," she said, admitting fantastically that he'd obviously thought of some way to get around Marina.

"I wouldn't say that," he murmured. "You used to like it quite well. You can go to Sakarya, darling." He paused and watched her eyes light up with delight, then he delivered the bomb. "And I'm going with you."

Aghast, Sallie stared up at him. Her thoughts whirled madly as she tried to think of some way out of this situation, but all she could say was, "You can't do that," in weak protest.

"Of course I can," he said, smiling in a predatory manner that gave her chills. "I own this magazine and I'm a newsman. Other than that, I'm your husband—all excellent reasons why I can go to Sakarya with you."

"But I don't want you along! I don't need you."

"Poor baby," he said in mock sympathy, then reverted to his normal tone. "There's no way out of it. If you go, I go. I want to make certain that silky skin of yours stays whole."

"I'm not a child or an idiot. I can take care of myself."

"So you say, but you still aren't changing my mind. Sorry if I've messed up your plans. Did you have it set for your boyfriend to go along with you? What's his name—the photographer?"

The skin on the back of her neck prickled as she caught the threat in his tone and she knew that he hadn't forgotten that day when he had seen Chris hug her. "Leave Chris alone!" she flared. "He's a good friend."

"I can imagine. He went with you to Washington, didn't he?" Rhy gritted savagely, abruptly catching her wrist and pulling her against him. "And he's the one you went to the airport to see off, isn't he?"

"Yes, he is," she admitted, surprised that he should remember that. She tried to release her wrist, and he anchored her to him with his other arm, sliding it about her waist.

"Here's another warning for you," he ground out. "You're still my wife and I won't tolerate another man in your bed. I don't care how long we've been separated. If I catch him with you I'm going to push his teeth through the back of his head and then I'm going to take it up with you. Is that what you want? Are you trying to push me into proving how much I want you?" Without waiting for an answer he bent his head and ground his mouth against hers, forcing a response from her and parting her lips to allow his deeper kiss.

The familiar taste of his mouth tore away the years

that had separated them, and she gasped at the lash of desire that sent her hands up to cling to his heavy shoulders as she pressed herself to him. It was their first kiss all over again. She melted, and her awareness of the world around her faded. Even as she responded to him she writhed inside with shame that she didn't have more self-respect than to be so vulnerable to him. He'd never really cared about her, he'd admitted it, but he liked going to bed with her, and she was too weak to resist him. It was odd that no other man had ever tempted her as Rhy did, but then, she'd never known another man like him. He was hard and brutal, but he was strong, and the force of his personality swept lesser people to the side.

But their attraction wasn't all one-sided, she realized dazedly a moment later when his hard hands slid down to her waist and clenched almost painfully on her soft flesh as he pulled her even closer to his taut frame. He groaned against her lips and a tremor rocked through him. "Sallie," he muttered, lifting his mouth a scant inch from hers. "Let's go to my apartment. We can't make love here, there are too many interruptions." His voice was a low growl, rough with his passion, and she shivered in sensual reaction.

"Let me go," she protested, her hands suddenly finding the strength to push against him as panic flared with the realization that it might be impossible to control him now. Their brief marriage had given her an intimate knowledge of his nature and now she admitted to herself that she'd forgotten none of it. She knew by the dark flush on his cheekbones, the timbre of his voice, the dilated glitter of his eyes, that he was half-wild with desire, near the point where he would take her regardless of where they were.

"No," he denied, his mouth twisting savagely. "I told you I'll never let you go."

She fought her way out of his embrace, but she had the uneasy feeling that he'd allowed her to gain her freedom, and spots of color also stained her face as she stared at him. "You'll have to," she told him fiercely. "I don't want you anymore!"

"I just proved you wrong in that!" he said on a short bark of laughter.

"I'm not talking about sex! I don't want to live with you. I don't want to be your wife. I can't stop you from traveling with me, you're the boss, but I won't sleep with you."

"Won't you?" he murmured. "You're my wife, and I want you back. Legally you can't refuse me my marital rights."

His determination, the steel in his gray eyes, alarmed her and she stepped back from him. Desperately she seized on Chris, throwing his name up like a shield to hide behind. "Look, Rhy, you're an adult, surely you can understand that my affections are elsewhere. Chris is special to me—"

A little muscle in his jaw began to twitch and she stared at it in fascination, forgetting what she'd been about to say. Rhy's hands closed painfully on her waist again and he ground out, "I told you what I'd do if I caught him with you and I meant it."

"Be reasonable," she implored, pulling vainly at his hands in an effort to ease the painful pressure. "For heaven's sake, I'm not demanding that you terminate your relationship with Coral!"

An odd expression crossed his face. "No, you're not, are you?" he said slowly.

He looked down at her with growing menace and to escape the impression she had of a time bomb ticking its way to the moment of explosion she managed a casual laugh. "I never thought that you'd live the life of a monk all these years." She tried to soothe the temper in him. "I've no right to object in any event."

Instead of soothing him her words seemed to inflame him more, and the tension in his arms lifted her on her toes. "I'm not that modern and openminded," he said almost soundlessly, his taut lips barely moving. "I don't want another man touching you!"

"Isn't that a dog-in-the-manger attitude?" she hurled at him and winced in pain as his fingers clenched. "Rhy, please! You're hurting me!"

He cursed vividly, then moved his hands from her waist in the manner of one freeing a bird and she swiftly moved a couple of steps from him, her hands automatically massaging her aching flesh. As he merely stood there watching her and made no move to break the silence that fell between them she decided that the best thing she could do was to get out of there. She couldn't handle Rhy when he was angry, he could reduce her to putty if he really lost his temper and she knew him well enough to know that he was on the verge of violence.

She edged toward the door and he moved suddenly, placing himself between her and her escape. "Don't fight me," he warned, still in that soft, nearly soundless voice. "You can't win and I don't want to hurt you. You're mine, Sallie."

Fear edged along her nerves. She'd seen Rhy in a lot of moods, in a lot of tempers, but she'd never before seen him with this wild savagery in his eyes. "I need to go to work," she muttered warily, watching him for any movement.

"You work for me. You go when I say you can go." He bit out the words, his eyes locked on hers, and she was helpless to look away. Was this how a snake paralyzed a bird?

Desperately she searched her mind for something to say that would break his concentration on her, but nothing surfaced and she squared her shoulders, ready to make a flight of it if necessary. She wouldn't be molested, not even by her own husband! All of the pride and dignity that she'd so painstakingly amassed for herself was in the tilt of her chin as she raised it at him. "Don't push me," she warned him evenly. "If you're even half the man you used to be you know that I'm not willing."

"You would be, after a minute," he retorted with brutal truth, but not by a flicker of her lashes did she betray the jolt he gave her with that statement.

"Don't confuse the past with the future. The days are long gone when I thought the sun rose and set on you."

"Good," he said, his mouth twisting. "I never wanted to be an idol. But don't make me out to be a villain, either."

With inner relief Sallie sensed that the danger was past, at least for the moment. She was tempted to try arguing with him about the trip to Sakarya, but she knew better than to provoke his temper again. "I really do need to get to work," she insisted.

After a moment he stepped to one side. "All right," he permitted, his tone at once tender and warning. "But we're not finished, baby, and when you go to Sakarya I'll be with you every inch of the way."

With that warning ringing in her head Sallie slipped past him and returned to her desk. She began trembling with delayed reaction and with difficulty she tried to concentrate on her writing. But she'd reached a slow spot. She couldn't decide just how the action should go and eventually her thoughts wandered back to Rhy.

Once she would have been delirious with joy if he'd announced that he wanted her with him, wanted her to have his children, but that was a long time ago, and she'd been a different person then. Why couldn't he accept that? Why was he so insistent on resuming their marriage?

She couldn't believe that he was motivated by jealousy. It had to be that possessiveness of his, because jealousy indicated caring, and she knew that Rhy had never loved her, not even in the early days. Their only bond had been a sexual one and he wanted to renew that bond now, but she was determined to break the weakness that made her respond to him.

Then the thought occurred to her that it was one thing to be an ordinary, quiet, stay-at-home little housewife and quite another for her to be a globe-trotting, successful reporter. She was more of a feather in his cap now, wasn't she? She hadn't been glamorous enough for him before! Was that why he was suddenly so interested after years of neglect? Rage burned in her for a moment; then she had the disquieting thought that if that was the case he wouldn't have grounded her, he'd have kept her in the limelight.

She didn't understand him; she'd never understand him. Why didn't he leave her alone?

It had to be the tension caused by her scene with Rhy that produced the pounding headache she had that afternoon when she went home. She wanted nothing more than peace and quiet, so she indulged herself with a hot bath and, rather than get dressed afterward, she merely pulled on her comfortable pink robe which zipped up to her throat and sat down at her typewriter to work her way out of the doldrums.

It was still early, not yet seven, when her doorbell rang and she frowned irritably as she switched the typewriter off. Just as she reached the door she thought better of opening it in case Rhy had decided to press his attentions. "Who is it?" she asked warily.

"Coral Williams" was the cool reply and Sallie's eyebrows rose in silent astonishment as she unlocked the door and opened it.

"Come in," she invited the striking blonde, then indicated her robe with a movement of her hand. "I'm sorry about the way I'm dressed, but I wasn't expecting visitors."

"No, that's true enough," Coral admitted, walking into the apartment with the prowling slink of a model. She was both cool and dramatic, dressed in a lemon-yellow evening gown that should have made her hair look brassy but didn't. "Rhy is taking me to a Broadway opening, so I knew he wouldn't be here tonight."

Aha! Sallie thought to herself. It looked as if Coral was checking out the competition, but who had told her? "He isn't likely to be here any other night either," she denied, and the amusement in her eyes and voice must have gotten through to Coral because the woman bit her lip and flushed.

"Don't try to hide it from me," she said huskily, her

voice growing thick as if she was near tears. "Rhy told me himself."

"What?" Sallie's voice rose in astonishment. Was Rhy going to start advertising their marriage? Did he think that public knowledge might weaken her stand?

"I know how hard it is to resist Rhy when he decides that he wants a woman," Coral was saying. "Believe me, I know! But you're not in his league and he'll only hurt you. He's had other women, but he's always come back to me and this time won't be any different. I just thought I'd let you know before you get in too deeply with him."

"Thanks for the warning," Sallie said, her inner amusement breaking out in a smile that made Coral look at her in disbelief. She couldn't help it; she thought it was funny that her husband's mistress should warn her about becoming too serious about him! "But I don't think you have anything to worry about. I'm not inter-ested in having an affair with anyone, and you'll be doing me a favor if you can keep Rhy's attention away from me."

"How I'd like to!" Coral admitted wryly, glancing at Sallie with disturbing honesty. "But I knew when I first saw you that Rhy was interested, and he won't give up easily. Why do you think he's going on this Sakarya trip with you? If I were you, and if you're on the level about not wanting an affair with him, I'd check into the hotel bookings, because if I know Rhy there'll only be one room available!"

"I know that," Sallie chuckled, "and I'm ahead of him. I've already thought of another place to stay. With a friend." She didn't add that the friend was Marina Del-champ and that she hoped to stay in the palace. She was fairly certain that Marina would offer her sanctuary and would, in fact, greatly enjoy helping her to thwart Rhy.

Suddenly Coral laughed. "Maybe I was worried about nothing. You seem more than capable of looking after yourself. It must be that braid that makes you look so young."

"Probably," Sallie agreed blandly, thinking that in all probability she was Coral's age.

"You've set my mind at ease, so I'll leave now. Rhy is supposed to meet me in half an hour and I'll probably be late." Coral glided to the door and Sallie opened it for her, feeling rather like a servant opening a door for a queen, but laughter still lurked in her eyes as she returned to her writing. Coral acting concerned for another woman was a performance worth watching! Not for a second did she believe that the beautiful model cared a snap of her fingers about another woman's feelings. What Coral so carefully guarded was Rhy's attention, his time, and with a shake of her head Sallie wondered what made Rhy so sinfully attractive.

Perhaps if she knew what made her so vulnerable to Rhy she'd be able to fight him, but she could pinpoint no concrete reason. It was everything about him, even the qualities that made her so angry. He was all man, the only man she'd ever wanted.

Realization struck and the force of it made her break out in a cold sweat, but she forced herself to admit the truth. She still loved him; she always had. She had tried to push her love away in self-defense against the crippling pain she'd felt when Rhy had left her, but she hadn't been able to kill it. It had flourished in the darkness of her subconscious and now she could no longer deny that it existed. She sat at the typewriter, staring blankly at the keys, and let the knowledge creep into her consciousness. She couldn't stop the tears that welled in her eyes, though she stubbornly refused to let them fall. Love was one thing, but compatibility was quite another, and she was no longer a starry-eyed young girl who believed that love could conquer all. She and Rhy were the mismatch of the century, even more so now than in the beginning. At least then she'd thought him the center of the universe and would gladly have followed him into the jaws of death if he'd only asked her.

But he hadn't asked her; he'd gone alone, disregarding her fears and clinging timidity. When had he ever cared how she felt? He was too forceful, too self-confident, to put her opinion, her feelings, above his own. It had been that way then and it was still the same. Wasn't that how he was acting now? What she wanted just didn't count! Look at the high-handed manner in which he'd stopped her career in its tracks and demanded that she resume their married life. What about her plans, what she wanted out of life?

Drawing several deep breaths, Sallie tried to force her thoughts into order. If she went back to Rhy what would she have? The answer was simple, she would have Rhy—for as long as he remained interested. Or perhaps she wouldn't even have his undivided attention at all. She couldn't discount Coral Williams, and Rhy had never promised fidelity. He'd made no promises at all, other than ones of physical pleasure. So, if she went back to him, she'd have sensual satisfaction and what joy she could find in his company.

On the other side of the coin, what would he gain from a reconciliation? Once again, the first thing that came to mind was sex. That fierce attraction was mutual, unfortunately, for it made him unreasonable. If Coral was pushing him for a commitment Sallie's return would put a stop to that particular demand, and from what Coral had just told her Rhy wouldn't have any worries that Coral might leave him. No, Coral would stay for as long as Rhy wanted her, and if he could have both women at once he probably would.

Sallie winced from that thought. No, Rhy wasn't like that. She didn't think him capable of fidelity to any one woman, but he didn't play games. A woman had to accept him as he was. That had been their trouble. She'd wanted him to be something he wasn't: an ordinary husband. Rhy had refused to change, or even compromise.

So she'd changed, slipped out from under his thumb, and he resented that even while she challenged him. She'd belonged to him once and he couldn't tolerate the idea that she no longer wanted to. That possessive streak of his had to be a mile wide. She'd been his once, and he wanted her back, and he'd move heaven and earth to get her, even if he had to destroy her career to do so.

She *couldn't* go back to him, though deep down she craved to do just that. Her own identity was at stake. Rhy would swamp her, smother her. Then, when he was no longer interested, he'd walk out, and she didn't think she could survive that again.

No, she had to follow her own path, and if it led her away from Rhy she had to accept that. Odd how she could love him and yet be willing to spend her life separated from him, yet that was the way of it. She knew instinctively that Rhy would destroy her sense of self, her confidence, if she allowed him control over her emotions again.

There was no hesitation; she had to choose the path

that was right for her, and that path didn't include Rhy. Perhaps no other man would ever make her heart pound madly as the lightest touch from Rhy could do, but if that was the price, she'd pay it. She had to.

When this trip to Sakarya was over she would turn in her notice and leave town. She couldn't wait any longer. Rhy was closing in, and she'd have to keep her guard up every minute.

CHAPTER SIX

THE NIGHT BEFORE they were due to leave for Sakarya Sallie went to bed early, hoping that she'd be able to get to sleep since the flight would be long and she'd never been able to rest on a trip. She was always too keyed up, too restless, and to her dismay she felt the same way now. The thought of traveling with Rhy, when every self-preserving instinct in her screamed to keep as far away from him as she could, had all her nerves tingling in mingled fear and expectation. It was rather like petting a beautiful tiger, wanting so desperately to touch something so lovely but knowing at the same time that the tiger could kill you.

She turned restlessly in the bed, tangling the sheets, and when the doorbell rang she jumped out of bed with a sense of relief and grabbed her robe, shrugging into it as she ran to the door. Just as she reached it she skidded to a stop and called, "Who is it?"

"Chris," came a muffled voice and Sallie's brow knit in puzzlement. What was he doing here? He'd been on the road a lot lately, due to Rhy's influence, no doubt, but he'd arrived back in town the day before, and he'd been fine earlier when she'd seen him long enough to say a quick hello. Now he sounded as if he was sick, or in pain.

Quickly she unlocked the various locks on the door

and opened it. Chris had been slumped against the door-frame, and he straightened, giving her a glimpse of his drawn face. "What's wrong?" she asked swiftly, catching his sleeve and pulling him in so she could close the door. She fumbled with the locks again, then turned to him. He'd jammed his hands deep into his pockets and stood regarding her with deep, silent misery evident in his brown eyes.

Sallie caught her breath. Had someone been killed? That was always her first thought, her deepest fear. She held out her hand to him and he took it, squeezing her slender fingers in a painful grip. "What is it?" she asked softly. "Chris?"

"I didn't know it would hurt so bad," he groaned, his voice so low that she could barely hear him. "Oh, God, Sallie, I didn't know."

"Who is it?" she demanded, grasping his arm urgently with her free hand. "Chris Meaker, if you don't tell me—"

He shook his head as if to clear it, as if he'd abruptly realized what she thought. "No," he said thinly. "No one's dead, unless you want to count me. She's left me, Sallie."

Sallie gaped at him, remembering that he was in love with a woman who wanted the same things she'd once wanted, a nice, normal husband who came home every night, who fathered children and loved them and was around to see them grow up. Evidently the woman had decided that she couldn't live with Chris's job, with knowing that every trip could be his last one. Granted, some of the assignments weren't that dangerous, but it was a high-risk job at best. She hadn't been able to take it, either, the constant worry about someone she loved desperately. Only by cutting Rhy out of her life had she been able to function again.

"What can I do?" she asked in quiet sympathy. "Tell me how to help."

"Tell me it'll get better," he begged, and his voice cracked. "Sallie, hold me. Please, hold me!" To her horror his face twisted and he began to sob, jerking her to him with desperate arms and holding her so tightly that she couldn't breathe. His entire body was shaking and he buried his face in her neck, wetting her skin and hair and collar with his salty tears. Great tearing sobs tore from him and she put her arms around him, giving him what he'd asked for, someone to hold him. She knew what he was feeling; dear God, she knew exactly what he was going through. She'd cried that way for Rhy, feeling as if he'd torn her insides out and she'd die from the pain of it.

"It'll get better," she promised thickly, tears blurring her own voice. "I know, Chris. I've been there."

He didn't answer, but his arms lifted her, taking her from the floor. He drew a deep, shuddering breath and swallowed, trying to control himself. "God knows it can't get any worse," he whispered, and lifted his head. For a moment his brown eyes, wet and miserable, stared into her wet blue ones, and then he dipped his head and fastened his mouth to hers, kissing her with silent desperation. Sallie understood and she kissed him back. He wasn't kissing her for any sexual reason; it was merely a reaching out for human contact, a plea for comforting. She'd always liked Chris; at that moment she came to love him. Not the deep, ravenous love she had for Rhy, not even a man-woman type of love. She simply loved him as a human being, a fellow creature who was vulnerable and who needed her. She'd never been needed in her life before; she'd been dependent on her parents, then dependent on Rhy. Certainly Rhy had never needed her!

Chris pulled his head back and sighed; then he rested his forehead against hers. "What can I do?" he asked, but she knew that he didn't expect an answer. "How long does it take?"

Now that she *could* answer. "It took me a couple of months before I could even begin to function again," she told him truthfully, and he winced. "But I worked at getting over it harder than I've ever worked at anything in my life, either before or since."

"I can't believe she did it," he groaned.

"Did you have a fight?" Sallie asked, leading him to the sofa and pushing until he sat down heavily.

His head moved wearily back and forth. "No fight. Not even an ultimatum. My God, you'd think she'd at least give me a warning! If she wanted to tear my guts out she bull's-eyed first shot!"

Sitting down beside him, Sallie took his hand and held it. With the insight of someone who had been there, she felt that she understood very well the motives of Chris's unnamed lady. He thought it was perfectly all right for him to risk life and limb while she waited patiently at home for him—how much warning did he think she'd have of his death? Did he think the pain would be any less for her if she was suddenly told that he hadn't made it back? Men were so arrogant and selfish, even Chris, and he was one of the most likeable people she'd ever met. Aloud she said, "Don't expect someone to give in just because you can't. You'd have made each other miserable. Face it, you're better off apart."

"I've never loved anyone before," he protested hopelessly. "It's not so easy to give up someone you really love!"

"I did, and I didn't have a choice either. He left me flat on my face."

Chris sighed and stared at the pattern of the carpet, and Sallie could read his anguish in the lines of his face. Chris had always seemed younger than his years, as if life had passed within touching distance of him but had never actually touched him, glancing off his inner calm like light off of a mirror. Now he'd aged and the boyishness was gone from his face.

"Her name is Amy," he said abruptly. "She's quiet, a little shy. I guess it took me a year of chance meetings in the hallways before she'd do more than smile at me when I spoke. Then it took me another year to get her into bed—" He stopped and glanced at her, his mouth going grim. "Forget I said that. I don't usually kiss and tell."

"It's forgotten," Sallie assured him. "Did you ask her to marry you?"

"Not at first. I've never wanted to be married, Sal, I'm a lone wolf, like you." He shook his head as if he didn't understand himself. "It kind of sneaked up on me, the idea of getting married. So finally I asked her and she cried. She said she loved me but that she couldn't take my job, and she'd marry me if I changed jobs. Hell, I love my job! Mexican standoff."

"And she cut her losses," Sallie murmured.

"She also hedged her bets." He gave her a wry, self-mocking smile. "She had another game going with a nine-to-five guy. She told me tonight that they're getting married later this year."

"Is she bluffing?"

Chris shook his head. "I don't think so. She's wearing a diamond."

After sitting quietly for a moment Sallie said frankly, "You've got a choice, you know. You can have Amy or you can have your job, but you can't have both. Decide which one's the most important to you and forget about the other."

"Did you forget about your guy when you chose your job over him?" challenged Chris.

"You've got it wrong. I was in Amy's shoes, not yours. He chose *his* job over *me,*" said Sallie. "I've never forgotten him, but I've done very well without him, thank you."

It wasn't until Chris spoke that she realized how much information she'd given him with her stray comments; or perhaps it was just that Chris was intuitive, sensing her moods and thoughts without any concrete evidence. After looking at her thoughtfully for a moment he murmured, "It's Baines, isn't it? He's the one who walked out on you."

Her stunned expression had to tell him the answer, but after a minute she gathered herself enough to admit, "He's the one. And let me tell you, when Rhy Baines walks, he walks *hard!*"

"He's a fool," Chris said mildly. "But he wants you back, doesn't he?"

"Not permanently," Sallie replied with a touch of bitterness. "He just wants to play for a while."

Chris looked at her for a long time, his brown eyes moving over her small face, shuttered now to keep from revealing any more of her inner pain. When it became evident that she had nothing more to say he leaned forward and gently kissed her, but this time he was offering comfort instead of taking it. Sallie closed her eyes and let the kiss linger, neither responding nor rejecting but letting time expand as his mouth moved lightly over hers. She'd never been kissed like that before, without passion, as a friend.

The strident demand of the telephone caused Chris to remove his mouth and with a murmured "Excuse me" Sallie stretched to reach the yellow receiver. When she answered she felt a tingle of alarm when a husky voice demanded, "Have you finished packing?"

"Of course," she said crisply, feeling insulted that he felt he had to check up on her. What did he think she'd do, wait until the last minute to throw everything together? Because of that, and also because of a certain streak of feminine perversity, she added, "I was just talking to Chris."

She could feel the thickness of the silence on the line; then the growing crackle of Rhy's anger leapt out at her. "Is he there?" he finally bit out, the words almost exploding from his lips. Sallie had a mental picture of him, his teeth bared in a snarl, his cheekbones taut and savage with his rage. The gray eyes would be flinty, with red sparks snapping in them. The tingle of alarm inside her changed to one almost of pleasure.

"Of course he's here," she responded, knowing that she was flirting with danger. What would she do if Rhy's temper roared out of control? The last thing she wanted to do was cause any trouble for Chris, but somehow Rhy goaded her past responsible actions. "I don't give up my friends just because you snap your fingers," she heard herself adding.

His voice was a low growl, almost too low to hear. "When I snap my something it won't be my fingers. Get rid of him, Sallie, and do it now."

Immediately she bristled. "I will not—"

"Now," he whispered. "Or I'm coming over. I'm not playing, baby. Get rid of him. Then come back and tell me you've done it."

Furiously she tossed the receiver onto the table and got to her feet. Without a word, not wanting Rhy to hear anything she said to Chris, she held out her hand to him, and with a puzzled look he took it, rising lightly to his feet. Sallie led him to the door, then stretched on tiptoe and kissed him gently. "I'm sorry," she murmured. "He's ordered me to get rid of you or he's going to come over here and get violent."

For a moment Chris looked like his old self, one eyebrow rising in mild mockery. "This sounds serious. Sallie, old girl, I think you've left a lot out of your story."

"I have, but there's no use in raking over old ashes. Will you be all right?" she asked, concern evident in her voice and eyes, and he quickly hugged her.

"Of course I will. Just telling you helped. Kissing you helped even more." He gave a crooked grin. "She knocked me for a loop, but I'm not giving up. She cried when she told me she's marrying this other guy, so it's not hopeless, is it?"

Sallie grinned back. "Doesn't sound hopeless to me."

He flicked her cheek with one finger. "Have a good time in Sakarya," he teased, and she stuck her tongue out at him. After he'd gone she carefully locked the door and returned to glare balefully at the telephone receiver lying there waiting for her. She was tempted to let him wait a few more minutes, but it was like a dose of bitter medicine: soonest done, soonest over with.

With that thought she snatched it up and nearly snarled, "Well, he's gone!"

"What took you so long?" he barked in demand.

"I was kissing him goodbye!" she retorted furiously. "And now I'm *telling you* goodbye!"

"Don't hang up," came the soft warning. "I'm going to give Meaker just enough time to get home, then I'm going to call and make sure he's there. For your sake, you'd better pray that he goes straight home."

"Your bully act is getting boring," she snapped, and slammed the phone down, then unplugged it. Marching into her bedroom she unplugged that phone too, but not before it began ringing. Muttering furiously to herself about what she'd like to do to Rhy Baines, she stomped around the apartment turning off lights, then flung herself on the bed and once again tried to go to sleep. If it had been difficult before it was impossible now. She was burning with righteous indignation, and she wondered how anyone could be such a hypocrite. It was perfectly all right for him to blatantly carry on his affair with Coral right in front of her, but he had no intention of allowing her the same freedom. Not that she wanted to have an affair with Chris any more than he wanted one with her, but that was beside the point.

Then her thoughts turned to the trip to Sakarya. After tonight Rhy would be his most demanding, his most seductive, and to her dismay she recalled that in the past he'd had no difficulty at all in getting her to bed. She'd been lucky that, since he'd discovered her identity, the only times he'd kissed her they had been in his office where there had been scant opportunity for a seduction scene; she had her doubts that she'd have been so successful in stopping him otherwise. She was too honest to delude herself even when the truth was painful. She loved Rhy, but even if she didn't she'd still want him physically. Only her pride and her deep-rooted fear of being hurt again kept her from giving in to him.

It was after midnight before she finally drifted into sleep and the flight to Paris, the first leg of the trip to Sakarya, was an early one. She was pale with weariness before she even left her apartment to meet Rhy at the air terminal. She was determined to be as businesslike as possible, both to keep him at a distance and to show him that he hadn't upset her with his jealous rage of the night before, but right from the start her attitude was difficult to maintain. When he saw her walking toward him Rhy got to his feet and came to meet her, taking her larger tote bag from her arm and bending down to press a brief warm kiss on her lips. "Good morning," he murmured, letting his dark gray eyes drift down over her body. "I like you in a dress. You should wear one more often."

So he was going to ignore last night, was he? Though she'd intended to do the same thing she felt a flare of irritation that he'd beaten her to the punch. Then she shrugged mentally and gave him a cool glance. "I thought the Sakaryans would prefer dresses over pants." She usually wore pants while traveling both for comfort and convenience, but considering the nature of the assignment she'd packed only dresses. For the flight she'd chosen a lightweight beige dress, sleeveless, with a low-scooped neckline, but the dress also had a matching long-sleeved jacket, and she was wearing it now, for despite the heat of summer in New York City she often felt cool in the early mornings, and she'd learned from experience that the temperature-controlled jetliners were too cool for her. She had also changed her hair from the informal braid to a neat coil on the back of her head. There wasn't a lot she could do with her hair, because of its length, but for more formal gatherings she always put it up.

"I also prefer dresses," he commented, taking her arm. "You have great legs, and I like to see them. You used to wear dresses a lot, as I remember."

That's right, remind me, she thought savagely, but she managed to give him an impersonal answer. "When I started working I found that pants are more suitable for the type of work I do." To change the subject she questioned, "Do you have the tickets?"

"Everything's taken care of," he assured her. "Do you want a cup of coffee before the flight's called?"

"No, thanks. I don't drink coffee while I'm traveling," she felt compelled to explain, and took a seat in an armchair. The glint in his gray eyes as he seated himself opposite her told her that Rhy was well aware why she hadn't chosen the sofa, but she ignored him and amused herself by watching the parade of early-morning travelers.

Their flight was five minutes late, and Rhy was already restless when the loudspeaker called their flight number. He got to his feet and took her arm, and suddenly he gave her a whimsical smile. "Those are some spikes you're wearing," he commented. "You come up to my chin…almost."

"They're also dangerous weapons," she said, her mouth curving.

"Are they? Are you planning to use them on me?" he asked, and before she could turn her mouth away he swooped his head down and captured her lips in a hard, hungry kiss that took her breath away.

"Rhy, please!" she protested, determined to hide the curling response she felt whenever he touched her. "We're in public!"

"I get more chances to touch you in public than I do in private, so I'm going to take advantage of them," he muttered in warning.

"This is business!" she hissed. "Try to remember that. It won't do the magazine any good if a reporter acts badly in public."

"No one here knows you're a reporter," he retorted with a grin. "Besides, I'm your boss and I say it's okay."

"I have standards, even if you don't, and I don't like being pawed! Are you going to catch this flight or not?"

"I wouldn't miss it for the world," he drawled, and she caught his hidden meaning and flushed. Beyond any doubt Rhy was planning on a reconciliation during this trip, and she was equally determined to prevent such a thing from happening. Marina would never turn her away, she was certain, and she relished the thought of Rhy's fury when he found she'd evaded him.

But for now she faced a long flight in his company and she didn't relish *that*. Not only did his presence make her nervous, she was a restless traveler under the best of circumstances. Before they'd been in the air an hour she'd flipped through several magazines and made a stab at reading a paperback she'd brought with her, then abandoned that for a book of crossword puzzles. When she discarded that and tried reading her book again Rhy reached out and took her hand.

"Relax," he advised, rubbing his thumb across the back of her hand, a gesture guaranteed to keep her from relaxing. "It's a long flight, and you're as jumpy as a flea. You'll be worn-out before we get to Paris, let alone Sakarya."

"I'm not a good traveler," she admitted. "I'm not good at sitting still with nothing to do." Already she was bored, and she yearned for her manuscript, but she'd been afraid to risk losing it, so she had left it behind.

"Try to take a nap," he advised. "You'll need it."

"I can't do that, either," she said with a rueful grin. "I'm just nervous enough of heights that I don't trust the pilot enough to go to sleep and let him handle it all."

"I didn't know you were afraid of heights," he said, and she bristled.

"I'm not afraid, I'm nervous. There's a difference. I fly all the time—or *used* to—and I've been in plenty of tight spots without going to pieces. I've even enjoyed some of them. In fact, I once took a few flying lessons, but that's another thing I didn't have the time to keep up."

"You've been busy," he said on an odd note. "What other accomplishments have you added since we parted company?"

He seemed to resent that and she suddenly felt proud that she had accomplished so much. At least he'd know that she hadn't been pining for him. "I speak six foreign languages, three fluently," she enumerated coolly. "I'm a fair shot, and I've learned how to stay on a horse. I've had to give up a lot of things I've tried—and that includes cooking and sewing, because I realized how boring they were. Anything else?"

"I hope not," he retorted, his mouth quivering with

amusement. "No wonder Downey sent you into so many hot spots, you probably bullied him into it!"

"Greg can't be bullied, he's tough as nails," Sallie defended her editor. "And he'd be in the field himself if he could."

"Why can't he? I remember him as one of the best, but he suddenly grounded himself, and I've never heard why."

"He was shot up pretty badly in Vietnam," Sallie explained. "And while he was recovering his wife died of a stroke. It was quite a shock, there'd been no warning at all, but all of a sudden she was dead. They had two children, a boy and a girl, and the little girl had a hard time adjusting to her mother's death, so Greg decided to stay home with the kids."

"That's rough," Rhy commented.

"He doesn't talk about it much."

"But he told you?" he asked sharply.

"In bits and pieces. Like I said, he doesn't talk about it much."

"A field reporter doesn't need a family. The old Pony Express advertised for riders who were orphans and had no family ties, and I sometimes think that should hold true for reporters, too."

"I agree," she said sharply, not looking at him. "That's why I don't want any ties."

"But you're not a reporter any longer," he murmured, his long fingers tightening around her hand. "Consider this your swan song, because after this your position will be that of Mrs. Rhydon Baines."

Swiftly Sallie jerked her hand away from him and stared out at the cloud cover below them. "Are you firing me?" she bit out angrily.

"I will if you force me to. I don't mind if you work so long as you're home every night with me. Of course, when we have children I'll want you to be home with them while they're small."

She turned furious blue eyes on him. "I won't live with you," she said bitterly. "I *can't* live with you and be more than half-alive myself. The thought of being a housewife again is nauseating."

His mouth turned grim. "You're lying to yourself if you believe that. You've changed a lot of things, but you can't change the way you feel about children. I remember how you were when you were pregnant with our son— "

"Shut up!" she flared, her fingers curving into her palms as she strove to control her pain at the memory of her dead child. "Don't talk about my baby." Even after seven years the pain of losing him was raw and unhealed, and for the rest of her life she would mourn that small, lost life.

"My son, too," Rhy said tightly.

"Really?" she challenged, lowering her voice to keep others from hearing her. "You weren't there when I gave birth, and you were seldom home during my pregnancy. The only role you played was to physically father the baby. After that, I was on my own." She turned away, swallowing in an effort to control the tears that threatened as she remembered her son. She'd never heard him cry, never watched him look about at the strange new world he'd entered, but for several magic months she'd felt his movements as he kicked and turned inside her and he'd been real to her, a person, and he'd had a name. She had somehow known she would have a boy, and he had been David Rhydon Baines, her son.

Rhy's fingers closed over her wrist so tightly that the fragile bones ground together and she winced with pain. "I wanted him, too," Rhy ground out, then almost flung her wrist aside. The next several hours passed in silence.

There was no layover in Paris and Sallie guessed that Greg had made the arrangements, because he always arranged things as tightly as he could, sometimes resulting in a missed flight when the first flight was only a little late. She and Rhy had barely checked through customs when their connecting flight was called, and they had to run to make the plane. From Paris it was another seven hours before they landed at the new, ultramodern jetport in Khalidia, the capital of Sakarya, and because of the time change, instead of the night their bodies were ready for, they were thrown into the middle of the Sakaryan day.

Their weariness and the long hours had largely erased the constraint between them, and Sallie didn't protest when he took her arm as they walked across the tarmac to the low, sprawling air terminal. The heat was incredible, and she was actually grateful for Rhy's support.

"I hope the hotel's decent," Rhy muttered beneath his breath, "but the way I feel right now I don't care what it's like as long as I can catch some sleep."

She knew the feeling. Jet lag was worse than simply missing sleep, it was total drain. She certainly wasn't up to battling with Rhy over where she would sleep!

They couldn't find anyone who spoke English, but several of the Sakaryans spoke French and both she and Rhy knew that language well. The taxi driver who took them to the hotel in a remarkably battered Renault spoke a rough French, and from what he said they gathered that Khalidia was being overrun by Westerners. Many Europeans had already arrived, and many Americans, including a man with a big camera, and it was said that the King would be on American television. He did not have a television himself, but he had seen one, and he thought that the big camera was one used for making the pictures for the television.

He was talkative, as taxi drivers the world over seemed to be, and he pointed with pride to the gleaming new buildings existing alongside ancient structures baked white by the merciless sun. Sakarya had the intriguing blend of old and new that so many developing nations displayed, with gleaming Mercedes limousines purring up and down the same streets used by donkeys. Camels were still used for travel in the Sakaryan desert, but overhead contrails were left by the sleek, screaming jets of the Sakaryan Royal Air Command.

The King had been educated at Oxford but, despite his absorption of European culture, he was by nature a cautious man, rather resistant to change. The Sakaryan nation was not a new one; it dated back to the day of Muhammad, and the family of Al Mahdi had held the monarchy for over five hundred years. There were deeply ingrained traditions to consider whenever modernization was discussed and for the most part life in Sakarya went on as before. Motorized vehicles were nice, but the Sakaryans had gotten along without them before and would not mind if suddenly there were no more automobiles. The jetport was too noisy and the people who arrived on the big jets had strange customs. However, the big new hospital was a source of pride and the children were eager to attend the new schools.

The man who had accomplished this modernization was the man Marina Delchamp had married, Zain Abdul ibn Rashid, the finance minister of Sakarya and a man of considerable influence with the King. He was a dark, hawklike man with the coal-black eyes of his race, and he'd been an international playboy since his college days in Europe. Sallie wondered if he loved Marina or was attracted only to her shining blond beauty. Did Zain Abdul ibn Rashid cherish Marina's gallant spirit, her natural dignity?

She worried over her thoughts like a terrier, for it wasn't easy for East to meet West. The cultural differences were so vast. Despite their spasmodic correspondence and the long intervals between their meetings Sallie considered Marina a true friend and she wanted her to be happy. She became so engrossed with her worries that she forgot to watch the scenery and was startled when the driver said in French, "The Hotel Khalidia. It is new and rich. You like it, yes?"

Peering around Rhy's shoulder Sallie admitted that she liked it, yes. The hotel was shielded on three sides by a row of carefully nurtured trees and beyond the trees was a high rock wall. The architecture wasn't ultramodern; instead, every effort had been made to insure that the hotel blended with its surroundings. The inside might offer every modern convenience, and she sincerely hoped it did, but the outer facade could have been ageless; it was clean and uncluttered in line, built of gleaming white stone, with deeply recessed windows.

Trying to keep up with Rhy, Sallie found that she was ignored when she tried to explain which cases were hers and which belonged to Rhy. A black-eyed young man in Western dress gave his attention solely to Rhy, not even glancing at her, and she received the same treat-

ment from the desk clerk. The young man disappeared
with their luggage and Rhy pocketed the room key.

When they were a few steps away from the desk clerk
Sallie caught Rhy's arm. "I want a room of my own,"
she insisted, looking him in the eye.

"Sorry. I've registered us as man and wife and you'll
have a hard time persuading an Islamic man to give
you another room," he informed her with evident satisfaction. "You knew what to expect when you came
on this trip."

"What do I have to say to get it through your head—"
she began in frustration, and he cut her short.

"Later. This isn't the place for a public argument.
Stop being difficult, all I want is a shower and a few
hours' sleep. Believe me, you're perfectly safe right
now."

She didn't believe him, but she had to retrieve her
luggage, so she followed him into the elevator, and he
punched the button for the fourth floor.

Even as tired as she was the charm of the room
made her catch her breath and she barely noticed as
Rhy tipped the young man who'd brought up their bags.
Though actually only one large room, it was separated
by intricate wrought-iron screens in two areas, a sitting
room to the front and the bedroom to the rear. A balcony
ran the length of the room and it was furnished with two
white wicker chairs with thickly padded cushions and
a wicker lounger. A small tea table stood between the
two chairs. Stepping onto the balcony, she could see the
huge swimming pool below, set among palm trees, and
she wondered if women were allowed to use the pool.

Returning to the room, she inspected the divan-style
bed and smiled at the number of vari-colored cushions

that adorned it. The parquet floor was covered in this area by a rug that looked Turkish but was probably a mass-produced copy. That made no difference, the effect was still stunning. Of all the hotels she'd stayed in she already liked this one the best. The food might be terrible, the service nonexistent for all she knew, but she adored the room!

Then she looked up and met Rhy's penetrating gaze and she paled. He'd removed his jacket and his shoulders strained at the material of his white shirt, and something in his stance told her that he was alert to her every movement. "Why don't you take a shower?" he suggested. "I'll make some phone calls and make certain everything's set up for the interview, which could take a while."

She wanted more than anything to grab her suitcases and run, but she knew that Rhy was waiting for just such a move. She would have to trick him and she wasn't certain just yet how to manage it. And a bath sounded like heaven....

"All right," she agreed wearily, picking up her suitcase and taking it into the bathroom that opened off to the right of the sleeping area, carefully locking the door behind her.

Despite her weariness, the bathroom delighted her. It could have come straight out of a Turkish harem with the black-tiled sunken bath, the mosaics, the rich jewel-like colors. She flung her dress off and peeled off her damp underclothing, sighing with relief at the sensation of cool air on her sweaty skin. She turned on the crystal taps that let the water pour into the huge tub and slid with a sigh into the cool water, then splashed about with a fantasy of having servants waiting to help her from the bath and prepare her body with perfumed oils for the coming night with the dark, exciting sultan....

Then reality intruded with the thought that she'd go mad under such circumstances, and she had enough to worry about now without bringing a sultan into it. She got out of the bath and toweled herself dry; then she debated what to wear. If she changed into street clothes Rhy would watch her like a hawk, but she had no intentions of parading around before him in a nightgown. She finally settled on a sapphire blue caftan and zipped herself into it, then took down her hair and brushed it vigorously.

She was too tired to braid it so she left it loose. After picking up her scattered clothing and tidying the bath she unlocked the door and carried her suitcase out.

Rhy was on the phone and he barely looked in her direction as she put belongings away, trying to behave as if she meant to stay. She wandered around the room, fighting to hold off the sleepiness that was growing stronger and listened as Rhy talked to several people.

After some time he covered the mouthpiece with his hand and said to her, "Why don't you go ahead and get some sleep? I don't know how long I'll be."

She didn't want to go to sleep, every instinct screamed against it, but she couldn't leave with him watching her. Besides, she was so tired; every bone and muscle in her ached from the long hours sitting in the plane. She could rest for just a few minutes until Rhy got off the telephone. She was a light sleeper; she'd hear him when he went into the bathroom.

She pulled the shades over the doors to the balcony and dimmed the room into semidarkness, then crawled among the pillows on the divan with a sigh of ecstasy. She stretched out her aching legs, turned her face against a pillow and was instantly asleep.

She was aroused some time later when someone muttered, "Move over," and she rolled over to make room for the warm body that slid next to her. Dimly she was aware that she should wake up, but she was so comfortable and the quiet hum of the central air conditioner lulled her back to sleep.

The time difference was confusing; when she woke it was dark, but she'd slept for hours. Still groggy, she peered at the dim figure coming out of the bathroom. "Who is it?" she called thickly, unable to clear the cobwebs from her mind. She wasn't certain just where she was, either.

"Rhy," the rough-velvet voice answered. "I'm sorry I woke you, I was just getting a drink. Would you like a glass of water, too?"

That sounded heavenly and she sighed a yes, then began struggling into a sitting position. In only a moment a cool glass was being put into her hand and she drained it thirstily, then gave it back to him. He returned the glass to the bathroom as she fell back among the pillows and thought drowsily that he must have eyes like a cat because he hadn't turned on any lights.

Just when the bed dipped beneath his weight again she remembered that she'd been planning on slipping out and her heart lurched with fear. "Wait—" she gasped in panic, reaching out to thrust him away, and her hand encountered smooth warm flesh. Shocked, forgetting what she'd been about to say, instead she blurted out, "You don't have anything on!"

In the darkness he gave a rough chuckle and turned on his side to face her, his heavy arm sliding around her waist and overcoming her futile resistance to pull her snugly against him. "I've always slept in the raw... remember?" he teased, his lips brushing her temple.

Her breath halted in her chest, and she began to tremble at the pressure of his strong, warm body against her. His male scent filled her nostrils and made her senses begin to swim. Desperately fighting her growing need to press herself to him and let him do as he wanted, she put her hands against his chest to push him away and instead found her slim fingers twining in the hair that covered his chest.

"Sallie," he muttered hoarsely, searching for and finding her lips in the darkness, and with a moan she lifted her arms to cling around his neck. She knew she should resist him but that had never been possible and even now, when she had such good reasons for fighting him, the temptation of knowing again such wild satisfaction kept her from shoving him away.

Nor was he unaffected; his big body was trembling against her when he lifted his mouth from hers, scattering kisses across her face and eyes. She felt him slide down the zip of the caftan and pull it from her shoulders, bunching it about her waist, then his shaking hands were exploring the delicately swelling breasts he had bared. Helplessly she buried her face in his shoulder, shuddering with the force of the desire he'd awakened, not wanting him to stop, knowing she'd go mad with frustration if he stopped.

Fiercely he stripped the caftan away from her and threw it aside, and she had a brief moment of sanity as he turned back to her. Her hands clutched at his powerful shoulders and she moaned weakly, "Rhy...don't. We shouldn't."

"You're my wife," he muttered in reply, taking her in his arms again and pressing his weight over her. She gasped at the wild, sweet contact of his bare flesh against hers, then the passion-tart possession of his mouth over hers sucked away her protests, and again her arms lifted and clung about him.

It was as if the years of separation had never been; their bodies were as familiar with each other as they had been long ago. Caught up in the whirlpool of his passion she could only respond, only return the passion he so freely gave. He wasn't gentle; except for the first time, Rhy had never been a gentle lover. He was fierce, tender, erotic, wildly exciting, and she was unable to stem her passionate reception of his lovemaking. It was just as it had been before—no, it was better; he drove her beyond sanity, beyond caring, beyond knowledge of anything except him.

CHAPTER SEVEN

SALLIE CAME AWAKE slowly, too comfortable and content to easily relinquish her hold on slumber. She felt utterly boneless, weightless, as if she were afloat. Her body was moving up and down in a gentle rhythm and beneath her head a steady, soothing drum kept time with her heart. She felt so marvelous, so safe....

The shrill ringing of the telephone was a rude interruption into her euphoric state and she muttered a protest. Then her bed moved beneath her and she clutched at it, only to find that instead of sheets her fingers were clinging to hard, warm skin. Her eyes popped open and she raised her head as Rhy stretched out a long, muscular arm and lifted the receiver from the bedside extension. "Hello," he muttered sleepily, his voice even huskier than usual as he wasn't completely awake. He listened a moment, said "Thank you" and hung up, then, with a sigh, closed his eyes again.

Hot color ran into Sallie's cheeks and hastily she tried to scramble away from him and pull up the sheet to cover her nude body. She was prevented from moving by his arms, which tightened about her, holding her in place on his chest. His eyelids, with their thick black lashes, lifted and he surveyed her flushed, tousled, early-morning beauty with a satisfied gleam in his gray eyes.

"Stay here," he commanded huskily. His hand quested down her side, smoothing her silky skin, and he murmured against her ear, "I feel as if I have a kitten curled up on my chest. You hardly weigh anything."

Involuntarily she shivered in delight at his warm breath in her ear, but she made an effort to free herself, saying, "Let me up, Rhy, I want to dress—"

"Not yet, baby," he crooned, brushing her long hair back to press his lips into the small hollow below her ear. "It's still early, and we don't have anything more important to do than getting used to each other again. You're my wife and I like the feel of you in my arms."

"*Estranged* wife," she insisted, trying to arch her head away from his insistent lips, but instead she found herself merely tilting her head back to allow him greater access to her throat. Her heart began pounding when he found the pulse beating at the back of her neck and sucked at it hungrily, as if he wanted to draw her life's blood out of her body.

"We weren't estranged last night," he murmured.

"Last night…" Her voice failed her and after a moment she managed to continue. "Last night was the result of memories, an old attraction, nothing more. Let's just mark it down to auld lang syne and forget about it, shall we?"

He relaxed back against the pillows but kept her cuddled close against him. Surprisingly her statement didn't seem to anger him, for he smiled lazily at her. "It's okay to surrender now," he informed her gently. "I won the war last night."

She almost winced with pain at the thought of giving him up again, yet she knew she couldn't be happy with him now. She let her head fall onto his shoulder

and for a moment she allowed herself to relish his closeness. He stroked her back and shoulders, playing with
her hair, pulling it all to one side to drift over his chest
and shoulder. His touch was sapping her strength, as
always, and while she still had the presence of mind
she raised her head from the haven of his wide shoulder and gazed at him seriously.

"It still won't work," she whispered. "We've both
changed, and there are other considerations now.
Coral's in love with you, Rhy. You can't just turn your
back on her and hurt her like that—or were you planning on keeping her on the side?"

"You're a little cat," he observed lazily as his hand
began questing more intimately, "always scratching and
spitting, but I've got a tough hide and I don't mind if
you're a little temperamental. Don't worry about Coral.
What do you know about her, anyway?"

"She came to my apartment," Sallie confessed, "to
warn me that you weren't serious, that you always came
back to her." She tried to squirm away from his boldly
exploring fingers and found instead that the friction
of her skin against his made her catch her breath in
longing.

He swore beneath his breath. "Women," he growled,
"are the most vicious creatures on earth. Don't believe
her, baby, Coral doesn't have any hold on me. I do what
I want to do with whomever I choose—and right now
I choose my wife."

"It isn't that easy," she insisted. "Please, Rhy, let me
go. I can't make you understand when you're holding
me like this—"

"Then I'll keep holding you," he interrupted. "The
bottom line is this, you're mine and you'll stay mine. I

can't let you go and I hope you're not in love with that photographer of yours because if you are I think I'll kill him!"

White faced, Sallie stared at him, at his suddenly narrowed eyes and clenched jaw. He reacted on a purely primitive basis to the thought of another man touching her, and abruptly she knew that it had been stupid to let him think she was involved with Chris. Not only was that a challenge to Rhy's virile domination, it wasn't fair to Chris to use him as a shield. Rhy was dangerous, he could hurt Chris and it would be her fault.

On the other hand, it went completely against her grain to let Rhy have everything his way, especially after last night. He'd certainly had everything his way then; except for that one feeble protest she'd made she hadn't attempted to ward him off at all. Even that lone effort hardly counted, because she hadn't tried to fight him off; she'd only said "no" and of course it had been a waste of breath for all the attention Rhy had paid to it.

Nor did she feel free to tell him anything about Chris. Chris's calm, lazy manner went hand in glove with such a strong sense of inner privacy that she was still surprised that he'd confided in her, and she refused to betray that confidence just to pander to Rhy's ego.

She still hadn't said anything, and suddenly Rhy's patience snapped. His hands tightened on her and he rolled, taking her with him and pinning her firmly beneath him. "Maybe you need to be shown again just who you belong to," he said violently, his mouth hard, his eyes glittering with an anger that wasn't quite anger.

Sallie's heart jolted as she felt his muscular legs parting hers, and she knew that he was going to make love to her again. Already she was drowning in the warmth that flooded her, and her heartbeat settled into a rapid pounding. But even as she slid her arms around his neck she heard herself insisting steadily, stubbornly, "I belong to myself. No one else."

"You're *mine,* Sallie! Damn you, you're *mine!*"

With his violently muttered words echoing in her ears she gave herself up to this overwhelming possession and even though her mind protested her senses were too enthralled by the delights he offered to let her argue with his blindly possessive instinct. She loved him, loved him so much that after those seven long, lonely years without his touch, now that he'd overcome her resistance and made love to her again, she wanted nothing more than to revel in the intimacy of their closeness. He couldn't give her love, but he could give her this, and it was as much of himself as he would ever give any woman. She clung to his broad shoulders and matched his fiery demands with her own, and when he finally moved from her to collapse on his back they were both satisfied and trembling with exhaustion. Unable to stand the space in the bed that separated them Sallie slid across to him and curled up against his chest, her lips pressing against his throat. As suddenly as cutting off a light she was asleep, her hands clinging to him even in sleep, as if she couldn't bear to let him go.

Awakening from her doze, Sallie stirred, opened her eyes and raised her head to find Rhy just awakening, too, his eyes still sleepy. Memories of the many mornings years ago when they'd made love and gone back to sleep made her feel eerily as if those intervening years had never been. His hand smoothed her hair back from her face, then slid around to clasp her slender neck with those strong lean fingers. "You never did tell me," he whispered. "Are you in love with him?"

She closed her eyes in resignation. He had the determination of a bulldog. But what could she tell him? Would he believe her or even understand if she told him that the way she loved Chris wasn't romantic or even sexual? The fingers clasping her neck tightened warningly and she opened her eyes. "Chris is none of your business," she said finally, tilting her chin at the grim temper that hardened his mouth. "But I haven't slept with him, so make of that what you like."

Silence followed that challenge and confession for several minutes, and when she summoned the nerve to look directly at him again she was jolted by the look of raw desire on his face. "Don't...don't look at me like that," she whispered, lowering her eyes again.

"I want you," he said hoarsely. "I'm going to have you. I'm glad that you don't have a lover now because I don't want any complications to stand in my way."

Wearily she shook her head. "No, you still don't understand. Just because I'm not sleeping with anyone doesn't mean that I want to take up our marriage again. For the record, I've never slept with anyone but you, but I just don't want to live with you. I don't think it'll work. Don't you see?" she pleaded. "I need my job the way you needed yours when we were first married. I can't be happy staying at home and cleaning house now, I need more, more than you're willing to give. I need my freedom."

His face was taut as he stared at her, his eyes restless. "Don't ask me to send you on a dangerous assignment," he muttered. "I can't. If anything happened to you and I was the one responsible for your being there

I couldn't live with myself. But as for the job—maybe we can work out a compromise. Let's give it a try, see how we get along together. All we ever did before was make love. We didn't get to know each other as people. We'll be here for three more days. While we're here let's just enjoy each other and worry about the future when we get back to the States. Can we manage three days together without fighting?"

"I don't know," she said cautiously. The temptation to enjoy those three days stole away her strength. She knew Rhy, knew that his idea of a compromise was to hem her in so that she had to do things his way, but there was nothing he could do while they were here. She had already taken the precaution of drawing out her savings, and once they returned to New York she knew she'd have to leave, but for now…for now why couldn't she simply enjoy being with her husband and loving him? Three days was so short a space in which to store up enough memories to last a lifetime! Why couldn't he see that they were hopelessly incompatible?

"All right," she finally agreed. "But when we get back don't expect me automatically to move in with you. I'll hold you to that compromise."

His strong mouth curved with amusement. "I never thought any differently," he said wryly, thrusting his fingers through her hair at the back of her head and pulling her down for his kiss. The kiss began casually, then gradually deepened until they were clinging together in mutual need that could only be satisfied one way.

As THEY DRESSED to attend the half party, half press conference that Marina was giving prior to the charity ball, Sallie was struck by how familiar it seemed, the same routine of so many years ago emerging without them having to talk about it. She used the bath first, then, while she was putting on her makeup and arranging her hair, Rhy showered and shaved. He waited until she'd put on her lipstick, then grabbed her and kissed her, smearing the color outside her lip line, chuckling to himself as she flounced back to the mirror to repair the job. How many times had he done that in the past? She couldn't remember. It was part of their marriage, and when she met his eyes in the mirror she knew that he was remembering, too, and they smiled at each other.

The gown she'd chosen was a pale rose silk, simply cut, as her lack of stature wouldn't permit anything frivolous or she looked like a doll. The color was extremely flattering to her dark blue eyes and glossy sable hair and Rhy eyed her with male appreciation as he zipped her up.

"I don't think it's safe for you to leave this room." He bent down to murmur in her ear. "Some wild sheik will steal you and take you into the desert and I'll have to start a war to get you back again."

"What? And ruin a good story?" she mocked, meeting his eyes in the mirror. "I'm certain I could escape, and just think what good reading that would make!"

"I would laugh," he said wryly, "but I know firsthand the kind of dangers you've faced, and it damned near curdles my blood. It's one thing for me to risk my hide and quite another for yours to be endangered."

"Not really," she argued, leaning forward to brush her finger under her eye and remove a tiny smudge she'd just noticed. "When we were together before, I was terrified that you'd be hurt and I nearly died when you were shot. Now I understand what sent you back to the field as soon as possible, because I became hooked on excitement, too."

"It wears off," he said, an almost weary look passing over his hard features. "The danger became almost a bore, and the thought of sleeping in the same bed for more than a few days in a row grew in attractiveness. Roots don't necessarily tie you down, baby, they can help you to grow bigger."

"That's true, if the pot's large enough so that you don't become root-bound," she pointed out and turned to face him. She was smiling but the expression in her eyes was serious and he tilted her face up to him with one long finger under her chin.

"But holding on to you is so much fun," he teased.

"Don't you ever think of anything else?" She shook her head in amusement.

"When I'm with you? Rarely." His gray eyes took on a glint of passion as he looked down at her. "Even before I knew who you were all I had to do was catch a glimpse of that sassy braid switching back and forth across your trim little rear and I wanted to chase you down in the hallways."

Sallie smiled, but inwardly she recognized that all of his words, his actions, were based on physical attraction and not on an emotional need. Rhy wanted her, there was no doubt about that, but the realization was growing in her that he was incapable of love. Perhaps it was just as well. If he loved as intensely as he desired, his love could be soul destroying.

THE PARTY WAS being held in another hotel as the Al Mahdi palace was being readied for the ball and Marina's husband did not want their own home opened to the public for security reasons. The circular drive in front of the hotel was choked with limousines and there was a confusing mixture of accents as Europeans and Americans mingled with the native Sakaryans. Security was tight; the doors and lower windows were posted with guards, fierce-looking Sakaryans in boots and military uniforms, with cocky little berets on their heads, watching the crowd of foreign visitors with their fierce black desert eyes. Their credentials and invitation were checked and rechecked as Sallie and Rhy moved slowly forward in the swarm of people.

But once inside they were guided smoothly into the suite being used and all outward signs of security vanished. There was soft, soothing music playing and the light tinkle of ice cubes against glass testified that many people were relaxing.

The suite was simply furnished in the Arabic way, but there were enough seats for anyone who preferred to sit instead of stand. The colors blended simply, golds and browns and whites, and Sallie discerned Marina's touch in the many plants and flowers that dotted the rooms and both cheered and soothed. She looked about for her friend but was unable to catch sight of her in the constantly moving flow of humanity.

"Why is the security so stiff outside?" she asked, leaning close to Rhy so no one else could hear her.

"Because Zain isn't a fool," Rhy growled. "A lot of people would like to see him dead. Relatives of the King who are jealous of Zain's influence, religious purists who don't like his progressive politics, terrorist left-wingers who don't need a reason, even Communists. Sakarya is an important hunk of real estate these days."

"I heard about the oil reserves," she whispered. "Are they that large?"

"Massive. If the surveys prove correct Sakarya will have reserves second only to the Saudis."

"I see," she mused. "And since the finance minister is married to an American woman his sympathies will naturally lean to the West. That makes his influence with the King doubly important. Good heavens, is it safe for Marina to live here?"

"As safe as Zain can make it, and he's a cunning man. He intends to die of old age."

She intended to ask more but a flash of bright hair caught her eye, and she turned her head to see Marina bearing down on her. Her friend was gorgeous, glowing, her lovely spring-green eyes sparkling with gaiety. "Sallie!" she exclaimed, laughing, and the two hugged each other enthusiastically. "I wasn't sure you were going to make it! I couldn't believe it. Someone kept wanting to send another reporter in your place. I refused to see her, of course," she said with laughing triumph.

"Of course," agreed Sallie. "By the way, Marina, let me introduce my publisher, Rhydon Baines. He's the one who tried to foul things up for us."

"You're kidding!" Marina smiled up at Rhy and gave him her hand. "Didn't you know Sallie and I are old friends?"

"Not until after the fireworks," he said wryly. "I soon found out. Is Zain here? It's been a long time since I've seen him."

Recognition lit Marina's eyes. "You're *that* Rhy Baines? Yes, he's here somewhere." She turned her head to locate her husband, peering around groups of people. "Here he comes now."

Zain Abdul ibn Rashid was a lean, pantherish man with a darkly aquiline face and a rather cruel smile, but he wore his exquisitely tailored suit as casually as an American teenager would wear jeans. Sensuality curled his upper lip and hooded his piercing black eyes, and with a shock Sallie realized that she'd only met one other man who exuded that aura of raw sexuality, Rhy. It was ironic but rather inevitable that she and Marina had married the same type of man, both untamed and unlikely ever to be tamed.

"Rhy!" Zain had transferred his gaze from his wife to glance casually at the couple with her and now his black eyes opened with recognition and he extended his hand. "I'd heard you were going to interview the King, then that the plans were changed. Are you going to do the interview after all?"

"No, someone else will do that. I'm here on a different matter entirely," Rhy said in a wry tone, nodding his head to indicate Sallie. "I'm here as a bodyguard for the reporter from *World in Review*. Sallie, let me introduce Zain Abdul ibn Rashid, the minister of finance—"

"And my husband," Marina broke in impishly. "Zain, Sallie is my friend I've been telling you about." Then she looked at Rhy. "What do you mean, bodyguard? I thought you were the publisher of the magazine?"

"I am," he admitted, unperturbed. "I'm also her husband."

Irrepressible Marina squealed and hugged Sallie again. "You're married! When did this happen? Why didn't you write me?"

"I haven't had time," Sallie blurted without thinking while she shot Rhy a glance that promised revenge.

He merely smiled at her, well satisfied with his announcement.

Zain was grinning openly. "So you finally got caught. We'll have to celebrate, but when I don't know. Marina has thrown the country into an uproar. I'll be glad when this is over." He gave his wife a look that held for several seconds before he jerked his eyes away, but Sallie had seen his expression and she heaved an inward sigh of relief. He'd looked at Marina with absorbing tenderness before pulling his sardonic mask back in place. He really loved Marina; he hadn't chosen her simply for her golden beauty.

"I can't stay any longer, I have to circulate." Marina sighed, putting her hand on Zain's arm. "Sallie, I promise that after the ball we'll curl up and talk our heads off."

Sallie nodded. "I'll see you then," she said as Marina left to attend to the other guests, with Zain a watchful escort.

"She's beautiful," Rhy commented.

"Yes." She glanced at him from under her lashes. "Even more beautiful than Coral."

"Am I supposed to argue with that?" he drawled.

She shrugged and didn't answer. Instead she questioned, "How long have you known Zain?"

"Several years," he said noncommittally.

"How did you meet him?"

"What is this, an interview?" he parried, taking her arm and steering her to the side. He signaled a waiter who came over with a tray of glasses. Rhy took two glasses of champagne and gave one to Sallie.

"Why aren't you answering me?" she persisted, and at last he gave her an exasperated look.

"Because, baby, I wouldn't like my answers to be overheard, and neither would Zain. Now be a good girl, and stop being so nosy."

She glared at him and turned her back, walking slowly among the ebb and flow of people as she sipped from her glass. Nosy! Asking questions was her job and he knew it. But he was the most contrary man she'd ever met, she thought idly, tracing her finger along the rim of a jade vase. Contrary and arrogant, he didn't know what it meant to be thwarted in anything he wanted.

"Stop sulking and start taking notes," he whispered in her ear. "Notice who's here and who isn't."

"I don't need you to tell me how to do my job," she flared, walking away from him again.

"No, what you need is a good spanking," he murmured, his long legs and greater strength making it easy for him to stay even with her in the press of people.

Perhaps he had hoped to get a rise out of her with that ridiculous statement, but she ignored him and continued her wandering progress through the suite. She rarely took notes at a function like this, having learned that it made people self-conscious. One of her assets was that she had an excellent memory and she used it, identifying the European blue bloods and financial giants. Social events weren't really her field, but she was able to put a name and a country to the important people and most of the not-so-important ones, as well.

Rhy caught her arm and leaned down to whisper, "There's the Deputy Secretary of State to your right. And the French foreign minister beside him."

"I know," Sallie said smugly, having already spotted the two men. "But I haven't seen a representative of a Communist nation, so I suppose Zain's influence is making itself felt."

Just then a tall, thin, distinguished gentleman with gray hair and kindly blue eyes approached them and extended his hand. "Mr. Baines," he greeted Rhy cordially in a clipped British-public-school accent. "Nice to see you again."

"It's a pleasure to meet you again, Mr. Ambassador," Rhy replied, taking the other man's hand. "Sallie, I'd like to introduce you to Sir Alexander Wilson-Hume, Great Britain's ambassador to Sakarya. Mr. Ambassador, my wife, Sallie."

The pale blue eyes lit as the ambassador took Sallie's hand and gently lifted it to his lips with old-world courtesy. "My pleasure entirely." He smiled as Sallie murmured a conventional greeting. "Have you been married long, Mrs. Baines?"

An impish smile curved her lips. "Eight years, Mr. Ambassador."

"My word! Eight years!" He gave her a startled glance and abruptly she wondered if he'd had reason to assume that Rhy wasn't married when he'd known him before. But if that was the case the ambassador covered his confusion with perfect poise and carried on without a hitch. "You hardly look old enough to have been married a year."

"That's true," Rhy agreed smoothly. "She's aged well."

The ambassador gave him a rather startled glance, but Sallie merely smiled at Rhy's impudence despite the hollow ache that had bloomed inside her at the thought of Rhy's blatant infidelities. She'd just have to get over that, she told herself firmly. Only a naive fool would expect a man like Rhy to be faithful; he was far too physical, and far too attractive!

It was several hours later, when they were at last in a taxi returning to their own hotel, that Sallie commented evenly, "Poor man, the ambassador covered up for you well, didn't he? But now he considers you a philanderer."

"I'd hoped you wouldn't notice," Rhy replied wryly, "but you don't miss much, do you? But don't paint me blacker than I am, Sallie. You said you never thought I'd live like a monk, but I very nearly did. I've had a lot of social dates that ended when I took the lady home, nothing more."

"You're lying," she stated without expression. "I suppose you expect me to believe that Coral Williams is just a friend?"

"She's not my enemy," he said, his mouth twitching in amusement. She didn't believe him when he continued. "I wanted to make you think she was my mistress to make you jealous, but I guess it didn't work."

She began to laugh in disbelief. She'd never heard such a ridiculous tale before in her life. Rhy was a sensual animal, his passions never far from the surface, and easily aroused. She'd have to be a fool to believe he'd been faithful to her during the seven years they'd been separated. She didn't even believe he'd been faithful to her while they'd been together! "Sorry." She laughed. "Try a tale that's more plausible. Besides, it doesn't matter."

He drew in his breath in a hiss, and glancing at him she saw the flare of anger in his eyes. "I'll make it matter," he promised her grimly. Or was it a threat?

She knew that he intended to make love to her as

soon as they were in their hotel room in an attempt to tear down her convictions, and she eyed him warily. She'd agreed to spend the three days with him and she'd known that they would be sleeping together, but she intended to limit their lovemaking to the nights. After all, his desire was familiar to her, even after all these years. What she wanted to do was talk to him, learn about him, get to know him in the way she'd never known him before. He was her husband, but he was still a stranger to her. Sadly she realized that even though she planned on leaving when they returned to New York she was still searching for some way to believe that they could be happy together even when she knew the search was futile.

They had just entered the hotel room, and Rhy was shrugging out of his formal jacket when the phone rang. With an impatient curse he snatched it up and barked, "Yes?"

Sallie watched him as he listened, saw the frown that darkened his brow. "I'll be right down," he said, and hung up, then pulled his jacket back on.

"Who was that?" she asked.

"The desk. There's a message for me. I'll be right back."

After he'd gone she undressed and hung away her gown, then put on a lightweight white blouson dress, all the while mulling over what he'd said. A message for him? Why hadn't they given it to him over the phone or, better yet, when they'd walked through the lobby not five minutes before? It didn't sound plausible, and without hesitation she left the room and made for the elevators. She made her living by being curious, after all.

But she was more than curious, she was cautious.

She left the elevator at the second floor and walked down the stairs the rest of the way. Her cautiousness was rewarded. She opened the door at the bottom of the stairs and looked out to see her husband standing with his arm around Coral Williams, who was staring up at him with tearstained eyes. Sallie couldn't hear what they were saying, but Rhy went with Coral to the elevators and the doors slid shut behind them.

Her lips pressed firmly together, Sallie returned to their hotel room and swiftly gathered her clothing. So much for his tale of being faithful! It had to be more than a casual relationship for Coral to follow him to Sakarya. And she wasn't going to wait for him to listen to any more of his lies!

She had to act swiftly; she had no way of knowing how long he would stay with Coral. She scribbled a note, not paying attention to what she was writing, but it was something to the effect of sorry, she just wasn't interested. Then she picked up her suitcase and purse and left, once again taking the stairs.

Finding a taxi was easy, a fleet of them was waiting outside the hotel; her problem now was finding a place to stay. She was aware that hotels were few and far between in Khalidia. In French she explained to the driver that she wished to go to another hotel but not one that was well-known. He obliged, and when Sallie saw it she understood why it wasn't well-known; it looked as if the French Foreign Legion should come swarming over the walls. It was small and old and simple, and the fiercely mustachioed man who seemed to be in charge looked her over thoroughly before saying something in his own language to the taxi driver.

"He says there is a room, if you wish it, but it is not

of the finest," the driver translated. "Also you must pay in advance and you must stay in your room as you are not veiled and your man is not with you."

"That seems fair," Sallie replied. To stay in the room was just what the doctor ordered; it would insure that Rhy couldn't find her. "But what shall I do for food?"

The Sakaryan's dark eyes slid over her, and then he revealed that he spoke some French by informing her rustily that his wife would bring food to her.

Delighted that she'd be able to communicate Sallie thanked him and beamed at him, her big eyes sparkling. When the driver had left Sallie lifted her suitcase and waited expectantly for her host to lead her way to her room. Instead he glared down at her fiercely for a moment, then leaned down and took the suitcase from her hand. "You are too small," he growled. "My wife will feed you."

Then he took her up the narrow stairs to her room and left her there, and Sallie examined what was to be her sleeping quarters for the next two nights. The room was spotless but contained only a single bed and a washstand on which stood a blue urn of water and a washbasin. But the bed was covered with an exotic spread and was strewn with cushions, and the mattress was comfortable, so she was satisfied.

The proprietor's wife brought up a tray loaded with cheese, bread, orange juice and coffee. She looked Sallie over from head to toe, her expression shocked at the sight of Sallie's slim legs, but she gave a timid smile in response to Sallie's grin.

After eating, Sallie took off her dress and shoes; if she was to be confined in this small room for forty-eight hours she might as well be comfortable. Digging in her suitcase she produced the long T-shirt that she had packed and pulled it on; wearing only that and her panties she was as cool as she could get and still have any clothes on. Then she unpacked her clothing and hung everything up to air.

With nothing else to do she lay down on the bed and tried to lose herself in one of the paperback books she'd brought, but the heat was becoming oppressive and she thought with longing of the air-conditioned comfort of the Hotel Khalidia. Flopping onto her back she raised the book to fan herself, and only then did she notice the old-fashioned paddle fan on the ceiling. "Shades of *Casablanca!*" she cried in delight, jumping up and looking about for the switch. She wouldn't even have sworn that the hotel was wired for electricity, but there was a switch on the wall, and when she flipped it the fan creaked into motion. The gentle movement of air against her skin relieved the sensation of smothering, and she fell back on the bed.

She tried again to read her book, but thoughts of Rhy kept breaking into her concentration, and suddenly a raw sob burst from her throat. Amazed at her tears and yet helpless to stop them, she bowed her head onto the bed and wept until her chest hurt and her eyes were swollen. Crying for Rhy? She'd sworn seven years ago that he'd never make her cry again, and she had thought she was over all her illusions about him, but seeing him with his arm around Coral had hit her like a sledgehammer. Was she always going to be a fool over the man? What was the old saying? "I have cried for these things once already," or something to that effect, yet here she was crying for them again. And it was a waste of time.

She should be glad that she'd seen Coral before she'd

allowed Rhy to make a complete fool of her. It was her stupid weakness for him that allowed her, even knowing that she was stupid, still to respond to his lovemaking—crave his lovemaking, if she was honest with herself. And subconsciously she'd been hoping that somehow things would work out between them. She might as well face the truth once and for all: the reasons Rhy wanted her back were not emotional ones; they were all physical. Sex between them was good. It was more than good. They were a matched pair with their needs, their instincts and responses, each knowing just how to drive the other wild. And it wasn't anything they thought about; it was inborn in both of them, whatever it was that made each of them so physically attractive to the other.

Having known his lovemaking, hadn't she refused all other men because she'd known that they couldn't compare with what she'd had with Rhy? She couldn't see Rhy refusing women like that; his sexual appetites were too urgent and strong, but there was no doubt that he had a weakness for her. But sex just wasn't enough for her! She loved him and she wanted that love to be returned. They couldn't spend their lives together in bed; there had to be something else.

With fierce determination she dried her tears and looked about for something to do. Reading couldn't help and she wished that she had brought her manuscript with her. But even if it wasn't here she could write in longhand, couldn't she, and type it up when she returned home? She knew that she could lose herself in writing, push the pain inside her away.

She never went anywhere without several pads tucked into her bag so she dug one out and sat down on the bed with it balanced on her knee, as there was nothing to use for a desk. Grimly she made herself recall where she'd left off, and after a few minutes the writing became easier. So what if Rhy had let her down again? She still had herself, her newly discovered talent and her integrity. She had learned how to live without Rhy, and she'd been a fool to have stayed with the magazine once she had learned he'd bought it. She was vulnerable to him, she always had been, but she knew that she didn't dare let him resume the prominent position that he'd once held in her life. It had nearly destroyed her, that mad need for his touch, his smile, his presence.

But what if she had a baby? The thought came out of nowhere and she dropped her pen, her hand straying over her flat stomach, and she wondered. Thinking back, counting, she realized that it was possible, even likely. But there was a difference now: she wouldn't be terrified at being on her own. She would gladly welcome a chance to have her child all to herself. Part of her longed for a baby, ached to hold a small wriggling body in her arms. She'd never been able to hold her son; they had taken him away immediately and she'd had only a glimpse of his blue little face. Another baby... another son. Suddenly she hoped it was so with a fierce, wild yearning. Perhaps she couldn't have Rhy, but she could have his baby, and she could give to her child the love that Rhy didn't want.

CHAPTER EIGHT

ON THE MORNING of the charity ball Sallie was a mass of nerves, partly a result of being shut up in that tiny room for two days and partly because she so dreaded facing Rhy again. She knew as well as she knew the color of her eyes that he hadn't left the city; he was waiting for her to surface at the ball. He would be furious, and that was an understatement.

But she dressed in the lavender silk dress that she'd chosen for the ball and noticed that it darkened her eyes to violet. A touch of mauve eyeshadow made her eyes pools of mystery and she underlined the air of sophistication by pulling her hair back from her face in a severe coil that was secured by three tiny amethyst butterflies.

It was almost time for her taxi, so she picked up her suitcase, since she would not be coming back there after the ball, and carefully made her way down the narrow stairs, not wanting to turn her ankles in her high heels. The Sakaryan proprietor was seated just to the right of the stairs, and he got to his feet as she descended. His gaze went over her thoroughly, and she sensed the tension of his powerful muscles. She had the uncomfortable feeling that this Sakaryan would like to start a harem, with her as his first concubine!

But he said, in his rough French, "It is dangerous for

you to be in this part of the city alone. I will walk with you to the taxi, yes?"

"Yes, thank you," she said gravely, and noticed that he didn't offer to carry the suitcase for her this time, but she was grateful for his escort even for the short distance to the taxi waiting outside. Her driver grinned and got out to open the door as they approached.

At the palace gates she had to leave the taxi as the driver wasn't cleared to enter the palace grounds. Her name was checked off on the list of guests and a hawk-faced guard escorted her to the palace and even stored her suitcase in a small cupboard before taking her to the enormous chamber that had been decorated for the ball.

Though she was early there were already a fair number of people standing about, the women dressed like so many butterflies, and the abundance of jewels made her eyebrows arch. To her delight there were also a number of Muslim guests, and she was certain that not all of the dark men, some wearing their native headdress and some in European clothing, were Sakaryan; probably Rhy could put a name to most of them. And there were a few Muslim women, too, well dressed, quiet, looking about with their huge, liquid dark eyes. She would have loved to talk to them, ask about their lives, but she had the feeling that her nosiness wouldn't be very well received.

Suddenly Sallie felt a tingle along the left side of her face, and she lifted a hand to touch her cheek. Then she knew, and she turned her head slightly to look straight into Rhy's furious gaze. His eyes were like flint, his jaw carved out of granite. Sallie tilted her chin and gave him back as good as she got as he strode toward her with suppressed savagery in every line of his muscular body.

She stood her ground, and when he reached her he encircled her slim waist with his hard fingers, a grip that didn't hurt but which she knew she couldn't break. A voice gravelly with temper growled, "You need to be shown who's boss, baby, and I'm just the man to do it. Where the *hell* have you been?"

"At another hotel," she informed him casually. "I told you from the beginning that I didn't want to resume our marriage, and I meant it."

"You agreed to give it a three-day trial," he reminded her grimly.

"So I did. I'd have agreed to rob a bank if it would have kept you from watching me. So what?" She raised her head and looked him straight in the eye. "I lied to you and you lied to me. We're even."

"How did I lie to you?" he snapped, his nostrils flaring in rage that he had to control because they were in public.

"About Coral." She gave him a wintry smile. "You don't seem to realize that I don't mind if you had other women—I really don't *care*—" that was a lie if she'd ever told one "—but I do object to people lying to me. So you've been a virtual monk, have you? Am I to believe that Coral followed you all the way to Sakarya with tears in her beautiful eyes on the basis of a platonic relationship?"

"I don't know how you found out about Coral—" he began impatiently, but she interrupted.

"I followed you. I have a nosy nature. It's part of being a reporter. So, my dear husband, I saw you comfort your mistress and take her to her room, and you didn't leave immediately or you would have caught *me* leaving!"

"It's your fault that I took her to her room," he snarled, his fingers tightening on her wrist. "I didn't ask her to follow me and I didn't lie to you. She isn't and never has been my mistress. But there she was, and she was crying, and I wondered if you'd been right when you said she was in love with me. I've never thought she was, she went out with other men, and I dated other women, but there was the possibility that you'd seen something I'd missed. I thought I owed her an explanation, so I took her to her room and told her the truth about us. Fifteen minutes later I went back to our room and found only that damned note of yours! I could break your neck, Sallie. I've been half out of my mind worrying about you!"

"I've told you I can take care of myself," she muttered, wondering if she could believe this or not. But she didn't dare believe him! How could she? She knew him too well, knew the strength of his sexual appetite.

Further conversation was prevented at that point by the entrance of the King of Sakarya, His Royal Highness Abu Haroun al Mahdi. Everyone bowed and the women curtsied, including the Americans in the group, and the King looked pleased. He lacked the stature of many Sakaryans, but five hundred years of rule were evident in his proud carriage and straightforward gaze. He greeted his guests first in perfect English, then in French, and finally in the Arabic tongue.

Sallie strained up on her toes for a better look at him, and for a moment her eyes were solidly locked with those of the monarch. After a second's hesitation he gave her a nod and a slow, faintly shy smile, which she returned with her own warm, friendly smile; then they were blocked from view by a group of people moving closer to him.

"You've made a hit," Rhy observed with narrowed eyes.

"All I did was smile at him," she defended crossly, for it seemed as if he was accusing her of something.

"Your smile is an open invitation, baby," he drawled.

He was going to be impossible; he would make the day as difficult for her as he could. "Isn't it time for the fashion show to begin?" she said, grateful for anything that would relieve her of his undivided attention.

"In half an hour," he replied, drawing her with him to the room where the fashion show would take place. Some of the top designers of the world had put together the show for Marina and already the chairs that had been placed about the runway were half filled. Exquisitely gowned women laughed and chattered while their suave escorts looked on with veiled interest.

A thought struck Sallie and she muttered to Rhy, "I suppose Coral is modeling?"

"Of course," he affirmed, his voice hard.

"Then we might as well find seats," she sniped. "I don't suppose wild horses could drag you away."

His fingers bit painfully into her arm. "Shut up," he snarled. "My God, can't you just shut up?" His head snapped around and before she could protest he was marching her firmly out of the room. He barked a question at a guard who saluted smartly, for some reason, and led them down a passageway to a small room. Rhy bodily pushed her into the room and closed the door behind them.

Hoping to divert him from the black rage she could see in his face Sallie said hastily, "What room is this?"

while she looked around the small chamber as if she was vastly interested.

"I don't care," Rhy replied, his voice so rough that the words were barely intelligible, and then he advanced on her with dark purpose evident in his face. Sallie backed away in alarm but had taken only a few steps when he caught her.

He didn't say anything else; he simply pulled her to him and covered her mouth with his and kissed her with such devouring hunger that she forgot to struggle. It would have been useless in any case; she was no match for his strength and he held her so closely that their bodies were pressed together from shoulder to knee. Blood began to drum in her ears and she sank against him, held up only by his arms.

Long minutes later he lifted his mouth and surveyed her flushed, love-drugged face. "Don't talk to me about other women," he ordered in a low tone, his uneven breath caressing her lips. "No other woman can excite me like you do, even when you're not trying to, you little witch. I want you now," he finished on a groan, bending his head to brush her lips with his.

"That—that's impossible," she whispered, but her protest was only a token one. The sensual fire that burned in him burned in her, also, and if he had persisted she wouldn't have been capable of resisting. As it was he retained some sense of their location and put her away from him with shaking hands.

"I know, dammit." He sighed. "I suppose we'd better go back if you want to see the fashion show—and not another word about Coral," he warned darkly.

Her fingers trembling, she repaired the damage he'd done to her lipstick and offered him a tissue to wipe the color from his mouth. He did so, smiling a little at the smear of color that came off on the tissue.

"What did you say to the guard?" she finally asked, obeying a need to make nonvital conversation.

"I told him you were feeling faint," he replied. "And you did look pale."

"Do I now?" she wondered aloud, touching her cheeks.

"No. You look kissed," he drawled.

The blood was still rushing through her body in yearning when they took their seats for the fashion show, and the parade of models barely registered on her consciousness. She was too aware of Rhy's tall body beside her, so close that she could feel the warmth of him, smell the unique muskiness of his body. Her heart pounded heavily in her chest. Only Coral made any impression on her, her eyes fastened on Rhy as if drawn to him, the pouty, sensuous smile on her perfect mouth meant for him alone. Glancing sideways at Rhy, Sallie saw that his expression remained closed except for a slight tightening of his jaw that spoke volumes to her, and she looked back at Coral with nausea boiling in her stomach.

THE PROGRAM WAS full, every minute ordered. After the fashion show there was a thousand-dollar-a-plate dinner, with all of the proceeds going to charity. Then dancing, then entertainment by a top American singer. Sallie lived through the hours feeling as if she was walking underwater. Rhy was with her every minute, but she couldn't forget the fleeting expression on his face when he'd seen Coral.

Why was she allowing him to torment her like this?

She had no illusions about him, and she had already determined her own course of action. When they returned to New York she would leave, it was as simple as that. But for some reason she couldn't shake her deep sense of misery, and as a result she drank more champagne than she meant to, realizing that fact only when the room swirled mistily around her and she clutched at Rhy's arm.

"That's enough," he said gently, taking the glass from her fingers and setting it down. "I think you could stand something to eat, a slice of cake maybe. Come on."

With tender concern he made certain she ate, watching her closely all the while. When she felt better she smiled thankfully at him. "How much longer before the interview?" she murmured.

"Not much longer, honey," he comforted, as if sensing her unhappiness.

But at last it was over with and Sallie and Marina were alone in a private chamber the King had donated for their use. "He's really a dear," Marina explained. "I think he's shy, but he tries so hard to disguise it. And of course he was brought up to disregard women in every way but the physical, and he can't quite become used to meeting them socially despite his English education."

"Did your husband go to the same school?" Sallie asked, thinking that Zain didn't seem to have any problem with women.

"No, and his attitude could bear some improvement, too," Marina said with wry amusement. "Listen, he kept a harem until we were engaged. I made him give them all up before I would agree to marry him!" she explained smugly.

Sallie choked on her laughter and gasped. "A harem? You're kidding! Do they still have those things?"

"Of course, why do you think the royal families have so many princes? Muslim religion permits three wives and as many concubines as a man can support, and Zain most definitely had his selection of concubines to occupy his nights!"

"What did you say to him to make him give them up?"

"I gave him a choice, he could have me or he could have other women, but I made it plain that I had no intention of sharing him. He didn't like the idea of giving up his harem, but he finally realized that my ignorant American mind just couldn't accept it."

Their eyes met and they went off into gales of laughter, and of course that was the moment when they were interrupted by Rhy and Zain. "I thought this was a serious interview," Rhy commented, strolling forward to drop his long length beside Sallie.

"And I thought it was a private one," she retorted.

Zain's strong mouth quirked as he stretched his long frame out close to Marina. "We couldn't resist," he explained. "I introduced Rhy to His Majesty," he said, flexing his broad shoulders as if he was weary, and he chuckled at the memory. "I think I made some diplomats jealous, especially when they had a long chat in voices too low to carry!"

"The State Department will probably try to debrief me," Rhy added.

A memory clicked in Sallie's mind, and she said casually to Zain, "How did you meet Rhy?"

"He saved my life," Zain replied promptly, but no explanation followed and Sallie's eyebrows arched.

"You don't need to know," Rhy teased. "We were both where we weren't supposed to be and we barely got out alive. Let it rest, baby. Tell us how you and Marina met, instead."

"Oh, that's simple enough." Marina shrugged. "We met in college. There's nothing unusual in that. Now, why don't you two run along? How can Sallie and I talk with witnesses present?"

Both men laughed, but neither made a move to leave, so they had to be included in the conversation. To be truthful, it was impossible to exclude them. Rhy wasn't there for an interview, but he was still a reporter and gradually he got one anyway. Despite her exasperation Sallie could only admire the way he posed his questions to Zain. Some were blunt, posed point-blank; others he merely hinted at, letting Zain evade the question or answer it as he wished. In response to that consideration Zain was open with his answers, and Sallie knew that she was listening to potential dynamite. He told Rhy things that perhaps even foreign heads of state hadn't been told, and he seemed to have perfect confidence that Rhy would know what he could report and what he should forget.

Slowly Sallie began to understand the razor-sharp brain of the man who handled the finances of a booming economy and was slowly easing his country into the twentieth century. He was an adventurer, but he was also a patriot. Perhaps that was why the King had such great confidence in his young minister of finance, why he was allowing Sakaryan policies to be shaped along Western lines.

The role that Marina played in those policies wasn't small, she realized. As Zain had vast influence with the King, so Marina had vast influence with Zain. She didn't know if he would admit it; a man who had kept a harem until fairly recently wasn't likely to admit even to himself that his wife was a major factor in the direction his politics had taken. Nor would the King be likely to be happy if told that Marina was the indirect influence behind his throne. Yet the smiling, beautiful young woman, so obviously in love with her husband, was playing a powerful role in a scenario that could affect the entire world through its effect of Sakaryan oil.

At last the conversation became more general and Marina asked if perhaps Sallie would be free to visit later on in the year. Sallie had opened her mouth to accept when Rhy broke in before she could say a word. "I'm set to be filming a documentary in Europe late this fall and early winter," he said, "and Sallie will be with me. I don't know yet how the schedule will be, but I'll let you know."

"Do," urged Marina. "We see each other so little now. At least when I lived in New York we managed to catch each other in town once every month or so."

Sallie didn't comment, but privately she thought that Rhy was taking a lot for granted. Was he in for a surprise when she walked out of his life and disappeared forever!

IT WAS LATE when they left the palace, and as they just had time to catch their flight Zain had arranged for an escort to the airport. Sallie and Rhy rode in Zain's personal limousine, and their luggage was checked and they were waved on board without pause.

Rhy had been ominously silent during the entire ride, and he was still not speaking when they buckled themselves into their seats. That suited her fine; she was tired and she didn't feel like arguing with him. Somehow she always came off second best when they fought. She was too impulsive, too reckless, unable to control her temper, whereas Rhy coolly plotted each move in advance.

When they were airborne the stewardesses began distributing the small airline pillows and blankets to those passengers who desired them, and because it was so late Sallie decided she would try to sleep and accepted them, then tilted her seat back. "I'm tired," she told Rhy's grim profile. "Good night."

He turned his head and his hard eyes burned her. Then he let his seat back, too, and slid his arm under her head, pulling her over to rest on his shoulder. "I've spent two hellish nights wondering where you were," he growled against her temple while he spread the blanket over her. "You'll sleep where you belong." Then he tilted her head back and his hard mouth closed on hers, claiming her lips in a possessive kiss that lasted long enough for him to be aware of her response. Then he drew back and resettled her head against his shoulder, and she was glad of the chance to hide her burning face. Why did she have to be so weak and foolish? Why couldn't she control her response to him?

After that kiss she was sure she wouldn't be able to sleep, but somehow she fell asleep immediately and woke only once during the long flight when she shifted and Rhy pulled the blanket up over her again. Opening her eyes in the dim cabin she looked up at him and whispered, "Can't you sleep?"

"I've been asleep," he murmured. "I was just wishing that we were alone." He pulled her close and kissed her again, leaving her in no doubt as to just why he wished they were alone. His kisses lingered and became hungry, pressing again and again to her mouth, until at last he muttered a frustrated curse and leaned his head back. "I can wait," he growled. "Barely."

Sallie lay against his shoulder and bit her lips to keep from whispering the words of love that sprang to her tongue. Tears burned her eyes. She loved him! It was so painful that she thought she'd scream. She loved him, but she couldn't trust him with her love.

They changed flights in Paris again and because the days they had spent in Sakarya hadn't been exactly restful jet lag hit both of them hard. Sallie had a splitting headache when they finally landed at JFK and from the taut, weary look on Rhy's face he didn't feel much better. If he had started an argument then she would have become hysterical, but instead he dropped her at her apartment and left without even kissing her.

Contrarily, that made her want to cry, and she lugged her suitcase up to her apartment and savagely emptied it. After taking a swift shower she fell on the bed and found to her fury that sleep eluded her. She remembered the sleepy sensuousness of his kisses during the flight, how comfortable she had been cuddled against his shoulder, the security of his arms. She burst into angry, aching tears and eventually cried herself to sleep.

But when she awoke the next morning her mind was clear. Rhy was driving her crazy, and if she didn't leave now, as she had planned, he would eventually wear her down. She would go to work today, type up the interview she had gotten with Marina and quietly turn in her notice to Greg. Then she would come back home, close up the apartment, pack her clothing and get on a bus going anywhere.

She dressed and took the bus to work, arriving a little late due to an accident that caused a traffic jam. When she entered the noisy newsroom the clatter dropped to almost silence, and it seemed to her that everyone turned to stare at her. A blush rose to her cheeks without her knowing why, and she hurried to her little cubicle. Brom was there, busy at his typewriter, but when she sat down and pulled the cover off of her own typewriter he stopped what he was doing and swiveled in his chair to look at her.

"What's wrong?" Sallie demanded, half laughing. "Do I have something on my face?"

In answer Brom leaned over and turned her wooden nameplate to face her. Aghast, Sallie stared at it. It was a new nameplate. And instead of SALLIE JEROME it blatantly declared for all the world to see, SALLIE BAINES. She collapsed in her chair and stared at it as if it would bite her.

"Congratulations," Brom offered. "That must've been some trip."

She couldn't think of anything to say; she just continued to stare at the nameplate. Evidently it had only appeared that morning, and she wondered at Rhy's motive. Uneasily she sensed that he was drawing the net tighter about her and that perhaps she had waited too long to make her break. But there was no help for it now, and her professional integrity wouldn't permit her to leave without finishing the interview with Marina.

"Well?" Brom prompted. "Is it true?"

"That we're married?" she replied crisply. "It's true enough, for what you want to make of it."

"And just what does that mean, Madam Sphinx?"

"It means that a wedding does not a marriage make," she mocked. "Don't take this too seriously."

"Listen, you can't be half-married, or casually married. Either you are or you aren't," he said in exasperation.

"It's a long story," she evaded, and was saved from further questioning when the phone rang. With a smothered sigh of relief she snatched it up. "Sallie Jerome."

"Wrong," Greg growled in her ear. "Sallie *Baines*. Your closet husband has gone public and it's a load off my mind. You had me in a tough spot if he'd found out I knew about you. But it's all over now and it's all between the two of you."

"What do you mean?" she asked warily, wondering if Rhy had done something else to hem her in that she hadn't yet heard of.

"Just that, doll. As far as I'm concerned you're not one of my best reporters now, you're his wife."

In blind anger Sallie forgot that she'd been planning on turning in her notice anyway and she hissed between her teeth, "Do you mean you won't give me any more assignments?"

"That's exactly what I mean. Take it up directly with him. For crying out loud, he's your husband and from what I can see he's more than willing to try a reconciliation."

"I don't want a reconciliation," she said, reining in her temper and keeping her tone low so Brom couldn't overhear. "But a reference will do just fine. Will you give me one?"

"I can't, not now that he's made it common knowledge that you're his wife. He's my boss, too," Greg explained dryly. "And he's made it clear that anything concerning you is to be okayed by him personally."

"Has he?" she demanded furiously as her anger broke out of control. "I'll have to see about that, won't I?" She slammed the phone down and glared at it, then turned her burning gaze on Brom, who threw his hands up in mock surrender and ostentatiously turned back to his typewriter.

She expected to be summoned to Rhy's office at any moment, and she couldn't decide if she wanted to see him or not. It would be an exquisite relief to unleash her temper and scream at him, but she knew that Rhy would also take advantage of her lack of control and would probably provoke her into revealing all her plans. The best thing she could do was to complete her report and leave. She knew her weaknesses, and the two worst ones were her temper and Rhy. The sensible thing to do was not to allow either of them to gain the upper hand.

She tried, but concentrating had seldom been more difficult. Her mind raced, going over her packing, the steps she had to take to close up her apartment, where she might go, and in the middle of all her plans would flash a picture of Rhy, naked, his eyes hungry as he reached for her, and her body would remember his touch and she'd tremble in reaction. She ached for him; why hadn't he come up to the apartment with her last night? Of course they'd both been tired, exhausted and irritable, but still… What a fool she was! The last thing she needed was more of his addictive lovemaking! It would be hard enough now to get over him, to forget again the wild sweetness that had consumed her.

The morning slipped past, and she grimly determined to work through lunch, but her plans were derailed when Chris stopped by her desk, his brown eyes shuttered as he silently lifted her nameplate and studied it, then returned it to her desk without comment. "Can you get away for a little while?" he asked quietly, but even so Sallie caught the undertone in his voice, perhaps because she was so miserable herself that she was sensitive to the suffering of others.

"It's lunchtime, anyway," she said without hesitation, turning off the typewriter and covering it. "Where do you want to go?"

"Will he mind?" Chris asked, and she knew who he meant.

"No," she lied, and gave him a cheeky little grin. "Besides, I'm not asking him."

He didn't speak again until they were out of the building and weaving their way through the hurrying, dodging, sidestepping lunch crowd that filled the sidewalks. He lifted his head and peered at the heat ball of the sun with slitted eyes as he commented, "Are you really married to him? It's not easy to get married that fast unless you detour through Vegas."

"I've been married to him for eight years," she admitted, not meeting the questioning glance that she felt him shoot at her. "And we've been separated for seven of those years."

They walked in silence for a while, then Chris caught her hand and indicated a coffee shop. That was as good as anything and they went inside, where they were shown to a small table along the wall. Sallie wasn't hungry and she chose only fruit juice to drink and a small salad, knowing that the salad wouldn't be eaten. Chris didn't seem very hungry either, for when their

food came he merely drank his coffee and stared broodingly at the tuna sandwich on his plate.

"It looks as if you're back together now," he finally
said.

Sallie shook her head. "It's what he wants."

"And you don't?"

"He doesn't love me," she said sadly. "I'm just a challenge to him. Like I told you, he just wants to play for a
while. It doesn't matter to him that he's destroying my
life in the process. He's already wrecked my career, and
he swears that he'll blacklist me, keep me from getting
another job as a reporter."

Chris swore, something he rarely did, and met
Sallie's surprised gaze with gold lights of anger leaping in his dark eyes. "How could he do that to you?"
he muttered.

She managed a careless shrug. "He says he's afraid
I'll get killed. That he can't stand the thought of me in
the middle of a revolution." But how many times had
Rhy left her to do just that, leaving her behind in a
frenzy of worry?

"Now *that* I can understand," said Chris, giving her
a wry smile. "I'll admit to having a few worries about
your pretty little carcass myself, and I'm not even married to you."

"But you won't quit for Amy," she reminded him
bluntly. "And I won't quit for Rhy—if I have any choice.
He's hemming me in, Chris. He's tying me down and
smothering me."

"You love him."

"I try not to. I just haven't succeeded very well so
far." Then she shook her head. "Forget about me. Is the
situation still the same with Amy?"

He tilted his head a little to one side. "I still love her. I still want to marry her. But she still won't marry me unless I quit reporting, and the thought of stifling myself in a nine-to-five job makes me break out in a cold sweat."

"Can you give in? Greg did, for his kids."

"But he didn't for his wife," Chris pointed out. "He had to lose her before he left the field. If she were still alive he'd probably still be out there chasing down a story."

That was true and she sighed, looking away from him. The demands made by children were so much harder to deny than those made by adults because children saw things only in relation to themselves and couldn't comprehend that their parents' needs should be as important as their own. They had no compunction about making their needs clear, demanding that they be taken care of, while adults for some reason drew back, refrained from pushing too hard, knowing that no one owed them anything and therefore they didn't ask. Except she had asked—she had demanded—that Rhy change his job and stay with her, and it had gained her exactly nothing. Rhy had made it plain that her happiness wasn't his responsibility. He had his own life to live. Nor could she offer Chris any hope, any solution, for she could see none for herself. No matter what they did, misery would be the result.

"I'm going to leave," she said aloud, then looked at him in horror, not having meant to announce her intentions.

He caught the look and waved his hand. "Forget it. It won't go any further," he assured her. "I kind of thought you might do that, anyway. You've got the guts to do what you have to do, no matter how it hurts. You're cutting your losses. I just wish I could."

"When you're ready you will. Don't forget, I've had seven years to get used to being without him." She gave him a tiny smile. "I'd even convinced myself that it was all over between us. It didn't take Rhy long to shatter that little fairy tale."

He looked at her as if he wasn't really seeing her, his dark eyes taking on the introspective blankness of someone walling himself up inside. He'd been hurt, just as she had. There was nothing so calculated to batter the self-esteem as to hear a loved one saying, "You have to change," the insidious little phrase that really meant, "I don't love you as you are. You're not good enough." There were deeper hurts, more violent hurts, yet somehow that particular hurt had such a nasty sting. She knew it well now, and she swore that she'd never ask anyone to change ever again. Had Rhy been hurt by her insistence that he change? She tried to picture a confused, hurt Rhy and failed utterly. He had a stainless-steel character that never faltered, never let itself be vulnerable. He'd brushed her clinging arms off like so many cobwebs and went on his way.

"I'll get over her," said Chris quietly, and on his face was the smooth blank look of acceptance. "I guess I'll have to, won't I?"

They walked back to the office in silence, and as they entered the empty elevator Chris punched the button to close the door and held his finger on it, staring fixedly at her.

"Keep in touch," he said softly. "I wish it could've been you, Sal." He curved his hand around her neck and bent to lightly touch his lips to hers and she felt tears sting her eyelids. Yes, why couldn't it have been Chris for her, instead of Rhy?

She couldn't promise that she'd be in touch, though she wanted to. Once she left she couldn't risk doing anything that might give Rhy a clue to where to find her, and anything Chris didn't know he couldn't divulge. She left the elevator with only a long look into his face that said goodbye; then she went back to her desk and tackled the report again with grim determination.

The sense of now or never gave her the concentration she needed and in less than an hour she sent the finished report on to Greg's office. She stood and stretched her tired, cramped muscles and casually got her purse and left the building without speaking to anyone, as if she was merely leaving for an appointment, when in reality she intended never to return. She regretted that she had to leave without telling Greg, but he'd made it painfully clear that his first loyalty was to Rhy, and she knew that he would immediately report her resignation.

Caution made her cash the cashier's check she'd been carrying in her purse and convert most of the money into traveler's checks. Who knew what means Rhy might use to hold her? She had to get out and do it now.

It was almost three-thirty by the time she reached her apartment and it was only instinct, but when she opened the door the hair on the back of her neck lifted. She stared around at the familiar furniture and she knew that something was different. Looking about she saw that several things were missing: her personal awards were gone, her books were gone, her antique clock was missing. Thieves!

Rushing into the bedroom she stared aghast at the emptiness. The closet doors stood open, revealing the lack of contents. Her cosmetic and toiletry items were gone from the bathroom, even her toothbrush. All of her personal items had disappeared! Then she went utterly pale and raced back into the bedroom to stare in horror at the uncluttered surface where her manuscript and typewriter had rested. Even her manuscript had been stolen!

A noise in the doorway made her whirl, ready for battle if the thieves had returned, but it was the landlady who stood there. "I thought I saw you," Mrs. Landis said cheerfully. "I'm so happy for you. You're such a nice girl, and I always wondered when you were going to get married. I'll hate losing you, but I know you're anxious to settle in with that handsome husband of yours."

A cold feeling settled in Sallie's stomach. "Husband?" she echoed weakly.

"He's the first celebrity I've ever met," Mrs. Landis rattled on. "But he was so nice, and he said he'd made arrangements for your furniture to be put in storage by this weekend so I can rent the apartment out again. I thought it was so thoughtful of him to handle it all for you while you were working."

By now Sallie had gotten control of herself, and she managed a smile for Mrs. Landis. "It certainly was," she agreed, her hands clenching into fists by her sides. "Rhy thinks of everything!"

But he hadn't won yet!

CHAPTER NINE

SHE WAS SO angry that she was shaking helplessly, unable to decide what to do. She got on a bus and rode aimlessly, wishing violently that she could get her hands around Rhy's throat. He'd literally stolen her clothing, all of her personal possessions. That was bad enough, but she could get along without all that if she had to. The one thing she couldn't leave behind was her manuscript, and she couldn't think of any way to get it back, either. She didn't even know where Rhy lived, and his telephone number wasn't listed.

But she had to find somewhere to spend the night, and at last she left the bus and walked the teeming sidewalks in the steamy hot afternoon sun until weariness prompted her to choose a hotel at random. She checked in and sat for a long time in a daze, unable to think of any action she could take. Her mind darted about erratically, trying to devise a way of retrieving the manuscript without having to see Rhy again. But to find the book she had to find out where Rhy lived, and to do that she had to talk to him, something that she wanted to avoid.

The theft of her book seemed to have paralyzed her, robbed her of her ability to act. She thought bleakly of simply beginning again, but she knew that it wouldn't be the same; she couldn't remember all of the details of her exact phrasing. She cried for a while, out of anger and despair, and when she finally decided to call Rhy at the office she realized that she'd waited too long; everyone would have gone home.

So there was nothing to do but wait. She showered, lay on the bed and watched television, then drifted to sleep with the set still on, only to waken in the early hours of the morning to the crackle of static.

She was starving because not only hadn't she eaten the lunch she'd chosen, she hadn't had dinner the night before, either, and her empty stomach was the last straw; curling up like a child she wept brokenly. How *dare* he!

But Rhy would dare anything, as she knew to her cost. She drifted back to sleep and when she woke again she had a pounding headache and it was nearly ten a.m. She took another shower and dressed, then breathed deeply several times and sat down by the phone. There was no way out of it. She had to talk to him.

Before her courage deserted her she dialed the office number and asked for Mr. Baines. Of course Amanda answered and Sallie managed a calm good morning before she asked to speak to Rhy.

"Of course, he said to put you through immediately," Amanda replied cheerfully, and Sallie's nerves screamed with tension as she waited for Rhy to come on the line.

"Sallie." His dark, rough-velvet voice in her ear made her jump and bang the receiver against her already aching temple. "Where are you, darling?"

She swallowed and said hoarsely, "I want my book back, Rhy!"

"I said, where are you?"

"The book—" she began again.

"Forget the damned book!" he rasped, and it was all her nerves could stand. She gulped, trying to swallow the sob that tore out of her throat, but it was swiftly followed by another and abruptly she was crying helplessly, clinging to the receiver as if it were a lifeline.

"You—you stole it!" she accused between sobs, her words almost unintelligible. "You knew it was the one thing I couldn't leave without and you stole it! I hate you, do you hear? I hate you! I never want to see you again—"

"Don't cry," he said roughly. "Baby, please don't cry. Tell me where you are and I'll be there as soon as I can. You can have your book back again, I promise."

"Written on water!" she jeered, wiping her wet cheeks with the back of her hand.

He drew an impatient breath. "Look, you'll have to see me if you want the book back. And since that seems to be the only hold I have on you, I'll use it. Meet me for lunch—"

"No," she broke in, looking down at her wrinkled slacks and top. "I—I'm not dressed."

"Then we'll have lunch at my apartment," he decided briskly. "I'll phone the housekeeper and have a meal prepared, so meet me there at twelve-thirty. We can talk privately there."

"I don't know where you live," she confessed, surrendering to the inevitable. She knew it was an error to see him again; she should just leave the manuscript and forget about it, try to start again, but she couldn't. Whatever the risk, she couldn't leave without it.

He gave her the address and instructions on how to get there, and just before he hung up he asked gently, "Are you all right?"

"I'm fine," she said bleakly, and dropped the receiver onto its cradle.

She got up to brush her hair and stared aghast at her reflection in the mirror. She was pale, hollow eyed, her clothing wrinkled. She couldn't let Rhy see her like this! And she didn't have so much as a tube of lipstick in her purse!

But she did have money, and there were shops on the ground floor of the hotel. Making up her mind, she took the elevator down and hurriedly purchased an attractive white summer dress with a tiny floral design on it and a pair of white high-heeled sandals.

In another shop she bought makeup and perfume; then she dashed back up to her room. Carefully she made up her face and repaired the ravages of tears and worry, then dressed in the dainty cotton dress and brushed her hair out; she didn't have the time to do anything with it so she left it streaming down her back in a rich sable mane.

She took a taxi to Rhy's apartment, too nervous to face the crush of a bus at lunchtime. When she got out at his apartment building she glanced at her watch and saw that she was a few minutes late. She paid the taxi driver and hurried to the elevator and punched the button.

As soon as she rang the doorbell the door swung open and Rhy loomed before her, his dark face expressionless.

"I'm sorry I'm late—" she began, rushing into speech in an effort to disguise her nervousness.

"It doesn't matter," he interrupted, standing aside to let her enter. He'd discarded his jacket and tie and unbuttoned his shirt halfway, revealing the curls of hair on his chest. Her eyes riveted on his virile, masculine flesh and unconsciously she wet her lips with her tongue. Just the sight of him weakened her!

His eyes darkened to charcoal. "You teasing little witch," he muttered, and his long fingers moved to his shirt. He unbuttoned the remaining buttons and pulled the shirt free of his pants and peeled out of it, dropping it to the floor. The sunlight streaming through the wide windows gleamed on his chest and shoulders where a light dew of perspiration moistened his skin and revealed all his rippling muscles.

Sallie stepped back, wanting to escape from the need she felt to touch his warm skin and feel the steelness of muscle underneath, but she made the mistake of raising her eyes to his. The hungry, blatant desire she saw there froze her in her tracks.

"I want you," he whispered, advancing on her. "Now."

"I didn't come here for this," she protested weakly, and made a futile attempt to evade him. His long arms encircled her and pulled her against his half-naked body, and she began to tremble at the erotic power he had over her. The scent of his skin, the warmth, the living vibrancy of him, went to her head and intoxicated her so that she forgot about pushing him away.

He attacked with his mouth, overpowering her with kisses that demanded and devoured, sucking all of her strength away so she couldn't resist when his shaking hands moved over her curves and renewed his intimate knowledge of her. She raised her arms and locked them around his neck and kissed him back, her response burning out of control and fanning his own fires.

She rested plaintively against him when he raised his head to gulp in deep, shaking breaths and the half smile that formed on his mouth before being quickly banished revealed that he was aware of his triumph, of her capitulation. With slow, easy moves, as if he didn't want to startle her, he unzipped her dress and slid it down to puddle around her feet. Sallie simply watched him in silence, her big eyes nearly black with desire. She couldn't resist; she couldn't make any plans. All she could do was feel, feel and respond. She loved him and she was helpless against his love.

But at least her desire was returned. She was dimly aware that he was shaking, trembling in every muscle of his big frame as he lifted her gently into his arms and carried her into his bedroom. He placed her on the bed and lay down beside her, his hands pulling at the bits of clothes that remained to separate skin from skin. He couldn't disguise his need for her, just as she had no defenses against him. Hoarsely he whispered to her, disjointed words and phrases that made her quiver in response and cling to him as she drowned in the tidal wave of sensation he evoked.

When the world had righted itself again she was lying in his arms while he slowly stroked her hair, her back, her arms. "I didn't intend for that to happen," he murmured against her temple. "I'd planned to talk first, eat our lunch together and try to act like two civilized people, but the moment I saw you nothing was important any longer except making love to you."

"That's all you ever wanted from me anyway," she said with simple, weary bitterness.

He gave her a brooding glance. "You think so? That's part of what I wanted to talk about, but first, let's see about lunch."

"Won't it be cold?" she asked, pushing her hair back from her face and sitting up and away from his arms.

"Steaks and salad. The salad is in the fridge, the steaks are ready to grill. And I gave Mrs. Hermann the rest of the day off so we won't be disturbed."

"You have everything planned, don't you?" she commented without any real interest as she began dressing, and he swung his long legs over the side of the bed to stand and watch her lethargic movements.

"What's wrong?" he asked sharply, coming to her and cupping her chin in his hand to look into her pale face. "Are you ill?"

She felt ill, achy and depressed after the soaring passion of his lovemaking, and she was stupidly weak. But she knew that her only ailments were an inability to cope with Rhy and the fact that she hadn't eaten in over twenty-four hours.

"I'm well enough," she dismissed his concern. "Just hungry, I suppose. I haven't eaten since yesterday morning."

"Great," he half snarled. "You need to lose some more weight. You must weigh at least ninety pounds. You need someone to watch you and make certain you eat, you little fool!"

He probably had himself in mind, but she didn't argue with him. In silence she completed dressing and waited until he had dressed also. Then she followed him into the neatly organized kitchen. He refused to let her do anything and made her sit on a stool while he grilled the steaks and set the places on the table in the small dining room.

He opened a bottle of California red wine to drink with the meal and for several minutes they ate in silence. Then Sallie asked without looking up from her salad, "Where is my manuscript?"

"In the study," he replied. "You've got a way with words. It's good reading."

She flung her head back as anger struck her. "You had no right to read it!"

"Didn't I?" he asked dryly. "I thought I had a perfect right to read what you'd been writing all those days when you were supposed to have been working for my magazine. You've been drawing a check every week and not writing a word of the articles assigned to you. If it hadn't suited me to keep you quietly at your desk I'd have fired you weeks ago."

"I'll repay every penny I've drawn since you bought the magazine," she flared. "You still had no right to read it!"

"Stop spitting and scratching at me, you little cat," he said in amusement. "I did read it, and there's nothing you can do about it now. Instead, think constructively. You've got a manuscript with strong possibilities, but it's also got some rough edges, and there's a lot of work that needs to be done on it. You need a place to work on it where you won't be disturbed, and you certainly don't need to worry about paying the rent or buying groceries."

"Why not?" she muttered. "Thousands of writers worry about those things."

"But you've never had to," he pointed out. "For your entire life you've had financial security, and it's something you're used to. You won't have a paycheck coming in now, because you're off the payroll as of yesterday, and it'll worry you when your savings begin shrinking.

It takes time to write a book and get it on the market. You'll run out of money before then."

"I'm not a helpless baby and I'm not afraid of work," she replied.

"I know that, but why worry about any of that when you can live here, work on your book without interruptions and keep your savings?"

She sighed, feeling trapped. On the surface it was a logical suggestion, but she knew that the proposal was only a way of getting her back under his thumb where he thought she belonged. If she had any sense she would leave at the first opportunity, even if she had to sacrifice the manuscript, but she'd already passed up one such opportunity and she painfully admitted to herself that it was too late for her to gain her freedom. She was caught again in her own stupid, helpless love for Rhy, knowing that her love wasn't returned except in the lowest form—physical desire. He desired her, and for that reason he wanted her around now, but what would happen when he tired of her again? Would he simply walk out as he had before? Knowing that she was leaving herself wide open for another broken heart she stared into her salad and said expressionlessly, "All right."

He drew in a quick breath. "Just like that? No arguments, no conditions? Not even any questions?"

"I'm not interested in the answers," she replied, shrugging. "I'm tired of fighting you, and I want to finish my book. Other than that, I don't care."

"You're great for a man's ego," he muttered under his breath.

"You trampled all over mine," she snapped in reply. "Don't expect kid gloves from me. You've got what you wanted, me out of a job and living with you, but don't ask for blind adoration because I'm fresh out."

"I never asked for it anyway," he rasped. "And for the record, I'm not trying to chain you down. It was that particular job that I objected to, for reasons you know. All I'm asking from you is time for us to be together, to try to work things out. If we can't stand to live together for six months I'll consider a divorce, but the least we can do is give it a try."

"And if it doesn't work out we'll get a divorce?" she asked cautiously, wanting to be certain.

"Then we'll talk about it."

Glancing at his implacable face she saw that he wasn't going to give her a promise of a divorce so she gave in once more. "All right, six months. But I'm going to be working on my book, not cooking for you and washing your clothes and cleaning this place. If you're looking for a little homemaker you're going to be disappointed."

"In case you haven't noticed, I'm a wealthy man," he said sarcastically. "I don't expect my wife to do laundry."

She lifted her head and stared at him. "What are you getting out of this, Rhy? Other than a sleeping companion, I mean, and you can have that anytime you please without going to all this trouble."

His lids shadowed his gray eyes and he murmured huskily, "Isn't that enough? I want you. Let's just leave it at that."

To SALLIE'S SURPRISE the arrangement worked rather well and they quickly fell into a routine. Rhy would get up every morning and prepare his own breakfast, then wake her with a kiss when he was ready to leave. She would linger over her own breakfast, then spend the rest of the morning in the study, working. Mrs. Hermann turned out to be a plump, gray-haired model of efficiency, and she took care of the apartment just as she had before, making Sallie lunch, cooking the evening meal and leaving just before Rhy arrived home.

Sallie would serve dinner herself, and while they were eating Rhy would tell her about how things were going with the magazine, what had happened that day, ask questions about how her book was progressing. She found herself remarkably at ease with him now, though their relationship never quite achieved true companionship. She sensed that they were both holding something of themselves back, but perhaps that was to be expected when two people with such strong wills tried to live together. There was always the thought that good manners should prevail or the frail fabric of their marriage would be torn beyond repair.

As the days turned into weeks and the stack of pages in the study kept growing she welcomed Rhy's advice and experience. Her own writing style was direct and uncomplicated, but Rhy had the knack of stripping an idea down to the bare bones. It became their custom after dinner for him to read what she'd written that day and give her his opinion. If he didn't like something he said so, but he always made it plain that he thought her overall effort was good. Sometimes she threw out entire sections and began anew, all on the basis of Rhy's criticisms, but at other times she stubbornly clung to her own words as she felt that they better conveyed her own meaning.

Her best work seemed to be done in the evenings

when Rhy sat in the study with her, reading articles and paperwork he'd brought home with him or doing his preliminary research on the documentary he was scheduled to film within three months. He seemed content, all traces of the restlessness she remembered gone, as if he had indeed burned out his need for adventure. In an odd way she was also content; the mental stimulation she received from creating a book was more than enough to occupy her imagination. They worked together in harmony and relative silence, broken only by the ringing of the telephone when Greg called, as he often did, and their own occasional comments to each other.

Then, when it was growing late, Sallie would cover the typewriter and leave Rhy still working while she bathed and prepared for bed. Sometimes he would work for an hour or more after she was in bed, sometimes he followed her closely to the shower, but always—always—he would get in bed with her and take her in his arms and the restrained civility of their manner would explode in hungry, almost savage lovemaking. She had thought his passion would wane as he grew used to having her around again, but his desire remained at a high pitch. Occasionally when they worked together she would watch his absorbed face, fascinated that he could look so calm now yet turn into a wild sensualist if she were to put her arms around him and kiss him. The thought teased at her brain until she would ache to do just that, to see if she could divert his thoughts from his work, but over the years she had developed a deep respect for a person's work and she didn't disturb him.

Only two incidents broke the surface harmony of those first weeks. The first occurred early one evening as she was clearing away the dinner dishes and putting them in the dishwasher. Rhy was already in the study, reading what she'd written that day, so when the phone rang she answered it on the kitchen extension.

"Is Rhy there? Could I speak to him, please?" asked a cool feminine voice and Sallie recognized it instantly.

"Certainly, Coral, I'll get him to the phone," she replied, and placed the receiver on the cabinet top while she went to the study.

He looked up as she entered. "Who was that?" he asked absently, looking down at the pages in his hand.

"It's Coral. She wants to speak with you," Sallie replied in amazingly level tones, and returned to the kitchen to finish her chores. The temptation to listen in on the kitchen extension made her pause for a second, but only a second, then she firmly replaced the extension.

She tried to tell herself that it was nothing but jealousy eating at her insides. Coral had enough self-possession that if she wanted to see Rhy she would have no scruples about calling him at home. Were they still seeing each other? Rhy never mentioned where he went for lunch—or with whom—and about once a week he was late getting home in the evening. As engrossed as she was in the progress of her book she hadn't really noticed or thought anything of it, and she also knew that deadlines had to be met and things could happen that would make a long day necessary.

But Coral was so breathtakingly beautiful! How could any man not be flattered that such a lovely woman obviously adored him?

She couldn't stand it if Rhy was still seeing her, Sallie knew. For a while she had convinced herself that it didn't matter to her if Rhy had other women because she was over him, but now she knew differently. She loved him, and all her defenses had been shattered. He had won a complete victory, if he only knew it, but somehow she had kept herself from admitting aloud that she loved him. He never mentioned love, so neither did she.

When she didn't return to the study Rhy came in search of her and found her standing in the kitchen with her hands clenched.

"Aren't you coming—" he began, then cut his words off when he saw her taut face.

"I can't stop you from seeing her," Sallie said harshly, her eyes black with pain and fury. "But don't you dare let her call you here! I won't put up with that!"

His face darkened and his jaw tightened with temper. It was as if the weeks of politeness had never been. At the first sign of hostility their tempers broke free like wild horses too long held under control. "Hadn't you better get your facts straight before you make wild accusations?" Rhy snarled, coming forward to glower down at her. "You should've listened on the extension if you're so interested in my activities! As it happens, Coral asked me to have lunch with her tomorrow, and I refused."

"Don't deny yourself on my account!" she hurled rashly.

His lips twisted in a travesty of a smile. "Oddly enough, I've been doing just that," he ground out between his teeth. "But now, with your permission, I'll show you just what I *have* been denying myself!"

Too late she moved, trying to avoid his hands as they darted out to catch her, but he swung her up in his arms and strode rapidly to the bedroom. Furiously Sallie twisted and kicked but the difference in their sizes and strength left her helpless against his powerful body. He dropped her on the bed and followed her down, capturing her mouth with his and kissing her with such angry demand that her struggles turned abruptly into compliance. They made love wildly, their pent-up frustrations erupting in the force of their loving.

Afterward he held her clamped to his side while, with his free hand, he stroked over her nude body. "I'm not seeing Coral," he muttered into her hair. "Or any other woman. The way I make love to you at night should assure you of that," he concluded wryly.

"It made me see red when she called," Sallie admitted, turning her head to brush her lips across his sweaty shoulder.

She could feel the tremor that ran through his body as her lips touched him and his arm tightened about her. "You were jealous," he accused, self-satisfaction evident in his tone. She gasped in a return of anger and tried to wiggle away from him, only to be hauled back against him for another whirlwind possession.

The second incident was her fault. One morning she decided to go shopping, the first time she'd done so since Rhy had moved her in with him. She needed several little things, and she passed the morning pleasantly, then decided to stop by and see her old friends at the magazine, maybe eat lunch with Rhy if he wasn't busy.

First she poked her nose into the large room where she'd worked and was greeted loudly and cheerfully. Brom was off on assignment, and for a moment she felt a twinge of envy, then the exuberant welcome of the others made her forget that she was no longer a free-flying bird. After several minutes she excused herself and went up for a few minutes with Greg. She wasn't certain that she'd ever forgive him completely for switching over to Rhy's side, even though she was now living with her husband in relative harmony, but Greg was an old friend and he was dedicated to his job. She didn't want any coolness between them.

After a restrained greeting she and Greg rapidly regained their former easy mood. They parted with Greg's grinning comment that having a full-time husband must be good for her, she looked contented.

Like a cow, Sallie thought to herself in amusement as she went up to Rhy's office. She was still smiling when she stepped off the elevator and literally ran into Chris.

"You're back!" he exclaimed in instant delight, holding her at arm's length and looking her over. "You're blooming, darling!"

Sallie's eyes widened in dismay as she realized that she hadn't let Chris know that she was still in town. Greg knew, of course, but Greg wasn't exactly talkative about personal details. "I've never been gone," she admitted ruefully, smiling up into his dark eyes. "Rhy caught me."

Chris's eyebrows rose. "You don't look as if you're wasting away," he drawled mildly. "Maybe the situation isn't as bad as you thought it'd be?"

"Maybe," she said laughing. "Greg just told me that I look *contented!* I can't decide if I'm insulted or not."

"Are you really happy, honey?" he asked in a gentle tone, and all of his joking was gone.

"I'm happy in a realistic way," she replied thoughtfully. "I don't expect heaven anymore, and I won't be destroyed when what I have ends."

"Are you so sure that it will?"

"I don't know. We just take every day as it comes. We manage to get along now, but who can say that it'll always be like that? What about you? Did you and Amy…?" She stopped, looking into the level, accepting brown eyes, and she knew that he was alone.

"It didn't work." He shrugged, taking her hand and leading her to the window at the end of the hallway, away from the elevator doors. "She's married to that other guy now, she won't even talk to me on the phone."

"I'm sorry," she murmured. "She got married so soon. I thought she wasn't supposed to marry him until later this year?"

"She's pregnant," Chris said rawly, and for a moment his face twisted with his inner pain, then he drew a deep breath and stared at Sallie with wry self-mockery. "I think it's my baby. Well, maybe it's the other guy's, I don't know, but I know that it could be mine, too. I'm not even sure Amy knows. I don't care. I'd marry her in a minute if she'd have me, but she said I'm too 'unstable' to be a good father."

"You'd marry her even knowing that she'd slept with another man while she was going out with you?" Sallie asked in amazement. That was love, love that accepted anything.

He shrugged. "I don't know what she did, but it wouldn't make any difference to me. I love her and I'd take her any way I could get her. If she called me now I'd go to her, and to hell with her husband." He said it in a calm, flat tone, then he shook his head. "Don't look so worried," he advised, a smile coming to his face. "I'm all right, honey, I'm not falling apart."

"But I care about you," she protested weakly.

"And I care about you." He grinned down at her and

suddenly lifted her in his arms, swinging her around giddily, laughing as she protested. "I've missed you like mad," he told her, his brown eyes turning impish. "I don't trust anyone else to give me advice on my love life—"

"Take your damned hands off my wife."

The toneless words were dropped like stones and Sallie struggled out of Chris's grip to whirl and find Rhy standing just outside his office door, his eyes narrowed to slits. Automatically she looked at his hands. They weren't curled into fists but were slightly cupped, his long fingers tense through his arms, his stance, relaxed and loose. Those hands could strike without warning, and Rhy looked murderous. She moved forward, casually putting herself between Rhy and Chris, but Rhy moved to the side and another clear path to Chris. As he moved Amanda came out of the office and stopped in her tracks at the sight of Rhy's bloodless face.

Chris didn't seem disturbed; he remained relaxed, his mouth curling into a wry smile. "Easy there," he drawled in his slow, humorous tone. "I'm not after your woman. I've got enough woman trouble of my own without taking on someone else's."

By then Sallie had reached Rhy, and she put her hand on his arm, feeling the rigid muscles there. "It's true," she told him, smiling like mad in an effort to hide the fear that had her heart thudding. "He's madly in love with a woman who wants him to settle down and stop dashing off to other countries at the drop of a hat, and he likes to tell me all about it. Does the plot sound familiar?"

"All right," Rhy uttered, his lips barely moving. His

face was still frozen in white rage, but he growled at Amanda, "Go on to lunch. Everything's okay."

After Amanda and Chris had left she and Rhy stood in the hallway staring silently at each other. Gradually he relaxed and said tiredly, "Let's get out of this hallway. The office is private."

She nodded and preceded him into his office, and no sooner was the door closed behind them than he caught her in his arms, holding her to him so tightly that her ribs protested in pain.

"I've never been out with him," she managed to reassure him as she gasped for breath.

"I believe you," he whispered raggedly, his lips brushing across her temple, her cheek, the corner of her eye. "I just couldn't bear to see you in his arms. You're mine, and I don't want any other man touching you."

Her heart pounding, Sallie lifted her arms about his neck and clung to him. She was giddy with hope. The violence of his reaction couldn't be simple possessiveness; his emotions had to be involved to some extent for him to be shaking like this, his hands almost punishing as he touched her. But she couldn't be certain, and she held back the most reassuring phrase of all that trembled on her tongue: I love you. She couldn't say it to him yet, but she had begun to hope.

"Hey, I came to see if you want to have lunch with me," she finally said gaily, lifting her head from its resting place on his shoulder.

"That's not what I want," he growled, his eyes straying suggestively to the sofa, "but I'll settle for lunch."

"I'm afraid we caused a scandal," she teased as she walked beside him to the elevator. "It'll be all over the building before the end of the day."

He shrugged negligently. "I don't care. Let it be a warning to any of your other pals who might want to hug you. I'm a throwback, a territorial animal, and I don't allow any encroachment into that territory."

At once she felt an icy shaft of pain in her heart. Was that all she was to him, a part of his territory? Thank heavens she'd kept silent a moment ago instead of blurting out her feelings for him! She was a fool to look for any deeper feelings from him; he didn't have any, and she'd always known that. He *was* a throwback, his instincts swift and primitive. He saw to the satisfaction of his needs and didn't waste time on anything as foolish as love.

CHAPTER TEN

THE SENSE OF accomplishment she felt as she stared at the last page of the manuscript surpassed anything she'd experienced as a reporter. It was finished! No longer was it a figment of her imagination. It existed; it had an identity. She knew there was still a lot of work to be done on it, rereading, correcting, rewriting, but now it was, for all intents and purposes, complete. Her hand reached for the telephone; she wanted to call Rhy and share this moment with him, but a wave of dizziness made her fall back weakly in the chair.

The dizziness was only momentary, but when it had passed she remained as she was, the impulse to call Rhy having faded. That was the fourth spell this week.... Of course. Why hadn't she realized? But perhaps she'd known all along and hadn't allowed the thought to surface until now. The book had claimed all of her attention, all of her energy, and she had pushed herself to complete it. But as soon as it was finished her subconscious had released the knowledge of her pregnancy.

Glancing at the desk calendar she decided that it had been the first night in Sakarya. "When else would it have been?" she murmured to herself. That was the first time in seven years Rhy had touched her, and she had immediately become pregnant. She gave a smile of self-mockery, then the smile became softer and she drew the calendar to her to count the weeks. Her baby would be due around the beginning of spring, and she thought that was a wonderful sign, a new beginning.

This baby would live, she knew. It was more than a new life, it was a strengthening of the fabric of her marriage, another bond between her and Rhy. He would make a wonderful father now, much better than he would have been years before. He would be delighted with his baby.

Then she frowned slightly. Filming on the documentary was scheduled to begin next month, and Rhy had planned on taking her with him. He might change his mind if he knew she was pregnant. So she wouldn't tell him until after they returned! She wasn't about to let him leave without her; it would be a rerun of their early days, and she wasn't sure enough of either him or herself yet to endure a long separation.

She realized that she had a lot to do before then; first and foremost she needed to see a doctor and make certain everything was normal and that traveling wouldn't hurt the baby, and begin taking the recommended vitamins. She should also buy new clothing, because by the time the filming was done she would probably have outgrown her present wardrobe. She pictured herself round and waddling and grinned. Rhy had missed most of her first pregnancy, but this time she would insist that he help her to do all of the little things she'd had to manage by herself before, like getting out of bed.

Of all the nights for Rhy to be late, she thought, he had to pick this one. He called at five and told her wearily that it would probably be eight or later when he made it home. "Eat without me, baby," he instructed.

"But keep something hot for me. I don't think I can face a sandwich."

Swallowing her disappointment, she agreed, then suggested jokingly, "Do you need any help? I'm an old hand at meeting deadlines."

"You don't know how tempting that offer is." He sighed. "But work on the book instead, and I'll be home as soon as I can."

"I finished the book today," she informed him, her fingers tightening around the receiver. "So I'm taking a break." She had wanted to tell him when he first walked in the door, but she couldn't wait that long.

"You did what? Oh, hell," he said in disgust and Sallie's mouth trembled in hurt surprise. Then he continued, and she brightened again. "I should be taking you out to celebrate instead of working late. But I'll be home as soon as possible, then we'll do some private celebrating, if you understand my meaning."

"I thought you were tired." She laughed and his low chuckle sounded in her ear.

"I am tired, but I'm not dead," he replied huskily. "See you in a few hours."

Smiling, she replaced the receiver. After eating her solitary dinner she took a shower and settled down in the study to begin rereading the book, scribbling changes and corrections in the margins as she went. The work was absorbing, so much so that when she heard Rhy's key she was surprised at how swiftly the time had passed. She shoved the manuscript aside and jumped to her feet, then had to cling to the back of a chair for a moment when dizziness assailed her. Slowly. She must remember to move slowly.

Rhy entered the study, his tired face breaking into a

grin as he surveyed her attire, a transparent dark blue nightgown and matching wrap. He tossed his jacket aside and tugged his loosened tie completely off, throwing it on top of his jacket. He began unbuttoning his shirt as he came to her. "Now I understand the charm of coming home to a negligee-clad wife," he commented as he slid his arms around her and pulled her up on tiptoe for his kiss. "It's like a shot of adrenalin."

"Don't become too fond of the practice," she warned. "I just took my bath early because I had nothing else to do. Are you very hungry?"

"Yes," he growled. "Are you going to make me wait?"

"You know I meant for food!" Laughing at him, she crossed to the door. "Wash up while I set the table. I've kept things warm."

"Don't bother with the dining room," he called. "The kitchen is fine with me, and a lot handier."

She did as he instructed and set his plate in the kitchen. He joined her there and while he ate they discussed the book. Rhy had already talked to an agent that he knew, and he wanted to hand the book over before they left for Europe.

"But it isn't ready," Sallie protested. "I've already begun making corrections for retyping."

"I want her to read it now," Rhy insisted. "It's a rough draft. She won't expect it to be word perfect right now."

"She?" Sallie asked, her ears pricking up.

"Yes, she," he mocked, his gray eyes glinting. "She's a bone-thin bulldozer by the name of Barbara Hopewell, and she's twenty years older than I am, so you can draw in your claws."

Sallie glared at him. She had the feeling that he'd purposely tricked her into revealing her jealousy and she didn't want him to gain too much of an advantage on her.

"Why are you in such a hurry?" she demanded.

"I don't want you worrying about the book while we're in Europe. Hire a typist, do whatever you have to, but I want the book out of the way before we leave."

Because she was feeling resentful over his gibe about jealousy she propped her elbows on the table and gibed back at him. "Has the thought occurred to you that now that the book's finished I'll be bored sitting around here all day? I need to be looking for a job, not jaunting around Europe."

If she'd wanted to rile him she succeeded beyond her wildest expectations. He turned pale; then two hectic spots of temper appeared on his high cheekbones. Slamming his fork down on the table he reached across and grasped her wrist, hauling her to her feet as he stood up himself. "You never miss a chance to twist the knife, do you?" he muttered hoarsely. "Sometimes I want to break your neck!" Then he jerked her against him and brutally took her lips, not allowing her a chance to speak even if she could have thought of anything to say, and with their mouths still fused he slipped one arm behind her knees and lifted her easily, her slight weight nothing to his powerful arms.

Sallie had to cling to him; the swift movement as he jerked her to her feet had made her head swim alarmingly and she felt as if she might faint. Neither could she understand why he had reacted so violently, or what he meant about twisting the knife. Confused, all she knew was that she'd made him angry when she hadn't really meant to, and she offered him the only comfort she could, the response of her lips and body. He accepted the offer hungrily; the pressure of his mouth changing from hurtful to persuasive, and he carried her to the bedroom.

Afterward she lay curled drowsily against him, wrapped in the security of his own special male scent and the warmth of his nearness while he lazily stroked her abdomen and pressed kisses along the curve of her shoulder.

"Did I hurt you?" he murmured, referring to his urgent lovemaking, and Sallie whispered a denial. "That's good," he replied huskily. "I wouldn't want to…" He paused, then after a moment continued. "Don't you think it's time you told me about the baby?"

Sallie sat bolt upright in the bed and turned to stare at him with huge eyes. "How did you know?" she demanded in astonishment, her voice rising. "I only realized it myself today!"

He blinked as if she'd jolted him in return; then he tipped his dark head back against the pillow and roared with laughter, tugging her down to lie against his chest. "I should've guessed," he chuckled, his hand smoothing her long hair away from her face. "You were so wrapped up in that book you didn't even know what day it was. I knew, darling, because I'm not a complete ignoramus and I can count. I thought you were deliberately keeping me in the dark because you didn't want me to have the satisfaction of knowing you're pregnant."

"Gee, you must think I'm a lovely character," she muttered crossly and, turning her head, she sank her teeth playfully, but firmly, into his shoulder. He yelped in pain and instantly she kissed the wound, but she told him defiantly, "You deserved that."

"Out of consideration for your delicate condition I'll

let you get away with that," he mocked, tilting her face up for a kiss that lingered.

"Actually," Sallie confessed a moment later, "I wasn't going to tell you just yet."

His head snapped around, and he cupped her chin in his palm, forcing her to look at him. "Why?" he growled.

"Because I want to go to Europe with you," she stated simply. "I was afraid you'd make me stay here if you knew I'm pregnant."

"Not a chance. I wasn't with you before, but I'm planning on being with you every day of this pregnancy—with your permission, Mrs. Baines, I'll even be with you when our baby is born."

Her heart stopped, then lurched into overtime. Too overcome to speak, Sallie turned her face into his shoulder and held him with desperate hands. Despite everything he had ever said—and all the things he had never said—she began to hope that Rhy really did care for her. "Rhy—oh, Rhy!" she whispered in a choked voice.

Misunderstanding the cause of her emotion he gathered her close to him and stroked her head. "Don't worry," he murmured into her hair. "This baby will be all right, I promise you. We'll get the best obstetrician in the state. We'll have a houseful of kids, you wait and see."

Clutching him to her Sallie thought that she'd be satisfied with only this one, if it lived. That, and Rhy's love, would make her life complete.

CAUGHT UP IN a whirlwind of activity preparing for the trip to Europe, which included readying not only her own clothing but Rhy's as well, as he was working late more and more often in an effort to tie up all loose ends before they left, and hammering the book into its final shape, Sallie hardly had a moment to think during the next few weeks. The doctor had assured her that she was in perfect shape, though she could stand to gain a few pounds, and the baby was developing normally. He was also in favor of the trip to Europe so long as she remembered to eat properly.

She had never been happier. Four months ago she had thought that Rhy meant nothing to her, and all she wanted was to be free of his restricting influence. She still fumed sometimes at the high-handed methods he'd used to restore her to her position as his wife, but for the most part she was glad that he didn't know how to take no for an answer. She was more deeply in love with him now than she'd ever been as an insecure teenager, for she'd grown in character in those years away from him. Her feelings were stronger, her thoughts and emotions more mature. Now he acted as if he never wanted her out of his sight, and he seemed so proud of the child she carried that she sometimes thought he was going to hang a sign around her neck announcing her expectant state.

Disaster struck without warning a week before they were due to leave for Europe. It was one of those picture-perfect autumn days when the sunshine was warm and the sky was deep blue, yet the air carried the unmistakable fragrance of approaching winter. Sallie made one last shopping trip, determined that this would be *it,* and took her purchases home. She felt marvelous, and her eyes sparkled and her skin glowed; she was smiling as she put away the articles of clothing she had bought.

Her senses had always been acute, but she still had

no warning of what was to come when the doorbell rang and she called out to Mrs. Hermann, "I'll get it. I'm right here!"

She pulled the door open, smiling warmly, but the smile faltered as she recognized Coral Williams. The model looked beautiful, as always, but there was a haunted expression on the exquisite face that made Sallie wonder uneasily if Rhy had been wrong, if Coral was suffering because he'd stopped seeing her.

"Hello," she greeted the other woman. "Will you come in? Is there anything I can do for you?"

"Thank you," Coral replied almost inaudibly, walking past Sallie and standing uncertainly in the foyer. "I…is Rhy here? I tried to phone him, but his secretary said he's out of the office and I thought he might perhaps…" Her voice trailed off and pity welled up in Sallie's throat. She knew all too well how it felt to suffer from the lack of Rhy's love, and she was at a loss as to what to do. She sympathized with Coral, but she wasn't about to hand over Rhy to the other woman, even if Rhy was willing.

"No, he's not here," Sallie replied. "He's often out of his office now. He's very busy preparing for our trip to Europe."

"Europe!" Coral turned very white, only her expertly applied makeup supplying any color to her cheeks. She was unnaturally pale anyway and the severely tailored black dress she wore only pointed up the hollows of her cheeks and her generally fragile appearance.

"He's filming a documentary," explained Sallie. "We expect to be gone about three months."

"He—he can't!" Coral burst out, clenching her fists. A sudden chill ran up Sallie's spine and unconsciously she squared her shoulders as if in anticipation of a blow. "What is it you want with Rhy?" she challenged directly.

Coral stiffened too, staring down at Sallie from her superior height. "I'm sorry, but it's private."

"I don't accept that. If it concerns Rhy it concerns me. He *is* my husband, you know," she ended sarcastically.

Coral winced as if Salllie'd scored a hit, then recovered herself to say scornfully, "Some husband! Do you really think he spared a thought for you when you were separated? The old adage of 'out of sight, out of mind' was never more true than with Rhy! He was out with a different woman every night, until he met me."

Sallie shuddered with the sudden violent desire to punch Coral right in that perfect mouth. The woman was only saying what she'd always thought herself, though privately she wanted very much to believe Rhy's assertions that his relationships with other women had been platonic. Certainly she couldn't fault his behavior since she'd been living with him again. A woman couldn't ask for a more attentive husband.

"I know all about your relationship with Rhy," she declared solidly. "He told me everything when he asked me to come back to him."

"Oh, did he?" Coral asked wildly, her voice rising in shrill laughter. "I doubt that. Surely some details are still private!"

Abruptly Sallie had had enough and she moved to open the door again so Coral could leave. "I'm sorry," she said firmly. "I'm asking you to leave. Rhy's my husband and I love him and I don't care what his past is. I'm sorry for you because you lost him, but facts are facts and you might as well face up to them. He won't come back to you."

"What makes you so certain of that?" Coral yelled, losing all control, her face twisting with fury. "When he hears what I've got to tell him he'll come back to me, all right! He'll leave you without even a consoling pat on the head!"

For a moment the woman's certainty caused Sallie to waver; then she thought of the child in her womb, and she knew that Rhy would never leave her now. "I don't think so," she said softly, playing her ace. "I'm pregnant. Our baby will be born in March. I don't think any of your charms can equal that in Rhy's view."

Coral reeled backward as if she might faint, and Sallie watched her in alarm, but the woman recovered herself and burst into peal after peal of mocking, hysterical laughter, holding her arms across her middle as if she found Sallie's announcement hilarious. "Priceless!" she gasped when she had enough breath for words. "I wish Rhy could be here. This lacks only his presence to be the hit comedy of the year!"

"I don't know what you're talking about," Sallie broke in stiffly, "but I think you'd better go." The amused, malicious glitter in Coral's eyes made her uncomfortable, and she wanted only for the woman to leave so she could be alone again and recapture her mood of confident serenity.

"Don't be so sure of yourself!" Coral flared, her hatred plain on her face. "You managed to pique his interest by acting as if you wanted nothing to do with him, but surely you know by now that he's incapable of staying faithful to any one woman! I understand him. Some men are just like that, and I love him despite his weakness for other women. I'm willing to allow him his little affairs so long as he comes back to me, whereas you'll drive him mad with boredom within a year. And don't think a baby will make any difference to him!"

Beyond Coral, Sallie saw Mrs. Hermann hovering in the doorway, her round face frowning with worry as she listened to Coral's abusive tirade. Instinctively disliking having a witness to the nasty scene Coral was creating Sallie jerked the door open and snapped, "Get out!"

"Oh, I'm glad to go!" Coral smirked. "But don't think you've got everything your way! Women like you make me sick, always acting so sure of yourselves and sticking your noses in where they don't belong, thinking some man will admire you! That's why Rhy pulled you off of foreign assignments, he said you were making a fool of yourself trying to act as tough as any man. And now you think you're something special just because you're pregnant! That's nothing so special. Rhy's good at getting women pregnant!"

Despite herself Sallie reeled in shock, not quite certain she understood what Coral was saying. The sight of her suddenly pale face seemed to give Coral some satisfaction because she smiled again and spat out, "That's right! The baby you're carrying isn't the only child Rhy has fathered! I'm pregnant, too, and it's Rhy's baby. Two months pregnant, honey, so tell me what that means about your perfect marriage! I told you, he always comes back to me!"

Having delivered her blow Coral stalked out with her head held at a queenly altitude. Unable to completely take in what the woman had said Sallie closed the door with quiet composure and stared across the room at Mrs. Hermann, who had pressed a hand over her mouth in shock.

"Mrs. Baines," Mrs Hermann gasped, her voice rich with sympathy. "Oh, Mrs. Baines!"

It was then that Sallie understood just exactly what Coral's words had meant. She was pregnant, and it was Rhy's baby. Two months pregnant, she had said. So Rhy had not only lied about his relationship with Coral, he'd continued it after his reconciliation with Sallie. In dazed horror she thought again of all the nights when Rhy had supposedly been working late. She'd never thought to call him at the office to check up on him. She would have been insulted if Rhy had checked up on her, so she'd accorded him the same respect and he'd abused it.

Numbly she went past Mrs. Hermann into the bed room, Rhy's bedroom, where she'd spent so many happy nights in his arms. She stared at the bed and knew she couldn't bear to sleep there again.

Without thinking about it she jerked down the suit-cases from the top of the closet and began filling them helter-skelter with the clothing she'd bought to take to Europe. She had money and she had a place to go; there was no reason for her to stay here another minute.

She paused briefly when she thought of the man-uscript, but it was safely in the hands of Barbara Hopewell, and she would get in touch with her later. Later…when she could bear to think again, when the pain had subsided from the screaming agony that was tearing her apart now.

When she carried the suitcases out into the hall-way she found Mrs. Hermann there, hovering, wring-ing her hands in agitation. "Mrs. Baines, please don't leave like this! Try to talk things out—men will be men, you know. I'm sure there's an explanation."

"There probably is," Sallie agreed tiredly. "Rhy's very good with explanations. But I just don't want to hear it right now. I'm leaving. I'm going somewhere quiet and peaceful where I can have my baby, and I don't want to think about my husband and his mistresses."

"But where will you be? What shall I tell Mr. Baines?" the housekeeper wailed.

"Tell him?" Sallie stopped and thought a minute, unable to think of any message that could adequately express her state of mind. "Tell him…tell him what happened. I don't know where I'm going, but I know that I don't think I ever want to see him again." Then she walked out the door.

CHAPTER ELEVEN

THE DAYS PASSED slowly, dripping out of existence. Like a salmon returning to the place of its birth to spawn and die she had returned to her own origins, the little upstate town where she'd grown up, where she'd met Rhy and married him. Her parents' house was empty and neglected and many of the old neighbors had died or moved on and she didn't know any of the children who played now in the quiet streets. But it was still home, and she moved back into the small house and tidied it up, refurnished it with the minimum of furniture for her needs. Then she waited for time to work its magic healing process.

At first she was unnaturally calm, numbed by her sense of loss and betrayal. She'd just gotten used to living with him, and now she was alone again with the solitary nights pressing down on her like an invisible weight. She didn't try to think about it or straighten it out in her mind; there was no use in driving herself mad with if onlys and might have beens. She had to accept it, just as she would have to if he'd died.

In a sense that was what had happened. She'd lost her husband as irrevocably as if he had died. She was as alone, as empty. He was in Europe now, half a world away, and he might as well have been on another planet.

Then she realized that she was neither alone nor

empty. His baby moved inside her one day and she stood with her hands pressed over the gentle fluttering, overcome by the feeling of awe that a living creature was being nurtured inside her body. Rhy's baby, a part of him. No matter if she never saw his face again she would always have him near. That thought was both painful and comforting, a threat and a promise.

The numbness wore off abruptly. She woke in the dark, silent hours before dawn one morning, and her entire body ached with the pain of her loss. For the first time she cried, weeping with her face pressed into the pillow, and she thought about it endlessly, trying to understand the hows and whys of his behavior. Was it her fault? Was it something about her that challenged Rhy to subdue her, then forced him to lose interest once she was captured? Or was it Rhy's own nature, as Coral had charged, an inability to be faithful to one woman?

Yet that denoted a certain weakness of character, and that didn't describe Rhy. A lot of adjectives could be used to describe him—arrogant, hot-tempered, stubborn—but weakness in any respect wasn't one of them. She would also have sworn on his professional integrity, and she felt that integrity was not an isolated thing in a person, restricted to only one field; integrity spread out, showing itself in every aspect of a person's behavior.

So how could she explain his infidelity? She couldn't, and the question tore at her. She forced herself to eat only because of the baby, but even so she grew pale and thinner. Sometimes she woke up in the middle of the night to find her pillow wet, and she wanted Rhy beside her so badly that it was impossible to get back to sleep. At times like that she wondered why she'd run off, like a fool, and left the field clear for Coral. Why hadn't she stayed? Why hadn't she put up a fight for him? He'd hurt her, he'd been unfaithful, but she still loved him and surely it couldn't hurt any more if she'd stayed with him? At least then she'd have had the comfort of his presence; they could have shared the miracle of the growing child she carried. During those dark predawn hours she sometimes determined to pack her clothes first thing in the morning and fly to Europe to join Rhy, but always, when the morning came, she would remember Coral and the baby that she carried. Rhy might not want her to join him. Coral might be with him. Coral was more glamorous anyway, more suited for a life in the limelight with Rhy.

It wasn't in her nature to be indecisive, but for the second time in her life she'd lost her bearings, and both times had been because of Rhy. The first time she had eventually found her feet and pursued a goal, but now she was unable to plan anything more complicated than the basic needs of living. She ate, she bathed, she slept, she did what had to be done. She had read enough to know that part of her lethargy was due to being pregnant, yet that wasn't excuse enough to explain her total lack of interest in anything beyond the next moment.

As the late fall days passed and winter drew closer she became aware that Christmas was near. Somehow every Christmas since the death of her parents had been spent alone, and this one would be no different. But next year, she promised herself, gazing at a brightly decorated tree as she made her weekly trip to the nearest grocery store, she would have a real Christmas. The baby would be about nine months old, bright eyed and inquisitive about everything in its world. She would decorate a tree and pile gifts beneath it that would fascinate a crawling baby.

It was a vague plan, but it was the first plan she'd made since leaving Rhy. For the baby's sake she had to pull herself out of the doldrums. She had a book in the works; she needed to contact the agent and see about publication and perhaps start work on another book. She had to have some means of taking care of the baby or the first thing she knew Rhy would be demanding custody of his child. Fiercely she determined that she'd never allow that to happen. Rhy had another child; she only had this one and she'd never let it go!

Two weeks before Christmas she finally made a firm decision and dialed Barbara Hopewell's office with her former briskness. When Barbara came on the line Sallie identified herself, and before the other woman could say anything she asked if any progress had been made in locating a publisher.

"Mrs. Baines!" Barbara gasped. "Where are you? Mr. Baines has been going mad, trying to complete filming in Europe and flying back here every free moment he has in an effort to trace you! Are you in town?"

"No," Sallie replied. She didn't want to hear about Rhy or how hard he'd been looking for her. Oddly enough, she'd expected that he would make an effort to find her if only because of the child she carried. "And where I am doesn't matter. I only want to discuss the book, if you don't mind. Has a publisher been found?"

"But…" Then Barbara changed her mind, and she answered in an abrupt tone, "Yes, we have a publisher who is extremely interested. I really need to schedule a meeting with you, Mrs. Baines, to go over the details of the contract. May I make an appointment?"

"I don't want to return to New York," Sallie said, her throat constricting at the thought.

"Then I'll be glad to meet you wherever you want. Just set the time and tell me the location."

Sallie hesitated, unwilling to divulge her hiding place, yet equally unwilling to leave it for a meeting at any other location. Then she quickly added up the dates and realized that Rhy would still be filming in Europe for another month. Barbara had said that he flew back as often as he could, but she knew that schedule, and it was a tightly packed one. The odds were that he would be unable to leave on a moment's notice even if Barbara did happen to be in touch with him and let slip that she'd talked to Sallie.

"All right," she agreed reluctantly and gave Barbara her address. They agreed on a time that Thursday for Barbara to come to the house.

That was only two days away and Sallie felt even more confident that Rhy wouldn't find out her hiding place. When she saw Barbara on Thursday she would get her promise not to tell Rhy; she hadn't wanted to discuss the matter over the phone, knowing that anyone in Barbara's office could listen in on an extension.

She couldn't sleep that night; she was too anxious that she had made a mistake in revealing her bolt hole to relax. Somehow she had the feeling that Rhy was one step ahead of her, as usual. Lying in her bed, tense and unable to close her eyes, she imagined all sorts of what ifs: What if Rhy had been in New York even then? What if Rhy had even been in Barbara's office and was on his way upstate now? What if she got up in the morning to find him on her doorstep? What would she say to him? What was there to say?

Tears seeped from beneath her lids as she squeezed them slightly shut in an effort to banish the picture she suddenly had of Rhy's dark, lean face. Pain pierced her sharply and she turned on her side to weep, hugging the pillow to her face in an effort to stifle the sobs. "I love him," she moaned aloud. That hadn't changed, and every day apart from him was an eternity.

Abruptly, desolate in her loneliness, she admitted to herself that she wanted to go back to him. She wanted his strength, his physical presence, even if she couldn't have his love. She wanted him there to hold her hand while she gave birth to their child and she wanted to have other children. The thought of Coral and that other baby tore at her insides, but gradually she was realizing that her love, her need, for Rhy was stronger than her anger. She had to accept him as he was if she wanted to live with him.

She dozed eventually, toward dawn, and woke only a few hours later to the steady, dreary sound of cold rain pouring down. The sky was gray, the streets stark and cheerless. Snow had not yet arrived and given everything its winter-wonderland effect, but the trees were denuded of leaves and the bare branches rattled against each other like bones of a skeleton. There was nothing to get up for but she did, and managed to occupy herself by trying to work out a sketchy outline for another book. This one would be more difficult, she knew, for the first one had been partially rooted in her own experiences. This one would have to be totally from her imagination.

By midafternoon the rain had stopped but the temperature had dropped, and when she turned on the television she learned that the rain was supposed to begin again later that night, then turn to sleet and snow before morning. Sallie made a wry face at the weatherman on the screen. It was possible that bad road conditions would keep Barbara from making their appointment and she felt horribly disappointed. Her interest in the world around her was returning and she wanted to get on with the business of living.

After an hour of pacing around, boredom overcame her and she felt stifled in the small house. It was cold outside, and damp, but she felt that a brisk walk would clear the cobwebs from her mind and perhaps relax her enough so she could sleep that night. Not only that, she told herself righteously, but the doctor had wanted her to take some form of exercise every day. A walk was just the thing.

She wrapped herself up warmly, pulling on knee-high boots and shoving her hair up under a dark fur hat that covered her ears. After buttoning her heavy coat up and wrapping a muffler about her throat she set off briskly, shivering at first in the cold air, but gradually movement warmed her and she began to enjoy having the streets to herself. It was almost sundown and the dreary sky made it that much darker. The water dripping from the trees onto the sidewalk and street was the only sound except for the clicking of her boots, and she shivered again but not from the cold this time. Why was she walking like an idiot when she could be back safe and snug in her warm house? *And why was she running from Rhy when all she wanted was to be back in his arms?*

Stupid, she mentally berated herself as she headed for home. Stupid, stupid, stupid! And spineless on top of that! She would be the biggest fool alive if she left the field clear for Coral! When this weather cleared up and she could travel safely she'd leave for Europe on the first plane out, and if she found Coral with Rhy she'd tear out all of that gorgeous blond hair. Rhy would not get off completely free, she promised herself, the light of battle sparkling in her eyes. She had a lot to say to him, but she meant to keep him! After all, hadn't these past seven years taught her that he was the only man for her?

Retracing her steps faster now, she turned the corner and came in sight of her house. She was so caught up in her plans that at first she didn't see the taxi in front of her house; it wasn't until a tall man who moved with the litheness of a panther ducked down to pay the driver that her gaze was drawn to the cab. She stopped in her tracks and the breath stopped in her chest as she stared at the proudly held dark head, bare despite the dripping trees. The taxi pulled away with a flash of red taillights and the man set a single flight bag on the wet sidewalk and stared at the house as if mesmerized by the sight of it. No lights were on and it could have been empty, she realized, except for the curtains that covered the windows. Was that what he was thinking? she wondered with sudden pain. That it was empty after all?

"Rhy," she whispered and began walking again. The sound of her boots drew his attention and his head turned swiftly, like that of a wild animal sensing danger. He froze for a moment, then began walking toward her with a purposeful stride. Just like him, she thought, trying not to smile. There was no self-doubt in that man. Even when he was wrong he was confident.

But when he was close, when he stopped with only three feet separating them, she had to bite her lip to keep from crying out with pain. His lean face bore the marks of suffering; there were harsh shadows under his steely eyes and lines that hadn't been there before. He was tired of course, and the grayness of exhaustion enhanced the grimness of his expression. He'd lost weight; the skin was pulled taut over the high, proud cheekbones.

He shoved his hands deep into the pockets of his overcoat and stared at her, his bleak gaze roving over her small, delicate face and her rounded form beneath her coat. Sallie quivered with wanting to throw herself into his arms, but he hadn't opened them to her, and she was suddenly afraid that he didn't want her. But why was he here?

"She lied," he said tonelessly, his voice even harsher than before and almost beyond sound. His lips were barely moving as he seemed to force out his next words. "I'm dying without you, Sallie. Please come back to me."

Incredulous joy rocketed through her veins, and she closed her eyes for a moment in an effort to control herself. When she opened them again he was still staring down at her with a desperate plea in his gray eyes, his lips pressed grimly together as if he expected the worst. "I was planning on it," she told him, her voice tremulous with joy. "I'd just now decided that as soon as the weather cleared I was taking a plane to Europe."

A shudder quaked visibly through his body; then he pulled his hands out of his pockets and reached for her at the same time that she stepped forward. Hard arms enfolded her in a tight, damp embrace, and she put her arms around his neck and clung desperately, tears of happiness running down her face. He caught her mouth with his and held it, kissing her deeply and reassuring both of them that they were together again; then he lifted her completely off the ground, turning round and round on the sidewalk in a slow circle as they kissed.

At some point it began to rain again; they were both soaked by the time Sallie glanced up at the pouring skies and laughed. "What fools we are!" she exclaimed. "Why don't we go inside instead of standing out in the rain?"

"And you don't need to catch a chill," he growled, putting her on her feet and leaning down to lift his flight bag. "Let's get dried off, then we can talk."

He insisted that she take a hot shower while he changed into dry clothing, and when she came out of the bath she found that he'd made coffee; two steaming cups were already on the table.

"Oh, that's good." She sighed as she sipped the hot liquid and it completed the warming job that the shower had started.

Rhy sank into a chair at the table and rubbed a hand over the back of his neck. "I need this to keep me awake," he said wearily.

Sallie looked at him, seeing his exhaustion etched into every line of his face, and her heart clenched painfully. "I'm sorry," she said softly.

He made a gesture with his hand, waving aside his weariness, and silence stretched between them. It was as if they were afraid to begin, afraid to say anything personal, and Sallie stared into her coffee cup.

"Chris is gone," said Rhy abruptly, not looking at her.

Her head jerked up. "Gone?" she echoed.

"He quit. Downey told me—hell, I don't know how long ago it was. Everything's a blur. But he quit, said he was moving on to another city."

For a moment Sallie had hoped that Chris and his Amy had gotten together, that he'd quit his job to settle down, but she knew that it just hadn't happened for Chris. A shaft of pain pierced her as she thought of how close she'd come to losing Rhy, and she quickly took another sip of coffee. She blurted, "I suppose Barbara called you?"

"Immediately," he acknowledged. "I owe her a lot to make up for that favor. I completely wrecked the shooting schedule to get on the first flight to New York. Everyone thinks I've gone berserk anyway, flying back and forth cross the Atlantic whenever we had a break. It drove me crazy," he admitted grimly. "Not knowing where you were, if you were all right, knowing that you believed what that vicious little tramp told you."

"Mrs. Hermann told you what she said?" Sallie asked, wanting to know if Coral's story had been related correctly. Wild hope was bubbling in her; he'd said that Coral had lied, and he certainly wasn't acting like a man who was guilty of anything.

"Word for word, with tears pouring down her face like a waterfall," Rhy growled. He reached out abruptly and took Sallie's free hand, clasping it firmly in his long fingers. "She lied," he told her again, his husky voice taut with strain. "If you've ever believed anything, believe that. Coral may be pregnant, but I swear I'm not the father. I've never made love to her, though she tried hard enough to instigate an affair."

The words jolted Sallie. His voice had an undeniable ring of truth to it, but still she squeaked incredulously, *"Never?"*

A flush darkened his cheekbones. "That's right. I think I was a challenge to her ego. She just couldn't believe that I wasn't interested in sleeping with her even when I told her I was married and that I'd never been as attracted to any other woman as I was to my wife," he said, watching her steadily. Sallie blushed under his regard, and his hand tightened on hers. "I think she hated you because of that," he continued, his eyes never leaving her face. "I turned her down in favor of you, and she tried her best to tear us apart, to hurt you. Maybe she didn't plan on doing what she did, if you want to give her the benefit of the doubt. If she truly is pregnant she probably wanted me to give her the money for an abortion. A pregnancy is poison to a model, and I can't see Coral as a doting mother."

Sallie sucked in her breath. "Rhy, would you have?"

"No," he growled. "And I could've killed her when Mrs. Hermann told me what she'd done."

"But...surely Coral has the money herself...?"

"Don't you believe it," he muttered. "She likes the high life too well to save anything and she loses heavily in Atlantic City and Vegas. She's not a good gambler," he finished starkly.

"But why did you go out with her at all if you weren't interested in her?" Sallie asked. That was the biggest flaw in Rhy's story. He and Coral had been constant companions, and she wasn't fool enough to think things hadn't progressed beyond hand-holding.

"Because I liked her," he replied abruptly. "Don't ask me for proof of my faithfulness, Sallie, because I haven't got any. I can only tell you that Coral wasn't my mistress, even before I found you again."

"Take it on trust?" she queried, her voice going tight.

"Exactly," he said in a hard voice. "Just as I have to

take it on trust that you haven't been involved with any other man. You have no proof, either."

Sallie scowled down at the tablecloth and traced a pattern on it with the hand he wasn't holding. "I've never been interested in any other men," she admitted with ill-grace, hating having to reveal that secret to him. "I've never even bothered to date."

"And for eight years you've been the only woman I could see," he replied in a strained voice, releasing her hand and getting up to stride restlessly around the small kitchen. "I felt like a fool. I couldn't understand why a timid little rabbit like you were then had gotten under my skin like that. I wouldn't have put up with one scene over my work from any other woman, but I kept coming back to you, hoping you'd grow up and understand that I *needed* my work. You said you were hooked on excitement, on danger, and that's exactly the way I was. A danger junkie.

"I never meant to leave you permanently," he said jerkily. "I just wanted to teach you a lesson. I wanted you to beg me to come back to you. But you didn't. You picked up and carried on as if you didn't need me at all. You even sent my support checks back to me. I buried myself in work. I swore I'd forget about you, too, and sometimes I almost did. I enjoyed the company of other women, but whenever things began getting involved… I just couldn't. It made me furious, but I'd remember how it had been with us, and I didn't want second best."

Sallie stared at him, thunderstruck, and he glared at her as if she'd done something terrible. "I made a lot of money," he said with constrained violence. "A lot of money. I bought some stocks and they went out of sight and I ended up a rich man. There was no longer any need to put myself on the line to get a story and getting shot at had lost whatever perverted thrill it had held for me, anyway. I wanted to sleep in the same bed every night, and finally I admitted to myself that if there was going to be a woman in that bed it had to be you. I bought the magazine and began trying to trace you, but you'd left here years before, and no one had any idea where you were."

"You tried to find me?" she asked, her eyes going wide with wonder. So Rhy hadn't simply forgotten about her for those years! "And this time? You've been trying to find me this time, too?"

"It seems like trying to find you has become a habit." He tried to make a joke, but his face was too tightly drawn to express any humor. "I didn't even think of hunting for you here. I've been checking with newspapers in all the major cities on the thought that you were likely to get a job as a reporter. You threw it in my face so often that you were bored without a job that I thought you'd go right back to work."

"I thought I'd be bored," she admitted, "but I wasn't. I had the book to work on, but most of all, you were there."

His face lightened curiously. "You sure put up a good fight, lady," he said wryly, and he gave her a wolfish grin that held no humor.

"I didn't have a chance," she denied. "Having me working for your magazine like I did gave you all the aces."

"Don't you believe it," he said roughly. "I caught a glimpse of a long braid swinging against a slim little bottom, and it was like I'd been kicked in the gut. Without even seeing your face I wanted you. I thought it was a vicious joke on me to find a woman I wanted just when I'd begun the search for my wife, but the few glimpses I had of you made me determined to have you. Then I ran into you in the hallway and recognized you. The dainty little elf with that bewitching braid was my own wife, changed almost beyond recognition except for those big eyes, and you made it plain that you weren't interested in anything about me. I'd spent eight years with the feel of you branded on my senses until I couldn't even see another woman, and you didn't care!"

"Of course I cared!" she interrupted, standing up to face him. She was trembling with strain, but she couldn't let him think that he meant nothing to her. "But I didn't want you to hurt me again, Rhy! It nearly killed me when you left the first time, and I didn't think I could stand it again. I tried to protect myself from you. I even convinced myself that I was completely over you. But it didn't work," she finished in a small voice, staring down at the tiled floor.

He drew a deep, shaking breath. "We're two of a kind," he said roughly. "We're as wary and independent as wild animals, the both of us. We try to protect ourselves at all costs, and it's going to be hard to change. But I *have* changed, Sallie. I've grown up. I need you more than I need excitement. It's hard to say," he muttered. "It's hard to deliberately leave yourself open to hurt. Love makes a person vulnerable, and it takes a lot of trust to admit that you love someone. Why else do people try so hard to hide a love that they know isn't returned? I love you. You can tear me to pieces or you can send me so high I lose myself. Trust has to start somewhere, Sarah, and I'm willing to make the first move. I love you."

Hearing him call her Sarah swept away all the long years of loneliness and pain, and she raised a face that was pale and streaked with slowly falling tears. "I love you, too," she said softly, making the words a litany of devotion. "I've always loved you. I ran away because I was hurt. I was insecure and didn't feel that you loved me, and Coral tore me apart with her vile insinuations. But today I decided that I loved you too much to just let you go, hand you over to her without a fight. I was coming after you, Rhy Baines, and I was going to make a believer out of you!"

"Hey," he said just as softly, opening his arms and holding them open for her. "Go ahead. Make me believe it, darling!"

Sallie dived into his arms and felt them enclose her tightly. She couldn't stop the tears that wet his neck, and he tried to comfort her, gently kissing the moisture from her cheeks and eyes.

They had been apart for too long. His kisses became hungry and his hands roamed over her gently swelling body, and Sallie cried out wordlessly as desire flamed through her. He lifted her and carried her to the bedroom, the same bedroom where eight years before he'd carried her as an innocent bride and initiated her into the intoxicating sensuality of his lovemaking. It was the same now as it had been then; he was gentle and passionate, and she responded to him with all her reserve finally gone. When the fire of their desire had been sated she lay drowsily amid the tangled covers of the bed. His dark tousled head was pressed into her soft shoulder and his lips sleepily nuzzled the swell of her breast. His lean fingers stroked the slight swell his child made and he murmured against her flesh. "Was it all right? There's no harm in making love?"

"None," she assured him, lacing her fingers tenderly in the thick hair that curled onto his neck. She couldn't get enough of touching him; she was content to lie there with him resting heavily against her, worn-out from traveling and their loving.

He was already half-asleep but he muttered, "I don't want to tie you down. I just want you to fly back to me every night."

"Loving you doesn't tie me down," she answered, kissing his forehead, which was all she could reach. And it didn't. She was surprised. Where had all her fears for her independence gone? Then she knew that what she'd really feared had been being hurt again. Rhy's love would give her a springboard to soar to heights she'd never reached before. She was free as she'd never been before, free because she was secure. He didn't hold her down; he added his strength to hers.

"You've got talent," he whispered. "Real talent. Use it, darling. I'll help you in any way I can. I don't want to clip your wings. I fell in love with you all over again when I found you, you'd grown up, too, and become a woman who drove me mad with your nearness and wild with frustration when we were apart."

Sallie smiled in the darkness. It looked as if all those crash courses so long ago had finally paid off.

He went to sleep on her shoulder, and she slept, too, content and secure in his love. For the first time she felt that their need for each other was something permanent. She had always felt the tug of the bond that held her to him, but until now she hadn't known that he was equally bound to her. That was why there had been no divorce, why he hadn't even made an effort to obtain one. They belonged to each other and they always would.

* * * * *

New York Times Bestselling Author

FERN MICHAELS

PAINT ME RAINBOWS

With nothing but her shattered pride and a wedding dress, Jill Barton flees town after the heartbreak of being left at the altar. While a charming country retreat offers her sanctuary, its hard-bitten owner, Logan Matthews, does not. And soon Jill realizes that nothing is safe around Logan—especially not her heart.

WHISPER MY NAME

Photographer Samantha Blakely is thrilled to land a job at *Daylight* magazine. Then she meets the owner, Christian Delaney, whose mere gaze leaves her wanting more. But how can she confess that she also happens to be the hated inheritor of his rightful legacy? And what will he do once he learns the truth?

Pick up your copy today!

Be sure to connect with us at:

Harlequin.com/Newsletters
Facebook.com/HarlequinBooks
Twitter.com/HarlequinBooks

www.Harlequin.com

PHFM900

From *New York Times* bestselling author

GENA SHOWALTER

comes the long-awaited story of Torin, the most dangerous Lord of the Underworld yet...

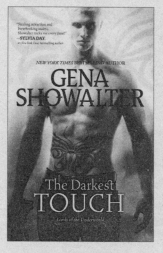

Fierce immortal warrior. Host to the demon of Disease. Torin's every touch causes sickness and death—and a worldwide plague. Carnal pleasure is utterly forbidden, and though he has always overcome temptation with an iron will, his control is about to shatter.

She is Keeley Cael. The Red Queen. When the powerful beauty with shocking vulnerabilities escapes from a centuries-long imprisonment, the desire that simmers between her and Torin is scorching. His touch could mean her end, but resisting her is the hardest battle he's ever fought—and the only battle he fears he can't win.

Available now wherever books are sold!

Be sure to connect with us at:

Harlequin.com/Newsletters

Facebook.com/HarlequinBooks

Twitter.com/HarlequinBooks

HARLEQUIN® HQN™

™ www.Harlequin.com

PHGS891

New York Times Bestselling Author

LINDSAY McKENNA

She was caught in her past until he showed her a future...

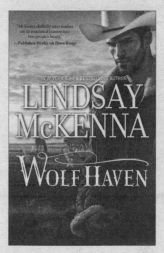

Some things can never be forgotten. A helicopter crash in Afghanistan. Capture. Torture. Now US Navy nurse Skylar Pascal is struggling to regain control of her life after a trauma that nearly destroyed her. After losing so much, an ideal job at the Elk Horn Ranch in Wyoming offers Sky something she thought she'd never find again...hope.

Former SEAL Grayson McCoy has his own demons. But something about Elk Horn's lovely-yet-damaged new nurse breaks something loose. Compassion—and *passion*. And even as Gray works with Sky to piece her confidence back together, something deeper and more tender begins to unfurl between them. Something that could bring her back to life.

But not even the haven of Elk Horn Ranch is safe from dangers. And all of Sky's healing could be undone by the acts of one malicious man...

Available now wherever books are sold!

Be sure to connect with us at:

Harlequin.com/Newsletters
Facebook.com/HarlequinBooks
Twitter.com/HarlequinBooks

HARLEQUIN® HQN™
www.Harlequin.com

PHLM903

New York Times Bestselling Author
ANN AGUIRRE

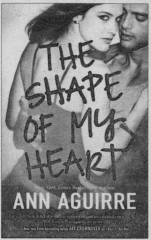

Some people wait decades to meet their soul mate. Courtney Kaufman suspects she met hers in high school—only to lose him at seventeen. Since then, Courtney's social life has been a series of meaningless encounters, though she's made a few close friends along the way. Especially her roommate, Max Cooper, who oozes damaged bad-boy vibes from every pore.

Max knows about feeling lost and trying to move beyond the pain—he's been on his own since he was sixteen. Now it's time to find out if he can ever go home again, and Courtney's the only one he trusts to go with him. But the trip to Providence could change everything…because the more time he spends with Courtney, the harder it is to reconcile what he wants and what he thinks he deserves.

It started out so simple. One misfit helping another. Now Max will do anything to show Courtney that for every heart that's ever been broken, there's another that can make it complete.

PIck up your copy today!

Be sure to connect with us at:

Harlequin.com/Newsletters
Facebook.com/HarlequinBooks
Twitter.com/HarlequinBooks

www.Harlequin.com

PHAA985

New York Times Bestselling Author

NORA ROBERTS

Two heartwarming stories about finding love in the most unlikely of places...

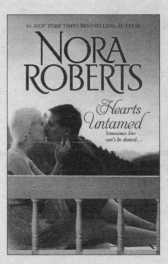

Pick up this 2-in-1 collection today!

Be sure to connect with us at:

Harlequin.com/Newsletters
Facebook.com/HarlequinBooks
Twitter.com/HarlequinBooks

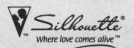

PSNR185

New York Times Bestselling Author

LAUREN DANE

Beyond passion. And beyond their control...

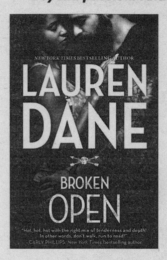

Five years ago, Tuesday Eastwood's life collapsed and left her devastated. After an empty, nomadic existence, she's finally pieced her life back together in the small Oregon town of Hood River. Now Tuesday has everything sorted out. Just so long as men are kept for sex, and only sex...

Then she met *him*.

Musician and rancher Ezra Hurley isn't the man of Tuesday's dreams. He's a verboten fantasy—a man tortured by past addictions whose dark charisma and long, lean body promise delicious carnality. But this craving goes far beyond chemistry. It's primal. It's insatiable. And it won't be satisfied until they're both consumed, body *and* soul...

Available now wherever books are sold!

Be sure to connect with us at:

Harlequin.com/Newsletters
Facebook.com/HarlequinBooks
Twitter.com/HarlequinBooks

www.Harlequin.com

PHLD935